BETWEEN LOVE AND LOATHING

BETWEEN LOVE AND LOATHING

USA TODAY BESTSELLING AUTHOR

SHAIN ROSE

Page & Vine
An Imprint of Meredith Wild LLC

Cover Design by Bitter Sage Designs
Editing: KD Proofreading, Salma's Library

Paperback ISBN: 979-8-9877583-3-5

Note on Content Warnings

As a reader who loves surprises, I enjoy going in blind with each book. Yet, I also want to give my readers the opportunity to know what sensitive content may be in my books. You will find the list of them here: www.shainrose.com/content-warnings

And to those who hate to love you ... but still do.

CHAPTER 1: CLARA

"We made a mistake." The doctor cleared his throat. "Well, we made a few mistakes."

That's never something a patient wants to hear during a visit. I stared up at the ceiling rather than at the doctor, trying to process as I held my own hand because no one was there to hold it for me.

"Some people manage this very well. It's quite a blessing we found out when we did."

I didn't think a disease could be a blessing. Especially one without a cure. One with fatalities every year. I hated that he'd said those words.

But I tried to accept them while he talked on and on. It was a good thing I hadn't driven because tears trekked down my face as soon as I folded into the Uber. Quickly, I grabbed my concealer and glanced in the compact's mirror to check my cherry lipstick, wipe at my eyes, and confirm my mascara hadn't budged. The redness of the rash on my cheeks was peeking through again so I blotted more cover-up on.

I had one more meeting today and tried to muster up the last amount of energy I had for it. *No more tears, Clara.*

When I showed up, my mother and sister were already gone and Mrs. Johnson motioned me into the room with no one from the extended family. Instead, the older woman smiled at Dominic Hardy, my stepfather's trusted architectural engineer. Dominic and his brothers were the sons my stepfather never had. He doted on them and loved them like his own, which was understandable. The Hardy Family was hard not to like with four charming brothers and twin sisters who'd married infamous men. Yet, out of the six of them, Dominic was different.

"Why is Clara's part of the will being read with mine?" His strong jaw ticked as he pointedly asked Mrs. Johnson without so much as a hello directed my way. I hadn't expected anything different. Every time I was near Dominic, he didn't even cast me a glance. He may have had the same dark, wavy hair, the same build, and the same color of green eyes as his younger brothers, but his were meaner. Colder. More ruthless.

Mrs. Johnson straightened her gold belt before tsking at him. "We'll get to that."

As he sat there with his piercing gaze and perfectly pressed suit tailored to his massive build, it was obvious he held himself in such a high regard that he couldn't even be bothered to grace me with a nod of acknowledgement.

Normally, that would have been fine, but my emotions were frayed on every edge. I was running on empty and ready to snap at him in order to protect myself. A wounded, tired animal can be dangerous, and today, I was emotionally spent.

She waved to one of the seats next to Dominic and murmured, "Have a seat, Clara dear. How was the drive?"

"Oh, fine. The traffic was a little bad because of an accident on the freeway."

Dominic checked his watch as if to draw attention to the time and my being five minutes late.

Immediately, the urge to apologize bubbled up. "I should have left earlier."

"Now, how would you have known there would be traffic?" She waited a beat but when Dominic didn't share in the sentiment, she hurried on, "Well, let's get to it then. I've discussed Carl's will with Dominic's brother and your stepsister and explained that each of his stipulations within the will are rather unorthodox. Yours are no different."

She slid papers across her desk slowly to both Dominic and me. My mother and sister would have lunged for the documentation, but I coiled away from it, not really wanting a gift in my stepfather's death. His heart had given out suddenly, but it was like he knew it was coming, like he'd been preparing this will his whole life, and with him being the type of businessman he was, he probably had planned it somehow.

Carl Milton had ruled one of the biggest hospitality empires of the country with the four men he thought of as sons—the Hardy brothers, hence the Hardy Elite All-Access Team brand, also known as HEAT. There were HEAT watches, HEAT resorts, HEAT technology, HEAT everything everywhere, and my stepfather owned half of it all.

Until now.

"Dom, you're the eldest of your siblings, and I think Carl trusted you to run the Pacific Coast Resort's reopening for that very reason. Plus, you designed it and took pride in it." Mrs. Johnson's eyes shined with unshed tears. "I'm so happy to tell you that Carl is leaving the final design, operations, shares, and management to you." She paused and flicked her eyes to me. "As long as you include Clara's bakery within the resort."

There was the twist. The knife in Dominic's back; the reason this felt all wrong.

His mouth dropped open. I glanced at him and saw how his sun-kissed skin reddened. "There's no room in the Pacific's blueprints for a little bakery like hers." He said the statement with disgust, his voice full of gravel and anger while his strong hands white-knuckled the arms of the chair he sat in.

"It's not just a *little* bakery." I couldn't help snapping. "It's a place that people gather and absolutely love, Dominic. It could be global." I smoothed the black maxi dress I'd decided to wear today to honor Carl even though the color weighed me down.

"Yeah, here. They love it *here*, Clara. In Florida. Across the country, at the Pacific Coast Resort—where Carl hasn't instilled your bakery for patrons to love—it's going to be a hard sell." So matter-of-factly Dominic Hardy threw knives at my self-confidence with his words. The man normally barely talked with me, but he had the audacity to now. With malice. With hate. "Are you up for that?"

Finally, he shifted his gaze to mine. Those green eyes with edges of dark jade seemed to cut at my mask of confidence, trying to find my weakness, to see if I was prepared for the challenge.

"Now, now," Mrs. Johnson said before she rearranged her wired glasses. The frames matched her belt and gold pen as she tapped it on the sheet in front of her. "As you know, Carl came in frequently to change the stipulations of his will. He had a standing appointment scheduled on a monthly basis, and it does seem he had the current blueprints submitted." The woman rummaged in a drawer before pulling out the papers and laying them out too. Then she took her pen and pointed to the middle of a blueprint in front of Dominic's face as if he couldn't see the gigantic space marring his perfect layout that read Clara's Bakery.

"That's going to be impossible. The construction to make that work would take—"

"Dominic, you're just starting renovations, right? Surely you'll be able to figure out where to fit a small bakery since you'll be going from midsize to large scale with an additional two hundred thousand square feet, bringing this resort to near half a million."

He crossed his massive arms over his chest. Everything about him was huge and hard as granite. He didn't seem to bend to anyone, especially not to Mrs. Johnson ... nor me.

Still, the elderly woman wasn't deterred. She smiled at me like she was my fairy godmother. Then, she laid her hand on mine. "And you'll own the bakery, Clara, because the one you have here will now be under your mother's management."

This was the biggest blow, the one that made it feel like my heart almost stopped. "That can't be right."

"Oh, honey, I know it seems harsh." Mrs. Johnson shook her head of perfectly coiffed hair. "But Carl wanted this new bakery to be all yours."

The bad day I'd thought I'd had at the doctor's office morphed into catastrophic in that moment as I shook with something very close to desperation. Had Carl understood that the bakery here was everything to me? That I not only lost him but now the bakery too?

The emptiness of losing a parent stabs at you every day. It never goes away, never really heals. I didn't know if he wanted me to cry or be strong here, if he thought I had the strength to do what he was asking.

"Right. My very own. I get it," I grumbled, trying to picture what would even work best in another resort. I'd built the bakery here on the East Coast, and within this specific hotel, it did well. Yet it had been completed under my stepfather's supervision, and the money went into a very large, very communal pot for the family.

"I'll have to discuss this with my mother and my sis—"

"Your mother will want nothing to do with this." Mrs. Johnson rolled her eyes and then it was like she was handing me glass slippers that would change my life as she continued, "Owning the bakery at the new resort will provide you with something that's completely yours, without being tied to your mother and sister."

I didn't snatch the slippers yet, although I was tempted. Instead, I glanced at the man who hated me more in this moment than he ever had before. We'd never gotten along. He was too broody and quiet and was constantly working. There was always another responsibility that needed his attention so much so that he never stopped to enjoy a little treat. Not even when I offered him my desserts for free. "What if I decide this bakery isn't for me?"

"It's not. We don't need it. We've planned for five restaurants and a whole pathway of shops weaving along the picturesque coastline. They are all within a block of the resort. Coffee, desserts, bakery, restaurants. Even ice cream. Housing another bakery within the resort doesn't make sense." He lifted a dark brow as he made clear that he didn't need nor want me anywhere near his precious resort.

"Even so," Mrs. Johnson said to Dominic, "it's what Carl stipulated." Turning her eyes to me, she said, "Otherwise, well, your mother still owns shares of the spa. You and your sister can always count on being taken care of by her."

Yes, my mother. Melinda Milton.

She hadn't explored doing something for her own success my whole life. She swam in different social circles and navigated the waters like a shark looking for blood. She'd found Carl probably when he was vulnerable and struck fast, sinking her teeth into an aging man who would help quench her hunger for elite status.

My stepfather delivered on most fronts for her and maybe he'd known somewhere deep down that this is what I needed. And maybe, just maybe, I'd be able to change the trajectory of my life.

"I'd like to make it work on the West Coast, too, then." I said it softly, nodding my head.

Mrs. Johnson smiled at me with a twinkle in her blue eyes as Dominic cleared his throat. When I glanced at him, I saw the tendons in his neck straining, saw how his temple moved as his jaw ticked up and down too. "You know, I'm not going to help you, and you'll have to follow all the design specs. You think you can handle that?"

My heart pounded as I replied, "Well, it's obvious you don't think I can."

"Of course you can't. You were spoon-fed your first business venture and are now being handed an even bigger opportunity." He pinched the bridge of his perfect nose. "This isn't some easy little journey, Clara. It takes work."

Despite how rude he was, I could admit he wasn't wrong. I took a deep breath and tried not to let him get the best of me.

"Mr. Hardy, this is her decision. The will does give her this space and states you both must approve the design. However, at the reopening, it will be hers."

"I'm sorry, can you repeat that?" I stuttered out.

Designing a place with *him*? The man could barely look at me, let alone work with me.

"You two must co-produce the plans for the bakery. And approval must be ..." She glanced down at the paperwork in front of her, blew out a breath, and chuckled. "'Harmonious.' Carl must not have realized how hard that one was going to be."

"Since it will be mine, it's probably best for me to get what I want ..." My voice trailed off as I glanced at Dominic, who was practically snarling at me.

His gaze flew to my hair and then traveled slowly over my body. This maxi dress usually made me feel comfortable, but it felt almost too revealing with him sizing me up the way he was. "It will be yours, Clara, but you can bet your ass it'll be my design."

Why did that statement cause shivers to travel down my spine?

***

"I'll drive you home. We can discuss the blueprints." I heard his voice behind me as I exited the building, punching in for another ride.

"Oh, I'm just going to grab a cab."

"You don't want to even discuss what the hell we have to do?" he asked, and anger laced through his tone enough that I gave in.

Once I stepped into the SUV, he told his driver where to go. Everyone knew the Miltons lived on a hill together, one wing for my sister and me, the other for my mother and Carl.

In my late twenties, the setup was getting old, but now my mother was mourning.

"I don't know if I'm going to even sign it."

"You have to." He pulled his phone out, typing away on it. "And then just let me handle all the details."

My heart squeezed at giving up another opportunity, but as we got closer and closer to my family's estate, I lost more and more confidence in being able to pull this off. My family probably needed me here anyway.

Dominic and I didn't say much to each other the rest of the ride. He must have figured he could convince me of everything later. Yet, when we got to the gated driveway of my home, my mother and the man I knew as her lover were outside.

Drunk.

Again.

"Oh, Jesus," I whispered because this time my sister was out there too, waving wildly at them. I shut my eyes once and breathed in and out before I said, "You can just drop me here and please don't ..."

I glanced at Dominic as he took in the scene. Melinda Milton was a put together woman in public. Beautiful blonde hair, high cheek bones, thin and willowy, but mean eyes. She'd always had a glint in them and now, as she approached the vehicle, I knew her and her lover's wrath would be turned on me.

When I went to open the door and get out though, Dominic pushed a button and the door didn't open at all.

I whipped my head to him. "Let me out."

He hummed as if he was considering and then shrugged. "She can talk to you here." And instead of giving me a choice, he rolled down the window.

My mom wasn't at all deterred. She and Hank peered in as she snarled, "Did Carl give you more than what I got?"

"Can we talk about this later, Mother? I had a doctor's appointment today, too, and—"

Her posture tightened as her hands wrapped around the window edge. "You want me to ask how that went?" When she rolled her eyes, her whole body moved and Hank's thick hand held her steady. "I hope they told you what I did. You're ridiculous, and you're fucking fine. Now, what did Mrs. Johnson say?"

The brush-off of my doctor's visit should have been the last straw, but I kept trying. "I've been given the opportunity to open a bakery outside of Florida with Mr. Hardy." I pointed to Dominic and tried to draw her attention to him, tried to make her see that having Hank out here right after Carl's passing, acting this way, wasn't acceptable.

"Are you kidding me?" she spit and then smoothed her blonde hair that was normally so perfect, so in place for everyone but us. "Where?"

"California. But, Mom, we have the spas, right? Nothing will change—"

"Everything changed the second Carl left us with less than everything he had. That man was always an asshole, but he really wanted to ruin my life when he died."

Carl Milton was never cruel to her. He gave her most everything she wanted aside from the more that she asked for. My mother had wanted every share of his company when he'd had the heart attack that took his life. When she didn't get it, she'd been furious. "It's not that bad—"

"Anastasia!" my mother screamed over her shoulder and then shoved at Hank. "Hank, get her out of the car."

Hank yanked at the door, his dark eyes wild. "Open this fucking door."

Chewing at my lip, I glanced at Dominic and whispered, "Please." But right as I did, Hank slammed his hand hard on the side of the car and I saw Dominic's eyes change.

Before, they'd been empty, devoid of any emotion for me. Now, there was anger as he peered around me to say quietly, "Hit my car again, and I'll be the one getting out of it. And you won't like the result."

My mother's lover wasn't big compared to Dominic. "Fuck this," he grumbled backing away and spitting at my mother, "Handle your stupid children, Linda. I'll be back later." Then he was stomping off to another car as my mother's tears started.

"This is all your fault, Clara." Her vodka cocktail sloshed back and forth in the glass. "Get inside so we can talk about this."

As Hank drove away, I closed my eyes. "Please unlock the door," I asked Dominic again.

"You giving in to them so easily?"

I hated that when I stared into his green eyes, I saw disappointment filling them as I nodded. He sighed and pressed the button, his gaze following Hank's car rolling down the driveway.

"You have my number and Evie's if you need it," he said softly before I opened the door and got out.

My mother was listening and scoffed as she yanked my elbow to pull me to her side. "She won't be calling. She'll be just fine. You can leave."

After a long look, he did. Rolling up his window, he disappeared down the drive and out the gates.

My mother wrinkled her nose and her hand tightened on my elbow. "Are you trying to leave us? Leave your *mother*?"

"No. Of course not. The opportunity was—"

"She's trying to leave us, Anastasia. I can't stand even looking at her. She's a disgrace."

"Mother, I didn't even do anything," I whispered, hating how desperate I sounded.

"Exactly! You don't ever do anything at all. That's why Carl didn't give you shit. I told you to be nice to him, didn't I? I told you to date his friends, put on a good smile, not act like your ridiculous baking meant something. Look what it got you. A fucking bakery."

Despite her harsh words, my heart swelled at the idea that the bakery could be my saving grace, that I could move away from her and work on my passion.

"Are you smiling right now?" She threw her glass down onto the cement, and I schooled my face immediately. My mother was the same height and same size as me, just much older. There shouldn't have been fear there, but when she stepped toward me, I stepped back. "Do you think this is funny, Clara?"

"No. Of course not."

"Anastasia, is your sister lying to me? Does she think this is funny?"

I glanced at my sister with pleading eyes. She knew I would never laugh at my mother. Anastasia sighed. "Clara, you have to learn. This is for the best." With that, she looked at my mother and said softly, "She was smiling, Mother. She thinks this is a game."

With that, my mother warped into a different woman. Gone was her soft tone, gone was her graceful movements, and gone was her will to reason. All that was left was a drunk monster who came at me fast and full of rage.

Maybe I should have fought her off, but this was a woman who had beaten me down for years, carefully crafting my fragile state of mind. As she hit me across the face, I was the one to apologize over and over.

"If you're so sorry, you'll go back and beg for more. That bakery isn't an option. So, don't even think about it."

I thought about that bakery as my salvation every single

day after that.

And I ended up signing on the dotted line.

SIX MONTHS LATER

Dominic: This design for your bakery won't work. Is that blown glass in the corner?

Me: Yes. I can get it imported.

Dominic: Your answer should be no. The resort is based on architecture from the Milwaukee Art Museum. Modern. Sleek. White and black, Clara. Redo it.

Me: Maybe I can be the splash of vibrancy and energy the resort needs.

Dominic: Maybe? I don't enjoy splashes of color. This isn't a kindergarten classroom. It's a luxury resort.

Me: Should I fly in and show you how I think it could work?

Dominic: I don't need thoughts on how it would work. Renovations are going to take another nine months. There's no point of you flying in now

when we're not working on it. Just seamlessly integrate minimalist aesthetics for a modern sophisticated look. Then, send it to my interior designer, Rita. She'll be your contact.

Me: But she's not getting how to mix our two designs.

Dominic: There's no mixing. If it's absolutely necessary, I can have a conversation at eight tonight. I'm in town.

Me: I have plans this evening, but I could do tomorrow.

Dominic: More important plans than your bakery?

Me: Noah's hockey game is tonight, and I promised I'd be there.

Dominic: So a boyfriend's game is more important.

Me: That's not what I'm saying. But it's important to him. And he's a good friend.

Dominic: Sounds to me like you're putting your boyfriend before the resort.

Me: Dominic, I'm trying my best.

Dominic: Right, but do you think that's good enough?

Seven months later

Me: I think the pastel pink leather seating will work well with a signature truffle I'll be making.

Dominic: No pink. Need I remind you Rita has been commissioned as the lead designer to bring modernism and a sleek look to the resort?

Me: But I'm going to be the head baker. You should want me happy in there.

Dominic: You have to learn to be comfortable anywhere when you're working with others.

Me: Is that what you do?

Dominic: No. I'm the boss of this resort. I don't bend to other's tastes, Clara. You bend to mine.

Me: I'll be flying to California tomorrow to start testing the kitchen. Maybe we could meet then.

Dominic: You sure your friend doesn't need you in the stands for his Stanley Cup bid?

Me: If you're insinuating I did something wrong by supporting my friend in the past, you're wrong.

Dominic: If you say so.

CHAPTER 2: DOMINIC

Clara Milton wasn't going to discuss a thing with my interior designer. She instead was hoping I would just hand it to her.

I wouldn't. When a person wanted something in life, they had to fight for it.

And Clara didn't know how to fight. At all.

I pinched the bridge of my nose, thinking back to how her mother had treated her when I'd dropped her off that day. Clara had been ready to walk right into that messed-up situation just to save her family's reputation.

She didn't fight it at all. And it had fucking bothered me more than it should have.

Now, she was ruining my resort and wasn't even really fighting me for her changes either.

Every text was a question, an idea, a "maybe." If someone was going to come in and change all my plans, they better believe in their vision. White-hot rage filled my blood just thinking about it. The only time she'd put her foot down was a half of a year ago to go look cute on her hockey player boyfriend's arm to placate him.

No one said no to a meeting with me in this industry to placate someone else, especially not another man. So, now, I didn't have time for nuancing Clara's idea for matching pink seating with her pink truffles or whatever the hell she said.

She needed to listen to me. I'd designed numerous buildings for the brand, and the Pacific Coast Resort was especially important to me. It was mine. The one I'd spent years perfecting, and the one I was most proud of. I'd designed how the cobblestone streets paved an ideal walkway to our restaurants, how they wove around the gardens and landscaping to the golf course, to the pools, to the beach, to the vineyards. Meticulously and tirelessly, I'd built it from the ground up. I'd sweated over every minute detail. I'd made sure to avoid any distractions so that I could present a damn masterpiece to the world that no one would question.

Never again would I be questioned.

And arguing over pink seating was ridiculous.

So, I'd put off the texts and approving the designs until the very last moment. We were opening the resort in a mere three months. But yesterday with Rita, it seemed Clara hadn't budged. She'd emailed her saying she was continuing with her design against Rita's recommendations.

So, I intercepted her in the lobby where she was supposed to meet Rita that day. "Ms. Milton," I grumbled out as she spun in a circle looking up at the crystal chandelier we'd made sure expanded across most of the lobby. With soaring cathedral ceilings, it presented quite a sight. That's what my whole resort was supposed to do.

She stood there, a goddamn beacon of color in my white-marbled lobby. Her thick dark-red hair was curled immaculately around her face, falling down her shoulders and stopping right at her curves.

Clara Milton was lethally beautiful. No doubt about it. Stunning with high cheekbones, smooth skin, and big green eyes, she appeared out of place and vulnerable without anyone by her side.

She didn't live in or understand the real world. But she was going to learn to live and fight for what she wanted in mine or she wasn't going to survive. That I would make sure of.

"Mr. Hardy?" Her voice was full of surprise as she stumbled over her words, but then she smiled at me, her eyes twinkling with what seemed to be hope. "Mr. Hardy. You came."

That hope was going to have to be squashed. This was simply a quick business meeting. "Rita called, Ms. Milton." I glanced at my watch.

"Oh." She frowned, her smile wobbling. "Well, that was nice of her to tell you when I'd arrive."

"I'm not here to welcome you to town." And there went her smile. Good. "I'm here because Rita informed me of your pushback."

"Right." She hesitated, then her fingers threaded together in front of her bright-green dress. "I thought she might," she admitted, but there was no remorse in her tone. Just that familiar rasp that I'd hated over the years, something about the way she let the words whisper out of her mouth made her sound dark and sinful but vulnerable all at the same time.

"I only have a minute, and then I'm sure she'll be here to discuss further with you, but I spoke with Mrs. Johnson, and she is aware of your unreasonable requests."

"Unreasonable?" Her eyebrow lifted like she was affronted.

"Yes. They're ludicrous, but besides that, Mrs. Johnson reiterated that in order to be in compliance with the will's requirements, we need to secure final approval from you for the design changes." I winced because it pained me to say it. Mrs. Johnson was taking her position as executor of the will much too seriously.

I was under her thumb and under Clara's, too, it seemed. The woman picked at the fabric on her dress that looked like a palm tree leaf and avoided my gaze for a second. So, I took her in. I'd known her for years, but only in passing, and I didn't mingle with women in high society anymore. It had proved to be toxic with a woman I thought I'd loved.

A mind can play tricks on you when you're distracted by bright colors, pretty eyes, and red lips. And Clara had checked all those boxes.

"You need to reconsider the backsplash above the sink." It was a small part of the bakery, true, but no detail was too miniscule.

"Like I told Rita, the soft pearl-pink color scheme will be an excellent accent there."

"We're not accenting color anywhere in the resort," I ground out. It's like she couldn't understand that stuffing a girly, Technicolor Barbie in the middle of my perfect, classic black-and-white film didn't work. There wasn't a place for her whatsoever. "The backsplash can be a checkered pattern of grays if you want something a little different but we need to stay on theme."

I heard her sigh, and then I saw how her chin actually quivered before she straightened and whispered, "Don't you think I should get one thing?"

Jesus, another request. And I wasn't a giver. Not anymore. Even when a woman with doe eyes the color of emeralds appeared to be about to cry.

I took, I executed, and I didn't look back. That's how empires were built. That's also how people got ahead while others were left behind. I knew that because I'd been left behind before.

Maybe that was Clara's problem. She needed more of a spine. "You're getting a bakery in a resort that's sure to be in every magazine in the country. Isn't that enough?"

She hadn't even sent me a real blueprint the first time I'd asked. I'd have fired her then if she'd actually been on my team.

"You know I'm going to have to be here after we're done designing it, right? You're aware that people will actually be walking around your resort wearing freaking color, right, Dominic? The place can't be pristine and untouchable forever."

I cracked my knuckles at the thought and paced away from her before I paced back. "I'm aware."

"So can you imagine that some people might even *like* color?" She mocked me by having her eyes bulge in feigned surprise.

She was trying to irritate me, and most people here didn't do that. They listened because I'd earned their respect. "What's your point?"

"There should be color somewhere. And I'm going to bring that here. If not in my bakery, I'll be wearing it." She spun in front of me. *Could I enforce a dress code?* "I'm going to wear what I want." She narrowed her eyes like she was reading my goddamn mind. "Also, my macarons are a favorite in Florida and—"

"Do you want a checkered backsplash or just white tile?"

Her eyes closed briefly, and I felt a tinge of loss, which was surprising. I never felt bad about snuffing out color. People used it as a crutch to draw attention away from their flaws. "This is the last thing I'm giving up, Dominic."

"Clara, it's what's best." I shrugged. "I don't want you to have to deal with the design critics. If you were down the street by our food trucks or out on the boardwalk, I'd let you do what you want."

"Are you saying my design isn't good enough?" I couldn't

tell if it was hurt or anger in her voice.

I pinched the bridge of my nose. "I'm saying you and I have different styles and they don't exactly go together."

"Oh, I'm well aware that nothing about you is like me and that we don't go together at all."

She grumbled it with such disdain I was caught off guard. I knew we were opposites but having her aware of it also suddenly sat wrong with me. "What the hell is that supposed to mean?"

"Well, isn't it obvious?" she snipped out before sighing. "I make desserts and you don't even eat them. It's like you're allergic to sugar."

There was no point in eating what was practically poison to the body when you could eat protein or something that was actually good for your health. I rarely went into her bakery in Florida, and I didn't plan to walk into this one either. "You might want to consider what food you're making within this bakery—"

The intake of her breath was sharp as she stepped back. "Do you think I'm so incompetent that I haven't considered the menu?"

Well, I wasn't so sure. "I haven't seen a menu sent to Rita."

"Because neither of you have asked for one." I heard the anger now, noticed how fast she snapped the words out before she exhaled, likely attempting to dissipate the emotion. "Nor have you asked for the marketing strategy, the name of the bakery, or the—"

"Is that a problem? We've provided a list of staff that can work morning hours with you, provided you the contact for weekly produce vendor, and Rita has handled most of the design. If you want to send over the rest, fine."

"No thank you," she replied fast.

"No thank you?"

"You'll just change it. I'm working with you on the design because it is required, and I want to be colleagues, not enemies. I'm set for produce and have hired someone from your list of staff—"

"Who?"

"Matt Connor will start training in two weeks."

"Matt Connor?" I knew of him because he had worked at the resort down the street and Valentino had interviewed him. I hummed, not knowing whether I had an actual reason to say no to him working there.

"He was on the list."

"Yes, I'm aware. He interviewed with Valentino's team."

"Why isn't he ... oh. So, you gave me Valentino's leftovers?" Her hand was on her hip immediately. "I thought you wanted the best of the best throughout your resort."

"I do. But I'm not sure your bakery is going to be a part of my resort for long." My words were pointed and cutthroat. She needed the practice of dealing with bad reviews. She'd be getting them. This wasn't her daddy's hotel anymore. People didn't know her like they did in Florida.

"You really mulled over my future here, haven't you?" Her words came out in a shaky whisper, and for a second, I considered whether I should back away now in hopes I wouldn't have to stand there while she cried.

But then Clara Milton did something I wasn't expecting. She bit her lip, dragged her teeth against the soft plumpness of it, and walked in a circle around me, slowly and with calculation. "You just sat there ... creating my space and thinking about how my coming to town would go. I'm happy you were here to at least welcome me to your lobby, Dominic. I think I've been accommodating enough on changes, though, and maybe my bakery will be out of your resort soon. Maybe I won't make it, just like you're hoping. And then you'll have the resort you dreamed of. For now, be happy I've been willing to compromise on some things. But the rest ..."

Her voice drifted off like she didn't want to say it. "The rest, Clara?"

We both waited in silence.

"It's nonnegotiable, Mr. Hardy. It's my bakery." Ah, there was the spine I thought she didn't have. She came alive with that comment—red stained her cheeks, power flew off her into the air as her glare held me hostage.

"You sure about that?" I'd conquered a lot over the years. People saying my designs weren't worth it, fighting with other engineers, ruthless competition, failure. Still, the last few years without meaningful pushback and true competition because I'd finally made it had left me content but bored.

Pushing Clara's buttons wasn't boring at all. Not when I suddenly saw the fight in her eyes.

"Why wouldn't I be sure?"

"People are paying for a Hardy-designed resort, not a—"

"Don't even finish what you're going to say," she whispered with venom. "Throw underhanded barbs somewhere else, Dominic. I'm done with them. This is the last thing I'll give you."

And with that comment, Rita's loud heels could be heard clicking across the otherwise empty lobby.

"Last thing you'll give me, huh?" I murmured.

Her gaze flicked to Rita before it latched back on to mine as she crossed her arms. "Yep."

"If you want to go head-to-head with me, you can try. You

won't win though, little fighter. This is my playground."

"We'll see," she said before Rita walked up with tall and lanky Matt Connor right next to her.

"Dom, you have a meeting." She then turned her eyes to Clara. I loved how Rita wasted no time. "Clara, it's nice to meet you in person ..."

I didn't say goodbye or spare them a backward glance.

I hadn't smiled the whole day, but I smiled the whole walk to my next meeting.

CHAPTER 3: CLARA

Paloma: You here? The meeting is in the lobby FYI

I frowned at the text while I listened to my stepsister, Evie, ramble on the phone. "One whole month you've been in LA, and the only pictures you've sent me are of those kittens you shouldn't have picked up in the first place."

I snapped another and sent it to her. Both of those gray-and-white furballs with gold eyes blinked up at me as I shooed them away. I needed to grab my laptop because I had no idea what meeting Paloma was texting me about.

"Oh my God. They're so small," she cooed. "They didn't have a collar or anything when you picked them up the other night?"

"Yeah and no microchip. They're eating kitten food now, after I took them to the vet, and they love their beds I just bought." That had been an ordeal considering I had no idea they needed a carrier to get into the cab because I didn't have a car to drive myself. I'd left mine in Florida.

"Can I see a picture of their kitten beds?" Evie asked innocently.

The girl was desperate to see any part of my place but with the worn furniture and tiny amount of space, I wanted to hold off on showing anyone until I decorated it fully. I sidetracked to the corner of the living room to send her a picture of the cat post and cushioned bed on the ground. "There. Stop complaining now."

"Oh, hardwood floors and that cute little end table with ... is that me with the babies in that frame?" The landlord had been very specific about hanging anything on the walls. Each nail would cost me about a hundred dollars, he said, and so I'd made sure to grab standing picture frames.

"Found it with one of my coworkers, Paloma. Remember, she owns the retail store connected to the resort. She's been great with introducing me to the area and invited me to go to some yard and garage sales over the weekend." And somehow finding a maroon rug to place on the scuffed hardwood floor, new blinds to hang over the ripped ones, and a framed mirror to lean on the yellowish walls had been more rewarding than buying red bottom shoes.

"She's bargain hunting without me, Declan," Evie whined to her husband, the nice Hardy brother—the one I loved for loving my stepsister in a way no one else could.

"Go to the damn boutique. It's free for you," I heard him grumble.

"It's not the same." She sighed. She was breastfeeding their first baby boy, and her husband was more than a little overprotective. Still, I heard the love in her voice and knew marriage suited them well in a way it never would me. "You know, if I would have come there, I would have been able to help you get settled in."

"The place is furnished, Evie." I sighed and smoothed a hand over the worn patterned couch before I went to my bedroom to open my laptop. The threading was torn on one cushion, and I couldn't quite tell if there was a leak in the bathroom or not, but the distinct smell of mold should have probably been a cause for concern. Instead, I opened the windows every night and enjoyed the breeze.

"Whatever. How are you feeling?" It was a question she always asked now.

"There's been small flare-ups here and there, but much better since I've moved honestly." I sighed, knowing she wanted an update on my symptoms, even if she didn't directly ask. "Being around Mom and Anastasia was difficult sometimes."

"Good. If you start to feel anything or get too stressed with opening this bakery, make sure you tell Dom, or I can have Declan talk to him about your diagnosis—"

I stopped clicking on my laptop immediately and almost shouted. "No. Do not have him say a word," I ground out. I did not want Dominic to hear from his brother anything about me. It was very clear he didn't care. "Honestly, it's a beautiful resort, and I'm very excited to have my bakery be a part of it."

Declan didn't hold back from shouting in the background. "Clara, don't lie. Bleed some color into that sterile place."

Evie chuckled, and I couldn't stop from smiling. "I know. I know. I just don't know that my bakery belongs here at all but—"

"Then make it belong there. You were never made to fit in, Clara. Stand the hell out. Honestly, it's probably why your dad wanted this for you."

"Our dad wanted a lot of things, and he was terrible at voicing them." She always did that, left herself out when she shouldn't. Evie had come into our lives a year ago after being estranged from her biological father, Carl, most of her life. She'd bore the brunt of Carl's "conditional gift" clause in the will, which forced an arranged marriage on her.

Or so I thought.

Dealing with Dominic Hardy proved to be very difficult. I wonder what she would say if I told her I hadn't seen that pompous disgrace of a man since the day I'd arrived a month ago. He'd written me off, apparently, since he'd never stopped by again.

And as I started scrolling through my emails, I knew dealing with him was about to get worse.

I hopped off the chair fast. "Crap, I have to go. I'm late for a meeting, I think."

"Oh, is it at your bakery? Send pics of that too!"

"Oh my God. Goodbye."

I hung up, and proceeded to scurry around like a madwoman, frustrated that I hadn't checked my email this morning. We were all working around the clock for the reopening, and I knew better than to take a day off. I ripped open my closet door and scanned my options.

I pulled out a flowy dress that was cream colored with coral peonies on it, took out a small Birkin bag that matched to throw just a few pieces of makeup in. I never wore a purse because I just had my phone with my credit cards and ID stuffed into my bra, but today, having the bag would make me feel the part. Then, I texted Paloma back.

Me: Thank you! I didn't see the email until now and haven't left yet. Is everyone there?

Paloma: Yes. Rita texted everyone too, but I just checked and you're not on the text thread. So hurry up.

"Of course she left me off the thread," I grumbled. I didn't care what anyone said, Rita hated me. Even still, I avoided thinking about it. My self-esteem didn't need another person to be wary about. That's why I moved away from my sister and mother in the first place.

I punched in for an Uber as I pulled on the dress, no time to iron out the wrinkles. I couldn't bother with curling my hair, so I threaded some cream through it and let my waves hang naturally before I applied concealer to cover my freckles, added red lipstick, and went to work on my eyelashes before I ran down the couple of flights of stairs in my apartment building and waited for the Uber to show.

Me: Well, at least she finally approved my pink seating.

Paloma: Oh really?! That's fantastic. Tell me about it when you get here. Did you leave yet? Dominic Hardy just showed up, and you know how he is.

Me: It's fine. There're a lot of us. He won't notice.

Paloma: He notices everything. Perfect example, my pink fitting rooms just yesterday.

I sighed. Well, he hadn't noticed me for the past month, right? So, one could hope.

Me: I'm still jealous of them. They're the perfect pink that I wanted in my bakery.

Paloma: Yeah. But my store is on the strip. Yours is in the freaking lobby, Clara. And plus, don't be jealous. I'm still wondering if I should change them just because he stared at it for an eternity.

I knew he stopped by other places to see how things were going too. Paloma was always on edge about it.

Me: He said he liked it though. Don't you dare change them.

Paloma: Well, right. I can't because when he hands out a compliment, it's a win.

As I got into the Uber and told him to take me as fast as possible to the Pacific Coast Resort, I sighed at the traffic. No way was I making it on time unless it parted like the red sea for us. So, I asked the driver about his life, learned a bit about his three kids and tried to make the best of our time. I even memorized a few new turns to take if I decided to bicycle to work in the future, considering I'd found a cute old teal bicycle at a yard sale.

"Traffic is usually okay on the weekends, but this is something," the driver mumbled as we came to a complete stop in traffic. "Want me to drop you off at the back of the resort?

Might be awhile otherwise."

"Would that be faster?" I asked.

"Maybe. You can walk around and avoid all this traffic."

I nodded, thinking I still had a chance. I'd attempted to navigate the resort a few times but mostly I'd just gotten lost, so I stuck close to the bakery and lobby where I was actually needed.

I realized my mistake as soon as I stepped out of the Uber and he sped off, leaving me feeling small by the magnificent but extremely large white building that practically loomed over the ocean. Every time I saw it, it stole my breath.

Though Dominic Hardy was an asshole, he was also a genius and a brilliant artist. He didn't ever talk about his accolades, but he didn't have to. He was by far the most callous, grumpy, infuriating man I'd ever met but everyone respected his opinion. Even me. You couldn't argue with perfection. His work spoke for itself, and then everyone in the world spoke for him too.

Magazine after magazine.

Award after award.

His engineering of resorts for the HEAT empire was unmatched.

I was on the side of the building and could see that it took up blocks and blocks. The traffic wasn't moving, but under the hot California sun, I probably wasn't going to move that quickly either. My ankles were already swollen from being on my feet so much lately and dealing with the fluid retention I had sometimes.

I sighed and hiked my dress up a bit. I'd thought cream, coral, and beige would have been a nice look. Now, I regretted grabbing a maxi dress to wear when, although light, the material billowed everywhere as I hurried along.

Dripping with sweat, I rushed into the lobby, my small Birkin swinging wildly at my side, in hopes they hadn't moved past introductions. Of course the revolving door didn't turn quickly enough, and I slammed into it much harder than I would have liked. Everyone's eyes flew to me even though they were all seated facing the man of the hour.

Dominic Hardy stood tall and confident in the suit I'd become accustomed to seeing him in when he passed by my bakery. The jacket was expertly fitted, showing off his broad shoulders, the lapels framed his chest well enough to draw attention to the fact that he maintained his physique. He looked classic.

And also annoyed.

His green eyes narrowed on me, and I saw his jaw tick under the five-o'clock shadow that added just a bit of ruggedness. My body betrayed me as I stood there and tried not to drool or get weak in the knees.

"Well"—his voice carried through the lobby, deep and in command—"Nice of you to join us, Ms. Milton."

Now he noticed me? Great. I hurried over to the seat that Paloma saved for me and sat down, grumbling a sorry.

"Let's hope there won't be any apologies from you all on the day our restaurants, stores, or bakeries open." The shot was warranted. So, I nodded without looking up, hoping that a hole might just appear in the ground for me to crawl into.

Thankfully, he moved on. "Keep in mind, coordinating restaurant hours with one another is ideal. Ms. Milton, please work with your staff and Rita to confirm that your menu and hours will complement the other restaurants. We have seventy-five floors of rooms booked in advance with guests, and I want all five of my restaurants available to them. Our beach strip has the go-ahead to open as soon as you're ready, hopefully in the next month."

Paloma nudged my arm excitedly.

Someone raised their hand, but Dominic glared at him, and the hand snapped back down quickly. "I'm not taking questions right now. We're going to have you tour the hotel, and after, all questions will be fielded by Rita."

It was 3:03 p.m. and already he was turning on his heel for us to follow him. Casual chat, praise, giving out attaboy high fives after a hard day's work—none of that was his strong suit. Even if seating had been arranged like we were going to be there for a long speech, everyone got up to flock after him like the sheep that we were.

As we all stood, I blinked and stumbled along as Paloma hooked an arm in mine. I guess that was it. No formal introductions were happening. No "let's all work together." No pep talk even. "We're not going to mingle or ...?"

Paloma didn't seem to mind. She bounced up and down by me like a child who'd just been given access to a candy shop. Her hair swayed with the movement, showing off the shine. It was cut razor sharp and black right above her shoulders, making her appear as lethal as a cute five-foot-nothing woman could. "We mostly all know each other. You're the one hiding out in that bakery of yours. Anyway, we'll meet everyone tonight on the beach. Supposedly it's catered. You think it's Valentino's food? I'd die if that guy cooked for me, for real." Valentino was an attractive man. But Paloma wasn't done. "Or you think Dominic Hardy will stay and hang out with us?"

She said his name like he was a deity. To her, he probably was. He was co-chairman of the board, along with his brothers, and most people looked at the Hardys as a celebrity family. When they'd bought into my stepfather's empire at just the right time, they turned the brand around quickly and made it their own. Dominic specifically was the mastermind behind most of the large resorts' architecture and was said to be ruthless in his pursuit of design excellence. To most, being in his presence was an honor.

To me, well, he was truly the one person in the world I despised.

"Don't make that face, Clara." She laughed. "We get it, you've been around the man and his brothers for years."

"Not me. My stepdad. Dominic and I don't know each other well at all." And we didn't get along in the least, either. Dominic Hardy hadn't even texted me after the first meeting we had in LA to say anything nice like "Did you find a good place to live?" or "How do you like LA?" Actually, he'd probably been hoping my plane went down in a fiery wreck so he didn't have to ever speak to me again. And then he'd happily get to nix my atrocious bakery from his blueprints.

Rita droned on in front of us about the five hundred thousand square feet of elegance Dominic designed, how the high lobby ceilings complemented one of the largest chandeliers in the country hanging above us made of all Tiffany crystal, how the east entrance walkway provided a skywalk and breathtaking views. We walked over the lazy river that wove through one restaurant's patio with foliage and skylights. I appreciated how they would open up to provide an outdoor feel. Following the lazy river past the restaurant, we arrived at the waterpark on the west end that even featured a wave pool.

Every aspect of the resort had been well thought out, and as people oohed and aahed, I glanced back behind all of us to where Dominic lingered. No smile. No outward display of pride in all he'd accomplished. His eyes scanned the perimeter as if he was looking for defects.

When we circled around to the lobby area and hooked a right to see my bakery, the small smile I'd had in anticipation of showing off my space dropped away like someone had smacked it off me. That's how it felt.

They'd ripped apart my designs time and time again over the last six months. Black and white was everywhere. The pink seating had been my last hope, the one concession I'd thought I'd been granted. And I'd grasped onto it, held it like a lifeline, and in many ways, it was the one small thing keeping me from throwing my hands up and walking away.

But black leather lined my booths and barstools. "Oh, fuck. Clara," Paloma breathed, sliding her hand into mine like she could take away my pain, "I'm sorry, babe."

Rita's lips spread across her too-white teeth as she announced, "Clara's bakery is coming along perfectly." She was essentially waving a damn red flag in front of me, hoping I acted like a bull. She started to drone on about the granite countertops, white and beautiful, the exposed piping that was all black.

"Is it bad that I hate her and this whole resort?" I grumbled only to Paloma, because I couldn't hold in my anger anymore. "It's like a sterile hospital with no life."

"What was that?"

I almost jumped seven feet when I felt his breath at the back of my neck, so close, in my personal space, and not at all professional. I whipped around, and there Dominic was, up close and personal, towering over me like a freaking CEO would. He was so tall, I had to peer up at him. Why did he have to look even better up close? I heard Paloma murmur a "Jesus" before I stepped back and muttered, "Oh, nothing."

"You sure, Clara?" He narrowed his gaze on me.

I nodded quickly.

Rita then said loudly, "Clara, we'll have the menu and hours soon to coordinate with Valentino and Justin, correct?"

Paloma's lip curled, like she was about to stand up for me, but I laid a hand on her shoulder. I turned and replied to everyone, "I'm finalizing the morning menu for opening day. Hours have been solidified as 6 a.m. to 3 p.m. every day. The staff is prepared."

That wasn't exactly the truth. I didn't really have a staff except for me and Matt right now who I'd given off until a week before opening day. I would get someone to work weekends hopefully soon. I just needed to iron out costs and everything in between. And I'd thrown out the last menu a week ago, furious that nothing felt right. Determined but also petrified, nothing seemed to be the perfect fit. How could it when everything I created here was shot down. My recipes were meant to be bold and vibrant with every bite.

This bakery wasn't.

"Clara, I need to discuss a few details. Please keep moving, Rita. We'd like to finish this meeting in enough time for everyone to handle priorities before the party tonight," Dominic commanded from behind the crowd, a lone wolf no one dared walk next to.

The man was an enigma. A larger-than-life loner here in California. In Florida, he was different. Approachable ... at least with his family. I'd seen how he smiled at his brothers, at my stepsister, at her baby. He hadn't smiled once today. Here, he was untouchable, and I didn't want to be alone in a room with him, not after how many times he'd found a way to cut me down.

Even so, I wrung my hands together, and my heels clicked on the tile of the lobby toward my sleek bakery.

One step and then another.

Dominic was this untouchable god to most of us here.

Click. Click.

To me, though, he was the devil.

Click. Click.

And there I went, walking right into hell with him.

CHAPTER 4: CLARA

He followed the track of my finger before he pulled his eyes up to meet mine. "How's your welcome to the City of Angels been?"

The man had the audacity to ask me that now? "I've been here for a month, Dominic."

"Right." He wasn't dumb, not by a long shot. And he wasn't socially awkward either. So, that left me to believe he was just being rude.

How sad that my stepfather had handed over this resort to him. A man that couldn't even greet me when I got off my flight or ask me to lunch or give me a walk-through of the place we'd both be working at. "The city is fine and so is your resort."

He hummed and leaned against the counter, swiping a hand over imaginary dust so that he didn't have to look at me. "You really don't like the resort or the bakery, do you? It resembles a hospital to you?"

I turned to look around me. The pink dishes I'd requested were white; the linens folded in the back were, I knew, white when I'd asked for red. Over and over, my desires had been rejected.

I was to blame, though, ultimately. I'd been compliant, merely requesting rather than demanding.

I pushed the tip of my stiletto into the rug in front of the register. That was black, too. "My taste in the resort doesn't really matter."

"If you say it doesn't, then it really doesn't," he concluded, agreeing with me.

"Well then." I shrugged. "Why even ask me then?"

"Because if you're going to work here, we need you to at least attempt to keep a leash on your ridiculously illogical opinions."

"I wouldn't say they're illogical. Other than the strip, this place is—"

"Luxurious, elegant, what people want."

"If you say so. No use arguing with you." I wasn't going to participate in such an exercise with an arrogant asshole who couldn't take criticism.

"Because?"

I frowned. "Because I've read you don't take constructive criticism well, and I've tried to argue my way into one speck of color in my own bakery to no avail."

"You read about me?" He seemed surprised.

"Everyone has." I tried to cover it up, not wanting to stroke his ego at all. "You're an amazing architect and designer. You've completed numerous resorts and also have a knack for managing them. People don't even know how you have time to sleep. You treat every design like your baby, and you're overprotective of them all. I get it. That's how I am with my bakery." I took a deep breath and tried not to feel pain when I glanced at those seats again. "I know what I sent to Rita wasn't perfect, but it was mine."

He nodded. "You realize it's a privilege to have Rita on the team, working on this with you. She's an MFA1." I blinked at him. "She has a Master of Fine Arts in Interior Design from the New York School of Interior Design." I blinked again. "It's one of the best schools in the nation"—he seemed slightly perturbed now—"and she knows how to capture the image of what we want."

She hadn't captured anything. "I don't think so," I blurted it out. Standing in that bakery was almost making me ill. I was going to have to work here, practically live here for the next year, and I had to make sure this bakery was profitable, that I could stomach my own backdrop, and that I could thrive here. My bank account depended on it. I took a deep breath before I murmured, "This wasn't what I wanted for my bakery. Not at all. Can't we consider changes?"

Dominic's eyes widened just a millimeter, before they frowned at my question. "You keep asking but nothing needs changing, Clara."

"Can you imagine someone coming in and destroying your whole architectural design of this resort?"

"It's happened a time or two. I did have to include a bakery that—"

"The bakery was a blip on your radar. You have half a million square feet, and the bakery doesn't even face the front of this building!" Snapping at him wasn't the right thing to do, but I couldn't snap at my stepfather since he was six feet under. "But my design, my brand's aesthetic? You and Rita destroyed it."

Dominic chuckled, then cracked his large knuckles. Even if I didn't enjoy his presence, his intense eyes, strong jaw, and muscles in all the right places were nice to look at. "If you think we did that, I'm sorry, but I will tell you ... fresh out of college, no one looked twice at my designs. My design pitches, site plan drawings, elevation drawings ... all of them were ripped apart over and over before I got any say in the builds I worked on. I worked my ass off from the ground up on my own and fought for each project."

There was the insinuation again, that I hadn't made my way to the top, that I wouldn't fight for any of it. "You do recognize that I also went to the best culinary schools, traveled the world to understand what works in the industry, and that my bakery in Florida was not a flop for a reason."

"I know the reason." He tapped a finger on the counter before he met my gaze with condescension.

"And what is it?"

"You and I both know that Carl handed you that bakery just like he's handed you the one here. I've interviewed countless chefs and bakers and worked with restaurateurs for nearly a decade. There are others who should have had that space instead of you."

I fisted my hand and put it over my heart that I knew would have broken or pounded out of my chest if I didn't control myself now. "Carl may have helped, but my menu, recipes, and brand's designs will speak for themselves. I guarantee it." He stared at me, his gaze hard as granite and as cold as ice. "You may not believe me, Dominic. But I will prove it," I whispered out.

I don't think I knew right until that moment how badly I wanted his approval, how hard I was striving for his acceptance. Dominic Hardy wasn't cruel. He simply knew what was the best. I think that's what hurt the most. He knew I wasn't it, that I hadn't earned my place.

But that's what I'd come to do. Not for him, but for myself. I'd decided to change my lifestyle and this was the first step.

He finally glanced away from me. "So what? You're unhappy with the added seating." He stood there with his arms crossed, a frown on his face.

"This isn't just about the seating, Dominic." Both of us knew that. "I'm trying to remain positive, and I would have at least given this a shot if Rita had given me one thing I'd asked for. One little thing after I sat with her and explained how much I wanted a few pink accents."

Yet, she hadn't even texted me to tell me she'd made the change. Instead, I got to find out on the tour today.

My desserts had bold color, at least. They'd pop against the stark white counter tops and shiny shelving encased in glass near the register. Not every appliance was in, I could probably brighten the place with those.

"But we're going for polished and modern. That will attract guests and uphold the Pacific Coast Resort standard," he said confidently. No amount of positivity would ease my frustration, though.

This felt like a last shot at my dream, and he was chipping away at it, tearing small pieces off and leaving me with a nightmare. He and Rita were setting me up for failure because I couldn't thrive here.

His phone vibrated, and I waved at him to answer as I glanced around and took in the eight hundred square foot area. The wraparound counter with the register on the end would work well, especially with half of it being glass where people could view desserts. The tables and chairs along the floor-to-ceiling window that overlooked the lobby was a plus.

Still, after seeing no pink booths, the white tiling felt like a slap in the face the longer I glared at it while Dominic bickered with someone on the phone. "I don't really care what they want. We did hardwood flooring to warm up the rooms when the sunlight hits. The end product is what they need for their brand. Let them know they will like it once it's finished."

He hung up and turned his attention back to me, his eyes full of vibrating energy I couldn't quite pin down.

"Rita is happy to make design changes where you feel necessary. We've ordered the last of the appliances which should be here in the next day or two."

I gnashed my teeth together and ground them back and forth. Even though tears pricked my eyes, I smiled through them. "Well, could I at least look at the appliances you ordered?"

He lifted a brow at my snark. I was beyond being polite though. "Is it a problem that I ordered those too?"

"I'd like to take a look at which models and brands specifically. I have certain tastes when it comes to the tools I use every day."

"Clara, I assure you we've ordered the best." He crossed his large arms over his chest. I tried not to glance down. I could list his accolades like most magazines did, but I would never repeat what they wrote about his appearance. They called him one of the most attractive men in the world next to Brad Pitt, and honestly, he'd probably beat him out. His dark hair had the perfect wave, his strong jaw had the perfect angle, and his large arms were perfect to have wrapped around a woman.

I took a step back so my body could distance itself. "Even so, if you happen to have a receipt for the appliances, I'll look it over and confirm—"

He sighed and grabbed his phone from his pocket. Two seconds later, my phone pinged. I scanned the list from the picture he'd sent and couldn't help but wrinkle my nose. Most of it was perfect, but none of it had a splash of color. Stainless steel, black, matte-black espresso machine.

"What's wrong with it?" He was scanning my features when I glanced up. For anyone else I would have given in. I was used to rolling over and not causing waves. But not this time.

"I don't like the colors of these appliances," I blurted out and felt lighter immediately. I didn't want to appease people here like I did in the past. So, I guess I was going to protect my new self at all costs.

"The color?" His question was asked in a higher pitch. "Jesus Christ."

"It's *my* bakery, Dominic." I threw back. "I have to work here. Do you understand that? Once you and Rita leave and move on to your next venture, I still want to be here. And I didn't pick the color scheme for any of this," I pointed out and then turned to wave toward the walls and the tables that had been set up. "Although you have the structure of the blueprint spot on, the mock-ups that I approved had bursts of color. Rita's changed every literal thing."

"Well, Rita has a vision. And she fought for it."

Was that a comment at how easily I'd given in to them? "Are you saying I should have fought more?" I narrowed my eyes at him. He knew the will's stipulations just as well as I did and I'd been trying to accommodate them by giving in time and time again.

"I'm saying you and Rita handled it, and we're here now." He sighed like this was all below his pay grade.

"Okay." I tried to pull back my feelings because lashing out wouldn't solve anything. Yet it was another chip at my dream. I'd just heard him micromanaging someone's flooring on the phone. There's no way he hadn't had a say in draining all the color from my bakery. "I'll talk with her about it."

"Keep in mind she's handling the lobby design and suites this week. I'll be covering some of the final construction and so we won't have much more time to spend here. The grand reopening of the resort is in just a few months. You have the dates in your calendar, correct?"

I nodded slowly, trying not to nitpick at the way his question demeaned my intelligence. "I'll be ready."

"See that you have extra staff working with you during the grand reopening. Rita gave you the list of hires available?" I nodded. "A lot of people will be coming through just to see the place and try things out. Are you staying close to the resort?"

"Close enough." I shrugged. If this was Dominic's small talk and attempt at smoothing things over, he had a long way to go.

He hummed like he didn't approve of my answer. I don't think he approved of anything in regard to me. "Shall we get back to the group and continue with this ridiculous party tonight?"

"I'm excited about the party," I told him, so he didn't think the idea was stupid. Whoever had planned it and placed importance on us all getting to know each other was building a good team of workers. "We'll all be much more helpful to one another if we hang out and are friends."

"You would think that," he grumbled and then waved me toward the door.

"It's true, Dominic. Think about if you'd come to me about your resort designs and I came to you with my bakery designs. We could have maybe come up with a better outcome than—"

"Better?" He glared. "As in not a hospital setting? You do realize magazines have said this is a brilliant display of opposition balancing, the straight lines with the curves, the black with the white—"

"I really didn't mean ..." I glanced up at him to see the passion in his eyes when describing the place.

"Also"—a small smile suddenly played on his lips—"I don't enjoy any sort of color. Not even on your dress."

I instantly grabbed the fabric of my dress, completely affronted. I loved flowers on dresses, color, and light everywhere. Glancing down and then up again, he started to chuckle "You're teasing me. That's fine. Whatever. I think you know this resort is beautiful. You don't need my approval."

He rolled his eyes and opened the door for me so I could walk out into the lobby. "Oh good. We done throwing insults at me now?"

"*At* you? I didn't say anything about you. I just said your resort—"

"My resort *is* me. We're one and the same, Clara." He said it with such conviction that I actually felt like we could relate for a second.

"Then you must know that me and my bakery are one and the same too. You realize that you and Rita upending my design was an insult every single time, right? If you change my design, you insult my bakery. And I am my bakery." I squared up to him, willing him to disagree.

He studied me for a few seconds before he stepped back, holding his hand out for me to walk out of the bakery with him. I grabbed my bag and brushed past him as he said, "Then own it and fight for it."

Little did I know, he shook something loose with those words, the way he said them like they were a command, like I needed to listen to him, like it was the best advice he could give me. I knew that was wrong. He didn't really want me to fight. No one did. It's why I was pretty much the pushover of the century.

Yet, that night, our fight began.

CHAPTER 5: CLARA

Anastasia called an hour later while I was at the party and told me to talk to her for just ten minutes, which I did, not because I wanted to but because I didn't want to say no.

I gave in again and again. It was how I was raised, what I was used to. Except, after listening to her blabber on and on about me coming home, those words kept rattling around inside my head. I told her I had to go, grabbed my keys with my bakery fob on them out of my purse, and then placed it down with the others near one of the tables before I decided to network with everyone.

I smiled, shook hands, and took shots with them. This was supposed to be a night of making all my colleagues like me, and as they got drunker and drunker, I found myself happy to be surrounded by each of them. No one seemed to care that I had the bakery on the lobby floor. They just wanted to make sure we all coordinated, had fun, and were all successful.

Except Rita. Rita glared at Paloma's clothing store sign on the beachfront like she wanted to start an argument.

"You'll have to change your shop name and if the sign can't be reworked by our deadline, I'll take my issue with it to Dom." She dropped his nickname like they were so close that she could get away with it. "He won't want such an eyesore for guests."

Paloma's eyes widened. We'd just been discussing how Frida's Closet fit her brand so well. She'd named it after her grandma who passed away just a year ago. I waited for her to speak up, to tell Rita to fuck off, to be the bold woman I knew her to be, but instead, her eyes filled with tears. She nodded without fighting back. Without even one peep.

"What exactly don't you like about the name?" I heard myself blurt out as I came to stand next to my new friend. Maybe I was getting bolder because of the drinks or maybe I was tired of Rita putting us down. I'd been near women like her all my life. My sister and mother had a great way of looking down at someone even when it would have been better for us all to work together. "What about the name don't you agree with?"

"Isn't it obvious, Miss Milton?" She turned her laser focus on me. "We've been very lenient with everyone's creativity on the strip, obviously, but Frida's Closet is not the look we're going for. Are you set on that name?"

"No ... No, of course not. I just thought it was cute and—"

"It *is* cute." I clarified. Paloma's bright brown eyes had lit up moments before as she'd explained the name to me. "People want a place to feel comfortable and at home when they shop. This is the perfect—"

"Are you an expert on people in LA, Miss Milton?"

This woman had some audacity to ask me that question. I crossed my arms over my chest, stepping in front of my friend. "I own a bakery on a beach in Florida, Rita, and I am about to own another here—"

"Yes, but the one here was designed mostly by *me*, was it not?" She didn't give me a chance to answer. "You may own it because your stepfather allowed for that, but I've built it to make sure it is up to standards. And it's taken quite the effort to make it fit in a place that it probably shouldn't. Do remember, we're trying to uphold a standard."

Paloma placed a hand on my back, hinting that I should

back down. But I was so tired. My eyes flicked around, and Dominic was nowhere to be seen. Yet, enough people were watching that I knew this story would get back to him.

I should have stopped. Rolled over. Maybe played dead.

Instead, I did what he'd said and owned it. I fought for it against his interior designer in a way he probably didn't want me to. "Then you should remember that standards are built from the designers and artists that create them. Paloma's store and my bakery included. Watering down our vision for the masses ruins the magic of originality that people want to experience."

I stormed past her, and thankfully, Paloma followed. She pulled me close to her, threaded her hand in mine, and whispered that we should go sit in her store for a minute. I nodded because I wasn't sure if I was tasting the salty air or the salt from my silent tears.

I needed a minute. Just one. And then maybe just one more.

Uprooting my life to move to the opposite coast and open a brand-new bakery that was meant to be all mine was supposed to have been fun. I squeezed my eyes shut in the darkness of Paloma's store and told myself I could get through how scary it was to put together something that was supposed to be yours and hope people enjoyed it.

And when I started considering how the venture was most likely abysmal with Rita breathing down my neck, Paloma slammed her store door behind us and squealed, "You're my fucking hero! You know how badly I've wanted to do that since I started here? Rita's the worst, and she never gives us any recognition. Did you see her face?"

No, because I was too busy stifling my urge to cry. I peeked over at my friend, "Was it bad?"

"It was epic." Then she squealed again and barreled into

me with a hug. "I ... I never stood up for myself like that, Clara. Legit was with a guy for ages who pushed me around and everything. Never once said a bad thing about him until right now. To you. Because you're a freaking boss."

I chewed the inside of my cheek, trying not to burst into tears for a whole different reason. I hadn't stood up for myself in a long time either. Too long.

"You know what," I whispered before I cleared my throat and said loudly, "I need the pink paint you used for your fitting rooms."

She frowned at me, confused, and then her eyes widened. "Well, that's ... I don't know if that's such a good idea. Telling off Rita was great but—"

"You don't even know what my idea is. If you don't tell me where it is, I'll just go through your store." I shrugged. String lights twinkled outside above everyone as they laughed and danced out on the beach, knowing they were getting the opportunity of their dreams. I wanted that opportunity, too.

And I was willing to fight for it.

"You're going to regret this in the morning. I already know it."

"I've known Dominic longer than the rest of you." That was only half true. "He's even worse than Rita, and they might have given everyone this opportunity, but they are suffocating us with their rules. And I'm so tired of not being able to breathe."

She took a deep breath. "Do you need help?"

She sounded scared and I chuckled as I reassured her. "I don't need help, and if anyone asks me, I'll tell them I have no idea where I got the paint. I was much too drunk to remember."

We both laughed as we disappeared around the corner into the back of her store. Within minutes, I was sneaking against the walls of the building and sliding into one of the doors to run through the lobby and down the long hallway to my bakery.

My heart raced, and I was filled with fear and adrenaline that someone might have been following me, but as I turned around, I found no one was paying attention. I had never been happier to not be important.

I laughed to myself and plopped down to sit on the clean white tile in my bakery—the bakery I'd dreamed about, the bakery I'd pictured in my head my whole life—and glared.

Disdain and anger at Rita's words swarmed my head. She was right, of course.

This bakery wasn't *mine*. It was *hers*. All hers. From the crisp white tile to the white countertops to the black leather in the booths and the checkered backsplash of the wall separating the back kitchen and the front of the bakery.

I stood there glaring at it before I stomped over to the white wall opposite the front doors. I stomped past the counters and went right to it.

I set the paint can down and opened it slowly before I took the paintbrush Paloma gave me and dipped it in.

The first swipe of the pink on that white wall felt like I'd wielded my weapon for the fight, and I was about to win.

CHAPTER 6: CLARA

"What in the actual fuck, Clara Milton?"

There was no denying what I'd done. Honestly, the paintbrush was still in my hand, pink paint dripping from it down into the can. The white back wall of my bakery now blended with pink creating a sort of ombre look. It was a soft pink but bold enough to throw off the black-and-white of the bakery. It was an accent wall of sorts. Different. Beautiful.

I wouldn't apologize. I wouldn't even give him the attention he felt he deserved. He'd done the same to me over the past year during renovations. I didn't turn around. "It's more perfect than I thought it would be."

He walked up behind me and swiped the paintbrush out of my hand and then stuffed it into the paint can. "Are you out of your mind? There's ... This ... We have to open in two months."

"I'm aware of the date, Dominic." My whole body was so tired just thinking about it. Working with him, near him, or even in the same proximity as him would truly be one of the hardest things I'd ever had to do in my life.

"You should probably stick with 'Mr. Hardy' while at work."

"Well, you should probably stick with 'Ms. Milton' then," I sneered back.

"God, I knew you were unequipped to run a business, but I didn't know you were this incompetent." He shook his head at the wall.

"Incompetent? Are you seriously for real? How about Rita being incompetent for her opinions on Paloma's sign—"

"That's been taken care of." He cut me off and right then a text came through on my phone. I felt the vibration before I pulled it out to look at it.

Paloma: Dominic told Rita the name of my shop stays, Clara. He freaking complimented it.

There were ten crying emojis after. I set my phone down on the counter and raised my eyes to look at him in bewilderment. "You let her keep the name?"

"It suits her store." That was all the explanation he gave.

I narrowed my eyes at him, unable to figure out his angle. "Okay. Well," I cleared my throat trying to come back from the fact that suddenly Dominic wasn't a complete asshole. "I'm sorry, but I'm here to make this bakery the best it can be."

"Is that what you're doing out there partying with everyone?" He questioned.

"Yes. It's called socializing with the staff and learning how this resort is going to run with their personalities. Incompetence would be disappearing even though you're the CEO of the damn resort."

"I'm the architectural engineer and designer first. Let's be honest, too, most CEOs aren't going to be mingling when they need to be working. Rita has that handled."

"Working real hard on that drink, huh?" I pointed to the tumbler he had in his hand.

He lifted it and tilted it a tad too much, showing me he was probably as tipsy as I was. "I deserve to unwind for a second,

Clara."

"Not when your assistant is out there ripping apart your staff."

"Rita knows what she's doing. If changes are needed—"

"You both wanted to put my espresso machine in the freaking kitchen, Dominic, and not out here behind the counter. Neither of you have any idea how to work that machine, bake in general, or run a kitchen."

"It doesn't take a genius," he grumbled.

If I had still had the paintbrush in hand, I would have thrown it at him. Instead, I leaned in and smirked. "You think you're so freaking good at everything, go into my kitchen and show me, then."

"What?"

"Go in there and make me a damn cupcake. You think I'm not good enough to be in your resort, show me that you can do it better than me. Or better yet, try my cupcakes for once and tell me it's not good enough to be next to your Michelin chefs."

He narrowed his emerald eyes. "You challenging me, Ms. Milton? Even after throwing paint on my walls?"

"They aren't your walls. They're *mine*." I said it boldly, and I even walked up and poked his shoulder like I had a right to. Maybe everyone else was scared of him but I wasn't anymore. This bakery was mine, and it would be my failure, too. I wasn't going to give it to someone else. I couldn't anymore.

"Oh, she's a fighter now," he mumbled to himself, like he wasn't sure what to do with me. I wasn't sure what to do with myself either, but the alcohol had given me courage and I was seizing it. "You want a cupcake, I'll play along. As long as you have all the right ingredients."

"I'll be impressed if you even know what goes into it."

The smile flew across his face fast. The man didn't smile much, and I sort of forgot how attractive he was right up until that moment. He leaned in close to my ear, and I smelled the ocean, sandalwood, and something wholly *him*. "I know exactly what goes into your desserts, little fighter."

The butterflies in my stomach erupted way too strongly for me to stay this close to him. I stumbled back and bit my lip, catching his gaze before he raked his eyes over my body boldly and without apology.

I didn't move, and I didn't break my stare. With any other man, I would have. I wasn't here to show anyone up, but this seemed like a challenge to see if I could hold my own and more than anything now, I wanted to prove I could. We were pushing each other's buttons, testing the limits, and seeing who would bend first. "Maybe you need to get back to work. Rita might need you."

His tongue dragged over his teeth like he was sharpening them. "Most of my staff can handle their jobs without me."

Another indirect shot at me. "Are you saying I can't?"

I didn't wait for his response. I spun on my heel and slammed through the steel door. I'd infused lavender in my last batch of chocolate cupcakes to see if they would be good enough for the menu. Most of the ideas I'd attempted yesterday hadn't made the cut, but those had. I grabbed a small cupcake with a flavorful infused flower on it. They were bite-size, mini cupcakes, but had such a burst of flavor I thought they might be worthy of being a signature dessert.

I spun around to find him inches away, hovering over me, so close I felt his breath fanning out on my cheek. He was ready to throw another barb my way, and I didn't care to hear any of it. I popped the tiny cupcake into his mouth before he had a chance to get a word out.

His eyes widened at my boldness.

I didn't care. I folded my arms and glared at him as he finally chewed. "If you can make a cupcake like what you have in your mouth, I promise you, Mr. Hardy, I won't complain about any of the changes made to the bakery again."

I might have been concerned about how my bakery would fit in his resort, but I was a damn good baker and pastry chef. I knew how to infuse chocolate, knew how to blend ingredients well enough that they melted in your mouth. I knew how to mix spices and create an experience through someone's body just from taste. I watched him closely, how he rolled the food in his mouth, and when he breathed out, I knew that's when the cinnamon and lavender would hit his taste buds. Normally when I got the ingredients just right, I would hear moans or whispers of praise. Dominic Hardy had never tried my creations, though, and so I'd never heard the low growl that seeped from deep within his chest and washed over me.

His eyes darkened, his muscles relaxed, and he leaned closer before placing both of his hands on the steel counter behind me. He hung his head as his eyes closed, like the flavor had overtaken him. "Fuck, Clara."

Him saying my name like that shot straight to my core and butterflies erupted everywhere in my body in a way they shouldn't have. "You mean *Ms. Milton*," I whispered.

He shook his head before he lifted it, not responding at all to my statement as he licked his bottom lip. "What is in that?"

I couldn't keep from smiling. "Hmm, secrets and revelations. Secrets of the recipe and the revelation that you won't be able to duplicate it."

"You enjoy challenging me, don't you? You know I'm

always able to do what they say I can't, right?"

I believed him. I never heard of his failures, only his successes. He'd solidified multimillion dollar contracts, and he'd created an architectural firm that was worth billions. And that was before he invested in my stepfather's empire. Even still ... "Making a chocolate cupcake isn't just technical, Dominic."

He hummed, "You mean *Mr. Hardy*, right?"

I shrugged. "I'm sure I won't have to call you anything much since I don't ever really see you."

"That right?" He tilted his head. "Who do you think is going to come back here and paint over your tantrum?"

"I know you aren't calling what I did a tantrum. Can you imagine if I ruined your baby over and over?"

"What's that supposed to mean?"

"I get that you can't stand that my bakery was plopped right in the middle of your resort. That I'm marring it in some way. I get it, but this space is a small portion of it. You still have the entire expansive exterior. Every floor. The lobby. Everything is yours. And you get it exactly how you want. You wouldn't have it any other way, right?"

"Sure?"

"Well, this is my only bakery. The one I can control, the one I've been given a shot at, and you and Rita have completely destroyed my ownership of it."

He didn't apologize, but I saw how his nostrils flared just a little as he breathed out deeply, like he finally had even a sliver of remorse before saying, "How about if I can make this cupcake just like yours, you stop asking for changes to this bakery for the next two months. How about that?"

Chewing my cheek, I tried my best not to laugh in his face.

"You think I can't make it, huh?" He chuckled and before I

could stop him, he'd grabbed my hips and picked me up to set me on the prep island's countertop. "Watch."

He turned round and round, trying to find all the ingredients I'd used. He got the cacao powder and butter right along with the sugar, salt, and milk. Quite frankly, I was impressed with that, but the spices and oils were the difficult part. I didn't even blink when he grabbed the lavender and held it up for me to approve.

"All you, big shot." I waved him on.

He laughed again like he enjoyed the challenge, like we weren't fighting for our dreams here. When I hopped off the counter, he asked where I was going.

"To get this." I grabbed a bottle of bourbon out of one of the white cupboards.

"You already stashing liquor to drink while on the job?"

"Bourbon adds a hint of sweetness to the chocolate. Some people like scotch better, but it's a little too smoky for my taste." I pulled out two glasses as he frowned at his ingredients. "Not for this specific chocolate cupcake, though. You're welcome for the hint."

I slid a tumbler his way as he turned on the stove to heat the cocoa butter. I didn't correct the temperature even though my hand itched to do so. He didn't have a heatproof bowl, either. Melting butter right in the saucepan was solidifying his defeat. "I'll give you one more. Cinnamon, lavender, and nutmeg were used."

"I'm fucking it up already, aren't I?"

Shrugging, I took a sip of my drink. "We'll have to see, won't we?"

"It's going to taste just like yours." He grabbed another cupcake from the wax paper and popped it in his mouth. He swore again. "Has Valentino tried these?"

I hesitated before answering. Valentino was on the seventy-fifth floor. He was another sort of celebrity in my mind. Sure, I'd met men like him before, but he was arguably one of the best in the world. I'd heard of his restaurants, how he ran his kitchens, how he became a legend in his twenties. Now, in his thirties, every food blogger and critic knew of him. His restaurants won awards, and he'd won the James Beard along with others.

"It's not on the menu yet. I'm just testing out the limits of this kitchen and seeing what I can do."

He hummed, still staring at the treat. "See that you discuss all desserts with him in the case that he wants to include this in the restaurant because there's nothing this good for a dessert up there."

Seriously? He hadn't said it in a way that I thought it was a compliment, and yet my heart warmed far too much at his assessment. "So you're saying you like something of mine finally?"

"Does it matter? This could be up there." Should I have said thank you?

"I don't know if our menus will harmonize that much. People will be going to his restaurant for a fancy night with their partner. My bakery is—"

"A fresh start to their morning with a decadent twist?"

I snapped my mouth shut at his near perfect description. I wasn't going to agree aloud ... even if I thought it.

He didn't seem fazed as he stared at the chocolate syrup he was trying to create. He hadn't even got to the flour and sugar yet. "I'm going to regret agreeing to this aren't I?"

"It's just the chocolate base. You can do that. I'm not making anything that special like your other chefs and bakers,"

I encouraged, starting the comment as condescending, but I felt a sliver of doubt at the end. "I'm just ..."

"You're what, Clara?"

I couldn't tell him I might have felt out of place, that I might not end up belonging.

I was here to fake it until I made it, right?

CHAPTER 7: DOMINIC

There was a new word I was starting to associate with everything Clara Milton.

Addictive.

I saw how she navigated people at the welcome event, how people gravitated toward her, took her opinion into consideration. *I* even did when she tore down my resort design. She had a refreshing eye and was honest with it. And then she'd stood up for Paloma more than she ever stood up for herself. It reminded me of what art was and what it could be.

I wouldn't dim that even if it meant giving into Paloma's store name. I told Rita, too, and of course she'd been pissed, but I didn't care. When Clara stood up for Paloma in a moment I'd been sure she'd stand down, that's when her light became brilliant, became irresistibly exceptional, shining so much brighter than the others that I couldn't look away.

I'd thought I'd fade off into the background at the party again, but instead, I caught her sneaking off.

She'd stepped up to the plate and fucking swung, too, when she painted *my* wall.

Mine. I wanted that clear. Everything in this damn resort was mine, and she'd vandalized it. Altered it. Changed it to her needs.

It was bold and completely rebellious. And my cock wanted to punish her or praise her for it, I wasn't sure which at this point. Something about Clara going against me and pushing boundaries when I knew she normally gave in to accommodate had me wanting more, craving more, needing more.

I'd fast become addicted to whatever she was serving. And that was dangerous. I didn't indulge in vices anymore. Sugar and sex were both big ones.

Clara Milton deserved a pink backdrop to the bakery she'd always wanted. She deserved probably everything she'd asked for. Yet, you had to be cutthroat to be at the top, vicious in pursuit of your vision, and willing to leave bodies behind. I was more than willing because I'd learned the hard way to do so. I wanted her to be that way too.

"You're what?" I asked again, harder this time. I wanted an answer. I wanted her to either fight or tell me she was something less.

I saw the desolation in her big green eyes and also the hunger; the hunger to be good enough, to fit in, to succeed. It reminded me of what I'd wanted so many years ago.

She'd gotten this bakery without working for it, and yet she still tried her hardest, had been on board to analyze every tiny design detail like me. I saw her effort and a part of me wanted her to fail so she understood that without failure, you couldn't truly reach success. She'd potentially fail over and over again with this bakery, but she only had to get up and keep trying.

She had to learn to fight.

I glanced down at the chocolate and saw it was clumping together. "Shit."

"Want to start again?" She sniffed the air. "If you don't temper it, you'll never get it right."

My jaw ticked. I hated failure even if it was small. "Show me the recipe."

Her mouth opened, the rosy color of her lips plumping out

into a pout as she shut it again like she was speechless. "I'm not ... It's too late to teach you a recipe right now. Are you serious?"

"I want to learn it. Right. Now."

"Maybe another day, Mr. Hardy." She rolled her big pretty eyes as she said my last name that I'd put between us as a boundary. Now, though, it was just acting as another magnet. I enjoyed how she tried to goad me. "We should get back to the party."

True, except I wasn't going anywhere now. "No." I shook my head slowly, my voice low, "Show me."

As she bit her lip, I knew she was considering it.

I pointed to the saucepan in front of me. "Come right here, little fighter. Let's see if you have it in you to do again."

There wasn't even a moment's hesitation when I challenged her like that. "Fine." She walked right up to the counter, shouldered me in my chest, and got to work. She handed me the saucepan and pointed to the sink where I dropped it, keeping my eyes on her. "That's all wasted so we're starting over."

She reached high above her, and I watched her stretch, noting that she was probably going to need a stool to reach all the way up in her own cabinets. Having her body against me, smelling the chocolate mixed with the flowery scent of her hair had my cock twitching.

She pulled out a thick bowl that I saw her practically glare at.

"Something wrong with that too?"

"I requested red bowls."

Also noted. "Could have been here to stop that order had you not been catering to your boyfriend's need to have you at his hockey game." She wanted to bicker about a damn dish, I'd meet her at her level.

No one fought me head-on anymore but she was ready as she slammed down the bowl. "He's not my boyfriend. He's a friend. Ever had a friend that's a girl?"

I let my eyes rake over her body, making sure she caught me. "He'd fuck you if you gave him the chance."

"Oh, he does when I do." Her smile was saccharine as she shrugged. "Still doesn't make him my boyfriend."

I felt it like a gut punch. *Fuck.* One point for her.

The tightening in my stomach was only due to the fact that I didn't actually like the desserts that I could smell everywhere, right? It definitely wasn't because hearing that Clara and Noah truly were fucking around pissed me off. I didn't get jealous about women anymore, and I definitely didn't get jealous over women I didn't even like.

"If you're fucking around with a guy, he's more than a friend."

"Really?" she countered. "So, when you sleep with women—"

"I don't stay over. I don't even fall asleep in their bed for a minute." I hadn't in years, not that it was her business, but a point needed to be made. "I tell them I'm fucking them, Ms. Milton, and that's it. I don't go to their games or wear their jerseys or end up in magazines with them. I make my intentions clear."

"As do I," she threw back. "Noah and I have always been very clear about the expectations. He's great that way."

"He's a fuckboy who has women circling him twenty-four seven. You should be careful with the men you're—"

"Mr. Hardy." She tsked. "*We* are colleagues. Not friends. I don't need your advice on anything but what you want in the bakery, and even that's mostly unwarranted."

I chuckled. Damn, she was something when she got a little alcohol in her. "Fine. You like reds and pinks and every color on the planet. Rita and I don't."

"You're depriving me of my dream." She said it with passion, and her eyes shined, like there was emotion behind them.

I actually contemplated soothing her. I took a deep breath. "Want me to change the bowls then?" Her gaze whipped to mine as she dropped the bowl into another saucepan and turned the stove way down. Her eyes shone with questions, curiosity, and hope. Why had I said that?

"Don't offer that unless you mean it, Dominic," she whispered, all joking aside as she murmured my first name this time. I loved hearing it across her lips.

"I don't normally say anything I don't mean."

We stared at one another for far too long as she stirred without looking. Then, she glanced down before grumbling, "Good luck telling Rita."

"Are you aware I'm her boss? You think she's going to have a problem with my request?" I smirked and Clara glanced up with a small smile, then she chuckled.

"I mean, probably." Another giggle bubbled up, and then she was laughing as she grabbed another cooking utensil and spun the butter round and round, adding in the cacao and sugar. Effortlessly, she salted the concoction and then dribbled in a few drops of an oil. "It's her bakery after all."

She admitted the last part with a sigh, letting her laugh die, and I couldn't stop myself from taking in the woman before me. Curves for days, dressed in heels and a cream dress full of flowers. She continued to drop in flavors even as I moved closer to dip a finger into the warm liquid that had turned to silk and caught her frowning. "What?"

"I just can't get over seeing you indulge in any of this, especially melted chocolate that needs to go into the cupcakes, when you never stop by the bakery, ever."

She didn't know me. She had no idea how much I would indulge in a vice, no idea about my ex, and how that led me to make fatal errors by doing so in the past. "Clara, I indulge when it's worth it to do so."

I found it harder and harder to hold back now as her cheeks pinkened under my scrutiny. The woman caught innuendo fast because her mind was probably exactly where mine was.

"Well, my chocolate is finally worth it, then? As opposed to all the years you passed by my bakery back home?"

"In my defense, now I need to know what will be in my resort."

She hummed and then murmured, "A touch of salt with three drops of lavender and sprinkling of cinnamon mixed with nutmeg is key. I add more some days and less others dependent on my mood."

"It won't be the same, then."

"It'll be mine though, and that should be enough." She quickly removed it from the heat and set it on the other burner, but she didn't step away from me. She met me with that burning gaze again. "I'm trying to prove that *mine* is enough here."

"And yet you let Rita run right over you for this bakery."

"I was trying to be 'harmonious' with your needs," she shot back.

"Ah. So sweet of you, Clara." That never worked if it was a designer's vision. "But, tell me, was it 'harmonious' when you called my resort a sterile hospital?"

She took a deep breath. "Well, I apologize for that—"

"Don't." My command cut through the air. She needed to learn something now and consciously pick a side. I leaned in, close enough to have my lips against her ear. "Are you sweet or spicy, babe? A pushover or a fighter?" I pulled back when she didn't answer right away. Her gaze glinted with embarrassment or anger or both. "Should we see? You as sweet as this chocolate or not?"

I was pushing her to the edge. I knew that. Maybe I wanted her to fold and step away. She needed to.

She needed to understand her place, but instead she stepped up to me and reached into the saucepan, swiping up melted chocolate on her finger and then dragging it across her collarbone. "I don't know, Dominic." She whispered, "Want to taste me and see?"

A challenge for a challenge. She met me head-on.

So, I guess the fighter in Clara didn't know when to quit. She'd met a formidable match, too, because I didn't even hesitate. I should have, but I'd had a hell of a day with structural problems and calls from overseas about another project. The last straw was listening to her tear apart the blood, sweat, and tears that went into designing and managing this resort.

Truth was it shouldn't have just been me. I had a whole team of restaurateurs, designers, financial advisors, HR, and every other possible person needed. Yet, I wanted my hands in everything. A person didn't get their perfection without doing it themselves.

I grabbed her neck and pushed her chin up so I could get better access to that sensitive part of her body. She shuddered when my tongue dragged across her collarbone and then my teeth. I wouldn't be gentle. When I shoved her against the counter and gripped her hip to lift her by her neck and thigh, she went willingly, wrapping her arms around my neck and spreading her legs for me to walk in between.

I didn't take my mouth from her neck. I couldn't. Her skin was smoother than the ribbons of chocolate, supple and full as I explored further down toward her breasts. Her hands were in my hair, pulling everywhere as she moaned that she needed this, that she wanted one more second.

"One second? Is that all you give your friend Noah?" I shook my head and she gasped at feeling my scruff against her soft skin. "I get more than that, Clara. I want to take my time tasting just to make sure I have it right."

"Wh-what? You just did."

I brought my thumb from her neck up to trace her lower lip, so plump and swollen, showing me she'd been biting it as I sucked on that neck of hers. I held her gaze as I shoved her dress up her thighs, higher and higher. The air in the room crackled with silent tension, and even though the lighting was dim, she vibrated with a bright electricity I couldn't look away from.

I'd ruin someone like her, and the idea of it had my cock rock hard against her stomach as my hand reached the lace under her dress. "When I said I wanted to taste you, I didn't mean your neck, baby. Or these fuckable lips."

I pushed the lace to the side and found her drenched for me. She gasped at how fast I found her clit, how I didn't hesitate to pinch it as I brought my other hand back around her throat and pushed her down so her back was flat against the stainless steel of her gourmet prep island. It gave me easy access to her pussy, to play and taste to my heart's content.

"I meant I wanted to taste you here." I slid one finger into her as I continued to work her clit. I loved how her eyes practically rolled to the back of her head, how her whole body arched at my touch. But I wanted more.

I wanted her to remember this—remember that the bakery and resort she'd called sterile could be dirtied up, that I could indulge, and I would right here and now when it came to her. But I made the rules. I'd bring indulgence here when it was needed. Tonight, it was.

I got on my knees, wanting the smell of her around me, her arousal to coat my face, to have her understand that I owned her here and not the other way around.

My tongue dragged against her slit, and she whimpered, "Dominic, please."

"Spread your legs wider, baby. I want full access. This is mine now. Mine to taste over and over."

She didn't fight me. Her thighs moved like her body belonged to me, and I smiled into my pussy. It was mine. All mine. I became intoxicated, drunk on it and not the whiskey I'd already had that night. I was high on the smell of her, ravenous for the taste of her, and vicious in my pursuit of stealing that orgasm. I sucked on her clit as I felt her body tightening. It was like she wanted to hit her high, but she wanted to fight it, too.

My little fighter. "Let go, baby." She started to work her hips faster and faster, but I knew she was still holding back as I looked up and saw her biting her lip. I pulled back to push a finger into her and she moaned. "That's it. You're going to give me all of you. I want to taste your orgasm on my lips, Clara. Ride my face like you fucking need it." She whimpered when I lowered my mouth to her again and thrust my tongue into her pussy.

Damn, did she move those hips like she'd been instructed to.

Her grip on my hair grew more and more intense as her

thighs tightened around my face like she could pull me closer, like I didn't already have my head buried as far into her as I could.

She tasted sweet and like she was mine. I pinched and rolled her clit so I was the one that pushed her over the edge, even if she was riding my face.

Her whole body clenched as she murmured, "Fuck." The swear sounded sweet on her lips before she screamed my name. The whole thing. Not just Dom or Dominic, but Dominic Hardy. And the raspy sound was purely sexual, filled with passion and surrender.

I drank in her arousal as it soaked my tongue, letting her aftershocks find a home on my mouth because I wanted to learn every taste of hers. I was thorough in all I did, but this was going to become an obsession. Getting Clara Milton to come was going to be a pleasure I wouldn't pass up in the near future. I knew that right then and there.

Clara Milton stretched her light and fun out everywhere. I'd seen it over and over again in the time since knowing her father—how she still smiled at Rita even though my interior designer railroaded her, how she agreed to changes on her design without me meeting with her, how her friend with benefits asked her to stay home for his damn games.

She was a people pleaser, giving herself away always, but tonight, I wanted her all to myself.

When her body finally relaxed, I stood over her, the taste of her still across my lips, her arousal still coating my fingers. I dipped one finger in the chocolate near us and ran it along her bottom lip telling her to taste it. Her green eyes were hazy, but I saw the spark in them as I commanded her to do it. "You are as sweet as your cupcakes, huh?"

She took a deep breath, holding my gaze as she dragged her pink tongue across her soft lips slow enough that my cock twitched twice watching. I didn't break eye contact as I dipped my finger in the bourbon, swirling the chocolate and her arousal around before I brought my finger to my mouth to suck them clean. "Sweet and Spicy just might be a fitting name for this bakery. Fuck, you taste good."

She shivered at my words, her breath coming faster again, and ... damn. Normally, I got what I wanted from a woman, and I didn't pursue much else. I made myself very clear and that included kissing them and whispering niceties after we fucked around.

Even so, when I bent to kiss Clara, it wasn't to be nice. I murmured, "Taste how much your pussy likes me and my resort now." I shoved my tongue in her mouth and thrust my hard length against her sensitive core. She gasped and quaked under me.

I was about to step back when her tongue darted out to meet mine. Then her arm wrapped around my neck, and she pulled me closer, grabbing at my belt to grind my hips to hers as she moaned.

Shit.

I didn't intend to fuck her tonight. I didn't even like the girl. And I hated her bakery being in my resort.

But damn, I liked the taste of her pussy.

CHAPTER 8: CLARA

I'd lost my marbles, okay? All of them. Dominic scattered my thoughts every time I was in his presence, and tonight I'd lost my cool, my control, and probably most of my morals.

Did I try to scrape them back up after he'd been on his knees and got me off?

No.

I, instead, wanted round two. I was going for gold, and I figured I already wouldn't be proud of myself later, so why not take the whole trophy home. I felt his hard cock rubbing against me and knew he was on the verge of fucking me. Maybe if we hate fucked, we could work together after, right?

I unbuckled his belt as he kissed me roughly. "You seem to love my resort now, little fighter."

I didn't. "I actually hate it," I said as he moved to suck on my neck more. He chuckled into my sensitive skin before he bit it and sucked harder.

With his belt undone, I fumbled over the button and then the zipper as I gasped at his hands running over my breasts. Jesus, he was rough, like he couldn't treat me tenderly, like he didn't want to.

I gripped his cock just as hard, though, squeezed it, and the low growl I received spurred me on. "You want to own me, cupcake?"

He thrust up, and I felt the size of him in my fist. I blurted out a "Jesus" before I could school my reaction.

"No baby. Just your boss." He was at the curve of my breast but hadn't pushed the fabric over, and yet I knew he could feel how my nipples had puckered, how they were practically begging for him to touch them.

Still, he sucked right at the edge, kissing my skin like we had all the time in the world. He didn't move his cock closer to my pussy either. Instead, he hovered just centimeters away with my hand stroking him, trying to urge him forward.

"Please," I whispered out, not even sure what I needed—his mouth on my tits or his cock inside me. I just needed more.

"Please what?" His eyes sparkled as he looked at me. He knew he had me at his mercy, that I would succumb to whatever at that moment.

"Please, Dominic. Please make me feel good."

"I won't fuck that pretty pussy knowing you drank. I'm not stupid. At least not tonight. What do you want instead?"

I whimpered and then glared at him. "Stupid? It's not stupid at all. That's what I want." I gripped him and pulled him forward. He allowed it by taking a small step.

We both tensed with the shock of his cock on my bare pussy. Did he feel the zing that shot through me too? My fist barely wrapped fully around him, but even as I pumped him, I still felt every part of him—the veins, the head of his cock, the pre-cum dripping over my fingers. "Would you rather I go find someone else who will have me?" He growled and his cock flexed against my sex. Whimpering, I whispered, "You want me too. I know it."

"Sure, but I want you sober. And then I want you on your knees, begging and pleading for my cock before I fuck the idea of any other man inside you out of your mind." He chuckled like I was ridiculous, and then he pulled the spaghetti strap of my dress over and sucked on my nipple.

His hot mouth and masterful tongue blurred my logical thoughts. Everything became fuzzy with heat and yearning as I begged him to fuck me over and over. The man didn't give in. He actually grabbed my wrist and pulled my hand from his cock when I tried to bring my pussy down on him. He raised one wrist and then the other above my head as he kept lapping at my exposed chest. He bit down on the nipple when I struggled against him.

It was like he was teaching me a lesson. He was in charge. Not me.

And then he stepped close enough that we were flush, his cock between my folds and against my clit. He moved once back and forth, and I felt so badly how much I wanted him to fuck me, tears were in my eyes.

"Need another orgasm, little fighter?"

He asked it so nicely, like he cared, like he wanted me to feel good. I knew he didn't. We were playing with fire, and I was about to get burned. "I need you to be quiet and fuck me, Dominic."

"No. You need to ride my cock. Ride it just how I tell you. Take what you want, baby, because being sweet here won't get you a damn thing." There it was. His insinuation that I'd been too sweet, I'd been a pushover. I'd let Rita take my bakery from me and therefore it was my fault. "Fight for what you want, and you'll get it, Clara. If you don't, I'll be sure to take it from you."

Screw him.

I did what I wanted right then and there. I rolled my hips and worked myself up, grinding my clit against his cock. I bit my lip and watched him, watched how his neck muscles strained. I was doing that, causing his suffering, pushing his restraint to the edge while I built up toward my pleasure and my high. This was for me.

I didn't back down this time, didn't fight his hand on my wrist or struggle when his other hand dragged across the fabric of my remaining spaghetti strap to expose my other breast. I let his eyes rove over my tits as they bounced with my every movement.

"Damn," he swore, "you're beautiful when you own it. How am I supposed to be professional after this?"

I didn't answer him. I didn't care how he went about it. I didn't care about anything in that moment but chasing my orgasm, and yet it evaded me even as I wiggled to-and-fro against him.

"Time to use your words, Clara. Demand what you need."

"Kiss me. Kiss me right fucking now, Dominic."

He smiled like he'd won before he bent down close to my lips and whispered, "So sweet to ask for a kiss. But your pussy wants my mouth more than your tongue."

Then he took his cock away and let his mouth descend on my core again. He didn't give in to what I wanted. I wanted him. All of him in me. And I didn't get anywhere near close to that. Still, I screamed for him. He was a pro at what he was doing. It was very clear at how quickly he got me what I couldn't get myself. I writhed under his tongue as exhaustion overtook me.

This time, he didn't come up to kiss me. He pulled my underwear back in place then rearranged my dress meticulously, covering my breasts, my thighs, and my body in a way that felt almost mechanical. Gone was the sexuality, gone was his hunger. The only thing that proved he still wanted me was his naked, rock-solid cock.

I sat up and stared at him as he shoved himself back into

his slacks. I was waiting for him to say this wasn't supposed to happen or to ask for the bathroom even though he knew exactly where it was. I'm sure he'd want to wash me from his face, maybe give himself a pep talk before he rushed out of here.

He didn't do any of those things. Instead, he let the silence fill the air as he continued to straighten himself up and then moved on to tidy the kitchen. The man was fine with a dark cloud of silence hanging over a room, but I wasn't. "Are you going back to the party?"

"What for?"

"Well, all your employees are out there. We should mingle, right?"

"You feel like mingling, Clara?" he said with a smirk, letting his gaze scan over me again.

I ignored my stomach dipping. "I do. I want to know everyone's face, understand everyone's personality, and learn all their weaknesses and strengths. We're about to be a team."

He scoffed. "How many people worked in your bakery with you before?"

Honestly, it had mostly been me. Carl didn't care when it opened and closed, and I'd been too anal about giving anyone else the reins. "It doesn't matter. Here, I'm on a team, Dominic. You can be on one, too, if you want. Or you can sit in the bakery you think is so delightful and stare at that pink wall you hate so much because, well, it's the only good thing to look at in here."

With that, I breezed by him to grab my phone from the counter to stuff it back in my bra. Leaving a man who thought he sat on top of the world behind in his own galaxy to contemplate his worth and decisions was a rather effective technique in getting them to follow, I'd found.

Before the bakery door had even closed behind me, I heard

it *whoosh* open with Dominic following, that grumpy frown of his back in place.

We strode through most of his resort in silence. Down some hallways, the lights would only flicker on based off our motion. "Once it's opened, the lighting won't be motion detected, right?"

"It could be. Why?"

"Too dark for guests. They'll feel—"

"Like we're cutting corners. It's definitely something I had the electrical team discuss. We want to be green, but it's an issue they'll have to work on more." I nodded, not about to say anything else. Yet he prodded, "What else do you hate?"

"I don't hate your resort, Dominic." I sighed. "You sound like me when Evie tries a dessert of mine and doesn't immediately bowl over in pure joy."

"You're more honest than most of my team. I need an honest opinion."

"I don't have opinions except on my bakery," I said. "Plus, I don't answer trick questions."

"Trick?"

"Be honest but not too honest, because you'll hurt that person's feelings, and then they'll lash out. I don't enjoy that game." I'd encountered it enough times with my mother and sister to know better.

"I don't lash out. And I don't really have feelings you specifically could hurt." I laughed at the way he said it, like he was proud his feelings were so in check, that he was proud he didn't give a shit about anyone else.

"Still, I'd rather not share any more opinions of your resort with you. We're done here." With that, I pushed through a tall glass door that opened to an expansive patio overlooking the beach. The music hit me along with the cool air off the ocean. Paloma waved to me immediately, her arm swinging back and forth wildly. The arm dropped when she saw who was behind me.

I didn't spare him even a backward glance as I rushed away. I had to leave the idea of him and what I'd done behind. It wasn't at all like me, and it wasn't at all something I thought I'd like so much.

CHAPTER 9: CLARA

"How's it going?" I whispered over to Paloma, trying to act like I hadn't just had my boss serve me the best orgasm of my life mere minutes ago.

"You missed Ed Sheeran. I can't even ... They brought *Ed Sheeran* here just for us, Clara." So, Dominic had spent some money on making his employees feel welcome after all. "And there were dancers, and I think there might be fireworks later, I kid you not."

"That's amazing." I glanced around and saw the buzz across the hundred people here. Laughter and smiles in the moonlight.

I found myself searching for him, wanting to see his reaction to the joy he'd brought people that night, but didn't see him anywhere. It was a reminder he didn't want to witness that with them, didn't want to mingle at all.

"So, did you do it?"

"Do what?" I whipped around, eyes wide as I smoothed my hair in front of Paloma. Did I look like I'd screwed around with him?

"Did you paint an accent wall in your bakery?" she whisper-yelled at me. "Did Mr. Hardy see? Is he mad?"

I let out a breath of anxiety and looked down at my heels in the sand. I probably should have worn something other than stilettos. I slid one foot out and then another, went to toss them over by my purse, and considered if it was a bad look.

Yet, no one was there for me to look good for or bad for except myself. Tonight was about me. I was on my own, and this was my chance to live just for me. "Yes, I painted it, and honestly, I don't care if he *is* mad."

I think my eyes got just as wide as Paloma's once the words left my mouth, but the ones that were knocking around in my head were Dominic's. He'd told me to take what I wanted, and tonight I was going to. Tonight was about making new friends, seeing how we would all work as a team, and having a bit of fun.

Paloma whooped and pulled me around to talk with everyone. I shook hands with Eddie, whose beach bar was the perfect addition on the strip for the nightlife. I hugged Paloma's store neighbor, Courtney, who was adorned with the beautiful jewelry she would be selling in a month to our guests. Garrett owned the vineyard to the east of the resort and offered me a glass of his finest. And when we came to Valentino, I think my breath caught in my throat at how attractive he was up close. His dirty-blond hair was naturally highlighted from the sun, his blue eyes twinkled like we had an inside joke already, and his strong biceps showcased that he worked out.

Paloma pointed between us. "You two are going to love each other. She makes the best desserts, Valentino. It's like Christmas and your birthday in your mouth at the same time, I swear."

"Christmas and my birthday, huh?" He held his hand out, and I knew I was blushing.

"Probably not both. Maybe one."

"And she's humble." He chuckled and I practically melted like the chocolate I'd made earlier with Dominic. "I'm sorry we haven't met sooner."

I finished shaking his hand and wondered why that

comment didn't sit quite well with me. Why *hadn't* we met earlier? He knew I was there, knew I was a new bakery owner, and knew I'd dropped off chocolates at his restaurant. "Yes. Sorry. I stopped by and left a note with chocolates ..."

"Ah, my team probably gobbled them right up." He shrugged, and that definitely explained it. He was insanely busy with a whole restaurant as opposed to just my bakery. "Don't be sorry, though, love. I'm happy we're meeting now. We'll have to get together soon, sample one another's plates, no?"

"That sounds great." My heart fluttered. Should I have told him how much I admired his work? That I'd followed his career?

Paloma pulled me along and then whispered, "Okay, down girl. You have stars in your eyes. Let's keep him wanting more. Time for us to have fun now."

Admittedly, I listened and had too much fun with too many margaritas, dancing well into the night with Paloma by my side. When she and Eddie started talking more, I leaned in to tell her that I was going to go walk on the beach for a minute just to enjoy the air. As I strolled down through the sand, the sound of the music got quieter, the lights faded in the distance a bit and the moon shined bright.

The water washed up to shore fast over the sand, and then pulled back like it was breathing in and out. In and out.

"You had enough of mingling with the team?" His voice rumbled out from the shadows, and I screeched before I lurched forward, losing my balance and stumbling straight into him.

Dominic's reflexes were faster than mine because he caught me against his chest, not letting me bounce off him into the water.

I looked up to thank him, and my body instantly reacted,

and not in a way that I would have liked. The way I melted for Valentino didn't compare at all to the electricity that coursed through my blood now. The butterflies in my stomach were free-falling, and heat flew over my cheeks as I turned to face him.

"Might be time for you to go home?" he said softly.

I shook my head no. "Oh. I'm fine."

"You fall into people all the time when you're fine?"

"You know what?" I poked him in the chest. "You scared me because you sneaked up on me."

"I don't sneak up on people."

"Yes, you've been lurking around all night instead of just going to the party."

"Oh I was at the party." He crossed his arms and continued. "I was at the party fucking around with the baker—"

I felt my eyes widen. "Be quiet." I threw my hands up. We might have been fifty feet away from everyone else, but I didn't want the chance of someone knowing what I'd just done. "I'm going back to the party."

But of course, when I started to walk back up to my friends, I stumbled. And he freaking caught me again. He sighed before he ground out, "We're going home."

My response was way too laid back as I covered my mouth to keep from laughing in his face. "God, you're way too good looking to be such bad company."

His jaw might have clenched at how candid I was being with him now, but I was a nervous talker, and the alcohol was flowing. "Come have a drink, Dominic."

"Remember what I told you about my name?"

"Um ..." The answer to that was no. The wheels were not turning perfectly in my brain since the margaritas froze them all up, apparently. I did remember how his cock felt against my pussy, though, and I smiled lazily at him. "No, but I do remember how you felt—"

"Go say goodnight to your friends," he commanded before I could finish my sentence. Then he leaned in to whisper, "I'm taking you home."

That had me sobering. "Don't ruin the party."

He eyed the beach like he had all the authority in the world to do just that. "Don't want me to? Then, let me take you home, or I'm shutting the whole damn thing down."

"Is that so?"

"Don't play with me, Clara."

"I'm not playing with you anymore. We already did that, and we barely even got started." I scoffed and pushed past him, done dealing with him popping up out of nowhere and demanding something from me.

It only took about two minutes for the music to cut out and Rita to announce, "Party's over, everyone. We'll be cleaning the beach, so please file out immediately. Fireworks have been rescheduled and ..."

I didn't hear anything else. Everything in me froze so my blood could boil as I felt the anger fly through me.

He wouldn't have.

Of course he would.

I pivoted around to find him standing there in the moonlight, glowing green eyes on me, his backdrop the ocean. He looked powerful. Cruel. And invincible.

Instead of filing off the beach with everyone, I murmured to Paloma that I'd call her when I got home. Then I stomped—or wobbled— right up to his selfish ass. "You're a complete dick, you know that?"

"I didn't claim to be anything else. Let's go." He started walking toward the resort, but I squinted out in the water.

"Are those my shoes?" There they both were, red-bottom heels, floating away. "And my bag?"

Crap. And of course, Dominic was no knight in shining armor. As I ran for them, he responded by yelling to hurry up or something.

"I have to get my purse," I screeched in determination. Those heels were my favorites too. I stepped into the water, but it was much colder than I thought it'd be. "Shit. Shit. Shit."

Waves rolled in and then receded back out. The water went back and forth, back and forth, and I felt my stomach lurch with it as I looked down.

"Jesus, Clara." I felt his big, calloused hands scoop me up then. "You're swaying, little fighter. You drink the whole bar tonight?"

"My purse, Dominic. And my shoes. Oh my God, I need my freaking shoes at least."

"I'll get you new shoes, cupcake."

"No. Those are Christian Louboutins. My only ones. And that bag ..." My stomach rolled at how much money was floating out to sea. "It was so expensive."

"Oh really?" He smiled down at me genuinely. A huge smile. I think it was the biggest one I'd ever seen on him. "How much?"

"God, you're disgustingly beautiful," I blurted out as I stared at his eyes twinkling down at me with mirth.

"That right?"

"It's very annoying." I pouted in his arms as he carried me like a baby through the sand. Everyone must have scattered and left, because I didn't hear a single sound except his heartbeat and mine.

He hummed, “What size shoe do you wear, Clara?”

“An eight but who freaking cares? Those were one of a kind. And so was the purse.” I groaned.

“I highly doubt it.” His voice was smooth, low, and hot. I felt the vibration of it all the way down to my sex. Wiggling, I tried to push the thought out of my mind but instead, I felt his muscles shifting to keep me from going anywhere.

“You have no idea.” I pouted, glancing behind us, as if I could grab one last glance. “That Birkin bag was at least $50,000.”

He laughed then. “So not expensive then?”

“Ew. Don’t brag.” I shoved him as he walked me through the resort again, laughing at how I curled my lip at him. “Honestly, my mother got it for me ...” I didn’t continue because thinking of the time we had when she wasn’t cruel to me brought tears to my eyes.

He frowned down at me. “How is she? You never called, so I assumed you two mended things.”

I didn’t understand this Dominic—one who might care underneath his hard exterior, the one who’d protected me against Hank and my mother, the one who gave Paloma her sign, the one who asked me things. I wrung my hands against my stomach and looked out into the dark night. “Sometimes mending things with certain people means you break yourself.”

He hummed without agreeing or disagreeing. “How far is home, cupcake? I’ll drive you.”

He’d drive me home even though he had no idea where I lived. And how ridiculous was that, because Dominic had moments of compassion but at the end of the day, he hadn’t even taken the time to meet me once outside of work. “Of course you will. Ditch me after not even fucking me, and then send me right on home." I was grumbling nonsense at this point. "Thank God my phone and my keys are in my bra or I would have had to call my landlord."

He said something like I should forget it and that it didn't matter.

"Where are we going?"

Of course he didn't answer. He wove in and out of hallways, not going toward the parking lot at all. Instead, he swiped a card on the elevator and took me to the top floor.

"My apartment isn't up here, Dominic," I singsonged to him.

"Guess you're not going to call me Mr. Hardy anymore?" he asked.

"Not when you're carrying me off into the night like you're a dream instead of my nightmare."

"Am I your nightmare, Ms. Milton?"

I didn't know how to answer as he swiped his fob over the penthouse entry keypad and carried me in.

Dominic Hardy was an enigma of a man, and I didn't think he wanted me to figure him out.

CHAPTER 10: DOMINIC

"I'm not going to talk with her," I ground out into the dumb FaceTime chat my siblings had me on.

My brother Declan sighed as he bounced a baby in his arms while making a protein shake. He'd really gone all in with Evie, and I couldn't even knock him for it. "You have to do something."

"Shut up and show me my nephew. I don't want to see your face anyway."

Atticus yawned and there was a collective aw over the FaceTime. All six of us were wrapped around the next generation's fingers, and we weren't too proud to deny it.

"Dom, you're changing the subject. She's making waves in the press. You can't just stay silent," Evie said behind him.

"The hell I can't," I grumbled.

"Don't talk to my wife that way," Declan snapped at me, and then both my younger brothers, Dex and Dimitri, snickered.

"Fuck all of you, okay? Evie doesn't care how I talk to her."

"That's right. I can lay you out next time and make you say sorry over and over if you want to mumble under your breath like a twelve-year-old."

I pinched the bridge of my nose. I'd barely gotten any sleep after carrying Clara to the penthouse, and I had a fucking headache from last night—not because I'd drank too much or got home too late, either. Instead, it was simply because I kept imagining how sweet she tasted, how I wanted to eat her and her cupcakes about a hundred more times to get my fix.

It was supposed to be a one and done.

"I don't have time for this."

"No, you're not hanging up," my sister Lilah said. She was the logical one of the six of us, and when she asked for something, we all listened. "You need to handle this, Dom. She broke your heart once before, don't let her break your business too. This resort is important to you."

I tried to cut her off, because Natya wasn't going to ruin anything with my resort. She knew better.

"No. Let me finish." She held up a hand and then pushed her dark wavy hair back. "You need to think about what would push her away enough that she'll leave you alone, that she'll understand you're done."

"I told her we were done three years ago." Natya was the most lethal ex of the century. She was an international entrepreneur of a woman. She graduated top of the same class as me, where I met her. When we'd started dating, she worked just as hard as me on those new building designs and I'd fallen hard. She'd been impressive in the business and so I let her infect my engineering firm with extravagant ideas, let her push limits within the business and outside of it.

She started to enjoy the attention our contracts got us and partied hard night after night. Then, she came to work tired day after day. I shouldn't have ever given her a team to manage. When I got the call about a work injury I'd given her permission to handle, the failure hit me like a freight train.

I pulled back hard and still remembered the headlines reading "Promising Young Architect Dominic Hardy Loses Billion Dollar Contract."

I rubbed at my heart, still feeling the pain of it. We tried to work through it until I found her in bed with someone else not much later. I told her I was done.

She'd told me she was pregnant.

God, that woman put on a good show, crying and pleading, and talking about a happy family. I was the eldest of the six kids of immigrant parents. They'd worked so hard to put me through college, to show I was worth something and I wanted to make them proud so badly. I wanted to prove to them and my younger siblings that we could all have the American dream.

The pain she inflicted the next time though, the way she lied again ... that was enough for me to walk away forever. Now, I wasn't stupid enough to fall for any of her breadcrumbs—or for any other women for that matter. I usually didn't indulge unless it was worth it, and I made my intentions pretty clear.

Except with Clara. I wasn't really sure what the hell my intentions were.

"Natya's not going away," Dex grumbled. He was just as jaded as me when it came to his exes.

"How do you know? Keelani went away."

"Man, fuck you for bringing her up."

Dimitri laughed. "Low blow, Dom. He's still not over her after, what? Like ten years?"

"I've been over her since the second we broke up. And it's not about me and her. It's about Natya and Dom, because I got a casino partnering with us in Vegas and they want nothing to do with Natya. She screwed them out of a contract years ago."

"Which casino? Tell them I've blocked her on all forms of communication. She knows we're done."

"Actually, she just said in the news that she's excited about the Pacific Coast Resort opening and that everyone should know you two will never ever be truly over." Izzy held up her laptop, pointing at Natya on the screen.

And Natya might have been right in a way. I'd never look at another woman as openly. She'd broken something in me enough to realize I was better on my own.

On Izzy's laptop, she stood tall, white dress pressed to perfection, with a small smile playing on her lips. She fiddled with a ring on her hand, and my heart dropped when I saw it was the one I'd given her years ago. Bile curdled in my gut at the audacity she possessed to wear it, to talk about the resort she knew would mean so much to me, to say we weren't over.

"Ignore her. She'll learn," I ground out. The woman wanted attention, negative or positive, and it's what we couldn't give her.

"You could tell that woman a lot of things," Izzy said, her husband's tattooed arm slung around her neck. Her fingers danced over his bicep as she shrugged at the screen. "Cade could have told me he was done with me, and I would have come for him anyway, Dom."

"Well, you two are a different breed."

She smiled like she was happy about it.

"You need to think of something," Dex repeated. "Figure out a way to make her stop talking about you and the resort. I need to solidify this contract. If they think you two are still a thing ..."

"If we just leave it alone—"

"Last time you did that, she almost ended your engineering career and your life, man," Dex threw back. "Find a girl or something. She thinks you still love her."

"I've found a lot of women," I growled. "Do you guys not know who you're talking to? I'm your big brother. I—"

"You set an example for all of us. Blah blah blah," Dex

said without even making eye contact through the screen. I knew he was working while talking, probably like most of us wanted to be doing. “Set an example by getting rid of your obsessive ex-girlfriend. She used to just be bad for you. Now she’s becoming bad for the HEAT empire. And that’s bad for the family business. We don’t need association with her if we intend to go public with our stock in the next couple years and solidify this casino deal.”

“I’m not—”

“He’s right. Listen to Dex,” Izzy said before Cade pulled her back while she giggled and clicked off her screen.

“What Izzy said,” Dante, Lilah’s husband, growled before he disconnected also.

Declan and Dimitri didn’t even attempt to wait for me to say anything, they just hung up too, leaving Dex as the lone caller.

“No one fucking listens to me.”

“Everyone in that resort listens to you,” my brother countered. “You got a whole team listening to you all the time and have a bunch of yes guys. Your family, though, will always give it to you straight. Find a girl for a while so she knows you’ve moved on, okay? What’s the harm in that? You know Natya never wants to look like a fool. She won’t bother you if you’re not single.”

I didn’t respond to that because it actually made some sense.

“Even if it’s only until the opening of the resort. Just figure something out, Dom. Your dumbass heart can’t take another beating from that woman.”

Then he was gone, too, leaving me to face my own thoughts.

That’s when the worst sort of darkness could overtake

a soul. I swore and ripped my sheets off, ready to get the day started and put Natya out of my mind.

I escaped to my personal gym and lifted weights before running harder than necessary. I wasn't running from the thought of Natya this time, though. I was running to get Clara out of my mind ... the way she'd moaned my name, the way she'd pushed back with her bakery, the way she'd stripped down in the penthouse and tried to pull me to the bed.

That moment—her standing in the city view and moonlight in front of an open window, nipples puckered for me, pink pussy on display—would replay in my mind forever. So would her saying, "If there's ever going to be a night between us, it's going to be this one, Dominic, because I don't hate a lot of people, but I sort of despise you."

She'd meant it too. The words had fallen easily from her lips. I'd thought I'd felt the same, but my heart lurched at her words, and then I found myself doing something I normally wouldn't. I kissed her forehead, "Save your begging for another night, baby. I intend to fuck you so good, you'll beg for rest."

She gripped my shirt with her small hands, her eyes already languid. "Why not now?"

I shook my head and smoothed a hand over her cheek. "Go to bed, cupcake. Please."

Her eyes drifted shut, and I set up water and ibuprofen next to the bed before I left her that night. Now, I stood in a scalding hot shower trying to burn away the memory. My cock throbbed at the thought of her and even as I turned the water freezing cold, I still hardened while I imagined her begging. I thrust into my hand, squeezing my length just as she had the night before.

Why hadn't I just fucked her and gotten her out of my

system?

I knew the answer.

I wouldn't be able to get her out of my system. I imagined her pouty lips wrapping around my cock, how they felt so soft and warm as she looked up at me with her forest-green eyes, determined but just a bit hesitant. She'd take my length all the way back, gag on me because she wanted to prove herself. I saw that little fighter in her, and it turned me on the more I thought about it. I pumped my cock harder, squeezed it tighter, brushed my thumb roughly over the head, and came more violently than I had in a long damn time.

Not once did I think of anyone else.

After I'd dried off and decided the only way I was going to get my mind out of the gutter was to work, I sighed at the black suit in the closet. We'd done most of the construction work, which meant that as the CEO of the resort, I had to look the part. I pulled the suit from the hanger, got dressed before calling my driver to take me to the resort. When a text came through, though, I caught myself smiling at seeing her name on my phone.

I rerouted my driver.

I had a stop to make first.

CHAPTER 11: CLARA

Thank every soul that was holy on the planet and in the universe that it was Sunday. I woke to a rising sun on my face in the soft down comforter and a fresh smell of clean linens. But drool lined my cheek, and it stunk like margaritas with strawberries and extra lime. It was getting all over me and the soft pillows. So soft they couldn't have been mine.

I shot up out of the bed and grasped at the sheet to hold it up over my body while I searched the massive room. A large television, floor-to-ceiling windows overlooking the city, and sleek black-and-white decor. I was in a penthouse suite at the Pacific. Had I booked this room last night?

The idea of how expensive that would be had me feeling like I might break out in hives, and I checked my arms immediately, groaning with the pain of the hangover.

"This was bad, bad, bad for your health, Clara," I breathed out. I'd gotten better about not drinking as much because flare-ups were the inevitable consequence of that particular indulgence. Minding my diet, stress level, and medication and vitamin routine got tiring though. It was painful to imagine life without needing to factor those things in, and those types of thoughts had me resenting the life I lived when I should have been grateful for it.

Moments with a disease were harder to enjoy, but they were still mine. I was getting them and that was enough, I told myself over and over. Most days I believed it, especially with my bakery.

I sighed and shook off my frustration, focusing on my bank account instead. If I booked this room ... That would be impossible. The resort wasn't open. So, I either broke in here or ...

And like a terrible movie, the memory of my night played through my mind. "Fuck."

That was not a memory I wanted, nor a moment I would ever enjoy reliving.

Dominic had carried me back. Jesus, what had I said to him? I groaned, then looked down and saw I had no clothes on. So, I'd also undressed in front of him. "Okay, today, is the day you hate yourself, Clara."

Even so, I knew now wasn't the time to succumb to gravity and throw the sheets back over my head. I had a million things to do before this bakery opened.

I only had two months to make this place what I wanted, and after dealing with Dom's arrogance, I was going to. Own it, he'd told me. He probably didn't mean owning the ridiculous display I'd put on the night before, but as my phone rang and I saw my mother calling, I owned that I didn't want to pick it up. I also owned that I didn't want to pick up my sister's call either.

My sister called about twenty more times that morning before I finally answered. "Yes, Anastasia?"

"You know, I'm getting really tired of you being there to pursue this idiotic dream, Clara? What the fuck?"

I winced because for some reason, I still wanted my sister's approval. I wanted to wake up one day and feel like she loved me how she used to. Somewhere along the way that had changed. Somewhere, we'd lost each other, and I hated that feeling. "Anastasia," I sighed. "I don't want to do this with you.

If you could be happy for me, I'd love for you to come visit and see why—"

How could I tell my sister that without her here, I was better. She was my mother's replica, but I swear she had to remember the days we would play outside together, run through the sand on the beach, and swim in the ocean like we were mermaids for hours.

"Do you know what those Hardy brothers did to us?" she asked, and I heard her voice shaking with anger. Anastasia hadn't only been cruel to me over the years, she'd also taken it out on Carl's estranged daughter, Evie. Evie had married Declan Hardy, and he was not about to have anyone be disrespectful to his wife. So, I knew they pulled her membership to the HEAT Empire. I agreed with their decision.

"Can we not do this?" I whispered, because in the past month, I'd made a sanctuary. I'd manifested change in my life, and I'd embraced not looking back. I didn't want to. I wanted my life here to be different.

There was silence on the other side of the phone.

"Why don't you tell me how things are going for you? How's Florida?" I tried to change the subject because my heart still wanted us to be seven again, back when we were the only ones who understood each other, who knew the pain that came from being under our roof, who could sympathize with one another.

I'd only had a few memories of my father and mother together when they were happy. He played with us when he was around, taking us to the park, to fancy dinners, and showering my mother with gifts. We had videos of him swinging me high up in the sky. He was a charmer who spoke beautiful Spanish and flew us around the world for a few years before we found out about his other family, leaving my mother with nothing.

It broke her and ultimately broke us. She never got over his betrayal, and I remember how she became obsessed with it being our fault.

"If you slouch at another dinner with Carl, Clara, I promise you won't get another dinner for a week." She had thrown the warning out, and it hadn't been just that. It had been a promise. My mother had starved Anastasia and I before.

Anastasia had been older and she'd been smart enough to hide food. She'd share it with me in the middle of the night. My mother made her pay for that when she was finally caught.

"*How's Florida*? Florida is fucking awful, and you know it. It's why you left me here to fend for myself."

I squeezed my eyes shut. "You can come visit if you want, Anastasia."

"Oh, so you leave without telling me, and now you want me to come visit? Typical, Clara. Make up your mind. One way or the other. You want me there or not?"

I glanced around the penthouse, the quiet and calm of it reminded me of what I had here now. "You're right. Maybe it's best you don't come."

I heard her gasp like I'd struck her. But Anastasia and I hadn't been close in a way that I'd wished for in years. She'd delivered metaphorical blow after blow since becoming my mother's sidekick. My stepfather hadn't known about my mother's physical and emotional abuse, but Anastasia stood by her and pointed out my faults every time, finding that it took the attention off of her.

I heard my sister grumbling to my mother then, and I sighed, a lone tear falling down my face. "No, I didn't tell her you were in the room, Mom. She just doesn't want me to come. This is what I mean about her picking our stepsister over me.

She's a—"

"I can hear you, Anastasia, and that's not true. It's—"

"I don't care if you hear me! You're fucking useless anyway. You're trying to leave us behind and get back into the HEAT empire. You think we don't see through your act?"

"Anastasia, can you stop and think about what you're accusing me of?"

She scoffed and hung up the phone. My heart cracked a little, but also the blocks I was building around it stacked up a bit higher.

I took a deep breath and tried not to even think about it as I showered off my makeup and used some mint-infused shampoo in my hair before the conditioner. Thankfully, the bathroom was stocked even though there weren't guests staying here yet. If nothing else, relaxing in the luxurious rain shower with unlimited amounts of hot water destressed me a little.

I'd give Dominic credit for this at least.

No credit for anything else though. Not even the orgasms he'd given me—although I thought about it once or twice as the water cascaded down my body.

Once I was out of the shower, I knew I owed him a thank you.

Me: Thank you for getting me somewhere safe last night.

Dominic: Good morning, little fighter. And a thank you? That's surprising.

Me: Well, the follow-up to that thank you is a question: Why am I in the

penthouse suite?

Dominic: Didn't read the note on the nightstand yet? You still in bed?

I glared at my phone and pounded out the next text.

Me: No. I'm showered and ready to go.

I walked over to the solid oak nightstand and my heart of steel toward him softened just a little. There was a large glass of water with Advil right next to it. Laying just below that was a crisp white sticky note with the HEAT emblem behind it that read, "So you don't claim I screwed around with you and then sent you on your way. Penthouse for a cupcake."

Me: You didn't need to put me in the penthouse suite.

Dominic: I know. But I did anyway. Do I get an extra thank you for that?

Me: Considering you cut the party short and that my kittens are probably worried sick, I think just one will have to do.

Dominic: Kittens? You've only been here a month, Clara. Why the hell would you get pets?

Dominic: Did you pick up strays? Those have fucking diseases.

I ignored that text, swiped the Advil off the nightstand and gulped down the water in hopes it would curb any sort of headache that was bound to come on without food or caffeine. I needed both sooner rather than later. It was still pretty early, only eight o'clock, and if I beelined back to my bakery, I could probably whip up coffee before going home, changing, and then getting back to work.

And getting shoes.

I'd lost my favorite heels and my purse last night, and I thought about crying over it. They'd been thousands of dollars, and my mom had said over and over again that I'd looked good in them.

What is it about wanting a parent's love so much that people would keep trying even when they didn't deserve it? Those shoes were that for me, and I hated that I'd lost them even if it was probably better to let them go.

I sighed and wove my way through the Pacific's halls without freaking shoes, hoping I wouldn't see anybody. I'd called my Uber and knew if I could hide away in the bakery with the lights off until he got here, I'd be just fine.

It was a terrible walk of shame that wasn't even a walk of shame because I hadn't gotten any the night before. But when I turned the corner into the lobby, I froze and felt the embarrassment of a million shameful walks.

Dominic Hardy stood right outside my bakery, leaning against the doorframe, beautiful in his tailored black suit and shiny Italian loafers, with a scowl on his face once he looked up from his phone as if he could sense my presence.

Why did he have to appear so completely put together? I tried to ignore the tension dancing between us in the air and the urge to dart away from him. No one here was supposed to make me feel that way. Here, I was taking control of my own life. So, I steeled my spine as I walked up to him completely barefoot.

And then he smiled as he murmured, "There's my little fighter."

It's like he was watching my every movement, learning me in a way most people didn't. He'd seen my hesitation and watched me overcome it to walk to him. Still, we didn't exchange good-morning niceties. I used my key fob to swipe us in and he jumped right into irritating me instead. "You didn't answer my text."

I rolled my eyes. "Sugar and Spice aren't strays."

"Where did you get them then?" He followed me in without an invitation.

"Outside my apartment. So, they aren't strays *now.*"

"Oh, fuck me." He groaned. "Do you realize that you can't—"

"I'm a big girl, Dominic." I wouldn't tell him that I'd just now realized they both needed to be spayed and get shots or about my mishap with the carriers.

"It's Mr. Hardy, Ms. Milton. We're at work."

"Right. Great." We needed that boundary anyway, and Dominic was great at creating them. "Anyway, I won't be here long." I immediately rushed to the espresso machine. Caffeine would give me life enough to get through these next ten minutes. "I already called an Uber."

"What for? Are you not working today?" He appeared disgusted that someone would take a day off even though it was

Sunday.

"I'm working. I just need to go home and change, get shoes, and—"

That's when I saw him reach for what was on the crook of his arm. Two bags. A Christian Louboutin bag—I knew that bag. Most women knew that bag—and a freaking orange one.

"What is that?" I whispered.

"Presents."

I narrowed my eyes, not believing it for a second. "For me?"

He held them out and then glanced at his phone when it vibrated. "Who else would it be for, cupcake?"

CHAPTER 12: CLARA

"Don't call me cupcake when I can't even call you by your first name." I tried to sound menacing, but it came out a whisper as I stared at the two bags he held out to me.

Then, I took a step back, and he frowned before snapping his arm out to grab my elbow and pull me forward. "Take the bags, Ms. Milton."

Was I seriously fighting to get away from him and expensive gifts? What was wrong with me?

But then I heard chatter outside my bakery, and I panicked, ripping my arm away from him and rushing to close the door just as I saw colleagues approaching the lobby. "Shit."

Dominic casually sat down on one of the barstools and eyed me warily, "What's wrong now?"

I shoved him up. "What are you doing? Go to the back kitchen. They'll see us."

"So what if they see us?" He shrugged.

Oh my God. Didn't he get it? I turned out the lights before grabbing the bags from him and pushing him into the back room. "I look like I got run over by a train, that's what, Dominic. I'm wearing my dress from last night, my hair is a mess, I don't have shoes or makeup on and—"

When we finally were through the back doors to the kitchen, he crossed his arms and looked down at me. "Check the bags."

Narrowing my eyes, I took in his gaze that sparkled on me.

Was he enjoying this? "Technically, this is your fault."

"Is it now?"

"Yes. I could have gotten my shoes out of the ocean at least."

"They were a hundred feet out to sea, cupcake. What were you going to do, swim in your already almost-see-through dress?"

"Are you that concerned, honestly? It would have dried." I scoffed.

"Not before half the world saw your ass," he pointed out without hesitation.

"It's my ass to show off," I threw back.

"Not if I have something to do with it."

"Oh, shut up," I said as I whipped the box out of the bag. When I lifted the cover, I murmured "Shut up" for a whole different reason. Beautiful new Christian Louboutin shoes sparkled up at me with what I'm sure were expensive diamonds. The next bag and orange box had something even more expensive. Beautiful leather, bright green and expertly crafted. I smoothed my hand over it as I murmured, "Shut the fuck up."

"So, you've got a mouth when you're impressed then?"

"What?" I whispered, still looking at the bag.

It seemed Dominic was making notes about me though because he said, "You swore last night when I tasted you and today when you got your Birkin. You must have been impressed that I can lick your pussy like—"

"Mr. Hardy!" I cut him off as my gaze ripped away from the beautiful purse to meet his and scold him. He was smiling again, and my heart lurched in his direction seeing him so openly happy in that moment. But then my heart dropped as I glanced back at the gifts. I couldn't afford these.

"This is very nice but I—"

"I lost your shoes and purse didn't I?"

"Well, yes." I wasn't going to back down from that, even if it was mostly my fault. "But I—"

"Then I owed you, so I got you new ones. Now, put them on."

"The shoes and purse you lost were not—"

"You said they were like fifty thousand dollars." He wrinkled his nose as he said it and mimicked my tone.

God, I'd made a fool of myself the night before. "That's a lot of money."

"Not for me."

When I still didn't reach for them, he sighed, set his phone down, and walked toward me. He grabbed my hips and lifted me onto the prep counter. His hand skirted down my calf, and I gulped, feeling his skin against mine again. "If your colleagues weren't outside, I'd probably ask for another round right now."

"You'd ask?" I blurted out, not sure I could imagine him doing that.

"You're right. I'd take." His hand brushed back up my calf and grazed over my thigh before his hand was where my panties had been. "Fuck me, little fighter. No underwear."

"Threw them in the trash. Couldn't wear them again this morning." I shrugged.

"So, when I have that penthouse cleaned, someone's getting your dirty lingerie?"

"Probably just garbage, Dominic." I breathed fast as his fingers brushed over my pussy. I knew this couldn't be happening again, but I spread my legs for him, and he chuckled into my neck.

"You're sober now, and I deserve this pussy after the hell you put me through last night." He sighed and rubbed my clit with his thumb before dragging his hand back down my legs back to my foot. "But I'll wait." I was dazed, confused, even a bit too disoriented to think of him slipping the shoes on my feet. "There. Now, you're ready to work."

Gripping the prep counter, I shook my head once, trying to clear the sexual fog in the back room. "I still need to go home."

I hopped off the counter and stared down at the shoes. "You don't need to go home. You look fine with your natural hair and freckles on your face."

I brushed a hand over my freckles and blew out a breath before I stalked past him to see if everyone had left the lobby.

Instead, Valentino stood out there. He was one man that I respected, that could probably make me give up my ban on dating. He smiled down at Paloma and Rita. Then they laughed at something he'd said. I couldn't help but smile too because Paloma had stars in her eyes as she gestured animatedly to him.

If the magazines and stories about him were true, he was a dream of a man. At just thirty-seven, he'd accomplished so much and was already giving back to charity by teaching kids how to enjoy healthy food and lifestyles. He'd been the head chef at numerous kitchens and every time someone was interviewed about working below him, they looked like they were in love with him. They all appreciated his laid-back style, his charisma, and his art.

"You aren't his type." I jumped at the rough voice behind me, against my neck.

"Huh?" I dropped my gaze and fiddled with the seam of my dress, stepping forward and turning around to play dumb. "Oh, I don't ... I'm not interested in him. Of course, I'd love to be mentored by him. I mean, he's a world-renowned chef and—"

"You don't lie well, Clara," Dominic cut me off, and I swear there was a hint of jealousy there. "Your eyes were glued to him the moment he came into view. Plus, I think you mentioned something about him last night in the hotel room when—"

I winced and ran a hand through my frizzy hair. "Okay, so what if I think he's attractive and a good catch? Can we not bring up last night ever again, please?"

"Why not, babe? Now, that Valentino's outside, you don't want him to know you enjoyed someone else's kiss?"

I pursed my lips and set my hands on my hips. "We barely even kissed."

"Oh, I'm not talking about kissing you here." He stepped to drag his thumb across my bottom lip. "I don't care to kiss a woman's mouth ever."

I couldn't respond. My insides were all jumbled, feeling too much from his touch and jealousy from thinking about him with someone else.

Then his gaze dipped down to my sex. "But I'll kiss your pussy and make sure you enjoy it every single time. I'm happy to inform Valentino of that—"

"Are you freaking kidding me?" I stopped him. Heat flowed through my body fast, turned on and pissed off at the same time. "Is there a reason you actually stopped by, Dominic?"

"Other than to save you from embarrassment by bringing you shoes?" His eyebrow lifted.

I think he enjoyed making me say thank you, but I ground it out anyway, because I would be polite even if it nearly killed me. "Thank you. I will pay you back."

I don't think he expected that response because he opened his mouth and then snapped it shut. He cracked his knuckles before he leaned close, his eyes darkening "You try to give me money for those shoes and that bag, fighter, I'll enjoy making you regret it. Don't disrespect me by acting like a few thousand dollars is worth shit to me or you."

One day he'd probably figure out I'd left my fortune behind, but today I didn't tell him because obviously I needed the money much more than him. "Whatever. Fine. We both need to get to work, so thank you, but now you can leave."

He glared at me for a second longer, his eyes still hardened with anger, but then he spun on his heel right before I grabbed his arm.

"Sorry. You can leave ... after everyone in the lobby leaves."

His phone buzzed again, and he glanced down with a grumble.

Maybe I was actually keeping him from a meeting. "If you really do actually have to go ..."

"No ... it's just my brothers and sisters trying to ..." His gaze narrowed on me. Then he stepped back and studied me as if I was suddenly an exhibit on display. "You might actually work."

"Um, work for what?"

"You want Valentino to *mentor* you and take notice of you?" He sneered the word because we both knew I wanted more than mentoring. "I know how to make him."

I scoffed and then laughed, thinking he had to be joking. Honestly, Dominic could probably tell Valentino to mentor me and he would. It was like everyone were sheep, and Dominic was the shepherd of this resort.

I went around the counter to pour some coffee that was finally ready. When I looked up, Dominic wasn't laughing with me. He'd simply folded his big arms over his chest and waited with such confidence, I knew he was actually very serious. He was giving me that look like he had a challenge ready to go, and suddenly I was hungry for what it might be. Why did I enjoy stepping up to the plate every time he threw a pitch my way? "I really don't think you know what a man like Valentino wants, Dominic."

We stared at one another as I took a sip of the coffee, not breaking my gaze from his.

"I do. He wants a trophy girlfriend. One that will take care of him and his restaurant, one that dotes on him, one that can share in his love for his career." He walked around the counter and grabbed himself a plain white cup to pour his own coffee. "He wants a partner, but he doesn't see that in any woman now, because he's focused on his career. He needs a blatant representation, and then he needs a woman that's so far out of his reach, he sees it as a challenge to get her on his arm."

"Okay." I dragged out the word. That was oddly specific, but I could probably be all those things, considering I loved his career, considering I was educated in exactly what he was and could clean up nice enough. "Well, maybe once the bakery is up and—"

"He's already dating Rita."

"Oh well, then, that ship has sailed." My heart didn't even feel that bad about it.

"No. You just need a few double dates with them to make him see you. His relationship with Rita is casual. It won't go anywhere."

"Why are you telling me all this?"

"Because I'll be your date on that double date." Then, his gaze flicked to the desserts I'd made a couple of nights before through the kitchen window. "You have anything to go with this coffee?"

The man had just dropped a ridiculous bomb in the bakery and expected me to go grab him a freaking cupcake?

"Wh–what? Did you just say we date? Are you still drunk from last night, Dominic?"

He chuckled as he stepped close before he whispered, "I was never drunk, baby. I remember every damn thing about last night, including you stripping down in front of me and begging to get your pussy fucked."

Dominic Hardy with a filthy mouth in my bakery had my heart beating faster than Valentino probably ever could. I didn't know if I was mad or turned-on.

"I asked you not to bring up last night."

"And I won't once you go on a few dates with me."

"Why would I ever do that?"

"Other than to show your dream boy you're the perfect girlfriend to me and could be the same to him?" He brushed a hand through my hair to push back some of the curls from my shoulder. Suddenly, my skin was extremely sensitive there and I shivered. I knew he caught the movement because he smiled at it. The man loved knowing he could affect my body in some way.

I rolled my eyes and crossed my arms over my chest. "Let's just say that plan actually works—which it probably won't. What's in it for you?"

"I need an appearance or two with a woman. I have an annoying ex on my hands."

"What does that have to do with me?" I wanted to ask more than one question. Was the annoying ex Natya? Most people knew of her, and she'd been linked to him and his family. And when I'd worked with the Hardy brothers, I'd read an article or two. Did he care about her?

"She'll back off if she thinks I've moved on."

"Have you?" I blurted out the question and saw how his

whole body locked up, his barriers flew sky high, and he wasn't letting anyone see past his mask as he played with the dress strap on my shoulder. "Does it matter if I haven't?"

I wanted to scream that it did matter.

But it couldn't. I didn't have feelings for him, just maybe wanted to know a bit more about his past, that's all. And I'd probably go into unhealthy stalking on my laptop later, trying to find news articles about them.

I cleared my throat as I also tried to clear away the thought of him with her. "I don't think your whole date idea will work with Valentino." And I didn't need the complication in my life, not when I was trying to find my own footing here in a new city. "So, the answer is no."

"You're turning down a date with me then?"

"Yep."

He stepped back and let his hand fall away from my shoulder. Immediately, I missed the electricity of his touch, a perfect indication that this was for the best. He wasn't the one I should be missing. Ever.

"So, any cupcakes left for my coffee?"

I chewed on my cheek before spinning on a heel and going to grab a few different sweets. I'd infused different flavors over the week, and they were still in the refrigerator. I'd also mastered adding chocolate flowers to the crème brûlée.

"Are those"—he narrowed his eyes at me when I came back around the corner—"orange and red poppies on that crème brûlée?"

I couldn't help but wiggle a little with a squeal. "Yes. California poppies are the orange ones. Red ones because, well, they'll match the pink accents. I'm going to try to make them my signature as long as they're good enough. I'll try other flowers too. But supposedly the fields here with them are gorgeous and—"

He sighed in disappointment. "We're minimizing color throughout the resort."

See, that's when all the electricity between Dominic and I died. We were back to colleagues trying to make my bakery in his resort work and not seeing eye to eye on a damn thing. "Yes, but in my bakery ..." I shrugged and set down the tray. He glared at all of them.

Next to the red velvet cupcakes were truffles that were coated in white chocolate that I'd infused with a strawberry syrup. The outcome was a light pink that I then topped with a single red heart. He wrinkled his nose at those too.

I didn't know if he was impressed or disgusted. Probably disgusted, but I didn't care.

Instead of hearing criticism I didn't need today, I followed up with, "I'm not sure if these will all make the menu, but the pink ones were *supposed* to go with the seating, so we'll see, and the flavors are delightful because"—I smiled at the mint leaf on top of one of the truffles as I pointed nervously now. I loved talking about my creations but was scared to share them too—"this one I actually ground and dried some fresh mint that blends well with the caramel I laced into the chocolate. Then when I added a hint of strawberry, it's this perfect dance of all the flavors in your mouth but still leaves you with fresh breath after."

He still didn't say a thing as he watched me. His lips didn't lift even a centimeter, and he didn't move to grab anything off the tray.

I was making a fool of myself. It was like sitting with my mother and sister, trying to get them to try things when they were on a diet. I skirted around the counter and grabbed the tray to take back to the kitchen.

"Where are you going with those?" Did he lick his lips?

"I'm putting them away. Paloma and I are going to taste test later if you don't want any and—"

"I'll try them," he announced, like I should be excited to have his expertise.

"Mr. Hardy, maybe we've reached our quota of hanging out for the day. I don't think you have the knowledge of what is going to be good on my menu anyway."

He clucked his tongue. "That's a pity. But you know who does have the expertise?"

"Who?" I asked, sort of confused as I stood there with the tray.

The man didn't even give me a second to prepare before he turned on his heels, opened the door to my bakery, and yelled Valentino's name. "We've got a few truffles we'd like you to try if you got a minute."

"Dominic Hardy, are you out of your fucking mind?"

He looked over his shoulder and shrugged, "Yeah, probably."

CHAPTER 13: DOMINIC

Damn, she was mad. The crimson over her chest rose up her neck to mingle with her freckles. I fucking loved seeing it.

I'd get her mad every day from now on just to witness her body's reaction. I'd also be coming here every day to watch her talk about her desserts because I couldn't see past anything when she did. Except for myself, I'd never seen anyone half as excited about their job. Clara sold me with her dream the second she said something about strawberries and mint in the truffle and looked about ready to cry with pride.

So, I was about to push our relationship and the boundaries I normally had with women. In more ways than one.

Valentino sauntered over as he waved to a few of the store owners and waltzed in like he owned the room. I'd liked the guy before last night. He was hardworking, had made a name for himself from nothing, and didn't cut corners. It's why I gave him the top restaurant in my resort. His food was divine, and he'd never given me a reason to dislike his character.

But when I saw Clara stare at that man, jealousy slithered through my veins, potent and vicious in its pursuit to suddenly want to claim her as mine.

"How's it going, Mr. Hardy?" He shook my hand hard and then combed it through his dirty-blond hair before he turned to Clara. I saw him take her in, saw his eyes register her dress and how different she looked without makeup.

Clara put a beautiful mask on every day, covered the

freckles, painted her lips deep red, and flared out her reddish lashes with dark black. Without all that, she was cute, like you wanted to fold her up and put her in your chest pocket to keep her close to your heart.

Valentino's eyes narrowed and ping-ponged between us. He was putting together a story in his head, and it's the exact one I wanted him to go with. "Nice to finally see your bakery, Clara."

"Right." She took a deep breath and stepped forward to set the tray on the counter again. "Sorry about the mess. I didn't really plan on having anyone but Paloma come in and taste today."

He hummed. "No worries. We're all working hard to get our places up to Hardy standards, huh?" He slapped a hand on my shoulder.

She nodded and played with a corner of the tray. "Your restaurant looks absolutely fantastic. I think the kitchen is laid out well for utilization, and the ambience is one in a million with the floor-to-ceiling panoramic window views."

"Thanks. Rita and Dom played a big part." Clara's gaze cut to me, and she lifted a brow as if to question whether I'd correct him using my abbreviated name.

I wouldn't. I didn't give a shit about the formality except with her. It was mostly to piss her off because she got a damn bakery here when I didn't want her to have one.

"And sorry I haven't been in to see your bakery. It's been a busy month. You've settled in quite well, no? And the accent wall, huh? Pink is soft but bold."

Valentino hadn't stopped by to see hers? *Fucking idiot.* She ate up his apology though. I saw how she practically melted at the sound of his freaking voice.

"The pink is still to be determined. We're undecided on whether or not we're keeping it." I announced and walked in between them to point at her truffles. "Which would you like to try first?"

"Pink, I think." He smiled slowly at her before he reached out and grabbed one. Then the fucker stared at her as he slid the chocolate into his mouth and moaned. I regretted my decision about bringing him in here immediately, especially when I glanced at her and saw how she was practically leaning in to get closer to him.

And did he just glance down at her cleavage? "It's ... Wow. The flavors, Clara." He looked fucking surprised. "Dom, have you tried this? I'm quite stunned actually. I'd love to have this on the restaurant's menu, Clara, for guests to order through the night if possible. I think—"

"You know what?" Shit. I needed to stop him right then and there. "I've got to get Clara home actually."

He glanced between us, confused. When I put my arm around her shoulders, though, he scanned her outfit, and I think it dawned on him officially then. "Oh, of course."

"I'm happy you approve of the truffles. Makes Clara's job easier. Let's make sure we all get together again before the resort opens."

"Of course, of course. Clara, we should do lunch. I talk with all the distributors. Did you get your mint from them?"

"Yes. But—"

"Ah. There's better mint around the corner. They sell it every weekend." His gaze flicked to mine. "Just local additions that help keep the food fresh. You understand?"

I nodded. "If we need them for distribution here, we'll adjust." It's why we had a team regulating imports.

"I'd love to check it out sometime," Clara confirmed.

"Yes, yes. Of course." Valentino hesitated though and looked at me. He knew better. "You'll come too, yeah?"

That's right. He was aware of his place. At least for now. I saw him trying to encroach on my territory already. But, fuck, I knew Clara wasn't really mine.

Maybe it was my stare that got him to back up, but he still waved before he said, "Let's chat soon."

And then he was gone, and she turned to glare those blazing green eyes at me as she shrugged my arm off her shoulder. "What in the actual fuck was that? He thinks we're sleeping together now."

"Yeah, although he probably thought that the moment he walked in and saw you wearing the same dress from last night." I leaned against the counter to watch her run through the ten emotions she was probably about to have.

"I ..." She hesitated, narrowed her eyes, then paced back and forth through the bakery. Then she shoved the tray so it slid a bit on the counter. "I don't think so."

"You know so. He wants to be the best man in the room, and you just became the best prize that isn't available."

"Well, that's stupid," she said and then stomped her foot like a mad little child. "I don't want a man like that."

"All men are like that. It's a pissing contest, but he respects you more now at least. You showed you know how to bake."

"Of course I do." She glanced at her chocolates and a small smile played on her lips. "I ... You know, I hate to admit it, and I know it's idiotic, but it feels good to know a guy with a Michelin star wants my food in his restaurant."

I grabbed a chocolate off the tray and took a bite because I wasn't about to resist either. They tasted almost as good as she did, and knowing she baked it gave me some sick satisfaction eating it too. "It's not idiotic. I sought approval of my superiors for years."

"And now?" she asked.

"Well, I'm the most superior now, Clara. So, I don't need anyone's approval anymore."

She rolled her eyes and then waved me toward the door. "Of course you don't. Anyway, I'm going home now that you've made a fool of me."

"Still want to pass on dating me? You might get the boyfriend of your dreams ..."

She wiggled one of the tips of her new heels into the ground as she thought about it. I wanted to hear *yes* and *no* at the same time, the feelings warring with each other in me. I could have her close, on my arm, maybe fuck around a time or two with her. But then she'd only be doing it for him, and I should have only been doing it to keep Natya away.

"You really need this girl to stay away from the resort? Will it hurt the bakery too?"

I sighed. "I'll handle her either way."

"But having me with you would be easier?"

"Probably." I nodded, hoping it was true. Natya had never seen me with another woman, but my siblings were right that she never wanted to look like a fool.

Clara stood there, fussing with her dress before she admitted, "I don't care so much about Valentino." Thank fuck. "But can we discuss changes to the bakery? And actually agree on them?"

"Of course my little fighter wants to raise the stakes. Fine. Give Rita three changes. Nothing big. No discussion necessary."

"You don't want a say?" she questioned, like she couldn't

believe it. Yet, in the past twenty-four hours, I'd seen her love and drive and now understood she cared for the bakery in a way I thought she hadn't. This wasn't a business her mommy and daddy gave her. She wanted this like I wanted what I worked for.

"My say is you get three changes, and I'll approve them as long as Rita can deal with it."

"Only three? How long am I dating you for?"

"Five months gives us a bit of time for the resort to be up and running. It needs to be public. You need to tell your friends and family about us. My ex—"

"Are we talking about Natya Fitch?"

"So you read the tabloids?"

"Like a fiend." She shrugged and when I scoffed, she just chuckled. "It's fun and relaxing, okay? So how much of that is true?"

"Enough of it." I cracked my neck, not wanting to go into details. "We need it to be public enough that she doesn't mention our resort anymore. We have partnerships that would disintegrate if she's involved. So, tell your friends, family. Even Noah." His name sounded like acid on my lips.

"Well, three changes seems a bit light if I have to fake it with everyone. Plus, people at work are going to think I'm getting favorable treatment."

"Well, you already are." I shrugged. "I don't let people change designs here."

"Five changes. One a month." Her voice was small but firm. Why was I bargaining with this woman? She was going to give me hell for five months, and even so, my damn dick was hardening just thinking about it. "And I get to keep the wall." Her smile was saccharine.

"Pushing your limits, baby. The edges of it have to be cleaned up and we might need to pull the color just a bit."

"Deal." She stuck her hand out to shake mine, but I slid my fingers through her hair and pulled her close.

"I don't shake hands with my girlfriend."

Then I took her mouth. I devoured those bare pink lips in the way I'd been wanting to all morning. She opened up with a whimper as soon as my tongue swiped over her bottom pout. She tasted of strawberries and chocolate, maybe a hint of that mint just like the truffle she had. I was going to crave chocolate for the rest of my life after this woman, I already knew it. Still, I kissed her without reservation, because I wanted to explore every taste she might have been hiding.

When I pulled back, she was staring up at me in question, and then she peered behind me to check to see if people were outside. "You said you don't kiss women, Dominic."

She was right. I'd never wanted to be involved with anyone since Natya, but I found myself wanting to now. "I kiss my *girlfriend*."

"Fake girlfriend," she corrected and then said, "And no one's watching."

"Sure they are," I said and ducked down to taste her again. We might have been fake dating, but I was going to kiss her for real every fucking time.

CHAPTER 14: CLARA

He came to sit there every day in my bakery, not saying much of anything. I don't know if Dominic Hardy was a man of few words or if we just didn't have much in common. Still, either way, I found myself nervously blabbing to him half the time.

"I don't know why the caramel isn't folding into the chocolate well enough," I scoffed.

He hummed but didn't look up from his laptop.

I continued the one-sided conversation throughout the day. "And if the mint is going to be withered when it comes to my door, why even send it?" I continued on about how my macarons weren't fluffing, how the coffee seemed to heat a bit too hot and then grounds tasted sort of burnt. I even offered him truffles and cupcakes.

He declined while he hummed along with my commentary the whole day.

Each day, I walked in at the same time, and every morning, he showed up like clockwork to find me fighting another recipe on my menu. One day, suddenly, he glanced up. "Do you have a final menu for opening week yet?"

I glared at him through my kitchen window. "Remind me why you're here again?"

"All for show," he replied and went back to his laptop.

Most days were the same. He didn't say good morning or even a hello. He plopped his laptop down on the counter, opened it up, and put on freaking glasses with his stupid expensive black suit. Glasses with black rims that framed his beautiful eyes and accentuated the perfect features.

He had no business wearing them. It was criminal that the man I was supposed to hate looked this good as he rudely dialed a number on his phone and got to work.

Like he belonged in my bakery.

He had such an audacity to him. I knew he was like that with everyone here. Most of my colleagues talked about him like he was a freaking god that couldn't be touched.

Still, a "good morning" in my bakery would have been welcomed and appreciated especially when I wasted my breath walking him through practically every recipe I made.

By the end of the week, I'd had enough. My heels clicked across the white floors as I found myself coming to stand right in front of him on the other side of the counter. Then, I watched my own hand, wide eyed as I closed his laptop.

His eyes bulged too like he couldn't believe I had as much audacity as him.

This was my home. And weren't we all supposed to feel relaxed in our homes? Plus, my joints had ached more that day and a rash had popped up on my arm. The tiredness ebbed and flowed but today it was there, strong, loud, and prominent.

I needed to get a doctor here in LA, but I needed this bakery to be a success first. And that meant if Dominic Hardy was going to be here, he was going to have to at least show me some respect.

I was building a world for myself and pushing for the things I needed. I had to, I reminded myself. This was for me. And if I couldn't live for me, I couldn't live at all.

I took a deep breath and glared at him. "When you walk into my bakery, you can say good morning or hello, Mr. Hardy."

His eyes cut fast to me, lethal in their pursuit of who'd ruined his view of his work. Then, they twinkled as he held his phone away from his mouth. "Ah, the little fighter woke up bright and early this morning, huh?" He then spoke into the speaker, "I'll call you back. My girlfriend wants me to properly greet her."

He hung up and stood. "No more 'Mr. Hardy' now that people think we're fucking, Clara."

I chewed my cheek as I watched him stalk around the counter, predatory as if he was after his prey. "Right. Fine. Well, *Dominic*, a good morning will do," I murmured as I backed up.

His smile was slow, and I knew immediately that man was looking for a way to antagonize me. "I don't say good morning to anyone, Clara. But since we're dating now," he grabbed my waist and pulled me close, "might as well take advantage of the situation."

When he kissed me in my black-and-white bakery, my eyes immediately drifted closed and colors burst everywhere. He tightened his hold on me and consumed everything I was. I felt his hands all over me, down my back, on my ass, gripping my hips and sliding up my breasts to my neck and then jaw where he held me at just the right angle. Dominic didn't give away any power here, not when I whimpered or moaned even as his tongue explored my mouth.

I was dominated.

I was ravaged.

I was owned by him while he kissed me senseless.

And then, just like that, he stepped away.

Still wanting him in a way it shouldn't, my body stumbled forward, as his body straightened like this was all business.

I brought my hand to my lips before murmuring, "What

was that?"

"Your good morning. And practice for when we're in public." He shrugged.

"So, okay." Was I gasping for air? "Warning me next time would probably be a good idea."

"You scared of a little kiss, Clara?" He sized me up and then shrugged. Was I so inadequate that he'd brush off a kiss that had felt like finding water in the Sahara Desert? My lips still tingled from tasting his, my skin still felt electric, and my heart was thumping at double its normal rate.

"It's just ... not how I imagined a kiss from my boyfriend would be in the morning."

His eyes were a darker green now than I'd ever seen. It was the only indication I'd affected him like he had me. He searched my gaze for more information before finally asking, "Did your last boyfriend not kiss you like that in the morning, Clara?"

I saw the way his jaw ticked, how he put his hands in his pockets and rocked back on his heels. Irritation looked good on Dominic Hardy as he waited for my answer. "I don't know if my last boyfriend was really even a boyfriend." I wrinkled my nose.

I was too worried about becoming my mother to fall in love when I went to culinary school, and back home, I had guy friends but we only hooked up occasionally. "I sort of like to leave before the sun comes up."

He quirked his head. "Interesting."

Then he walked back around the counter and sat down to work. He even put those ridiculously hot glasses back on.

That was it? "Why do you keep coming here?"

"Well, we need people to start talking before we're seen out together."

I sighed and figured I might as well use him while he was here. "Want to try a mocha?"

"No." He typed away without looking up at me.

"Do you want to try a cappuccino instead?" He had to want something to drink.

"I'll take coffee black if you have it."

Of course he wanted something with no flavor in it. I wasn't here to deliver him what he wanted though. What I handed him in his cup today was going to be what I was going to hand him with my bakery: something he never thought he needed.

I turned on the frother and let the rhythmic sound soothe my scattered thoughts of handling him here. It was difficult to feel his presence through my soul while I worked,and worry over him judging my every step. I fell into step when I knew that adding the syrup and chocolate and caramel at just the right time was necessary with the espresso and frothed milk. Within minutes, I smiled down at the cup. It was perfect, and I'd be damned if he thought less of it as I set it down in front of him.

When his eyes flicked over to the concoction, I saw his large hand tense into a fist and then his jaw muscle popped.

"You'll love it, I promise," I said before I went back to the kitchen and got to work. There were a million different things I had to bake. "If you're going to keep coming here, you might as well try some things."

I started with a breakfast sandwich, making sure to grab the paprika for my homemade hollandaise. "Everyone in Florida loves this sandwich, I swear."

There went his humming again. When I brought out the sandwich and set it in front of him, I saw he'd finished half his drink.

No comment though. Next, I cooked up bacon but added cracked pepper and a dollop of honey. When I took that out to him, the sandwich was gone.

He still typed away, without any mention of the food.

We worked most of the day with me talking his ear off. And somehow, I felt lighter, like this worked, like we weren't completely dysfunctional in my bakery. When I placed three truffles in front of him and he ate every single one in front of me, I waited for the verdict that time.

He didn't take those eyes off me, and every bite he took bit into my resolve to avoid him. He was delighting in this, probably knew my mouth was watering as he licked his lips, that my sex was clenching as I watched him suck his fingers clean, and that my body heated while he hummed around the last bits of dessert. "I like the third one best. Reminds me of how sweet you taste."

"Dominic," I warned.

He leaned over the counter. "Your chocolate rivals how sweet your pussy is, baby. If I could marry the two flavors, I'd eat your truffles every day ... and I don't even like indulging in chocolate."

My mind scrambled every which way at his freaking dirty mouth before it hooked on to one thing. "Wait. You don't like chocolate at all?"

He chuckled before shoving away from the counter, closing his laptop and saying, "That's not what I said. I said I don't like to have it. Put everything you served me on the menu."

"So it's good enough?" I lifted an eyebrow, wanting to admit he liked something.

"It'll do." Of course he couldn't say it. "I'll see you tomorrow, little fighter. Same time, same place. Pick out the color of dishes you want and send the request to Rita."

With that he was gone.

CHAPTER 15: CLARA

Other managers got curious enough that Dominic kept coming around. Paloma's texts ended with a lot of exclamation points about the boss being in my bakery.

Then, she finally stopped in one day and just wide-eyed us both and then mouthed to me, "You owe me an explanation." When Dominic looked up, she smiled and backed away fast.

"They're all scared of you," I announced.

"Rightfully so."

"No," I countered. "You're supposed to be helping the team come together in the final days before we open so we have a cohesive brand, look, and flow."

He sighed but didn't say anything. When I offered him a truffle later, he glared at it for three seconds before turning it down.

The next day, Paloma was there again. This time, he asked her if they figured out the front displays. "We went with green apparel in the front like you wanted." She plopped down right next to him and said, "Oh, let me show you. Green or burnt red earrings for the front display?"

She held out her phone, but he didn't even look before he answered, "Burnt red."

"Really?"

He pushed up his stupid perfect glasses that weren't even falling down his face. "It works with the aesthetic."

"Fine. You're right." Again, my new friend mouthed "I want

answers," then she was out of there.

Every day after that, she was there, blabbering our ears off. She asked if we were a thing and he answered, "yes," she glared at me some more, but I was too nervous to say anything further.

And then one day, Dominic wasn't there, and I got a text from him.

Dominic: I'll be gone for the rest of the week. When I get back, we should go out. Be seen.

Me: I'm ready when you are.

Dominic: Rita said you're requesting paint colors. What happened to keeping your wall?

I scoffed at his text message. There was no way I was admitting I was wrong.

Me: I'm going for a softer hue and then fading into red.

Dominic: Technically, that's a change.

Me: No it isn't. Screw you, Dominic.

Dominic: Little fighter, if you're talking dirty, feel free to call me.

Me: Goodbye.

Dominic: Did you hire a team to paint?

Me: I'm capable of doing it myself.

Dominic: Hold off until I'm back.

Me: Do you think I can't? We have a month and a half until we open, Dominic.

Dominic: I'm aware. I'll help you when I get back, then you can fuck me to thank me.

Jesus. I thought about that text all week. Even when Paloma was sitting there asking for all the dirty details of our relationship. I explained it had come on fast, but we'd had a history. She bought the whole thing, and now I had to make sure Dominic knew it too.

Still, I didn't make an effort to text the man. He hadn't made an effort to tell me where he was going, why he'd gone, or anything of the sort. We weren't really dating. Honestly, Dominic Hardy was a terrible fake boyfriend and would be a catastrophic real one. Not one I'd ever actually want in my life.

Instead, I worked. All day, every day without any news from him.

"I'm sorry. So, you're telling me that coffee bean isn't available to be shipped here?" I gnashed my teeth together, pacing up and down the lobby.

I didn't have enough space to dissipate the frustration in the air from phone calls this morning.

The resort's food distributor continued to list off different types of beans just like he'd done for my cacao, my fruits, and some of my herbs. Setting a bakery apart from others meant we needed fresh produce, top-of-the-line ingredients, and fast shipping.

"I'm sorry, ma'am. Like I said, it's just not doable."

Trying not to feel defeat, I ended the call only to look up and see familiar, deep forest-green eyes that pulled me in even when I fought them. His black suit, as always, made me feel underdressed in the coral sundress I'd chosen that morning.

"Clara," he murmured as he walked right up to me, wrapped an arm around my waist and lowered his head to kiss my cheek. "Miss me?"

"Want the fake girlfriend answer or the real one?"

He waited a beat and pulled back to catch my glare. His eyes scanned my face, and it took every ounce of control not to turn away from him. I knew I was makeup free. No one showed up to my bakery during the day with the resort still being closed, and I'd been baking in peace.

The sound that he made vibrated so low and deep through my whole body that I felt it in my bones. "Is it the real Clara I'm looking at today?" He murmured it softly as his hand went to my chin to tip my face up to him. He dragged a thumb across my cheek where I knew freckles dotted my face. "If so, I'll take real. Always."

I licked my lips and his eyes zeroed in on them. "Dominic," I whispered and stepped back. Being in his arms with his eyes looking hungry like that was dangerous. "You need to hear the fake girlfriend version though." I emphasized the word to make sure we both stepped back into reality.

One side of his mouth kicked up. "Go on then, fighter." It's like he knew what was coming.

"Well, since my boyfriend went somewhere all week and I haven't seen or heard from him, I don't miss him. I loathe him. Especially considering your distributor is giving me hell, and Rita is still pushing back on my next change." I'd requested hanging floral decor that would match the soft pink wall. She'd emailed back that it wasn't an option.

"I'll remind Rita that you've been allotted five changes at your discretion." He was smirking at me. The man, who never cracked a smile had the audacity to think all this was funny.

At least we were on talking terms and making headway with the bakery though. I stepped back, trying to distance myself from him. "You have fun on your little vacation?"

He sighed and pinched the bridge of his nose. "Honestly?" He then pulled at the back of his neck and looked toward the high ceilings. "A design of mine is going to shit, so I needed to be there."

"Oh." What do you say when a man that never makes mistakes admits to one? "Want to talk about it?"

"The glass bridge is of architectural brilliance, but it's outside, and when it rains—"

"People slip and fall?"

"Right. It's been taken care of though. So, now we take care of getting you in magazines with me so the reopening of this resort doesn't turn into a PR disaster." He threaded his hand through mine and started to pull me toward the revolving doors.

"Where are we going? I'm work—"

"You need a dress for the reopening or just a dress so we can be seen out. It'll solidify that we're serious."

I wrinkled my nose at the idea. Dresses were expensive.

Thousands upon thousands of dollars that I didn't have. And why did the idea of doing anything with him make me utterly nervous? I combed a hand through the hair I hadn't even curled this morning because I thought no one would be seeing me. "Maybe we should do it tomorrow." I glanced back at my bakery. I wasn't doing much food prep today and would be busier tomorrow but ... "I need to get ready. I can't be seen like—"

"Like what?" he scoffed and then pulled me towards the entrance again.

"People are going to look at us together, and I didn't do my hair or put makeup on—"

"And without the makeup, I see the imperfections that make you perfect." He said it so easily, in that decisive tone that was meant to propel everything forward without emotion.

"Huh?"

"With nothing to define you, you're just like everyone else, Clara. Your freckles, the way you blush, the way your lashes are a hint of red is what defines you. You're painting over a perfect canvas."

"I ..." What did you say when an artist described your imperfections as perfect and pointed out your flaws as flawless? I tried to ignore the fluttering in my heart, the lurch into this relationship being real when it wasn't. I huffed. "I need lashes and concealer and my hair curled. Did you know my mother—"

He opened a black SUV's door for me without letting me finish my sentence. "Clara, I don't give a fuck what someone else has said. You're beautiful. Stop worrying about stupidity from your mother, who, if I recall, wields her beauty as a weapon quite a lot."

"You think that of my mother?" I almost tripped getting into the car. "But she's—"

"An elitist who probably taught you all the rules of high society?" He followed me in. "Am I correct?"

Why his take-no-shit attitude worked for me, I didn't know. It felt straightforward without any twists and turns, no passive aggressive comments, no smoke and mirrors.

"Probably too correct," I grumbled. I figured I wouldn't fight him on going back to the house but when he tried to direct his driver, Callihan, to a small boutique, I stopped him. "Oh, Callihan, I'd like to try the department store over at the Promenade."

Dominic eyed me curiously, and my heart beat fast as he did. I'd been creative in hiding the fact that I didn't have much more than pennies to my name at this point. Shopping at a haute couture boutique wasn't a luxury of mine at this point.

When he didn't pry, I breathed a sigh of relief and changed the subject. "So, how did you fix it?"

"Fix what?"

"The flooring?" I asked, because I was curious how he navigated those things he didn't plan for, how I would handle them.

"Why?" He scratched his head, trying to figure out my angle. We were only fake dating. I didn't need to know so much about his life, right? Still, I wanted to know everything.

"If we're gonna sell this whole fake dating thing, we need to make everyone believe it. I need to know what you're doing. Why you are frustrated one day, why you're proud the next. And by the way, I told Paloma how we've always had tension between us and when I came here, it all sort of combusted. So, that's our story."

"Combusted?" he asked, his tone suggestive.

"Seriously, Dominic. Relationships deal with your

emotions, and your emotions seem to always deal with your job. I need to know about *you*. We don't even know anything about each other."

"You think I don't know anything about you?" He frowned at me and then slowly his lush lips lifted. "I know how you sound when I lick your pussy and you moan my name, cupcake. We definitely know something about one another."

Jesus, his mouth was filthy sometimes, and my thighs clenched together trying to not be turned on by it. When I bit my lip, his thumb was there pulling it out of my mouth.

"Stop chewing your lip, baby. I'll tell you whatever you want to know, okay?" He rubbed over my bite mark once before he pulled back, and I missed his touch immediately. "We added raindrop pebbles onto the bridge outside that are a sort of rubber material, which allows for much more traction."

"Still maintained your vision with the transparent drops, I'm assuming?" I couldn't help but be impressed. "Owning that your design was still perfect."

"With a few alterations, yes. I'll always own that." Dominic Hardy, completely and utterly arrogant without any apology was a sight to see.

When we pulled up to the department store, I tried to hop out fast. "You can wait—"

"I'm coming in." He eyed me curiously but followed as I hurried through the store, trying to find a dress that would work. I still winced at most of the prices.

"Why are we shopping here?" he finally asked as if it was a complete waste of our time.

"This place has great deals and beautiful dresses, Dominic."

"Do we need a deal all of a sudden?" he asked, incredulous. "We don't have time to be looking for sales, Clara. Do that with

Paloma." He didn't wait for me to respond. Instead, he scoffed and pulled me from the store and then demanded that Callihan take us to a boutique up the road.

When he walked me into the boutique, he waved a saleswoman over. "Mr. Hardy, to what do I owe the pleasure?" She was my age, perfectly manicured and fluffed in a way I would have tried to be once while standing with my sister and mother. Now, my hair was all frizzy natural waves, and my freckles were on display with no makeup covering them whatsoever.

Dominic didn't even glance at her. His hand was on the small of my back as he looked down at me. "Get my girlfriend whatever she wants. We have a gala type event, so make sure it's appropriate for that."

"Oh, sure." She threw a glance my way and then ushered me into a fitting room. She wasn't deterred at all by my title as his girlfriend as she directed one of her employees to pull dresses for me. She asked how his career was going, offered him champagne, and had the audacity to offer her number, too, in case he needed to have anyone else fitted for an event in the future.

"I have a lot of great designers that give us exclusive products and—"

"I'm sure my girlfriend has most of your contacts," I heard him mumble.

When I came out of the dressing room, even though I'd no intention to do so before, he was looking down at his phone. It was as if he wasn't at all influenced by the fact that the woman was shamelessly flirting with him.

When she turned to me and literally rolled her eyes, I felt like shrinking back into my dressing room. My mother and sister had always critiqued me ruthlessly, and I didn't expect anything less from this woman. "Probably should try a different fit. This one isn't flattering. And what's your budget?" She lifted a brow, like she was challenging me.

"Oh, probably not more than this dress." Which, at a couple thousand, was more than I could afford.

"That's only five thousand. So, we won't be able to find many others that can—"

"Pull every dress in her size, Miranda. And don't tell my girlfriend what's flattering and what's not. She decides that. Not you." Miranda blushed as she backed away. "Cupcake," Dominic breathed out my name as his eyes raked over my body. "Turn around. Give me a full view?"

The way his eyes scanned me, how I saw him rearrange himself in his seat, and then how he flexed his hands, I couldn't deny him his request. Before I'd made a full spin, he was up out of his chair to stand right against my back as we faced the fitting room door mirror. "This dress accentuates every curve on your body. It's mine, and *only* mine." I felt his length against my ass as he continued, "I don't need other men enjoying the curves of my woman too much."

I chuckled as his hands danced over me, giving me a confidence I should have had the moment I walked in. "Scared of a little competition, Dominic? They're only looking."

"Looking at what's mine is disrespectful. I can either go out and knock heads around all night or enjoy you in my bed. I'll do either if that's what you want." He turned to Miranda, whose mouth was hanging open, and repeated, "All the dresses to her fitting room. Now."

After that, she backed off, and I didn't come out with too many other dresses to show. He didn't need a fashion show, and I didn't need to be tempted to drag him into the fitting room with me.

There was just one last dress to try on, and I knew it was the one I'd love but also the one I shouldn't have even considered with its price tag. I chewed my cheek and tried to figure out what to do right as I heard the old-fashioned bell over the boutique's door jingle.

My heart sank when I heard the saleswoman squeal, "Oh my God. Natya Fitch. Weren't you two just an item?"

"Just?" A soft laugh sounded on the other side of my curtain. "We've always been more than that, right, Dom?"

Her voice sounded like a kitten's purr, purely sexual when she said his name, almost like it could lull you into a trance. And wow, had the saleswoman's tone changed. She sounded like Natya was royalty and she wanted to cater to them both as a couple.

My heart raced in the fitting room as I listened to that woman's voice, soft and calm, tell Dominic how she'd so missed seeing him.

We were supposed to see her at the reopening together. Now wasn't the time for a show. Yet, I shook in that fitting room, contemplating what to do. She might have been his ex, but she needed to know who I was. Fake or not, it was time to make an introduction. It could have been his words before to own it, it could have been the saleswoman already making me feel less than, or it could have been my heart suddenly feeling tired of being walked on over and over.

I was going to lay down a boundary. He'd asked for this, and now he was going to get it. I grabbed the dress I was saving to try on. I might have loved color, but I understood how nudes and black lace swirling strategically over fabric could be used to somebody's advantage. I slid the skintight fabric up my body and felt the weight of it. With rhinestones and beads threaded through the lace, the Valentino dress reminded me of red carpet showstoppers. The plunging neckline and high thigh slit hinted at the confidence in a woman who wore it too.

I took a deep breath, trying to channel that confidence. Then I opened the door and looked at my fake boyfriend, staring at his beautiful ex. She was so beautiful she was almost statuesque. She wore black and white, exactly how he would have wanted, and the lines on her pantsuit sculpted lethally around her to demand respect for her beauty.

Every angle of her face was precisely in the right spot, her high cheekbones, her straight chestnut-brown hair pulled back in a ponytail, and her dark eyes shadowed perfectly to add a sort of mystery. Her gaze caught mine, and we stared at one another. No part of me ever really stood up to people unless it was Dominic and me fighting over my bakery. Here though, I didn't break eye contact, and I didn't look away as I cleared my throat, hoping Dominic would turn to face me, hoping that I wouldn't be made a fool of.

When he did, I didn't break eye contact with her. I just asked, "Dominic, could you zip my dress?"

Natya narrowed her eyes and the hand on her small designer clutch clenched as the other that was on Dominic's arm tightened. She leaned in to say softly to him, "To think I was missing you and then you showed up to our favorite boutique. Destiny, my love, or the universe is trying to tell us something, no?"

A small gasp escaped my lips. He'd brought me here knowing it was her favorite place? Was I the fool? Or had he made me one by not even telling me that?

"Natya." Dominic shook his head, his muscles coiled even

when he shrugged her hand off him. "The universe doesn't speak. So, excuse me, my girlfriend needs a bit of help."

She clucked her tongue and then gave me a tight-lipped smile. "The universe always speaks, Dom. But I'm glad you've found someone new. Your name?"

She stepped toward me and held out a hand. I took it even as Dominic walked up to me and put his arm around my shoulders. "I'm Clara."

"Ah, Clara. Be good to him. He and I ... Well, I still love the fool." She chuckled like this was some small girl talk. "And we'll always have something between us, right, Dom?"

He didn't answer her or say goodbye as she walked off to shop and he steered me into the fitting room.

He might have been my fake boyfriend, he might have been a man I was supposed to hate, but the pain of seeing him standing there with his ex and the look on his face when she said they'll always share something ... that was very, very real.

CHAPTER 16: DOMINIC

I didn't give Clara a moment to respond to Natya because I saw the emotion on Clara's face all of a sudden. Instead of me dwelling on Natya's words, I yanked Clara into the fitting room and closed the curtain. "Don't engage with her."

Clara narrowed her eyes at me, and I knew she was gearing up for a debate. "She's instigating, and you know it."

"Of course she is. That's what she does. She wants attention, and if we give it to her—"

"Is there still something between you two?"

"No." I said it loud and fast, mostly because I didn't want to share my heartache but also because I was starting to believe it.

Clara scoffed and then whisper-yelled at me, "Don't lie for my benefit, Dominic. Better that I know what I'm dealing with than you lie for truly no reason. I don't care one way or the other."

"Is that right?" I growled because if her ex had come waltzing in the way Natya did, I'd have cared. I'd have dragged her to the fitting room and fucked her loud enough for him to hear. "You're telling me you don't care if I want to have relations with my ex?"

"It's your life." She stepped back, crossing her arms.

The dress bunched her cleavage together and my hand shot out to drag across her collarbone and down against the edge of the fabric. "You know, *this*, between us, whether it's fake or not, it's exclusive, Clara."

Her breath hitched as I dipped my finger between her tits. She stepped back, but I followed her, and she lifted her chin to keep my gaze. "I didn't agree to that."

I hooked a finger on the V of that dress and yanked her forward. "You'd better agree to it now, little fighter."

"Or what?" The challenge in her eyes was there. "Shouldn't I be the one who's worried? She stood out there fawning over you and practically foaming at the mouth when she saw me. She'd have gotten on her knees for you in a second."

"She's not the one I want on her knees," I murmured, my hand going to the slit in her dress. Her pussy had dripped arousal past her panty line and onto her thigh. "Do you know how much I fuck my hand while thinking of your pussy, baby? How hard my cock gets imagining how tight you'll be for me?"

She whimpered and bit her lip as I pushed her panties to the side and rolled her clit between my fingers. She grabbed the lapels of my suit and moaned, "I want you, right now."

"You know I won't. This isn't the place." Her eyes narrowed, turned almost cunning before they flicked to the curtain shielding us from the boutique. "But I'm happy to make my girlfriend relax, huh? Ride my hand, baby. Let me take care of you."

My tone was teasing, but she glared as she whispered back, "Not really your girlfriend. Only fake."

I was starting to hate her saying it, reminding me of it. It'd only been a few weeks, but I thought of her all the time, wondered what she was doing in that bakery, wondered if she'd sneer at me for not eating her sweets that I was already addicted to or talk nonsense to me all day while I worked there.

I yanked the side of her dress down and bit her nipple

before I sucked it and lapped at it to soothe the bite, then I did the same to her neck over and over, leaving marks everywhere. She clawed her fingers through my hair, arching into me. "You want this?"

She didn't answer, but her muscles clenched every time I put pressure on her clit, and when I slid my middle finger into her sex, she cried out.

"That's what I want to hear. Tell me, little fighter, your pussy want your boyfriend now?"

She shook her head no and repeated softly, "It's fake, Dominic."

Right. "Your orgasm isn't about to be fake, baby."

I thrust another finger in her as I grabbed her thigh to hitch it onto my hip, then I curled my fingers up and down in her as she rode them. Her pace was just as fast as mine, so hungry for that orgasm that her round, luscious tits bounced exquisitely just for me to stare at.

When she was about to hit the high she wanted, though, when I felt her sex tightening around my fingers like a vice, I stopped. "Feel *real* yet?"

She gasped, "Fuck you, Dominic. Finish me off or—" She pulled me close as she rode my hand instead of me moving it, and said, "You're trying to control me, trying to get your way. I hate that everyone does that with me, you know that?"

"Something you want instead?" I lifted a brow.

"You didn't even let me say a thing to her out there." Her leg on my hip flexed, pulling me closer. "I didn't even get to tell her *you* were *mine*."

"Oh, now I'm yours?" I antagonized, not apologizing for controlling her here. It was to protect her, to keep her out of the line of fire of my ex. "Not just a fake boyfriend?"

But Clara was done playing games. That Clara had left and this Clara—she was possessive and jealous—was a sight to see. Her green eyes vivid, her makeup-free face flushed with passion, and her lips rosy from nibbling on her bottom lip. She licked it again before she did something I wasn't expecting.

She took control and she dominated me. Her hands went to my belt buckle, undoing it like she was racing against time as she pulled me close. I tried to grab her wrists. "What are you doing?" I knew what she was doing, knew that I'd pushed her too far.

"Be quiet," she commanded before she freed my cock. I didn't have much say in the matter because before I could reply, her small hand was wrapped around me, her fingers barely long enough to fully grip on. Still, she pumped me once, and I groaned immediately. With the sound, she came fucking alive, the smile that whipped across her face was powerful and all-knowing. Clara had me at her mercy, and my cock pulsed in her hand at the sight of her this way. Her long red hair fell in natural waves around her face, her skin glistened with a soft sheen of sweat, her lips parted to accommodate her rapid breathing. She stood tall, though, her chin tipped up like a queen, ready to rule the man she'd conquered.

Her thumb rolled over the head of my dick as she continued, "I deserve this, and you're going to let me have it, Dominic. You deserve it, too, you know that?"

"A fitting room probably isn't the best place for—"

She got on her knees in that dress. "Are you going to deprive your girlfriend?"

This time she left out the word I'd decided I hated. For that alone I knew I was going to give her what she asked for. "You going to take it all, baby?"

She bit her lip and when she let them pout out, I rolled my hips to move the head of my cock just right so that it coated them with my pre-cum. Her tongue followed like this was what she'd craved. After pumping me one more time, my veins protruded in damn anticipation and she murmured, "I don't know if I can take all of you."

"You'll take all of me, baby. You'll learn."

She swallowed once and then opened that mouth. I saw her pretty pink tongue extend right before she wrapped her lips around me. I was lost to everything but Clara after that. Her tongue swirled around my head, and she moaned as her eyes drifted shut.

No way was I going to last but I needed to see her. "Eyes on me always, little fighter. Make it known who owns my cock."

Clara dragged her tongue up my length so slow, I fucking shuddered at the feeling and slammed a hand onto the fitting room mirror right behind her. Even with me leaning over her and her on her knees, she reigned supreme in that room. I was going to come way too hard here; was going to lose control in a damn fitting room with my ex standing outside.

My hand went to her face. "We should go home, little fighter."

She smiled and shook her head no. "When we argue, Dominic, I think you're starting to learn that I always win."

She took me further into her mouth then, eyes watering, and her rhythm picked up as she worked that mouth up and down, up and down. "Fuck, you're beautiful." I couldn't stop from saying it over and over as I looked down at her, lips so red, I'd never look at the color the same, freckles on display for me because she'd listened even if she didn't have to. I dragged a finger across her cheek over them. "Fucking flawless. My girlfriend is so damn good and—"

The gasp on the other side of the curtain was audible before I heard Natya seethe my name. "Dom, how could you?"

Most women would have stopped, but Clara must have known I was on the brink, and when I looked down at her, her gaze was on Natya where we'd accidentally left an opening in the curtain. She sucked on my cock hard instead.

"Fuck." I dragged out the word. Clara owned me here, not anyone else, and I didn't give a fuck who saw.

"Is she really—"

That wasn't true. I didn't care who saw me vulnerable to Clara, but no one was going to make this woman feel less than again. I knew that right then and there. "Go the fuck away, Natya." I slammed the curtain shut as I said through clenched teeth, "I'm going to come down your throat if you don't back off, baby."

Her cheeks hollowed around me, no stopping on the horizon.

I gripped her hair as I thrust in. "Take it then. Take all of me, Clara. Fuck, baby, my girlfriend is good at sucking cock." Damn, damn, damn. "Good girl. Such a pretty fucking mouth."

She hummed and the vibration sent me over the edge. I exploded, not able to control myself for a second longer. The high was so damn good, I thought I'd black out. Instead, I saw the color of Clara everywhere. Bold, bright, and as epic as a grand finale of a firework show.

She drank every part of me she could, and I slumped over her for a minute, breathing heavily. When she pulled back, the come that had dribbled onto her chin was evidence enough of her being mine. Even still, I rubbed my thumb over it and then dragged it down onto her cleavage. "Oh my God, Dominic.

What are you doing?"

I just shook my head. "I think I'm going a little crazy, cupcake. And honestly if I could, I'd paint you with it." I took a breath. "I don't think this dress is appropriate for the reopening."

"Come on." She laughed. "It's absolutely appropriate. Women wear stuff like it all the time."

"But I'll be imagining you on your knees in it and not be able to function. Plus, every damn man will be staring at you the whole night."

"You can't take a few guys staring?"

"I can. I just don't know if they can take me knocking them out."

She tried to hide her smile, but I caught it. "So, you want me in a different dress?"

"No." I shook my head. I couldn't be that crazy about her that fast, wouldn't dictate what she wore because I wanted to keep the attention off her. She deserved to shine, and she was just getting started. The confidence in her was growing, and I wasn't sure I would be man enough to handle it.

I helped unzip the dress and stared at her while she got changed. "You can leave, Dominic. I can get dressed on my own."

"Probably, but this is purely selfish. Anytime you want to go shopping, count me in as long as I can be in the fitting room with you."

We were laughing as we walked out, her hand in mine.

The fact that my ex stayed until we came out of the dressing room was a problem. She wanted a fight, exactly like my siblings had foreseen, and she proved three things by walking into that boutique to confront me.

One, our love had always been a game to her. My happiness wasn't important to her in the way hers had been to me. She could have kept walking when she saw me in here today.

Two, she put her ugliness on display when she saw Clara standing there, but it only served to showcase Clara's light.

The dress, the way it hugged every part of Clara and the way the black crisscrossed over the nude made her look wild, in power, and untouchably stunning. Even the salesperson admitted, "That dress is the winner on you. Wow."

Natya hated it, and that brought me to ...

Three, she proved I no longer cared about her.

When she walked up to us again as we went to the register, she murmured to Clara, "That's a great Valentino dress. Probably the most expensive in the store." She scanned Clara's face and came to a conclusion she shouldn't have. "I wonder, does this boutique do loans or financing? Or is he buying it because of what you did for him?"

Clara visibly flinched, and I saw the pink on her skin before I stepped in front of her, ready to put myself in Natya's line of fire. Sure, Clara was my fake girlfriend and I wasn't supposed to care about her. We might have agreed to be done in a few months, but the timeline didn't seem to matter anymore. Something was shifting between us, and no one was allowed to irritate my little fighter besides me.

She was mine. And no one made what was mine feel anything but fucking flawless.

"Natya, is there a reason you're looking into fitting rooms you shouldn't be? Because if my girlfriend feels violated in any way ..." I turned to the saleswoman who immediately started to ask Natya to leave but I held up a hand. "And why the fuck would the woman I'm serious about need a loan or financing?"

"How serious?" she asked.

Instead of Clara staying quiet, she peeked around my body and spit out, "Pretty serious considering what I just did in there."

When I whipped around in surprise to stare at her, her eyes sparkled with mirth before we both started chuckling, and then she was full-on laughing.

I turned to the saleslady and paid for the dresses. "Please make sure to keep my card on file," I told the saleswoman and then turned to Natya as I said, "in case my future wife ever wants anything else here, got it?"

Natya and Clara both gasped at my words even as the salesperson mumbled, "Of course."

I knew the news would spread fast, but the only person that needed to hear it was Natya. I was making it clear that Clara wasn't just some fling that I hooked up with in the fitting room. I wanted a boundary set; I wanted respect for Clara to extend far and wide.

Natya may have proved three things when she'd walked into that boutique, but Clara proved more important points. She proved she was a force to be reckoned with, that the fighter in her didn't quit, and that she could bring any man to his knees to prove his love for her.

I wouldn't have anybody say otherwise.

I was falling for Clara Milton, and I had to make damn sure I stopped. Love between her and me would end up being a battlefield, and I didn't want her wounded.

I had already been wrecked by love before and lived in a darkness now because of it. I'd accepted that I didn't want love. She, on the other hand, was just finding her light, fighting for what she wanted and for herself. The way she owned me in that fitting room, the way she didn't have any remorse about it either, she was a phoenix coming to life, and I was scared I'd ruin her.

She needed something I couldn't give her. But despite that, I smiled the whole way to our car as she smacked my shoulder and told me I was an idiot for saying something like that. "Now, she'll think we're getting married. What if they tell the media? Are you completely mad?"

I was. Truly and utterly mad for Clara Milton, and it had started to feel a lot like love when I thought of her as my wife.

I repeated those words over and over again in my head.

My future wife.

It had a nice fucking ring to it.

CHAPTER 17: CLARA

His future wife?

What the hell was wrong with him? He'd conveniently dropped the statement like Natya wouldn't have heard it. Like the saleslady wouldn't immediately turn around and post the juicy tidbit on her social media.

I bickered with him about it the whole way back, then I insisted he drop me off at the bakery, and when he left me to my own devices, it was with a loopy smile on his face.

For another whole week, I woke up, stretched out the aches and pains of working my butt off in the bakery, and then I bicycled there. I figured I was so sore from the addition of my secondhand bike, nothing more.

I took my meds and vitamins and tried my best to avoid unhealthy foods. I avoided the media and calls from my family too because I knew the news about us was out now.

Of course, Dominic showed up with that same smile even when they started printing things about us, *serious* things. Much more serious than me being a girlfriend. Instead, I was his future wife.

For that whole week, my phone rang off the hook. Every time it did, I snarled at it. Evie wanted details, so I texted her. We'd talk more later, but the bakery kept me busy.

My sister and my mother wouldn't stop calling. Over and over, they called like I owed them an explanation. Maybe I did, but I was too overwhelmed to give them one.

Then Dominic would sit there in his ridiculous glasses that I decided didn't even look that good on him and chuckle as I glared at it, vibrating on the counter. "Don't you have an office?"

"Sure, but I'm trying to spend time with my future wife."

I rolled my eyes. "You're an asshole. You know that? You keep joking about it, but we're dealing with the blowback already. You know how many times my mother has called me?"

He tsked. "Want me to answer and talk to her?"

I did kind of want to make him deal with it. "You have no idea how ridiculous it is dealing with her." When my phone rang again, I sighed, but he snatched it off the counter. "Dominic, don't you dare."

He had already answered. "Ms. Milton, how are you?" Silence. "Yeah, I'm dating her. She's proven to be a joy in my life I'd missed out on for quite some time." Silence. "Of course her bakery is going to do well here. She's made a cupcake that has a poppy on it—" Ah, my mother couldn't stand talking about that. "No. She'll definitely continue baking, Ms. Milton. Why would I do that?"

My heart fell and I shook my head, trying to grab the phone away. I knew what my mother would say. I should be staying home, taking care of him, and my investment in baking was a frivolous one.

Dominic stood up and backed away from the counter, keeping the phone out of my reach as he frowned. "Ms. Milton, your daughter loves baking. It makes her happy, and what makes her happy should make her mother happy, right?"

As he waited, he hummed low, and I knew that look. He didn't agree with anything she was saying.

"Well, I'll see what we can do. Clara's been very busy because

I do have her work hard. We also haven't sent invitations for the reopening to outside guests yet. Exclusive HEAT members at this time have access. And that means you'd have to talk to Evie—"

I saw the phone light up, saw that she'd hung up on him, and he was smiling when he set it down on the counter. "She's a real piece of work, huh? How long haven't you been talking to her?"

"Very sparingly since I've been here." I shrugged.

"Why?" he asked softly, coming around the counter to pull me close.

"Because I'm trying to create something healthier for myself. I just... I was stressed there. Seriously in pain." I truly felt it in my bones sometimes, there was no other way to describe it. "Here I feel lighter. I'm trying to do what's best for me, and sometimes that means ..."

"Means what?"

"Means making a choice to choose me." To choose yourself sometimes wasn't selfish, right? It was necessary.

He whispered, "Own it, cupcake." And then he kissed me like it was what we should be doing.

I stepped away from him, too comfortable in his arms, left him with a small smile, and went back to reorganizing the spices in the back kitchen. "I emailed Rita with my next change. She's not happy. You'll have to talk to her. Again," I informed him.

"Am I going to have to argue with her?" He lifted a brow and then actually wrinkled his nose. Fuck, those glasses were so stupidly hot. Who was I kidding?

"I'd told her I wanted pink and red dishes."

"She's going to flip out then. I should be rewarded for the

shit I'm going to take for getting you these five changes."

"Isn't this your resort?" I quipped.

"Rita thinks she owns my resort, along with your bakery," he admitted, and that actually made me chuckle.

"Want a treat for your efforts?" I pointed to one of the chocolates I'd just made. He eyed it longer than normal. Then he shook his head and closed his eyes.

He dug into his pocket and popped one of his dumb mints instead. Then he mumbled, "I want a treat, but I want it to be your pussy, not a damn truffle."

"Oh my God." I rolled my eyes and went back to work.

***

Not much later, Paloma twirled in, waving her phone at both of us. "You two move fast, don't you?"

"I think Dominic just accidentally said that. Right?" I stared at him pointedly. "They're making it much bigger than it should be."

Of course the man hadn't said anything in an hour, but he had the audacity to speak up right then, "If you say so."

I ground my teeth together. "Knock that off, Dominic Hardy. We have a resort to open, not a freaking wedding to plan. Stop creating gossip for no reason."

He smirked at me. "Want to go gossip in the back room for a minute?"

Paloma squealed and plopped down next to him. "She's fucking furious, and you love it. You two are so cute."

I huffed at them both, "Neither of you are getting any food from me today."

Paloma groaned and Dominic grabbed another of his

stupid mints as he shrugged. The two of them had me needing a moment of fresh air. There was too much gossip and too many whispers about me going around, so silence was what I wanted. But then I turned toward the lobby doors and saw another person I'd been avoiding texts from because he was too good of a friend to lie to about my fake relationship.

His blue eyes shone bright, and he had a smile that was so infectious, I squealed with delight. "Noah freaking Romero, what are you doing here?"

He opened his arms and bellowed out, "Lucy, I'm home."

There wasn't an ounce of hesitation when I ran to leap into his arms, and he caught me like I was lighter than air. Immediately, I felt home. He smelled like ocean breeze and spicy cologne and his hair was shaggy enough for me to rub back and forth as I nuzzled into his arms. He'd been a laid-back friend long before we did more than just hang out. He was supportive and fun and never had one expectation of me other than being there when it meant a lot to him.

My pink hydrangea-printed maxi dress swung around us as he spun me in circle after circle until I stopped giggling. "You didn't say you were coming. Why didn't you tell me?"

"What? I've called you damn near fifteen times." He let me slide down his body but kept his arm around my waist. "If I'm not one of the first to see Clara's Bakery in California, I'll always regret it."

I laughed. "Not the name." I sighed as I looked above the doors. "We actually don't have a name yet. I just put in a request for approval."

"What is it? Am I the first to know? Tell me I'm the first to know, and I'm going to be the first to see this finished place of yours."

I rolled my eyes. Noah wanted to be the first at everything, the best, and the person that would always be on your mind. He would have been for a lot of girls. For me, he was a friend who'd filled a void for a while. I did the same for him, and that's as far as it went.

"Clara? You going to show me?" He crossed his arms over his chest, waiting.

Damn. I knew Noah also loved to stir a pot big or small, and Dominic was a big-ass pot to stir.

"Fine." I grabbed his arm and pushed through the doors fast.

"Clara Milton," Noah breathed out right when he walked in. He did not turn to Paloma or Dominic, he gave my bakery his attention first, which made my heart swell and brought tears to my eyes right away. He ran his big hands over the leather seating and said, "The pink seats suit you. You about to blow it up with color in here?"

I bit my lip. "I'm trying."

"You better, babe." He snatched a chocolate cupcake off the table and moaned when it hit his tongue. "Goddamn, I missed these."

Paloma snatched one too before I could smack her hand away.

"And this wall you did, right? Damn, I love it."

I waved off Noah. "It needs to be fixed. I'm fading it a bit and cleaning up the edges."

His eyes checked the corners, and he started laughing. "Guessing that got your ass in trouble."

I wrinkled my nose. "But you like it?"

"Of course. I'm here for a day, going up to Vegas after. Want help?"

I went to stand by where the pink bled onto the white, dragging a finger over it.

"I've already told Clara I've got it handled." Dominic's voice was low, quiet, and completely dominating in my small bakery. He closed his laptop slowly and turned in his seat to stare down Noah.

Noah didn't seem at all deterred. He just turned back to me and flicked his eyes to the wall and then to me. "Proud of you, little dancer." His nickname had Dominic standing up slowly. "You know, pink's your fucking color."

"Don't start, Noah." He had that look in his eye.

"But you blush and it shows up all over you." He smiled and his eyes glinted as he went to stand right in between me and Dominic, cutting off my line of sight to him. Instead, I was staring at my old friend, giving me a look I knew very well. I'd enjoyed that look for years. We were friends with benefits after all. "See. Like right now. Bet I know for a fact that under that dress, you—"

"Clara." Dominic's voice cut through the bakery, loud and authoritative. When he used it like this, my body jumped to attention.

Why did I feel guilty immediately when I peered around Noah's massive shoulders to see Dominic standing there?

"And Noah Romero." He said the name carelessly, like it didn't hold any real weight. "What are you in town for?"

"Hey, man." Noah walked up to shake his hand. They were cordial, had met before when Dominic was in Florida, even trained once or twice together at the HEAT gym. It should have been an easy handshake, quick and friendly, except Noah continued, "Here to see my girl and her bakery, of course."

I'd never seen Dominic stand taller and really size someone

up. He didn't even do it here. He was utterly confident in his ability to outshine another man, and yet I saw the way his jaw ticked when Noah said *my girl.* Would he correct Noah when there was no need? He was respected and feared around here because he threw the truth fast and ruthlessly. Yet, Noah wasn't talking to him about the resort, only about me.

"Your girl and her bakery?" Dominic questioned and must have squeezed Noah's hand hard because Noah visibly frowned as he glanced down and then smiled.

"Yeah. Clara here has been working hard." He squinted at Dominic, catching the tension but continuing forward. He threw his arm around my shoulder casually.

I wide-eyed Dominic and shook my head just a tad. The man lifted an eyebrow at me, and I swore now they were both smiling.

Dominic wouldn't, I thought at first. He didn't care one way or the other about my friend with benefits. "Dominic, want to show Noah around?" The resort was the thing he cared most about anyway.

His eyes didn't break from Noah's arm around mine. "You like *your* girl's ideas for the future design here too?"

"I intend to find out." Noah's eyes narrowed.

"So I assumed." Dominic's green eyes held fire. They licked between us before he said softly but loud enough for both of us to hear, "Your girl tell you she's *my* girl now?"

My jaw dropped while Noah tilted his head in confusion. I felt his body tense as he looked at me and then back to Dominic. "That shit in the tabloids true then?"

I cleared my throat to start explaining, but Dominic beat me to it. "She's my girl. So remove your fucking arm from her shoulder."

"Dominic," I chastised immediately and rushed to correct him "we're friends and he was just—"

Noah cut me off with a smile and then squeezed my shoulder before he dropped his arm. Then his blue gaze hardened. "I came here to support a friend, but you can bet I was looking to support her in all different types of ways."

There was the Noah the NHL knew and loved, searching for a freaking fight. I saw how he cracked his knuckles and tilted his jaw one way and then the other.

"He was *not* going to be supporting me in that way, Dominic." I stepped between them, glaring up at Noah, who just winked down at me.

"Fine, little dancer. I'll play nice."

"No need to play nice for me. You touch my girlfriend, I'll break every bone in your body, on the ice or not," Dominic threw back.

I spun and snapped at him, "Are you joking?"

"Noah knows who'd win in a dogfight, baby. I'm just reiterating it for him, right, Noah?"

"What's that supposed to mean?"

"It means you and I both know the last time I was in Florida sparring with people at the gym, your ass wouldn't even step inside the ring."

"It was the beginning of hockey season and—"

"Care to go down to the ring now?"

"Guys!" I threw my hands up between them. "For what? Are we measuring something here? Dominic, you know I'm with you. Noah, we've had our fun."

"Still here to have fun when you want," he threw out, which just made Dominic growl like a caveman.

"Stop. Right now." I flicked Noah in the shoulder. "You

don't care about who I date, and you know it. You've got puck bunnies in literally every state."

"Yeah"—he combed a hand through his hair—"came to talk to you about a specific one, actually."

I saw how his gaze drifted away for a second, and I rolled my eyes. "See. Stop glowering at each other for no damn reason."

"Fine," he grumbled and plopped down on a barstool, ready to submit like the good friend he was. "You'll come out tonight with me?"

Paloma had been sitting there silently the whole time with wide eyes, but she chimed in right then. "Yes! Let's all go out and have a good time dancing. I'm Paloma by the way."

Dominic didn't give in so easily. When I glanced at him and whispered "You good?" he pulled me close and held my gaze.

"I'm not sharing you, cupcake. I've told you that before." Then he proceeded to kiss me like he was laying claim every which way. I couldn't stop him either. I didn't even want to try.

The kiss was too good.

And that was a problem.

CHAPTER 18: DOMINIC

"You're staring." My brother Dex had flown out to LA and then decided to come to the club with me primarily to discuss the meeting he'd had about his casino deal. Instead, he was bothering the shit out of me because he knew I didn't want to be here.

How I'd agreed to meeting here was beyond me. "Of course I'm staring. He's dancing with my girlfriend," I ground out, watching Clara and Noah spin in circles as she laughed wildly at his antics. We'd all agreed to meet at the club later that night. She'd insisted she had to go home and get ready with Paloma, because I guess that's what every girl did. I knew my sisters historically did the same—get ready with their friends for hours.

In her defense, Clara walked into that club looking goddamn divine in an orange floral maxi dress that swayed with her every movement. Two slits at each of her legs teased my eyes every second. So, I wasn't going to look away even if it was obvious to my brother.

Plus, Noah was glued to her side. Loud, over the top, and too happy and charming to be in our vicinity. I hated that fuckboy with a passion. Was he good to her? Sure. Was he still a fuckboy whose eyes roved over every good-looking woman in the club? Absolutely.

She deserved the best and it wasn't him. Not that they were dating. But they had a romantic-type relationship in some sense of the word, and I was starting to think Clara didn't hold herself in a high regard if she'd been linked to him for this long.

When he dipped her low and she hooked her arm around his neck, his eyes were only on her. On her mouth. On her body. On her flawless face.

"He's being respectful. That guy hasn't even grabbed her ass once."

"What the fuck?" I shoved my brother. "If he fucking grabs her ass, I'm killing him."

"Jesus, our brothers-in-law rubbing off on you?"

"I'm starting to understand it." When my little brother chuckled darkly, I knew we were all going down the wrong-ass path. At least we accepted it. My sisters had married men who'd allegedly been in the mafia. I said it that way to anyone I was doing business with. At home, we fucking knew they killed people. The sad thing was I understood why now.

Someone had hurt my sisters, and for that they deserved to die. My brothers-in-law loved them so they'd reacted, swiftly and without mercy. I wondered if they also reacted when they were jealous too. I was verging on exactly that watching Noah with Clara now.

I didn't give a shit what Dex said, I saw how Noah's eyes lit up. He had some sort of feelings for her. It's why he was here even if he blamed that shit on wanting to hook up with another woman. He'd blabbered on about some woman that was giving him the cold shoulder, how he'd fly around the country after her if he had to and how she was supposedly at a casino on the Vegas Strip.

Given his proximity to my girl, I didn't care about what he said about another. He leaned in to whisper something in her ear as he pulled her close, and that's when I'd had enough of them both tonight. Leaving my brother behind, I stormed over without a word, and clapped Noah on the shoulder. "Time for the boyfriend to cut in."

Before Noah stepped away, he groaned, and Clara looked torn before she said, "Dominic, you get me all the time." It was a great excuse, but one she was using to avoid the inevitable.

"And still, I want more of you, Clara." The words that left my lips weren't a lie. I wanted her close, wanted to smell her, wanted to learn about where she was taught to dance like that. I held out my hand. "Dance with me."

Noah stepped back, probably because he knew he wasn't going to break the connection I had with her now. No one was. Something about Clara and her light and her damn colorful dresses had infected me, and I was hooked on making sure everyone knew it.

It was for the good of the company, right? I could indulge for the time being too.

She stepped up to me, taking my hand with a small smile playing on her lips. "You think you can keep up? Noah's been dancing since he was a child."

"I see." I stepped with her, immediately taking the lead, and turned her to the music. I could waltz, salsa, and foxtrot.

Her eyes widened as I led her around the floor. "You dance?"

"I keep up," I murmured in her ear.

She chuckled and then she let me spin her out. We moved to the music. Song after song.

Her lines were much cleaner than mine, her body much more trained in controlling movement. She was practically a professional. She'd probably done ballet or dance most of her life, and I loved watching her do it. Whatever sadness I'd seen in her eyes earlier that day was gone. She was alive with the music, with the laughter around her, with Noah cheering her name. When I pulled her close after a slower song came on, I whispered against her hair, "You're divine when you dance. But let's give them the show they want."

Her emerald eyes glanced at me. "Dominic," she warned.

I wasn't thinking about a warning. I was thinking about her lips, her body up against mine, how she felt like a bright light to my soul when I'd been happy with the mediocre flickering of it for a while. The tabloids thought the news was fake, that we might be joking. I didn't want even a sliver of a question. It wasn't about Natya anymore. It was something else.

I kissed Clara Milton for everyone to see that night, and we made a statement that wouldn't be forgotten. Even with our eyes closed, flashes went off. It meant the paparazzi caught it. It meant our coworkers, my brother, *everyone* caught it. Natya would too. I didn't give a damn about any of them.

I let her go mingle again when she pulled away from me, flustered and saying she should hang out with Noah a bit more. Appeasing her friend was what she wanted, what I was finding Clara needed to do to feel comfortable. I let her go to talk more business with my brother.

It wasn't much later that Noah proved to be the true idiot I'd always thought him to be. He lifted my girl up and set her on the bar and then put Paloma right up there with her.

"What the fuck?" I swore again and stood up.

"Calm the hell down. They're just having fun. Plus, you can't be the big brother to everyone," Dex grumbled and pulled me back into my seat.

"Fuck you. I'm not her big brother. I'm her goddamn boyfriend."

"So you're really into her then? It's real?"

"As real as it gets with me," I said, and I don't know if it was to my brother or myself.

Dex had all the same features as me, but his hair was longer, his eyes more mysterious. My brother kept to himself most of the time. So, when he whispered, "How did you know?" I immediately studied him harder.

"Bro, I know because if I didn't, it wouldn't be real." I leaned to knock my shoulder into his. "You got something real over there?"

He sighed. "I think I might."

We all knew about Dex and Keelani, his long-lost love. Him thinking he might meant it wasn't real, meant he was still pining over her, trying to fill the gap with someone new. I should have let it be but, chalk it up to my being the eldest ... "Don't make a dumb mistake and give up on her for someone that's less than her. I don't have dumbasses for brothers."

He narrowed his eyes. "I should fuck this casino deal up just because you said that."

I wasn't listening to him though. I was staring at Clara, staring at how more and more men walked up to that damn bar. When a guy hollered at them, I felt my muscles tense. But her muscles were all loose, languid, full of sway and movement. Her eyes met mine over the crowd, and her smile was slow.

I shook my head at her and mouthed, "Get down."

She pouted and before I knew it, she was doing exactly what I didn't want her to. Her hip rolls got more animated, her stare sultrier, her eyes on fire with a damn challenge.

"Goddamn it," I growled as I stood up again.

My brother didn't even attempt to stop me. He knew it was getting out of control, guys were swarming the bar as she dipped low, her maxi dress to her ankles but still showing every curve she had. Paloma wasn't helping with her hooting and hollering for Clara to continue, but Paloma's yelling died when she saw my face.

She hopped down immediately, but Clara kept on. That mesmerizing red transfixed every man there, and she even waved a guy up and glanced back at the bartender. "Give him a shot."

Everyone listened to her. The whole damn place was hyped up on my little fighter's energy.

I yanked the guy back as he tried to grab her ankle and flirt with her. "Mind if I cut in?" I growled before jerking him away from her. It was loud enough that she whipped her head toward me, and Noah was right at the bar immediately.

"She's having a good time," he declared, but there was a knowing smirk on his fucking face.

We both looked up at her lifting her hair off her shoulders, and her cheeks were rosy and alive with excitement, her mouth in a full-on smile that dropped just a centimeter when she met my gaze. It dropped all the way off as the guy I'd moved just a second before tried to lunge for her leg. I had him by the throat and pinned on the bar in seconds while the bouncer was a moment too late.

Noah told me to let go and Clara instantly gasped, stopping her dancing to crouch down. "Dominic, let go of the man's throat."

"You think you can touch my girl after I removed you once? Twice and I'll kill you."

"Fuck you, man," the guy spit at me.

"Dominic, let go," Clara repeated, her hand now on my shoulder, eyes suddenly sobered.

The problem with me that people didn't seem to get was that I was the ruthless one in my family. Maybe I'd hardened over the years after what Natya had done, maybe I'd always been this way. I locked my emotion down because I knew what happened when I let it out. I felt the rage deep in me. I felt it more maybe than my other brothers. Declan smiled, Dex handled our tech, Dimitri was quiet until he wasn't. I protected them, protected what was mine. Clara was now that.

I squeezed the man's neck harder as I held her gaze. "Clara, he was about to assault you. Had that been my sister up there—"

"I'm not your sister," she countered, "I'm just me, Dominic."

"Yeah, she's just a fucking slut," the guy wheezed. "Let me go."

Clara was pleading now. "I'm not worth this. Think about your name on your resort. It's not worth it."

Her words rattled me. Like she didn't know her worth. Did she expect me to not know it either? "You're always worth it, cupcake," I whispered before I lifted the man up by his neck and pounded his head down into the bar.

It took not one but two bouncers and Dex to get me off the man, and when the manager of the bar hurried out from the back to see what the commotion was, he pointed to the man immediately for the bouncers to remove him. "So sorry, Mr. Hardy. Please, I don't want problems."

No one wanted a problem with the Hardy empire. We owned most of these clubs in some way anyway. He and I both knew it. "Make sure he's never allowed back in here," I ground out.

Dex had turned to the people with phones and muttered "shit" before he quickly got on his.

The lights flickered, and I knew exactly what was

happening. My brother was working on clearing the footage. "Leave it," I commanded. "I don't give a fuck."

Dex mumbled to himself before he glared at me. "My deal goes through, I won't care either. Till then, I'm keeping your dumb ass in line."

Someone had to, I guess, because as I looked up at Clara still kneeling on the bar, I knew my mind wasn't operating right with her. She was the sweet to my sour and the calm to my storm. I couldn't have her balancing me out when I had to be more on top of my game now than ever before. "Come on, Clara. No more bar dancing."

Squinting at me, she put her hands on my shoulders so I could grab her hips and swing her off. "You're not going to reprimand me?"

"For what?" My hands were at her waist as I set her down and didn't let go right away. I pulled her close and whispered, "My girl wants to have every guy's eyes on her. I told you, they just have to be ready to fight."

She scoffed. "I was only dancing, but maybe—"

"Go, keep dancing." I smacked her ass and smiled when she gasped. "Paloma looks about ready to combust. So go have fun with her."

Smiling, she rose up on her tiptoes and kissed my cheek before whispering, "I think I might combust, too, if I don't get away from you."

Watching her make her way over to her friends had my neck on a damn swivel now. I didn't want any guy near her, not after that.

"Okay, so, no bars in the future when we go out. She can go on stage, but not—" Noah started, suddenly back by my side like he was going to mend a fence that he broke the second he put her up there.

"Fuck off, Noah," I said, my voice low and quiet, but I knew he heard it even with the music loud. "I'm not here to play with you. I don't even like you. So, don't play with me. You'll lose."

"I'm aware. I already lost her to you, not that I really had her anyway." He frowned. "I never wanted her that way. Even so, I don't really think there's more to lose here tonight."

"How about your damn ego? I'm happy to bring you to the ground after the shit you just pulled." I cracked my knuckles, still ready for a fight. My body itched for it at this point.

He sighed and pinched the bridge of his nose. He knew he was in the wrong. The man could have assaulted Clara, and he'd instigated it. "You know what? I like you, Dom. I really do. But you just started seeing her, right?"

Clara and I hadn't gotten through the details of what we'd been doing. I wasn't going to elaborate with him now. "Not your business, Noah."

"Fine." His shoulders sagged a little as we both stared at Clara animatedly describing something to Paloma over the table. "But I'm going to tell you something in case you don't know. Clara doesn't get up on the bar. She doesn't have the fun she's having here. Ever. She doesn't do anything for herself. You know that, right? She's quiet and sweet and does everything for her mom and her sister. She gives them the limelight when she should be in it."

"What's your point?"

"Let her shine here, man. She fucking deserves it."

So, he cared about her more than just wanting to sleep with her. I filed that thought away for later. I still wanted to punch his dumb ass, but not as much. "I know how to take care of my girlfriend."

"We'll see." He shrugged and we both watched as she laughed at something Dex was saying to her and then turned to Paloma. "Honestly, if you don't know how to take care of her, Dom, I'm coming for you." Before I could reply, he cut me off. "Not because I want her. I don't. I actually came to tell her that specifically. I got a girl I'm going to wife up if it's the last thing I do."

"You ..." I stopped. "What the fuck, man?" He chuckled as he backed away from me. He'd been irritating the hell out of me for no reason. "If you intend to wife up some girl, better make sure she doesn't know that you came to visit your friend with benefits, dumbass."

His face fell momentarily, then he murmured, "Fuck." He glanced up at me. "You got Clara tonight?"

I rolled my eyes. "Yeah, man. Go do damage control."

He went and hugged her, then was gone. Dex chuckled next to me, "She's going to give you hell man."

"I'm more than aware." I shook my head as we both stared at her coming over to our cocktail table. Clara sauntered up, her laugh light and airy as she looked at my scowl. "Relax, Mr. Hardy."

I hummed when she dropped low in front of me, that dress of hers was long but had slits going up to the thighs allowed me a direct line of sight to her soft supple skin. Then she brought her ass right up against my cock. Fuck, my body instantly reacted as I pulled her against me and then caged her back to my front against the cocktail table. I felt how she rolled her ass right against my length. "Jesus, cupcake, we need to leave." My patience had frayed at every edge.

"We?" She looked at me, confused, and then her small mouth formed a little O. "That's okay. I'll just, um ... get an

Uber?" She glanced around like she needed help getting out of the situation.

I leaned close. "My girlfriend would never take an Uber home, cupcake. Tell your friends bye."

Instead, she peered over at my brother. "Dex, tell your brother that of course I would go home in a cab. I could potentially be so very angry at you for making such a scene in a club with all our colleagues and friends."

"And I could be so over your shit that I'll throw you over my shoulder and carry you out of here if you don't listen."

"Yeah, I'm avoiding this one." Dex shook his head and took two steps back. "But give him hell, Clara." He winked at her and walked away.

"We go home or I'm taking you to a bathroom to bend you over a sink to teach you what happens when you don't listen."

She bit her bottom lip slow, her eyes dipping to my pants. "What happens?"

I leaned in as I wrapped my arm around her stomach to pull her close and whispered against her ear, "I fuck you so good, the only way you get home is with me carrying you out of here. That what you want?"

Her green eyes had misted over as her ass rubbed back and forth on my cock and we swayed to the music. I was right on the edge now, ready to drag her to a dark corner.

"You came!" Paloma yelled loudly from two tables down and both Clara and I snapped our attention that way. Then she smiled at us and waved us over. "Clara, didn't I tell you he would come if I said you were here?"

At this point, we were well into the night and Clara was stifling a yawn as she rubbed at a spot on her shoulder I knew must cause her pain. She massaged it a lot. Even so, she smiled brightly and pulled me over to her friends, saying, "Valentino, I'm so happy you came."

Valentino combed a hand through his hair and smiled softly at her. "Didn't want to miss a moment with the delightful woman who makes delightful desserts."

Goddamn, when she blushed at his compliment, I knew right then. I'd be damned if I let Valentino or anyone else have her attention for a second longer. "We're headed out actually."

He had the audacity to look hurt, like Clara meant anything to him at all. "Well, the market is tomorrow, Clara. We could meet? How about I give you the address?"

Before I could tell her no, she handed over her phone as she vibrated with joy while he added details.

I wasn't going to deny her the perfect ingredients at whatever this so-called market was tomorrow, but she damn sure wasn't going to be going without me. As he handed her phone back, I leaned close to her, "We going to your house or mine?"

She frowned and pouted out her bottom lip, like she was so sad about leaving all her friends. "It's rude that we're leaving when more people just showed up," she grumbled as we exited through the back doors into an alley.

"I'm not staying just to appease people, Clara." The woman would have stayed all night and well into the next morning to make everyone happy.

"Well, maybe you should try every now and then." She folded her arms over her chest, and as I saw the goose bumps rise on her skin, I sighed at her lack of foresight.

I shrugged off my suit jacket to drape over her shoulders. "And you should try not appeasing people. Your happiness shouldn't be reliant on theirs."

"It's not," she retorted much too fast and then stomped her foot, drowning in my jacket now. "I just know things go more smoothly when you try to accommodate—"

"What about yourself? You willing to sacrifice your comfort for theirs?"

"I'm not uncomfortable."

"You've been kneading at your neck and shoulders for the past ten minutes," I pointed out and massaged her shoulders for a second. She gave in enough that she closed those emerald eyes and sighed. "You were yawning too, cupcake."

"Whatever," she grumbled because she knew it was true.

I pointed over to the corner of the street and said, "Callihan will pick us up over there. Don't want to block this alley."

I steered her that way as she went on and on about how I of course didn't care about other people's feelings. "And if you'd just let me take a cab home—"

"Not happening."

"Fine." She threw her hands up. "We have to go to my place though because my cats need to be fed, but I don't want you staying over."

I never stayed over at a woman's house. It was a damn rule. Yet, I was immediately pissed she didn't want me to. "You can't have your boyfriend stay at your place now?"

"My *fake* boyfriend is rude."

"Because I left a few people at the club early?" I scoffed.

"No. You're rude all the time. You're rude about my bakery too. You have Rita just run over all my ideas." She waved wildly around, getting animated now. "And I'm so sick of it. And I'm sick of her emails signed as the 'head interior designer' and her—"

"Are we listing off everything you're angry about right

now?" I lifted a brow as I tried to hold back a laugh.

Under the streetlights, away from the crowds, and with the cool ocean air whipping through her hair, Clara tipsy and crabby was extremely flawed. She wobbled in those heels, one tendril of her dark-red hair was low on her forehead, and her green eyes sparkled with a little extra fire. Flawed so perfectly for me that she was flawless.

If I could have built a building of her curves, drawn her into a blueprint, designed her into some structure, I would have. "What's wrong with the designer, little fighter?"

"She just changes everything last minute."

"She has a right to do that, Clara. She's invested in the opening of this bakery."

Damn, I nearly felt the blood rise to her cheeks, I felt the wave of fury flow through her to me. She wasn't just Clara anymore, she was Clara with fire, with a vengeance.

"I really hate that you're standing here on these cobbled stone streets that are supposed to be beautiful, shrouded in late-night fog. I read this romance novel once and they had such an epic kissing moment in just the same place. Instead, I'm with you, telling me your designer needs to be listened to even though she has no actual stake in the business but her paycheck."

Her eyes widened, blazing green in fury and, fuck, I loved to see it.

I'd make this woman hate me over and over just to see her unleash that beautiful fire on me any day.

I didn't indulge much, but I was starting to find I was going to indulge with her over and over.

CHAPTER 19: CLARA

Yup, I'd just said that and then slapped my hand over my mouth.

"She gets paid very well, Clara. For a job that she takes pride in." I swear he was egging me on in his stupid perfect suit saying all the logical things that weren't supposed to be logical at all. Didn't he know that I took pride in my freaking bakery too?

I looked down and stepped up on the curb so I could face him head-on.

No one deserved to stand over me now, not when it came to my business, and I was going to meet him at his level, his height, and tell him so. Even if I was still inches shorter than him, I felt more powerful up there as I poked him in his shoulder. "No one is as invested as I am, and how dare you give anyone the authority to override my decision after how hard you know I've worked on it. Have you completely lost your mind?"

"No. I've navigated this whole negotiation with a completely rational and sound mind, although I would have liked to have tantrums like you numerous times," he said matter-of-factly.

"Of course. Because you're a big baby when it comes to your resort. Wa-wa. Someone else has plans as good as yours and wants to implement them into a tiny bakery. You still get the massive resort exactly how you want it all around that bakery. Plus, this bakery is a damn good addition. I've agonized over every detail probably more than anyone else. You haven't combed through Valentino's restaurant like this. Nor has Rita.

I swear she wants it to fail because I've changed her plans, and now she sees this as a way to point and say, 'See, I told you so.' Just like everyone in my life."

I wobbled on the curb. The man kept glaring at me, but his arm immediately shot out to wrap around my waist.

I frowned and looked down. "What ... what are you doing?"

"Making sure you don't fall, cupcake. The ground could be slippery."

I bit my lip because immediately I wanted to thank him and kiss him for protecting me even while I bit his head off. I didn't though. Instead, I crossed my arms and huffed, "Fine." He smirked. "I still want all my changes and we're getting closer to the reopening which means flowers are next, Dominic."

"Don't I know it, babe. I'll make it happen. Now, tell me, who's saying I told you so?"

"I ... what?"

"You said everyone does that to you? Your mom?"

"And Anastasia and probably Rita and I know you will too. That's fine. I need to know I tried my best anyway. If it's a failure, I want it to be my failure and no one else's."

"Why?"

"Because at least it's my own then, right? And have you ever heard of someone successful not having any failures? If I don't make it here, I'll learn from it and make it somewhere else." I meant it too. I'd found myself wanting this bakery more and more, wanting to prove myself. "I'm going to fight for my success, Dominic, and fight to belong somewhere."

He hummed but didn't say anything. How could he? He was always needed somewhere. He was the best of the best and also had family that loved him. His staff definitely didn't, but they respected him. I didn't have any of that. It was a sad realization, but his thumb rubbed up and down on my arm like he was trying to soothe me, and I focused on that instead.

"Clara, let's go into the car, huh? You're getting cold."

"No. I'm not finished telling you everything I'm mad about." I stomped my foot. I was on a roll.

He sighed and pinched the bridge of his nose. "Right." Then he picked me up like I weighed nothing and threw me into the SUV.

I immediately started complaining, but he cut me off to ask for the address. In a fit, I blurted it out and kept going on my rant, but he stayed silent until I quieted down too.

Now, I sat there twisting my fingers, staring out the window. Why had I said my apartment again? My apartment from the outside didn't appear to be old or under construction. Inside, though, the elevator was out of order, so we had to climb a flight of stairs, and the ventilation barely worked in the hallways, so the blazing summer heat of the day got trapped between the walls. It created a weird vortex of warmth even after the night and ocean breeze cooled everywhere else off.

"The lobby door always open without a key?" he asked behind me as I pulled it and turned to him before he walked in.

"They're working on it." I blocked the path into the building. "Thanks for dropping me off."

He smiled down at me like I was truly ridiculous. "I'm coming up to your apartment, Clara. So get your ass moving."

I groaned. "What for? I'm not sleeping with you!"

"Such different words from the last time you were drunk." He chuckled.

"Shut up, Dominic. That was a colossal mistake." I wrinkled my nose and then sighed when he wasn't deterred at all.

"How's it going to look if a pap trailed us home and you left me at the door? We should be making out right now, little fighter." Was he serious? I looked over his shoulder and didn't see anyone, but then again, I'd never been good at spotting cameramen the way my mother and sister had been.

"Fine. Come up for a minute until we think they've left."

He hummed a *sure*, and I let him trail me to the stairs before he asked, "No elevator?"

"The landlord said they're working on it." I shrugged.

We didn't say much of anything as he followed me. Stair after stair. He was most likely wondering what the hell I was doing climbing up and down them in heels daily. It was only one flight though. Not too bad for most people. For me, my joints ached every single day. That served as a reminder to call a doctor here ... when I had time after the bakery opened.

We passed my neighbor, Martin, on the way in. He licked his lips as he mumbled a hello, but Dominic grabbed my waist and pulled me close, causing Martin's hungry eyes to turn cowardly. He grumbled "Excuse me" right away and hurried down the steps.

"He live in the building?" Dominic asked as he watched him leave.

"Next door to me. Harmless, but a little slimy." I shrugged and went to unlock my door. He leaned against the frame, eyeing me curiously. "A lot of the buildings are older around here, and I didn't plan well for moving so—"

"You're not telling me something." He stated it casually, but I felt his scrutiny.

What could I say? I had no money and even this place wasn't really affordable. Nothing in LA was. I swung open the door after fumbling way too much with it. "Do you think the paparazzi are gone?"

"No chance," he said and walked right in without waiting for me.

Sugar and Spice ran toward us, and I bent down to greet them and give them all the love they usually gave me. They both defied me. Pure betrayal as they rubbed on Dominic's legs instead of mine, meowing like he was the love of their lives. "Sugar and Spice!" I reprimanded them. "Your mother is home."

They didn't even look over at me. I frowned. Those kittens loved me more than anyone. Well, more than the outside, I guess, considering I never really had anyone over. And they'd hissed at Martin and the landlord when those men came to the door. Dominic knelt down to pet them both as I took off my shoes. Then, I watched them for much too long as his large hands glided over their fur.

"You like cats?"

"I don't particularly like animals at all." Still, he continued to pet them, rubbing their necks at the exact part I knew they loved.

"They like you."

He let out that low sound before he stood, and then put his hands in his pockets as he glanced around. Magnified under his scrutiny now, I saw the scuffs on the floor, the worn furniture, the lightened wood of the table and chairs where people had gathered one too many times before me. Most of the living room was doused in deep colorful tones. The pillows were red and purple and blue, patches sewn together from a small art fair I'd been to weeks ago. Paloma had helped me find a rug that spanned most of the living room, woven color, too, used but still bright with life.

Dominic eyed the pictures I'd put on the counter and the

tables. "Declan and Evie look happy with my nephew here, huh?"

"They're so happy. Who wouldn't be with a baby like that?"

Nodding, he set the picture back down and grabbed another. It was of Carl, my mom, and Anastasia, all of them smiling with hats on. "You like the Kentucky Derby?"

"Not so much." I shrugged. "But they looked like they had so much fun, right?"

"You're not in the picture. You're not in any of your pictures."

"I ..." I looked around. "I guess I hadn't noticed." It wasn't really something I was particularly concerned about. While he eyed a few other ones, I walked around as fast as I could, fluffing a few of the soft pillows and picking up some of my dirty laundry that was in the hall. When I caught him glancing at it, I blurted out, "Sorry, didn't expect—"

One side of his mouth lifted. "Don't apologize. I love seeing your lingerie whether it's dirty or clean."

I glanced down. "You're ridiculous," I snapped before storming down the hall to my bedroom as I yelled behind me, "You can leave now. I don't think the paparazzi are still outside."

Instead, he stomped after me. "I'm not leaving. We have things to discuss."

"Like what?" I started to unbutton the back of my dress once in my bedroom, knowing I needed to shower and prepare for the early morning at the market with Valentino.

"We're going to start getting questions. Dex asked me about you tonight, and Paloma seems to want every damn detail." He leaned on the doorframe and watched me fiddle with the buttons before he stepped close to brush my hands away. Down the dress were about fifty small buttons, but I only need about ten of them undone. "Like what's your favorite color and why you wear dresses that are so damn hard to get off when your boss and boyfriend likes easy access."

His voice was low when he said the last part, and I shivered while I held my dress up as it loosened with each button. "I don't care about how you want to answer questions. Just tell me what to say and I'll say it," I said over my shoulder and frowned at his eyes trailing down my body, my insides immediately heating at his perusal. "Turn around, Dominic."

"What for?"

"I'm dropping my dress."

"I've undressed you, Clara. And I told you in that fitting room, I won't miss an opportunity ever again."

"That's not ..." God, I wanted him, and that was bad. This was bad. Bad. Bad. Bad. "We need to stop what we're doing."

"Do we?"

"Yes. Lines are getting blurred. You're supposed to hate me being in your resort, remember?"

"I don't hate making you scream my name though. And a fake relationship can have benefits." He smirked and his eyes scanned my body. "We can have a lot of fake benefits."

"Get real." I rolled my eyes and let go of my dress. I didn't care if he saw me in my lingerie or naked for that matter. I wasn't very modest when it came to my body as long as I wasn't having a flare-up, which might be the case tomorrow. Tonight, well, there was something about knowing his eyes were on me that made me feel powerful.

And hungry.

And hot.

I dragged my teeth over my bottom lip as I watched him watch me. Then, I turned to slide the doors of my closet open to grab some pajamas. He continued his reasoning. "You know, if we're not comfortable physically, we'll never sell that this is real. People already will think it's for publicity with the resort reopening."

He was probably right. And as I heard his feet pad across the floor, I tensed up when his chest met my back.

"This." He put his hands on my shoulders and massaged them, pushing his thumbs right into the pressure points. "The tension in your body when I'm against you, can't be a thing."

Resisting how his hand kneaded the muscles in my back with precision and strength would have been impossible. I normally didn't even do it. Yet, here and now, with the emotions flooding every part of my mind, I froze. My heart wasn't supposed to want love.

I moaned as I slumped against him, letting his large fingers spread over my shoulders to my collarbone, and then one of his hands drifted to the strap of my bra, sliding under it before nudging it off my shoulder.

I gasped when his calloused hand cupped my breast as he lowered his head to suck on my neck. He stepped us both back and turned us toward the door he'd closed behind him. The long narrow mirror on it showed how his body almost enveloped me. His eyes looked up, catching my gaze in the mirror as he bit into my sensitive skin. He penetrated my soul, held me captive, and snuffed out the embarrassment I would have normally felt from standing there with barely any clothes on next to a fully clothed man.

Still, I tried my best to hold out even though I'd thought about him all night, witnessed him lay a guy out for coming near me, and felt his green eyes follow me around that club like I belonged to him. Feeling wanted, feeling desired, and feeling like I could hold his attention was addicting, hypnotizing, and dangerous.

The hand that massaged my shoulder slid to my waist and then to my panty line. "We need you relaxed and ready to fuck me always, Clara. Is that how you've been all night?"

I wouldn't admit that even if it was true. "Maybe it wasn't you I was ready to fuck."

His eyes darkened, and he swore before his hand dipped under the lace and slid over my pussy. "Right. So wet for a woman who barely glances at her boyfriend through the night. Was your pussy dripping like this at the club? Was it really for someone else?" When I didn't answer him immediately, he growled. "Should I fuck you so good, you'll never think of anyone else?"

I whimpered but didn't answer him and bit my lip to keep the confession from bursting out of me.

He chuckled darkly as he watched me, pinching my nipple and my clit at the same time. "Clara, I want an answer."

Giving him an answer would only serve to feed his ego, give him the upper hand, give him the edge he had on me already. How could I tell my fake boyfriend I'd wanted him to fuck me all night? That's all I'd thought about when his cock was grinding against me as we danced for just a little while, I'd thought about his eyes latched onto me as I dragged my hands across my dress on the bar, I'd thought about his mouth on mine for much too long.

When I shook my head no and whimpered, he must have realized the challenge. Dominic Hardy was ruthless always. He strived for perfection, wanted everything of his to be desired, and needed to be the best even if this was a fake relationship. He'd make me feel wanted, he'd make me feel desired, he'd make me feel like I was his and he was mine. He'd make a relationship of perfection.

Even if it was fake. Even if I'd start to believe it was real.

Yet, my attempt to stop the train wreck I knew would occur after this was feeble at best. I moaned out, "I don't think this is a good idea." But my hips rolled back as I pressed my back further into him, his length so big against it that my pussy clenched at the thought of having him try to fit within me. Yep, my body screamed that it was a fantastic idea, but I ignored it. "Do you want a drink or something to eat?"

"I intend to eat, cupcake." His hand massaged my breast, and I knew that look, knew as he leaned his head down that he would go right to my neck. When he did and sucked hard again, I moaned. "But I only want dessert, Clara. And all you have to do is sit on my face to serve it to me."

"Things will get too complicated, Dominic," I reminded him. "This is only for a few months and not at all real."

He thrust against my back. "That feel real to you, baby?"

God, I wanted him. Wanted this. And why couldn't I? What would it really hurt? The words left my mouth softly, "Only this once."

"Once won't be enough." He stepped back to unbutton his shirt, then discarded it before he was back against me. "You need to look in love with me anyway. I need to look ravenous for you. It's the only way people will believe it."

"I don't know what ..." He slid one finger in me and watched me with those piercing green eyes as I whimpered out, "Oh, God."

"That's right. You only want one time? My pussy seems to be begging me for more than that, baby. My pussy loves when I take care of it," he whispered against my ear as he curled his finger into me. Gasping, I bucked against his hand. “Tell me how you don’t want the orgasm I’m about to give you.” No words left my mouth as I stared at him while he rolled my nipple between two fingers. “That’s right,” he whispered darkly and then chuckled, “You can’t, can you? So say what you really want, cupcake. Say you want me to lick your pussy nice and slow, baby. Say you thought about it all fucking night.”

I shouldn’t have given in. I should have walked away before the destruction barreled through our lives and ruined us both. But I said, “I thought about your cock sliding into me all night.”

CHAPTER 20: DOMINIC

Clara had unhinged something in me.

Unhinged and unleashed something too possessive and hungry to cage. And it was a deadly combination.

I'd felt it in the club, but here, in her little apartment she had no damn business living in, something in me snapped.

She didn't take care of herself the way she should. She took care of everyone else, took in goddamn stray cats, said hi to creeps in the hallway, and didn't complain about the fact that her apartment was barely habitable. The way her ceiling bowed wasn't right and neither were the leaks in the corner. It didn't take an engineer to see that.

I was going to rectify some things the next morning, that was fucking for sure. She wouldn't be living here for another week, even if I had to drag her out. She was too selfless, but I was unbelievably selfish.

Fucking her tonight wouldn't be good for either of us even though it's all I wanted. I reminded myself of that over and over again as my hand worked her pussy. "You wanted my cock all night and yet you danced with and for other men for half of it."

She smirked before she threw out, "Well, Noah is a good dancer."

Goddamn. I loved to see the challenge in her eyes when she teased me, made me jealous, made me irrationally unstable for no other reason than to irritate me. Somehow, the woman I'd despised just a few weeks prior was the only one I wanted to be around now, the only one I wanted to stare at, listen to, fight with, and fuck.

"Is he good at eating your pussy, too, Clara?"

She frowned as I stopped for a second to see how far she wanted to push this game. "I ..." She bit her lip. "He's good, Dominic. Maybe the best I've had."

So she wanted to fight and to infuriate me. "Careful, little fighter," I said slowly and then stepped back, breaking off my touch with her. She gasped and then frowned as she tried to hide her rapid breathing. I stared at her. "You don't want to regret how far you push me tonight."

She narrowed her eyes and put her hands on the curve of her hips, standing there in lace lingerie, hot as hell. "I think if I'm going to go that far, I might as well go all the way." Her breath was shaky as she breathed in and out, but still she said the next words slow and clear, so I heard every single one. "He's given me some of the best orgasms of my life. And I'm not sure anyone will live up to the way he licked me here." She pointed to her sex.

My whole body shook with her statement, vibrating with a jealousy I wasn't at all used to. I growled at her boldness, whipped the tie from my neck, and took one step toward her.

"Dominic, okay, actually I was just—"

"You were just what?" I grabbed both of her wrists, and she didn't fight me at all. I didn't want her tied up but I did want her blindfolded and at my mercy. I wrapped the fabric around her eyes.

"What are you doing?" she whispered.

"You think a guy gave you what you wanted, but I bet you've never listened to your body properly. I bet you never asked for what you needed." Clara's body was already reacting to not seeing and just feeling my touch, my breath on her lips, my body close to hers. Her skin had goose bumps, she was biting her bottom lip, and her sex was dripping through her lingerie.

I walked in front of her, grabbed her thong, and ripped it off fast. She gasped but I wasn't saying sorry. "Your pussy bare in front of me looks good, Clara."

I dragged the piece of fabric up her stomach and then roughly over her cleavage before it got to her face. "You smell yourself, baby? How aroused you are?"

She whimpered and said, "please" before I threw the fabric onto the ground and grabbed her thighs to yank her up. Wrapping them both around my head, she scrambled to catch herself. Her fingers threaded through my hair as I licked at her clit fast, wanting to bombard her with the right sensations, wanting her to scream for me and for only me. I turned and walked us over to the bed where I lowered us down, the iron of her headboard clattering against the wall.

"Oh my God. Dominic, hold on. That's going to be too loud for the—"

I sucked her clit hard and saw her immediately reach above her to grab hold of the bars. I chuckled as I squeezed her ass and then murmured, "Oh you're going to be loud. Hold that headboard and ride my face, little fighter. I want that iron banging into the wall. Your neighbors are going to know this is the only boyfriend that makes you come like this."

"I don't think—"

I smacked the side of her ass. "Don't think."

Then, I licked her pussy slow, tasting everything I wanted. She moaned loud and arched off the bed.

"Say what you want, Clara."

She shook her head and so I licked her even slower, softer

this time and only rolled my thumb over her clit once.

"Dominic, please."

"Please what?" I murmured, "Tell me exactly what you want."

When she didn't, I licked and then blew on her clit instead of pinching it and she gasped, wanting to give her the sensation of going from hot to cold instantly.

"I need you, Dominic. Please."

"Need me to what?"

"Give me an orgasm, asshole. And lick me the right way. Now."

"That's it. That's a good girl, finally telling me what she needs." I descended on her pussy, sucking on her clit first and then sliding my tongue between her lips to taste her. I took my time, savored her flavor.

When her body started to tremble as she whimpered, I grabbed her ass and flipped her over so that she was straddling me. Then, I said, "You feel how your thighs are shaking for me, baby, how your pussy is dripping down your leg?"

She bit her lip and nodded.

"Focus on what your body wants, on your own pleasure." I slid a finger in as I looked up at her and watched her arch as her pussy clenched around me. "What do you want, baby? You want to ride?"

She nodded again, her hips rolling over my hand before I slid my finger out. "Then, ride, baby. Hold the headboard tight and ride my face like you want to."

She ground her hips down and moaned my name over and over, letting me taste how sweet she was as she started to buck over my tongue. Clara needed me to eat her out as much as I wanted to. But I felt how her thighs clenched and knew she was holding back just a bit probably to try and keep her vulnerability or her heart.

I was taking it all from her.

I smacked her ass hard and then gripped her waist. "If you don't sit all the way down on my face, I'm going to bring you to the brink all night without making you come. Let go, and fuck my mouth like a good girl, baby. Don't make me tell you twice."

"Please, just shut up, Dominic." Her hands were white-knuckling the iron headboard this time when she dropped onto my face, her arousal ran down the side of my jaw as I worked my tongue around her clit and then into her sex, thrusting it in and out, in and out, as she gyrated harder and harder.

The headboard knocked into the wall louder and louder as she screamed my name. Her tits bounced in that lace bra, and her nipples puckered as her whole body tightened on the edge of orgasm. This is how I wanted Clara. I ripped the blindfold from her so I could see her eyes. They burned bright as she watched me sucking on the most sensitive part of her, her skin glistening from the electricity that vibrated between us, and her lips swollen from biting them to keep from screaming. When I curled my tongue in her, that raspy voice of hers belted out my name again, and it was music to my ears, better than winning a fucking award, better than getting a damn resort built, better than most everything I'd done.

Watching Clara unravel on top of me as her pussy clenched hard around my tongue shifted my world. Fake boyfriend or not, I'd make sure she'd forget every man she ever had before me.

CHAPTER 21: CLARA

"I want to take care of you now, Dominic," I whispered as I slid off his face and released my grip from the headboard. I moved across his chest, then his hard abs, and onto the bulge in his trousers.

He was still wearing pants after giving me the best orgasm of my life, and I wanted to return the favor. He'd given me orgasm after orgasm and then denied himself pleasure I was more than willing to give.

The fitting room had been the only time he'd allowed it. And I didn't even get him the way I wanted to there. We'd had another woman's eyes on him and not enough time to really enjoy it, for me to learn how to really take him all.

My hands were at his belt buckle when he stopped them. "You need to shower and get some sleep before the market with Valentino, remember?" He sneered Valentino's name like he suddenly hated the man.

"You eat me out and then deny yourself of getting any." I rolled away from him. "Why? I want to have your—"

"You drank tonight, little fighter. Tomorrow, if you want, I'll bury my cock so far in your mouth, I'll touch the back of your throat."

Normally, I would have rolled my eyes at such a statement, but I'd felt how big Dominic was in my mouth already and knew he'd actually be able to do that, no problem. My mouth watered at the thought, and I tried to breathe in deep as I turned to him and propped myself up on an elbow. "I'm not drunk."

"Not sober either," he retorted and lifted a brow.

"So what? You'll only fuck me when I'm sober?" My voice was high-pitched in surprise.

"Don't drink when you want cock, baby. Not that hard."

I glanced at the bulge in his pants and my hand shot out on its own accord to touch the length of him. I wrapped my fingers around it over the fabric and squeezed. "Very hard, Dominic."

"Careful, Clara."

"Or what?" Every time I fought him, his eyes darkened, his muscles bunched, and his voice deepened. I was becoming obsessed with every single one of those changes I saw when I pushed him.

"Or I'll remind you who's the boss here."

I stroked him as best I could and the tendons in his neck tightened. "Are you sure you are?"

He sat up fast and grabbed my hips before throwing me over his shoulder and stomping his way to the bathroom.

"Dominic, seriously," I laughed and smacked his back, "I don't want to shower!"

He didn't care, just turned on the shower in my bathroom and tested the temperature before he set me under the water's spray. He dragged a hand over my bare stomach and then up my breast and around my back to undo the hooks of my bra, the fabric's color deepening as water hit it. When the bra gave way, he slid it from my arms and then stepped back. I didn't close the curtain when he started to undress.

His abs were defined, the V toward his cock pronounced and strong. "Take in your boyfriend, Clara. I'm all yours."

I watched as he unzipped his trousers, shucked them down with his boxers, and then stroked his massive cock. Once, twice. And one more time before he stepped out of the rest of his clothing and crowded me into the shower. I reached for him immediately, wanting him on me, in me, and all around. I kissed him with passion, lost in him more than I'd been lost in anyone in a long time. I gripped his cock again, hoping he'd changed his mind.

He pulled back and dragged a hand from my waist to my breast. "So pretty. So sweet. Still, you don't listen." He circled my nipple but didn't give it any attention. It tightened and I whimpered. From there, his hand went to my throat. One by one, he softly wrapped his fingers around the column of it before he pushed me back against the tile, the cold at my back and his heat and the water at my front. He hovered over me, his hand tightening.

Instinctively, my hands went to his wrist, and he smiled, his eyes filled with a new type of hunger I'd never seen there. "Want me to stop?" he whispered.

He asked me that question right as his other hand brushed over my sex again.

I couldn't tell him no, my legs were already spreading, and he was already chuckling at how soaking wet I was for him again.

"I think you're going to like your fake boyfriend showing you how comfortable we can be together."

"Comfortable or not, we need rules for this."

"Should I show you the rules, little fighter? One of them will be that you don't even think about other men."

I lifted my chin and raised an eyebrow just to piss him off.

"See, and already I think you'll like defying my rules. I can put you in your place nice and rough though."

On the last word, his fingers thrust up into me, and he cut

off my oxygen supply. He whispered in my ear to squeeze his wrist three times if it was too much. I just shook my head over and over, my eyes shutting as fireworks burst through my body, the adrenaline of not breathing but having pleasure delivered instantaneously wasn't too much like I thought it would. It was too good.

I clawed at his wrist, tears streaming down my face, and then he lowered his head and bit one of my nipples just hard enough. The pain, pleasure, and adrenaline moved through me as he let go of my neck so I could gasp and then scream in ecstasy.

I crumbled against him as he murmured, "That pretty pussy is only going to want me from now on. I'll fuck you soon, little fighter, but only if you listen."

All I could do was nod as he grabbed some soap and added it to the loofa. He rubbed it softly over my body, practically holding me up as I shivered at his touch.

Honestly, I might have blacked out or fell asleep once or twice as he washed me, his hands massaging every part of my body, getting rid of aches and pains I didn't even know I had. I coughed a little when I stirred in the shower where he'd sat me down to finish shampooing my hair. "Let's get you to bed, cupcake," he murmured.

Then, he toweled me off, mumbling something about mold in the bathroom.

"Oh, right. The landlord is—"

"Working on it?"

"Um. Yes."

"It's a health hazard. You should move. If you need a place to stay for a while, I've got room."

Did I hear him right? I chuckled and pulled the towel tight

as I stared at him drying off. "I don't really think it's that big of a health hazard. And this is LA. You can't find an apartment that fast." Well, not one within my budget. I yawned and coughed a bit again.

His jaw muscle ticked up and down, up and down. "I'm not kidding, Clara. How long have you had that cough?"

"Oh. No, not long. I think it's just allergies from—"

"You always cough like that after showering in there?"

"I ..." Now that I thought about it, probably. "No. Are you the health police?" He was worrying me with his eyes roving over my body like he was checking for ailments.

"You're a fucking terrible liar, Clara. I swear to Christ."

"I'll figure it out tomorrow, Dominic. We need to put boundaries in place. This sleeping over isn't realistic. So, just this once you can sleep in my bed." Because my heart wasn't going to survive much more of it. I grabbed a sleep shirt and didn't bother with much else as I plopped into bed.

He barked out a laugh and didn't even consider putting clothes on as he slid under the blankets. "You know I never sleep with women in their bed?"

I frowned, half asleep and half confused. "Why?"

"No reason to get close."

"So why are you now?" I asked softly.

"Well, you said just this once, cupcake."

"Right. And I'm serious. And I'll probably be up early, but feel free to sleep in. I have to make sure I'm on time when I meet Valentino at the market for produce."

I was drifting off to sleep when I heard him mumble, "When he meets *us* at the market."

CHAPTER 22: CLARA

I hadn't dreamt him saying that. I also hadn't dreamt that Dominic took me home the night before and that the cats loved him. They were purring loudly in the room with me bright and early the next day. Except I didn't feel their fur.

And I'd swear he closed the door last night to my room.

I peeked over and saw the door was now open and both cats were beside him.

Also, a large muscular arm was draped across my waist. I tried to slide away, I felt the scruff of his five-o'clock shadow as he nestled into my neck and yanked me closer. "Go to bed next to me, you wake up next to me, cupcake." I felt his cock and the length of him immediately made my body react by rolling my hips. "Don't tempt me unless you want to deliver."

I sort of did.

But I needed to remind myself that this was fake. I sighed. "Stay in bed if you want, but I have to get up and get ready for the market. Plus, Sugar and Spice are here. Did you let them in?"

"They were meowing at your door this morning." He shrugged. "I fed them, and they scarfed it down like two full-grown dogs."

"Yeah, I think they were starving outside when I picked them up," I murmured, trying to stop the pitter-patter of my heart. Did people know the Dominic Hardy I did? Or did they just know Mr. Hardy? Because Mr. Hardy was quiet and ruthless but had earned respect. Dominic Hardy on the other hand, didn't wait for respect. He'd taken it last night, swiftly and unapologetically before he came here to worship me and then took care of my freaking kittens.

He rolled over to pet both of them, whispering something only they could hear.

I evil-eyed them both. "You two slept next to him when you know your mother feeds you every single day?"

"They know when there's a good man in their bed." He claimed to hate animals, but he wasn't acting like it as he scratched Spice's neck.

"You should be ashamed, Spice." I swear she narrowed her eyes at me before I huffed and got out of bed right as my phone rang. I knew that ring tone, and I winced before I silenced it.

"Who are you avoiding?" He glared at the phone, probably hoping it would announce an answer to his question. With a stare that inquisitive, I was surprised it didn't.

"Anastasia."

The usual vibration from deep in his chest rumbled out before he said, "Not talking?"

"She doesn't approve of my being here. So, I don't really talk to them much at this point."

"But she's calling because ... ?"

"I don't really know." I shrugged. This was my new start, and I was trying my best not to taint it. Boundaries were built through blood, sweat, and tears. Mostly tears here because I wanted something with my sister that I couldn't have. "I'm avoiding it right now. I'll answer later, but I have enough going on with this bakery. I realize my boundaries are probably—"

"Just what you need. Keep establishing them, babe." He said it with conviction like he knew.

"You have boundaries over there too?"

"Well, you met my Natya," he offered, and I waited for him to continue, my whole body tensing at her name. Muscles that were conditioned in feeling heartbreak, feeling like second best. A mind can ready itself for that type of thing after enough time spent with people who tore them down.

"I met your ex," I said softly.

"Well, the woman is good at wiggling between every boundary but I made quite a few of them after I left her."

"Most women in love are good at that." I picked at the fabric of my bed. If I was being honest with both of us, he needed to consider what he might be doing, passing on Natya for a fake relationship with me. "I think she loves you and you should probably be sure—"

"Sure I want her out of my life?" He chuckled and pulled me close by the wrist of the hand I was using to fidget. "You hedging on whether or not I want to keep dating you, little fighter?"

"I'm not ... I'm trying to make sure you don't make some catastrophic mistake in your life by pushing her away if you really—"

"I'd be making a catastrophic mistake losing you. How about that?"

I sighed and tried to smile as I glanced at Dominic staring at me and shook my head before I got out of the bed. "We'll stay in bed all day if we don't move."

"I don't mind," he grumbled, but that was a lie. Dominic worked harder than anyone I'd ever seen. His eyes roved over me before they froze halfway down and widened on my body.

He was up and out of the bed so fast, I jumped. "What?! Is there a spider?"

"Not a spider." He growled, snapping his hand out fast to catch my arm. Then he said in a grave tone. "What is this on your arm?"

Looking down, I saw the culprit of his worry and immediately relaxed but slapped a hand over it to hide it away. Wrinkling my nose, I turned around and went digging through my closet to find a light long sleeve. "I get rashes sometimes."

"Sometimes?" I heard rustling but didn't turn around. "Since when?"

"Since I was a teen." I chuckled, trying to brush off his concern. It was the first concern I'd witnessed over my health in a while. I'd been the only one to go to the doctor, the only one to listen to the signs and pursue more tests, being the most concerned about the results.

"Everyone has ailments, Clara. We can't worry about them now," my mother had said over and over.

I got tired even thinking about that conversation.

"Did you ever get it checked out?"

"Dominic," I glanced over my shoulder. "You do realize people have ailments they live with, right?" It was something my mother would have said, a way to downplay the truth, but I was facing it and handling it.

His face hardened, "You do realize if something's wrong, you should be seeing a damn doctor?"

"I have and I do when necessary," I shot back fast, somewhat defensive. And when he tried to say something else, I shook my head. "Leave it, Dominic. I take care of myself just fine."

He hummed. "Maybe it's time someone else starts taking care of you too."

"I'm *fine*," I reiterated and then I turned away. Owning it. Living with a disease meant learning to not dwell on it. I'd come to terms with what was healthy for me and moved forward with capturing the beauty of life rather than dwelling in the ugliness of it. Both actions took up the same amount of time, yet one was much brighter than the other.

Dominic would have done the same, which was why there was no use burdening him with it. "If you're fine, then—"

"There's towels in the bathroom if you want to shower," I pointed at the bathroom and lifted a brow. We were changing the subject whether he liked it or not. His glare showed that he didn't and I saw his brain working as he frowned then and stomped into the bathroom.

I went to the kitchen and started cooking, trying to shake off his concern, how he wanted to be more than most were to me, how he cared. When he entered the living room and walked over to the table, I set a plate of scrambled eggs and a cappuccino I'd whipped up with a dash of cinnamon on the dining room table for him. "You can stay as long as you'd like—"

"I'm coming with."

"Um ... what?" I asked, but Dominic was already scarfing down his eggs double time, not even taking a second to enjoy the taste. "What for?"

He mumbled around another mouthful, "You ready?"

"Do you always eat like that?" I needed to stop this. He needed to understand flavor if there was at all anything I could teach him.

"When we have somewhere to be, sure." How did he still look good in yesterday's suit? He'd lost the jacket and rolled up his sleeves, leaving one button undone, and it made him look disheveled but properly so. The veins of his forearms were on display under his sun-kissed skin with his massive hands that I knew were skilled at everything they did.

I snatched the plate back fast when his fork went to his mouth again. He lifted a brow. "Problem?"

"Can you sit down and just enjoy the food?"

"Am I bothering you by not?" One of his dimples showed up when the side of his mouth curved.

"I think it might be better if you take one extra minute and tell me what you taste in those eggs, Dominic." I chewed my cheek, suddenly feeling like I shouldn't have dictated how he ate my food.

"Hm." He studied me. "You think or you *know* it would be better, little fighter?"

Combing a hand through my hair, I busied myself with wiping down the counter before turning to grab some lemons and slice them up. Squeezing a few of them in a cup, I filled it with water. I took my time so I could diffuse some of my anxiety at answering. Then, I murmured, "I know."

"There she is." He sat down then as I put the cup in front of him. He took a bite slow and held my gaze as if he wanted me to experience it with him. The way his lips closed over the fork and the way he savored the bite now was intentional, and the air freaking crackled with tension. "Tastes divine, Clara. Did you add dill? Probably a couple other things—"

Kicking out the chair across from him, I shrugged. "Yep. With minced garlic and parsley. Does it work together?"

He tsked. "You know it does. Own it."

"Okay." I crossed my arms. "I know it does. And you should enjoy your meals, not rush them."

"I'm fine enjoying a meal all damn day rather than going to meet your future *mentor* at the market."

I chuckled. "Yeah, maybe my future mentor, Dominic, if he wants."

He squinted around another bite and pointed his fork at me. "He'd be lucky to have you, cupcake. He's mastered main courses, but he's still yet to nail a dessert menu."

"His desserts are—"

"Not as good as yours. And I've told him so."

My knees buckled, and I almost fell over onto my worn kitchen tile. "You what? You didn't."

"He knows what I like about his restaurant, and he knows what I don't like. I disclose that to everyone when I bring them on." He shrugged like it was normal. "Your desserts would be a phenomenal addition to Valentino's restaurant, and he knows it."

My mouth dropped. "Was that a compliment about my baking?"

He cleared his plate before answering. "You're passionate and good at what you do. You're an asset."

So casually he said the words. So honest and sure of himself when he said them.

"Thank you," I murmured before making a grab at his plate, but he nudged my hand away and got up to wash it himself. Then, he took the pot from the stove and did that too. "You don't have to clean up—"

"Of course I do. You cook, I clean, Clara." He smirked. "My mother was dead set on that. Equal households whether we're fake dating or married."

The HEAT empire and the Hardy brothers who owned it were in the news enough that I knew they came from Greek immigrants, that their parents were still married, and they didn't like the limelight. His parents didn't even do interviews and wouldn't move from their home in the Midwest. "Guess that must be the key to their happy marriage."

"Probably," Dominic chuckled. "They've got good hearts on their side too."

"What do you mean by that?" I leaned against the counter and waited for him to answer.

His shoulders tensed and his back straightened enough that I knew there was more to the answer than he gave me. "It just means my father and mother always wanted what was best for the other person. They're selfless because they're in love. To love someone more than you love yourself and risk them not feeling the same."

Talking about love shouldn't have seemed so intimate, not with a man I'd despised just weeks ago, and yet I wanted to know ... "Have you been in that type of love?"

His eyes cut to mine, forest green layers of so much emotion he never shared with anyone. "You read the magazines, Clara. You tell me."

"I ..." Magazines and the media lied. Instead, I coughed a little, clearing a tickle in my throat and shrugged. "I'm never going to get a whole story from the tabloids, right?"

That low rumble he always did when he was lost somewhere in his head came out.

"Anyway, the market shouldn't take long. You don't have to come. I don't think—"

"Are you still wanting to date him?" His pointed question flew at me so direct and out of nowhere that I didn't know how to respond.

"Well, I ..." I hadn't even thought about it. "That was never my main goal, Dominic. If we ..." I stopped myself just in time. What was I going to say? If we don't work? If this fake relationship doesn't turn into something more? This wasn't real. "If I get my five changes to the bakery, that's all that really matters. Your resort will be saved from Natya, and I'll get what I need. Valentino maybe would be an added—"

He frowned and cut me off like suddenly he didn't want to hear the rest. "Let's go."

***

The sun was shining bright and beautiful in the sky when we finally met Valentino, who was already at a vendor sniffing and tasting some mint. He held it out to me, but Dominic snatched it from him and put it near my mouth.

The man kept a firm arm wrapped around me the whole time. Even when a vendor smiled politely my way, Dominic introduced himself and me as a couple, saying we were considering produce for my bakery. Loud and proud. He even snapped a few pictures of me looking at produce, telling me it would be good for the social media pages.

The whole morning, he didn't say one word about his resort unless it was in reference to my bakery. Or Valentino's restaurant. He boasted about my bakery instead. He didn't compliment my design, but suddenly he was adamant that I was the best baker in town and needed all the best produce. He haggled prices, confirmed shipping if I would need it that day, discussed who would be picking produce to make sure it was the very best if he invested.

Gone was my fake boyfriend who was putting on a show and in his place was Dominic Hardy, ruthless businessman that would do right by his resort which now included my bakery. For a second, I felt a part of it all.

And Valentino chimed in a few times, too, even complimenting my truffles while I boasted about his restaurant.

After a couple hours of walking around, Valentino told me he was so happy to be working with me. Then, he shook Dominic's hand respectfully. "I'll be at the restaurant most of the week if you need me."

"Have you discussed the lighting changes with Rita?" Dominic asked.

"We've agreed upon a few changes. You know Rita's been accepting of some of my designs considering we both went to school together."

Dominic nodded but I was shocked. "You did interior design?" I'd never read that about him.

He smiled at me and leaned in. "Guess it helps with how I design a plate."

"That would have probably helped me with Rita." I sighed. "She's very good at keeping her vision but ..."

"But she won't bend at all to yours?" He chuckled and then winked. "Let me know if you'd like me to look anything over. She's got a bit of a soft spot for me."

Dominic didn't add any commentary, but he studied us both. When I turned to him, he lifted a brow and shrugged as if to say, "If that's what you're into." I rolled my eyes and gave Valentino a hug.

It dawned on me right then and there. My heart didn't flutter, and my stomach didn't react to Valentino's touch the way it did Dominic's.

Ignoring the blatant feelings that grew in me for the man I couldn't have, I continued to let Dominic skip around the market with me well after Valentino left. He wanted to check every stand, to confirm we'd gotten the produce right, to make sure it was the best.

At one point, a vendor asked for the name of the bakery,

and Dominic turned to me. "What's the name you're going with, babe?"

I sighed. It'd been a freaking point of contention since I'd gotten there. Rita had asked once or twice and when I'd mentioned a name, she shot it down immediately. "Unknown," I said loudly with a smile to the vendor before we bought the food.

Dominic frowned. "Name's got to come faster than where we're at, Clara."

"I'm aware, Dominic." I singsonged. "You and your interior designer have to agree to something first. I've considered a few. All of which Rita hated."

He hummed and smiled. "Rita's picky. But you'll get changes. So, let's hear them."

I smirked and rattled off different names. All of which he would shake his head to. "No. No. No."

More and more, I felt the heat boiling in my veins. "You're kidding right?"

"They don't work with the resort."

"If I hear that one more time, I'll scream."

"But I like when you scream."

I rolled my eyes and glanced at the last vendor down the alley of tents as I said, "They're *my* changes, Dominic. I'm not giving you a damn say when I choose the name at the end."

When he didn't respond, I glanced back at him and saw he was smiling big. At me. At my fighting him.

Before I could point it out, he glanced at his phone and the smile dropped off. Dominic didn't wear his emotions on his sleeve, but right then and there I saw a pain that was almost tangible. When I whispered his name, his green eyes glanced up at me with a castle full of torture in them before he closed the gates, lifted the bridge, and built up walls around his fortress. "Well, news travels fast."

I narrowed my eyes before sliding my own phone out and reading the headline. "Is She the New Natya?"

What I hated was that I was being compared to her, being thrown into a sort of feeding frenzy the gossip magazines loved. Before the fight at the club, Dominic and I had been a rumor. Now, it was fact, and they wanted blood. I'd been pitted against my own sister before. Who was the prettier sister, who should have been the Milton heiress? They didn't know that neither of us really won from that.

I wouldn't win this either. There was no winning in a competition like that. Only pain. "Well, Natya will believe it now, right?" I whispered.

He nodded. "She's already texted me about it."

I closed my eyes to hide the knife to my gut at his confession, but I think he caught it.

He must have as he growled, "I'm getting rid of the fucking article." He started tapping into his phone. I grabbed it from him and held it back.

"It's for the good of the resort, right?" I lifted a brow. "That was the goal. Your ex will be taken care of, and the resort will prosper. Dex gets his casino deal, huh?"

"Dex told you about his fucking casino deal?"

"Yes, at the club. He's very excited, Dominic."

I saw him glance away, probably to hide the softening he felt when we talked about his siblings. That was his weakness as their older brother, I think. He'd do anything for them. "If they start writing bullshit, we're pulling the articles."

"Fine. But it's not bullshit that she was with you before and I'm with you now." I sighed. "You loved her once. So, it's good they're comparing me to her, right?"

Even as he nodded, I knew it wasn't.

My words shook me back to reality, reminded me that this was all a facade, that we might want her to believe it, but I'd better stop what I was doing because I was starting to believe it too.

Instead of inviting Dominic back over that day, I told him I had work to do. I tried to build up a barrier between us. I tried to be just a fake girlfriend because being a real one wasn't an option.

CHAPTER 23: CLARA

He never mentioned Natya again, but I still thought about it every single day when he came to sit in my bakery the next week.

Especially when my sister's text came through.

Anastasia: I've been calling you. You didn't tell me you were dating him. Are you really? Call me back. Please.

Was it sad that I wanted to actually do it? To bridge the gap between us somehow. And I gave into it, dialing her number with a shaky hand and a heart full of hope.

"Clara." Her voice sounded cheery. "Is it true? I was on socials and got a million DMs this week about you two."

"Yeah, well, they're making it bigger than it is."

"Did he really get in a fight for you?" she whispered like we were conspiring together, two sisters just sharing gossip, and I smiled.

"It was mostly my fault."

"Then, it's totally true," she exclaimed, and I heard the excitement in her voice. "We have to come visit you. It'd be so fun."

I sighed. We'd gone over this before. "I know. It's just—"

"I'll visit soon. Don't worry about Mom. I know how that's hard for you." She said it with emotion. "Everything's been so crazy lately. It's no wonder you felt all this stress, and I'm sorry because I've been stressed too."

When the weight that's been suffocating you gets lifted by a sibling, the feeling of relief is euphoric. Someone who loves you took the burden and removed it, hurried to help you get rid of it. It's that feeling of being loved that blinds you.

"Thank you," I whispered.

She went on and on about how she wanted to come visit, how she wouldn't talk to our mother about it, and how it'd be wonderful. She didn't give me dates, but I felt connected to her again, felt happy, carefree.

It was a dangerous place to be. Then she said she was handing over the phone to Mom and to be prepared because she was on some sort of new mission. I smiled. With Anastasia on my side, Mother was manageable. Even though, my mother had already texted me to try harder to look better in magazines, especially if I was going to be compared to someone like Natya. The insult was there, I just chose to ignore it.

Dominic seemed to ignore all the magazines and news about us. He just worked quietly every morning, and every time I asked him if he wanted to taste test anything of mine, he said no. I'd nearly perfected the menu and was excited to have anyone try anything. "Want a poppy cupcake again? I'll make them special for you."

"No poppy cupcakes, cupcake," he responded and went on drinking his black coffee with his black soul that never ate any sweets.

Every day, I tried to rush to work before he'd arrive. I'd purchased a secondhand bike and was making an effort to bicycle in rather than Uber to save on costs.

Of course, he got there before me nearly every day, but

I set my bike around the corner, rearranged my dress, and walked through the lobby. Unfortunately, on that fine morning, Dominic arrived at exactly the same time. "You're bicycling into work from where you live?"

I sighed, "Just trying to stay in shape."

I said it as I started massaging a part of my neck that had been giving me pain over the last few days. He stepped close and immediately started rubbing there for me. "You're a terrible liar."

I moaned at how good his hands felt, allowing myself a minute of it before waving us on to get to work. He didn't say much about it until we were about to leave for the day. "I'll give you a ride," he announced. "It's dark."

"Oh ... that's okay." I scrambled for an excuse. The longer I was near him, the more I wanted him, the more I thought about his hands on me, the more I wished I could invite him into my bed again. "I'm not sure my bicycle will fit in your car. I'll need it to get to work in the morning."

That was believable, right?

"If you don't take the ride, I'll follow you home instead. My sisters have made it quite clear how dangerous it is for a woman alone at night."

Another angle. "I can take care of myself."

"Even so, at night, I take care of you too."

"You're not going to do this every night, Dominic," I pointed out.

"I'm very aware of that, Clara." He grabbed my waist as I turned out the lights, spun on his heels, and pulled me along with him, not dropping his arm from me for one second. I hated how much I enjoyed the feeling.

And I doubly hated how flattered I was that he went directly to my bike like he knew exactly where I parked it that day. "You should get a lock for your bike."

"Why? You think the construction workers want it?" I threw out. I knew I was being catty, and I didn't really care. It was a used one that I'd found at the Goodwill. I highly doubted anyone would want it.

He hoisted it up with one arm as we made our way to the parking garage. "I'm actually more concerned about the well-being of the person stealing it and you seeing them on the street, little fighter."

The drive back to my apartment was filled with silence. So much silence as he stared at his phone texting away that my mind drifted to Natya again.

Was he texting her? Should I have cared?

Tension bounced back and forth between us so much that I opened a window in hopes to dissipate some of it. Finally, I did the stupid thing and asked the question. "Did Natya reach out to you specifically about us a week ago?" I asked quietly. Would it be rude to ask what she texted? To want to know?

He nodded without elaborating, continuing to text away like he had a million things to handle now. "Want food?" he asked halfway home.

Thinking of eating anything after my stomach had been in knots felt ridiculous, so I shook my head no. "I ate at the bakery." Which was true. I ate way too much when I worked.

His jaw clenched but he didn't push any further. It occurred to me why he'd driven me home as we pulled up slowly to my apartment building. Huge-ass construction machines were everywhere. Caution tape was all around. Posted across the lobby door was a No Entry sign.

"What the hell?" I murmured.

Dominic glanced up from his phone and rubbed at the scruff on his face. "Maybe you should call that landlord of yours."

No shit. I grabbed my phone from my purse and looked up the number. He answered on the first ring. "Clara. So happy you called. I can't thank you enough for your help with this problem."

"This problem?"

"Well, your request for that mold removal was, I will say, a bit concerning, as I didn't have the means to accommodate you. I'm happy Dominic Hardy and his team were able to aid us in getting a team out here so fast and at his expense."

"I'm sorry. What exactly are you—"

"I believe most everyone has been relocated by the movers he brought in today."

"I haven't!" I screeched. "My cats are—"

"I had a team get Sugar and Spice this morning, along with most of your belongings," Dominic murmured before I could jump out of the car.

I glared at him but continued with my landlord. "So, I've been relocated? For how long?"

"Yes, well ... most everyone has been moved to Hardy Tower West but Mr. Hardy explained you will be staying with him. Our residents are very appreciative to stay in the new apartment space at the same rental price as in their agreements here. We didn't realize the health concern, but we are more than happy to take care of the problem."

"Right. Thank you," I said like a freaking robot, and then he said goodbye and hung up.

Something in my blood curdled, something in my heart pounded, and something mean, ugly, and angry flew out. "You asshole! Where exactly did you take my kittens?"

"They've been delivered to my house," he said, crossing his arms over his chest. Was he fucking smirking?

"Without my permission?"

"Well, they had to be moved." One brow lifted. He wanted a fight, and I was ready to give him one. "You want them to die from mold inhalation?"

"I'm not staying at your fucking house, Dominic Hardy." Jesus, the mold inhalation couldn't have been good for anyone. I'd ignored it the first time I'd seen it, and now I felt guilty for doing so, especially because of the kittens. Because of my health. Because of trying so hard to give myself a fighting chance. Even still, what he'd done wasn't acceptable. "We can barely agree on what we want in a damn bakery, let alone in a home."

"Your apartment is unlivable. So, you either stay with me or you rent another place." He waited a second. "Unless for some reason, you can't do that?" Silence filled the car before he said, "Callihan, take us to my place."

His driver pulled away from my apartment building immediately. "Callihan," I shouted, "do not take us to his place. Take me back to the Pacific."

His stupid driver looked at him for the okay, and Dominic smirked and nodded like he had all the time in the world.

I just kept going. "You can also have my things sent to—"

"Where, Clara? They're starting demo on that apartment, and I'm not relocating you to another one. So, stay with me a few days, see how you like it, and look for a new one if you want." He waited again. "If you can afford it."

"I ..." My mouth snapped shut, and then my eyes narrowed. Every time he'd looked at his phone today, that man had been working. Not on his actual job. He'd been researching me. "Did you break into my bank accounts or something?"

"You should have told me your mother cut you off."

"For what reason?"

"So, I could have made sure you were living somewhere suitable."

"Like you cared!" I fumed and threw my body back into the seat.

He didn't say another word to me as I flung the door open as soon as we were in front of the resort. I heard him murmur to Callihan to wait. He could wait all he wanted, but I wasn't getting back in that car with him.

Instead, I stormed through the lobby and swiped my key fob before hurrying to the back of my kitchen. I was going to fury bake and think before I said words I regretted.

The man ambled in a few seconds later and plopped down on the bar to work, like he freaking belonged there.

"You can leave, Dominic."

"Well, I figured I'd just wait for my girlfriend to be done baking so we could leave together since we live at the same place."

I was chopping some fruit and pointed the knife at him. "You can give me the penthouse here again until I find a place since this is your fault."

He hummed. "I think that's technically against some rule in the HR handbook."

"You mean *your* handbook? Considering it's your fucking resort."

"Right. Better not risk it." He pulled his glasses from the bag he'd carried in with him and opened his laptop.

No. I literally couldn't deal with him right now. I stomped out in front of the counter between us to slam the laptop shut on his hands. He was quick enough to pull them back.

I got a smile from him right then and there. It was brilliant, and I hated how my heart reacted.

"Don't come in here and work. I'm too mad at you right now. You upended my life more than once, and you're not thinking right when you say I should live with you for a while. It's preposterous considering you can't even stand the design of my bakery."

He chewed his cheek. "You're right. We don't have the same taste. And your additions are—"

"Are what?" I narrowed my eyes at him. Would he dare?

He pointed to the pink seating. "This is too soft. If you want to go bold, do it. The leather should probably have been velvet. And the glass countertops looking in at your bakery items will probably add more color that doesn't flow with the balance of white and black in here, most likely clashing with the pink wall you're so insistent on keeping."

This is why I couldn't be around him or live with him or probably even fake date him. Dominic Hardy threw out honesty like sharp darts coming for your soul. He knew this meant something to me. And he pinched the bridge of his nose when he saw my chin wobble. "That being said—"

He was cut off by his phone ringing, and he stood, mumbling he had to take it.

I spun around to go back into the kitchen.

Everything was falling apart. And I didn't know what to do about it other than try not to cry and unload some of my frustration on Evie when she called. I was furiously telling her how Dominic had just ripped apart my whole bakery and looked disgusted with me for almost crying when I heard him come back in. I told her I had to go and straightened my spine.

If I was going to be here, I was going to get through this. I just had to figure out how. I took a deep breath and walked out with my arms crossed, a shield now up to ward off any stupid feelings I had toward the man who was so hot when he fake dated me and then ruthless when he worked with me. "Dominic, I don't want to fight with you."

"Sure you do, little fighter. We like fighting, and we like fucking around too. It's probably what we do best together."

"We actually haven't even fucked," I said, irritated all over again for continuing down this petty path. "And we won't. I'll stay with you a couple nights while I figure out another living situation—"

"I have a whole wing you can stay in, Clara. It won't be that bad." He said it softly, consoling, like suddenly he was remorseful for his actions. "Plus, it will look good for our fake relationship."

Ah, there it was. I took a deep breath, trying to will back the tears that were hot behind my eyes. "I get that I'm an asset to you. That this fake relationship is benefitting the both of us. But"—I held up a hand when he started to say something—"don't treat me like a toy you can fuck around with. I've been a toy and a damn accessory for most of my life. I won't be that here. Not again."

"Clara," he frowned, and I knew he didn't understand. How could he? "I didn't mean for you to feel—"

"I don't care how you meant it. You didn't think about it." I crossed my arms over my chest. "You ruined what was mine. My mother and sister ruled my damn life, Dominic. You might not understand it, and I'm not going to sit here and cry about it with you, but I left so I could have something that was mine. Just mine! I bought the stuff that went in that apartment, I made it a home, I made it what I wanted, and you fucking destroyed it."

"Clara." He whispered out my name as an apology, but when he reached out to wipe my tears, I stepped back. "Fuck, baby. I didn't know it would hurt you."

"No. Because you didn't ask." I shook my head. "It doesn't matter." I took a deep breath. "I'm changing that right here and right now by telling you that you'd better ask in the future if you want this dumb fake relationship to go over like it should. This *won't* happen with me again. Give me your word." I stuck out my hand for him to shake.

His jaw worked up and down, up and down. "I don't shake hands with you, cupcake."

"Don't you even dare—"

He came for my mouth, and he wouldn't be denied. I enjoyed the kiss from him too much even if it was filled with hate.

CHAPTER 24: DOMINIC

Clara was so worried about the damn resort and what I wanted out of it that she barely worried about herself. She'd basically sold her soul to those tabloids when she'd pushed me to let them continue to be printed. She was doing it over and over again in front of me, putting someone else before her happiness.

She mentioned her mother and sister, and again, I knew there was more to the story, that one day I'd have to pry it out of her. Now, though, I just wanted to shake out the trait of her letting others run over her and then hug her for all she'd done in the past for everyone else.

I knew the paparazzi would be ruthless once they got wind of our living situation, so I took it upon myself to make sure my PR handled some of it. Nothing negative was to be printed about her, I didn't give a shit if it helped fuel the resort's opening.

And now? I was so worried about her well-being that I'd pulled every string to get her out of that apartment and into my own house. Was I supposed to care this much about a fake girlfriend? Never had I imagined I'd be worried about her well-being over the resort or over how Natya would lash out, and yet, I went to bed and woke up worrying only about her.

Did her damn cupcakes turn out right today? Did she get the stupid vanilla extract she wanted from the distributor? I should have been worried about the call I'd gotten on another project at a resort an hour away. I had a million things to juggle, to consider, to fill my head. Over the years, I'd been satisfied to let work consume me.

Yet, nothing took over my mind and haunted it in the way Clara's broken face had. I watched her puffy eyes take in the greenery surrounding my private drive. We wove through the hills and the land, getting farther and farther from LA. I lived outside the city limits to get away from the crowds of people, or maybe I was just trying to preserve a semblance of my soul. I'd bought the home in an auction from a late architect's estate. Supposedly, he'd built it for his family, but never got to share it with them. The story was morbid but maybe so was mine.

She didn't say a word one way or the other about the structure as we pulled up and waited for the gate to open. It was all brick—brick driveway, brick stone, gray and melancholy. I'd never livened the place up because my heart didn't want that.

When she walked in, all I heard her mumble was, "Of course there's no color," before she bent down and scooped up the kittens that had already made themselves at home. My personal assistant had got the cats food bowls, set up their beds in the study, and there was no mold anywhere in my home that I knew of.

"Where would you like me to sleep the next few nights?" she said in a clipped tone.

Damn, I'd hurt her by relocating her without asking. I'd have to make it up to her over time.

Taking over that apartment was necessary though. I knew health hazards when I saw them, and too many people were being taken advantage of. High rent made their health take a back seat to housing.

She still had that cough, but it was less now. I swear she didn't even notice it, but I did. I noticed every damn thing about that girl. The way she looked away when I pushed her on her money situation, the way she hid the hell people put her through to accommodate everyone else.

I just didn't know how much that apartment had meant to her. Peeling the layers back on Clara's life suddenly felt like a necessity. The woman was going to be living in my house, and I knew nothing about her except that I wanted to know everything and that she belonged by my side until further notice.

Instead of asking for a tour or acting at all interested in the place I'd redesigned and lived in, she'd demanded to know where she'd be sleeping. That was it. My team had dropped off her belongings into the guest room.

When I pointed down the hall, she called Sugar and Spice and made kissing sounds in hopes they'd follow her. They didn't. Both cats seemed to have abandoned their owner for me, preferring instead to weave in and out of my legs.

She glared at me, betrayed all over again. "Bring them to my room and then leave."

I'd take any way of getting time with her that I could right now. I whispered a thank you to both the kittens and stalked down the hall.

When they filed into her room, she glared. "Leave." I took a step back and gave her the space she rightfully deserved. She shut the door right away, and I murmured, "Good girl." At least to me, she was learning to stand up for herself.

Her outburst in the bakery told me so. She'd cracked enough that I saw through her facade. She'd been overlooked in more ways than one, but here she wouldn't be. I'd make sure of it.

That night, I worked out in the fitness center across the house harder than I should have. Punch after punch. Weight after weight. I worked away the stress, the frustration at how I'd handled Clara that day, and the text messages I knew were weighing down my phone.

Natya pursued what she wanted viciously—a lot like me. We'd been a phenomenal team before we were a catastrophic disaster.

Unknown Number: Is she a fling to fuck around with, or do I really have competition?

Unknown Number: You can't avoid me forever. We have to visit Susie soon.

Those were the only texts I received, and I hadn't responded. Natya didn't understand that I didn't have to be in love with someone else in order to not love her. There was no competition with my heart where she was concerned. Too much pain lived there now that she'd inflicted.

I knew she was right though. I wouldn't miss my visit with Susie ever, even if it meant Natya would come too.

The text messages hadn't stopped coming in though. My brothers and sisters weren't going to let up until I responded. I swiped my phone off the floor and went to shower before making my way to my study where I could answer them.

Dex: So I guess the news is out.

Me: You talked to Clara about the damn casino deal? What did you say?

Dex: That's what we're discussing? Who cares? I just told her she's great. Natya never helped solidify deals the way she will.

Me: Why the fuck are you comparing her to Natya?

Dex: Damn. Calm down. It's not like the whole nation isn't doing the same thing.

Izzy: Don't compare women. It's rude. We're not objects.

Dex: It wasn't like that. Jesus.

Me: I don't care how it was. We're not doing it as a family to my girlfriend.

Dimitri: So it's real?

Lilah: I think it's real only because Dom never dates anyone but Natya.

Declan: It better be real. Don't fuck with Clara. You know Evie loves that girl.

Me: Why wouldn't it be real?

I winced. We normally didn't lie to each other. But I wasn't exactly lying. Clara wasn't only doing it for publicity. We were doing it for the resort, for her bakery. Not for her getting a date with Valentino. Because that shit wasn't happening now. I was making sure of it.

Izzy: Seems mighty coincidental.

Me: Worry about something else. We're grown-ass adults.

Declan: How about you worry about not pounding people's faces in so we don't have to deal with a PR shitstorm next time.

Izzy: Dex and I handled it mostly. A few people lost some pictures and videos. Big deal. Tell us more about you loving Clara. That's what I want to know about.

Lilah: Should we talk to Evie about this?

Declan: Fuck no. She's nursing. She doesn't need the stress.

Izzy: Seriously? Her breastmilk isn't going to be affected by stress, you idiot.

Me: Would you all just calm down? I like Clara's company, she likes mine. Don't meddle when everything

is working out with flying fucking colors.

Dex: Yeah. The casino deal is looking solid.

Me: Exactly. I've got shit to do. Bother someone else.

I didn't check for notifications from them again. I didn't check the news or the magazines from the reports that were flowing in either. I wore a HEAT watch and knew the technology was sending me updates regarding my own name. The articles had gone from comparing Natya and Clara to "Another Hardy-Milton Merger" because Evie and Declan were the first to have been caught in the tangled mess of Carl's will.

I knew none of the articles had pictures of the fight at the bar, although some of them claimed an eyewitness saw one or two things. Every article was swooning though. The spin was good. Our PR teams were doing their jobs like I told them to. Yet, I'd somehow fucked up mine as a boyfriend.

A fake one.

I sat in my study for what seemed like days. The minute hand on the clock ticked slower and slower by the second. What was she doing in her damn room? If she was angry, she should have been out here fighting with me about it.

She had to talk to me. She may have been frustrated with me now, but we were bound together for the next few months. Apologizing to her for taking care of her health wasn't an option, but I made the first effort by texting:

Me: You want to have dinner?

Clara: Not with you.

I growled up at the ceiling, pulling at the back of my neck and then pounding a fist on my oak desk.

Me: Should I deliver food then?

Clara: I'll take french fries and crab rangoon.

Me: No place serves both of those things.

Clara: Well then. Guess I'll stay mad.

Clara: And just so we're clear, food delivery won't make this better.

Me: What will?

Me: The moving team will have all the furniture and decor that was yours here tomorrow. I'll try my best to make you feel at home here, babe.

Clara: As you should since you upended my home.

I had to smile at her boldness, at her not being at all accommodating, trying to put me in my place. She was right to do so.

Me: I took control of my girlfriend's life a little too fast, huh? I'll apologize for that. I should have moved slower.

There were dots for a minute. On and off, and on, and then off. My move since she wasn't sending.

Me: I know how I can apologize further if you let me, little fighter.

Clara: How?

I was definitely going to hell for sexting her in hopes of forgiveness. I'd either get her in that big white bed in the guest room with the down comforter fluffed up around her or she'd storm out of that room mad as hell.

Me: I'll get you the food and make you feel good.

Clara: You don't know how to make me feel good.

Me: Now we both know you're lying. Bet your pussy is wet already from the idea.

Clara: Not after you ripped apart my bakery and said you hated everything in it.

Me: Shit, cupcake. I never finished what I had to say. It's not my taste,

but your bakery shouldn't be. It's got the flair you do.

Clara: Is that a compliment?

Me: As close as you're going to get to one.

Clara: How close will I get to an apology for what you did today?

Me: My actions speak louder than words and apologies, Clara.

Clara: Is that so?

Me: Want me to elaborate further?

She knew where this was going. I saw those dots going and then disappearing again. And instead of waiting for her to respond, my hand went to my cock. Rock fucking solid as always when I thought about her. The pre-cum was already dripping down onto the head of my dick, practically weeping to fuck my fake girlfriend, given that I'd passed on the chance over and over again at this point.

I kept telling myself it was because of her needing to be sober and it not being the right time. I'd wanted her sober, wanted her begging, wanted her to remember. Here, in my home, I couldn't think of a better time. I wanted it to be real.

And that was a problem. Clara and I were fake but somewhere somehow my boundaries had blurred. I slept in her bed and wanted her in mine every night after. I upended her life so she could move in with me even though I never wanted a woman in my home.

I'd wanted Natya the same way and she'd made me believe a damn lie.

Keeping my distance was probably best and I'd done that effortlessly with others in the past. I just had to do it again.

Tonight, though, for just one night, I had some making up to do, and I intended to do it just right.

When my phone finally buzzed on my desk as I pumped myself slowly, I snatched it up with one hand to see just one word.

Clara: Yes.

My fake girlfriend wanted to fuck me as much as I did her.

CHAPTER 25: CLARA

Dominic: If you're not in your sleepshirt, get in it now. Nothing else.

I bit my lip, not knowing how far I should take this. I was surrounded by Dominic Hardy. He'd invaded every aspect of my life to the point where even my kittens were meandering around his home.

My suitcase had been packed for me. I ran to it to see if all my bathroom essentials were there, including my vitamins and medication. I caught a sob when I saw them and breathed out once and then twice.

Did he have any idea? Would he have put two and two together? But Dominic was straightforward and would have asked. Most people asked that sort of thing, right? Maybe I shouldn't have cared, maybe I shouldn't have cared about him moving me here either. I didn't know. My mind was still angry, scrambling to take a stand on what he'd done, but my heart kept circling back to him protecting my health—the one thing no one had done for so long. And then he'd said my bakery had flair.

I'd witnessed Dominic in his element now. I knew he didn't hand out empty compliments. He'd torn down Valentino more than once at the market, told more than one person on his business calls that they were incompetent, and he really wasn't exaggerating any of his assessments.

He said what he meant to say. Having him seeing even a sliver of my vision had my heart bursting with pride in a way I couldn't control.

And my body was a complete freaking slut for him. My hand had already slipped under my sleepshirt, whispering over my panty lace to where I was dripping wet for him.

Me: Yes. I'm going to bed after I eat.

Dominic: Want me to eat you out first?

Me: You probably don't deserve that after what you did today.

I gulped because it felt like he was telling my fingers to slow down, and then he followed up on his last text.

Dominic: Are you touching yourself nice and slow, baby?

I bit my lip. This wasn't how the texting tonight was supposed to go.

Me: If I said I was?

Dominic: If you did, I'd tell you to slide one finger into that pussy. Feel how wet you get for me. Know I'd drink it all up and then kiss you after, make you taste how sweet you are.

I whimpered at what I was reading because I knew he was only in the other room. We could be doing exactly that instead of this.

I stared at the wall of his room, ran one hand over the white down comforter that pillowed out around me and growled up at his white ceiling. Everything in this room was so clean, so perfect, and somehow so frustrating. I jumped up and messed up the bed, then took some of my clothes and threw them out of the black suitcase they'd been neatly packed into. I wanted me here. My color. My life. My energy. I wanted what was supposed to be my life here in this city.

Maybe my body wanted it even more. To be healthy. To be living my fullest life. To be taking what I wanted without waiting for an okay. Without waiting to see if I'd have a flare up, without tiptoeing through things. It was a confession I'd not even admitted to myself yet. I was trying to hard to hold on to what I was making here that I wouldn't even call the freaking doctor. I wanted nothing to change which was why I was so mad he'd changed my apartment.

I was just becoming me and he'd disturbed that.

I swung open my door and stomped down the hallway to his study. I didn't even knock as I pushed through the entrance.

There he sat, Dominic Hardy, glasses and a smirk on his face as he pumped himself once. His cock completely bared to me, long, hard, thick and throbbing. I gulped as I stood there. Seeing Dominic Hardy in the world he'd created for himself, surrounded by beautiful carved white crown moldings, all the books had been turned with the pages facing out too, all white. The black bookcase holding all of the books in their rightful place. His desk was glass, his chair black leather. Everything, black and white, clean, precise.

Dominic Hardy wanted a world devoid of color, and I stood there in the middle of this study bursting with it. "Should I go?" I whispered.

"I don't know, Clara," he said pointedly. "Should you?"

He'd instigated me taking more control lately, and I realized I appreciated it. "No. I won't go."

"Good. You leave, I'll drag you right back here anyway." He looked down and I followed his line of vision, whimpering at the sheer size of him, large and full, completely ready to fuck someone. "See what you do to me, Clara? Even when you're mad in your room, I'm out here thinking about fucking you. I can't seem to think about anything else."

"Then, maybe you should do it."

"You'd like that wouldn't you?" he growled, his muscles tense, his eyes so dark and piercing, I should have been scared. "Don't you see that if I do that, cupcake, I'll never come back from it?"

I shook my head. "I don't understand."

"This isn't real. I'll never be able to give you the real damn thing, Clara, but I get a small taste of you, and it's all I think about." He shook his head, his forearm flexing as he gripped himself harder. My nipples puckered, and my pussy clenched just watching. My mind was lost to him. I took another step into the study. "Stay where you are," he commanded, his voice loud enough that it bounced around the room. "You stay right there, and you watch. Watch what you've done to me."

I could see the sheen of sweat forming on his forehead, could see the veins protruding now from his thick, long cock, could see how the pre-cum gathered into a drop that pebbled and dripped from him. My breath came faster as he picked up the pace. "I want to touch you, Dominic."

"Come here. Come sit on my desk." When I listened and then tried to reach for him, he rolled his chair back enough that I couldn't. "You'll watch me first, little fighter. Watch and touch yourself for me."

"What?" I whispered. Gone was my shame or pride. I wanted him and I was going to get him here and now even if it was only once. "You can't be serious. I want you to fuck me—"

"You know how long it takes to build something to perfection? Years. Took me years to build that resort, years to rebuild this place, and I'm building this between us now. Here, you don't fight me. You listen."

I whimpered with his command but obeyed anyway. He was a sight to see, unraveling in a place he'd probably worked so tirelessly to create with control. For Dominic to lose it, that was the true masterpiece that no one, not even me, could pass up.

I'd given up a lot for the sake of others, but here I was going to be greedy. My hand slid up my thigh as I watched his thumb roll over the head of his cock.

"That's it. Touch yourself for me, Clara. Tell me if my pussy is wet. Lift your shirt." I lifted it enough for him to see my damp underwear. His jaw tensed and his other hand went to my thigh. He gripped it tight as he murmured, "Push them to the side."

I was already losing control with him so close, right between my legs. When he shoved my thigh further over, my legs were almost fully spread for him. Then, he rolled his chair between us and I did as I was told because my clit was throbbing, aching, and begging for relief. My fingers brushed over it, and I immediately gasped, my eyes closing.

"Eyes on me, little fighter. Show me how you touch yourself when you're thinking of me."

"You don't know if I always think of—"

"Don't lie, Clara." He didn't even give me time to finish. "Go on. Slide a finger in. Moan my name, baby."

My eyes were locked on his as I did. My other hand drifted to my breast to squeeze as I arched and moaned his name, rolling my hips to give him the same show he gave me.

He encouraged me. "Look at how you play with your own pussy for me. Such a good girlfriend, aren't you? That body belongs to me." I shook my head no and felt the hum of disagreement he let out before he stood from his chair. He hovered over me before he murmured, "You belong to me."

When I shook my head again, biting my lip to keep from agreeing with him immediately, his eyes darkened with possessiveness, with what I thought might be anger.

"Say it, Clara." This time one of his hands threaded through my hair and yanked it to turn my gaze up to his. "Say it."

"I'm yours ... only for a little while." I pushed him because he deserved it. He'd pushed me into his house, and I was going to push all his buttons while I was here.

"Fuck. Don't goad me right now," he whispered against my neck before he bit and licked it.

"I'm giving you brutal honesty, like you give everyone else."

He hummed. "If you want honesty, I'll give you some. I'm going to fuck that pussy so good you'll always be mine. You know that, right? Once I have you, you won't want anybody else."

I was actually concerned he might be right about that. Still, I wouldn't admit it. "If you say so, Dominic."

He must have heard the hitch in my voice, heard that I was concerned about it because he smiled. "Go on, little fighter. Roll those hips a little more. Fuck your hand like you'd fuck my cock. Get my pussy nice and wet."

His mouth was filthy, and I told him so. Then I said, "And it's not yours. It's mine."

He chuckled as his hand drifted to my neck where he gripped me firmly before shoving me down onto the desk. "Everything of yours is mine, Clara. When will you see? I am taking ownership of you. Now, lift your shirt so I can see everything that's mine. I want those tits on display."

His hands went to them immediately when I lifted it. He pinched my sensitive nipples, pulled at them how I liked. He knew my body better than I knew it myself, and I continued to indulge, continued to let him learn more and more because I couldn't stop myself. Even if I had to remind us that we were limited on time with each other, I was taking every second of it with him that I could at this point. And I wanted him as lost to me as I was to him.

I worked my pussy, feeling my arousal everywhere on my legs, on his desk, on my hand. I moaned his name and let myself indulge in every sensation. My thighs trembled against his, and I watched how the head of his cock swelled, how his forearms tensed, the veins snaking around. He muttered swear after swear with his eyes locked onto my sex. When I was almost there, I grabbed his belt loops and commanded him this time, "Get us there together, Dominic."

"Clara—" he warned. One of his hands was still at my throat and the other slowed the rhythm of pumping his cock.

I didn't give him an out. "Please," I begged. I wanted him lost with me at that moment. "I deserve it."

His cock throbbed against my clit, and my body moved on its own accord, trying to get closer to him, trying to get him to slide in like he'd give me life, give me ecstasy. It was his turn to lose control, and when I looked into his eyes, they were wild. Gone was the man who didn't indulge. Here, I saw how he wanted everything.

Dominic Hardy was a taker, vicious in his pursuit of conquering the world, and I wanted him to conquer me now.

"You want this?" he ground out as he squeezed my throat, his other hand moving his cock back and forth over me. Then his thumb brushed my clit, and I wiggled against him faster. I nodded. "Say it, baby. Own it."

He let go a little on my neck. "I want you, Dominic. I'm on birth control and my tests are clear," I whispered.

He smiled and leaned close. "Good, because nothing is going to be between us when I fuck you. Ever. You realize that, right?" His statement felt deep, too intimate for what we were doing. "Tell me again. Louder this time, little fighter. What do you want? Own. It." His voice was full of force, ruthless in his pursuit to make even our fuck perfection.

"I want you to fuck me. I want it now." I slammed my hand on his desk, frustrated that he didn't just give me what I wanted.

He let go of my neck to run his thumb up my jaw. I gasped as he slid the head of his dick inside me. My pussy clenched immediately, feeling full already. "Jesus." I closed my eyes. "You're bigger than—"

"Big enough to fit you just right, baby. You scared I won't fit?"

I nibbled at my bottom lip, not sure I wanted to voice my concern.

He dipped down and licked my breast, bit my nipple, tugged it with his teeth. I whimpered, but my legs spread further as he pushed himself in another inch. "See how your body listens. You're made just for me."

For some reason, I wanted it to be true. Even if it was just for a few months. He thrust in and out of me, slow at first, like he was giving me time to adjust as his hands swept over my body, touching all the right places. My walls clenched around him, feeling him everywhere. He was hard, solid, thick, and pulsing just for me. Stretching me. Making everything just right.

He pulled out again, thrust in harder this time, and the pleasure was instant and all consuming. I felt myself shudder as I moaned loud, building toward destruction or salvation, I wasn't sure which.

Either way, I wanted us to reach it together. I was vulnerable here, baring my soul like a woman who'd finally figured out she was confident enough to do so. And sex with him shouldn't have been that. Dominic Hardy was becoming my safe place, and I knew that meant he would be my catastrophic disaster too. "I want you like this every time, Dominic," I blurted out and held his gaze, trying to make it clear. "Show me it's me you want."

"I fucking want you spread on my desk every night. I want you screaming my goddamn name and no one else's ever," he growled as his cock pumped in me again, the sound of our skin colliding grew louder.

Believing him was ridiculous. A man would say anything after feeling good. Plus, Dominic's mouth worked in a charming and filthy way. Even still, my legs looped around his backside and held him close for another minute.

I'd indulge in our fake fantasy for a minute longer.

Just another minute was all I wanted.

"Come on me then, Dominic. I want you in me, on me, all around me. Show me."

CHAPTER 26: DOMINIC

She was demanding her needs now, pointedly and with authority.

Gone was my cupcake and in her place was the little fighter, brilliant, beautiful, and completely naked on my desk.

Fuck, her pussy felt good. It felt like it was made for me, like she'd been designed by the very best to fit my every need.

Her words were gasoline to my already on-fire obsession with fucking her. I stepped back, pulling myself from her to stare at her sex. She didn't close her legs, didn't hide herself now. She just glared at me. "What are you doing?"

"Staring at what's mine, thinking I should have been fucking that pretty pink pussy the whole time."

"You aren't done fucking me yet." She lifted a brow.

I hummed low and I loved that she shuddered with the sound. "You want me, baby? Take me exactly how you want then."

Her emerald eyes widened as I sat down in my chair again, my cock glistening with her slick, shiny arousal. I flexed it and her eyes immediately locked on to it.

"Come sit on my lap, baby. Put your little pussy on me and ride my dick like you want to."

She slid off the desk slowly, like she was mesmerized with the sight in front of her. Her tits bounced when she hit the ground, her hips flared out from her waist and swayed as she took the two steps to me before climbing onto my lap. Without hesitating, she sheathed herself on me fast and hard. "I've wanted this for so long." She murmured, riding me fast, her pussy so tight that every muscle in my neck, back, and whole fucking body strained not to come in her right then and there.

Her hands used my shoulders as leverage, the nails digging in tight as she moved faster, her hair swaying fast over her tits, her eyes drifting closed. Her pouty mouth formed an O as her ass and pussy bounced up and down on my lap until that final moment.

She shifted back, her gaze on mine fast as she took my cock, pulled me from her body, and squeezed as she cried out.

Seeing her lose it, having her hand milking my cock as she pointed it toward her stomach had me coming hard. I shot myself out over her stomach, unable to control myself for a second longer as her arousal gushed onto my leg. My hand went to her pussy immediately, wanting her on me as much as I was on her.

We marked each other, and a primal part of me loved it, relished in knowing I'd brought this need out of her. She'd wanted this, wanted me on her as if she couldn't have it any other way. I ran my fingers over her again and again letting her ride out the aftershocks. All the while, I smoothed my other hand over her stomach, rubbing myself into her skin. "You're mine, little fighter. No one else's. Do you understand? I should leave my cum on you as a reminder."

She slumped against me and nodded over and over. "Maybe but this relationship is–"

"I'm taking you to your bed," I cut her off. I didn't want to know what she was going to say because suddenly I was sure that this was a relationship, that I'd created something authentic with her, something I wouldn't be able to back away from clean and easy.

I didn't want to.

I put her to bed that night and tried my damn hardest not to crawl into it with her. It'd been my own rule once before and now I fucking hated that I was having a problem following through with it when it came to her.

That night, I tossed and turned thinking of her down the hall and hoped once I woke the next morning, it'd be better. I got to have sex with her. That should have gotten her out of my system.

It didn't.

***

Of course I still expected a little bit of a disruption from Clara moving in the next morning. I told myself it would showcase why we actually would never work; it would be a reason as to why I needed to keep her and everyone at arm's length.

And disrupt she did. Like a storm barreling ashore, she hit me like a tsunami.

The next day, she padded into my study and grumbled, "Until this facade of a relationship is over, I'll stay. Then, I'm out with Sugar and Spice."

I petted both cats that had already claimed my lap in the study while I sat at the desk and worked. "Fine."

"Are you wearing sweats?" She sounded completely bewildered.

"Sure. It's my house."

Then a frown formed. "And a T-shirt?"

I lifted a brow. "You've seen me in Florida working out, Clara."

"I know. But here ... you're always in a suit."

"Again, I'm at home." I shrugged and eyed her attire. "Are you wearing a sleepshirt?"

She crossed her arms and popped a hip. "I just woke up because ..." Her face turned a bright red, and I smirked. She shook her head at me, her long red hair swinging back and forth in disarray, like I'd fucked the well put together out of her last night.

"Because what, baby? You got fucked so good last night you wanted to sleep in?" I licked my lips as she bit hers. "I like this look on you best, by the way."

"Oh my God. You know what? There are rules if I'm staying." She cleared her throat. "One, you don't talk about the sex we shouldn't have had."

I chuckled. "I'll consider it."

She scoffed. "And you don't come into my room unannounced, and you let the cats roam free."

I glanced down at them. "Obviously. They're not trained well at all. They've wandered in here already like they own the place."

She rolled her eyes, but I saw how she chewed her cheek like she couldn't get enough of how they loved me. "And you stop wearing those glasses."

"What for?" I barked out a laugh.

"They're distracting."

"Noted but not in agreement unless you promise to only wear the dresses my hands can disappear under quickly and with no underwear so I can—"

"Stop." She held up a hand as she dragged her teeth over those red lips. I pushed the cats off my lap and rearranged myself. Now that I had her, I wasn't going to think of much else.

"Sure you want to stop, or are we just getting started?" I

saw the way her nipples were hardening under that sleep shirt.

"I want to decorate a room or two where I'll be."

I started to object, but she held up her hand.

"I don't want your input. It's yes or no."

"Clara, our tastes are—"

"Different, and I need—" She took a deep breath and I saw pain in her eyes before she glanced away. Then she massaged a part of her shoulder that I noticed always bothered her. "I need a place I'm relaxed in, Dominic. I was trying to make that at my apartment."

Silence filled the room between us as I warred with giving in and giving up what I felt I'd perfected. The home wasn't full of flair and eccentricities of color like she would have wanted. Yet, it flowed. It was a Dominic Hardy design, and it was mine.

Not hers.

I'd taken what was hers.

"Fine, but—"

"I'm not done." She held up one tiny finger, and I had to keep from smiling. "You don't say a word when I'm baking in the kitchen. You let me do what I want in there. And you get used to my bakery name being Sugar and Spice because I already told Rita it's one of the changes, and after arguing for way too long about it, the sign is coming in a few days."

I glanced at the kittens that were already growing on me somehow.

"Don't hurt their feelings, Dominic," she warned.

"That it?" I said. She could have asked for the world, and I would have given it to her at this point to make her stay.

She frowned. "I think so."

"Good. I intend to walk in the bathroom every time you're taking a shower."

She rolled her eyes. "Absolutely not. What if I'm—" When she stopped immediately, I knew exactly what she was about to say.

"What if you're what?"

"Well, um ... In there with someone else?" she squeaked out, trying to distract me from what she was really going to say, but it did its job.

My brows slammed down, and I shut my laptop before pacing slowly over to her. She leaned back as I caged her in and dipped my head down close to her face. "You're not having other men here ... or anywhere, Clara. You're mine."

"Well, I'm fake yours," she corrected, as if she could stop the blurring of lines between us at this point.

"Tell me." I thrust my cock against her stomach. "That feel like my dick thinks this is fake to you? You're here for three more months. You're exclusively mine for all of them."

"You're counting down?" she whispered, then she shook her head. "It doesn't matter. If you want me to be exclusive, are you going to be also?"

"Don't ask stupid questions. Of course the same goes for me. I'm not in the business of sleeping with a woman I'm not attracted to and it seems the only one I'm attracted to right now is you. I woke up thinking about you in my study, and I'll go to bed thinking about you coming on my cock with your pretty hair draped over your tits in my bed. Want to go fulfill my fantasy now or later?"

She chewed on her bottom lip. "I've got only a few weeks left until this opening. And you do too. We need to work, not mess around. Plus, being professional is—"

"Overrated when I know how you taste."

She stepped away from me. "Don't be ridiculous, Dominic.

You're probably smarter than most when it comes to toxic relationships. Ours would be a whole keg of poison if we kept indulging the way we are now." She breathed out fast and then looked at me with those big green eyes. "Right?"

Fuck, my dick wanted me to say wrong. But my mind knew she was right. My ex had stirred up a pot of poison and fed it to me. I was lost to love and relationships and the hope that they would ever end well.

I stepped back and whispered, "Right."

She echoed it back again, her face falling, and her walls flying up. She took a deep breath before she excused herself to go unpack. Somehow, that one word of confirmation restructured our relationship.

We let the days tick by as we passed one another by in the hallways without touching. Without eye contact. With only soft hellos and small talk. Still, if she stayed late at the bakery, I made sure my driver went back for her, and I paced in front of her room half the time. I also wandered into it once or twice and saw she'd set up the pictures she'd had in her apartment on the dressers here.

Something about her having other people—even Evie, Declan, and my nephew Atticus—in a picture without her frustrated the hell out of me.

Her disruption to my everyday life shouldn't have been huge with how quiet she was and how she moved around me. She even thanked me for having my assistant set up her bright rug in her room and move her small amount of furniture and pillows in there. She didn't ask to have it in the living room. She just walled herself off with all her belongings every day in that room when we got home. But Clara couldn't contain that she was brilliantly alive or that my attention was always drawn to her, even if she didn't want it to be.

Every day, I'd offer to take her to work and she'd quietly worry her hands in the car. She kept her nails short but always painted in red or a pink to match what she was wearing. They matched the walls of that bakery, too, and her poppy cupcakes I was having a fucking hard time avoiding.

When I worked late in my study, I heard her tiptoe out to the kitchen to get water every night at some random point, never the same time, like she just remembered she needed it rather than planned for it.

When I met her footsteps with mine one night, I saw her taking pills with the water. "What are those for?"

She spun around fast, probably shocked that she hadn't heard me sneak up on her. "Just birth control?"

The woman literally couldn't tell a lie without about five movements that gave her away. Not only did she blush, she looked anywhere but my eyes, fidgeted on her feet, picked at a nail, and then combed her hand through her hair.

"Try again, little fighter. This time, no lies."

She curled in on herself when she said softly, "I get joint pain sometimes. I have medication to help with it."

"Joint pain—"

She shook her head and didn't wait around to explain herself more. She just rushed past me with a soft *good night.* Suddenly, I couldn't think of anything else. Did she wake up with the pain? Go to bed with it? Was it something more? Every question felt too intrusive for a woman that was living in my home but not sleeping with me. For a woman that barely talked with me now that we'd drawn some fucked-up line in the imaginary sand.

Every night after, she rushed past my doors like I wouldn't

see the deep-green or blue or red flurry of silk pajamas she was wearing. She was quiet, but the disruption was huge. All I thought about was her on my desk, how she tasted, how she'd wanted everything I gave her.

When she cooked in that kitchen, I ate copious amounts of little chocolates to try to curb the addiction I had to her. That very night, I'd shooed the cats out of my study and actually closed the doors, hoping to bar off the temptation of Clara Milton and get back to my work.

And when I heard clanging around from my study, I should have let it be. Instead, I sighed and ended a call with colleagues. Something was missing from the damn resort, and I couldn't put my finger on it. I couldn't reopen it without it being perfect either. The Hardy name was stamped on it.

It was also the resort I'd finally given my all to after the incident within the workplace, after Natya lied to me over and over again. I couldn't let my family or anyone down this time.

The last thing I needed was to be bothering my fake girlfriend about whatever racket she was making in my kitchen. Still, I went. There, on her tiptoes on top of the counter, trying to reach the highest cupboard shelf stood my tiny fighter. And around her was the biggest mess I'd ever seen.

"What the fuck?" I whispered. Every one of my dishes had been pulled from the shelves, all my spices, all the food.

"I'm going to clean it up," she responded loudly before she hopped and grabbed the bowl, and then landed with skill like she did this all the time.

Fuck. Had I invited this into my home? "Clara," I warned.

"You said I could redecorate a few rooms. This is one. And you said you wouldn't complain about what I did in the kitchen," she quipped, a hand on her hip while I took in the mess. "So, please don't."

The black countertops were cleaned weekly even though I never used them, the dishes always in place, the stainless steel industrial appliances immaculate because, again, they were never used.

Except now flour was everywhere. In her hair. On her face. All over the counters and all the dishes she'd taken out. Probably in the crevices of the tile on the floor.

"What the fuck happened in here?" I started forward, reaching for a bowl just to see what she was working on.

"Ah!" She swatted her cooking utensil at me. "Don't come in here. No taste testing until it's done."

"You let me taste test in your bakery before—"

"This is my ..." She cleared her throat as she glanced away and then continued, "my home kitchen for the time being, and here I will not be critiqued. I need this time and space. I do not need you to toss negative comments about how you don't like something I'm doing right now. I need to relax." She sighed at me and then wrinkled her nose. She was all freckles and red blush after she said it. "It's silly, but I do."

I held up my hands. "Pastry chef's kitchen then."

The smile that flew across her face was worth flour and sugar and egg yolk all over my kitchen if need be. Clara, carefree and happy, was showstopping.

"Come back later." She shrugged like I would be happy when I did.

"Will it still look like this?" I couldn't help but ask.

She narrowed her eyes. "That's a negative thing. You can leave."

She didn't even glance at me for the next five minutes as I stood there watching her stir ingredients. I hated that my mouth watered even as she poured fucking milk on top of flour. There wasn't a single thing I wanted to eat in that kitchen. Well, except her.

My mouth watered for her specifically. "Something's wrong with my resort," I blurted out.

She stopped stirring. "What do you mean?"

"I can't figure it out. I'm racking my brain, and I don't know what."

She glanced around the kitchen. "Something's wrong with my menu. So. I'm making everything and having Paloma try them all." She hesitated to continue.

"What?"

"Maybe you should try that. Have a meeting. You have the best colleagues in the industry around you. Ask for feedback and try everything."

"Clara, that's—"

"Remember you're in the kitchen. No negative feedback," she reminded me.

I nodded and stepped back once and then again and then again. "I trust that you'll clean this up?"

"Obviously. You dragged me into your home, Dominic. But I will make it better, even if you think it's already perfect." She winked at me and went back to stirring.

I left with every doubt in my mind that I wouldn't be happy with what I saw later. Yet, the next day, it was completely cleaned, dishes in different places, more spices on display, small appliances moved, but everything was still functional. Maybe even more so.

She somehow perfected my perfection, and I saw her doing it every day. She'd bring in the mail and put different piles together for me so I didn't have to reorganize them myself.

I saw her planting seeds outside one day, and she even waved enthusiastically. "You'll be smelling beautiful things in no time."

I didn't question her. If I hated them, I could rip them out in a few months, right? My heart beat faster thinking about the fact that in only a few months she'd be gone. She was planting seeds and they were growing roots but she wouldn't be here to water them.

None of this would last. None of it was going to thrive. Not without her.

She stopped my train of thought when she announced, "I have a few changes I sent to Rita and one specifically that I think I need your help on."

I shook my head. "Your changes, Clara. Not mine."

We weren't in a relationship. Her partnership was with Rita. Our boundaries were all muddled, and my mind was too.

I was going to have to learn to be without her soon and I felt the panic of it suddenly, like I had to disentangle myself fast.

"Right, but I really would like your expertise on picking out these flowers for the ceiling." She emphasized by waving her hand full of dirt above her head. The sun shined down on her in my grass, planting a fucking garden, and I think my stress level went through the roof. Suddenly it was fucking hard to breathe.

"Whatever. Fine. Send it to my email." I waved her off and tried to hurry inside. And then I made another idiotic decision by calling a brainstorming meeting with staff to discuss final changes to the resort.

When I walked out of the study and saw her, I couldn't decide if I wanted to fuck her or flee from her.

"Are you okay?"

"Fine," I muttered. "Just fine."

I was not in fact fucking fine.

I was falling in love with my fake girlfriend.

CHAPTER 27: CLARA

I already got the sign hung that week, worked on clarifying menu changes with Rita and the team, and had to fight tooth and nail for Rita to approve my floral decor.

That morning, I almost gave in and called a health professional about the increased pain that I was experiencing. Baking was becoming more and more difficult, and the medications weren't working like they should be since my flare-ups were getting worse. It was not too much longer until the opening, then things would get better.

It should be easy enough, I told myself. But even getting out of bed was pretty difficult actually.

Thankfully, Dominic had informed me he was going in to work early but Callihan would be waiting for me when I was ready. I didn't want to bike to work, so I was happy to take an extra-warm and extra-long shower to help ease all the stiffness. Then, I tried to paste a smile on my face for the day.

I wasn't expecting to walk out and freeze in the living room to stare at a few pictures Dominic must have hung while I'd been asleep. Some were of his family. Some were of his buildings. And a few were of me at the farmer's market. One of us at the club dancing together. Just mixed in. Like I was a part of his life. Like it wasn't a big deal at all.

I tried to tell myself the pictures weren't a big deal, but I stared for far too long before going to work and trying to shake it from my mind. Instead, I mulled over why he'd hung them up while I tried to muscle through my tasks for the day, telling myself over and over I'd be fine.

Paloma waltzed in later and didn't believe me for a second. "You're sick. Go home."

"I'm not." I sighed and flexed my fingers before stirring some of the chocolate into her coffee like I knew she enjoyed.

She snatched it away and did it herself. "Be honest with me. Because you're not honest about half the stuff going on with Dom and you."

"What?" I whispered and she glared before pulling her phone out and reading me the header of a new article. "Heiress Moves in With Hardy Brother."

"Well, that's just not—"

"Clara, I'm sure someone's told you before that you don't lie well."

I sighed and then slumped into the bar stool next to her. "Fine." I practically face planted into the bar as I groaned. "I moved in with him. And it's very stressful but my apartment has a mold problem and I'm dating him and it's gotten very complicated."

"No shit," she grumbled as she patted my back. "So, go home to his mansion and take a sick day."

"I'm not sick," I admitted but I was so tired of keeping secrets. "I mean ... I am. But I always am. Perpetually sick."

"Explain." She narrowed her dark eyes at me and tilted her head so that her bone-straight black hair fell away from her face a little.

How did you explain something you didn't quite believe yet yourself? "So, I was diagnosed with lupus a while ago, and I know it's not as serious as cancer or—"

"Wait, what?"

"What do you mean what?"

"Not as serious as ..." She scoffed. "Who fed you that line of bullshit? This isn't a competition about who hurts more, Clara."

"No. I just mean, I don't want to complain, and I don't want someone to think I can't function or anything, but I'm very tired—"

"Obviously." She frowned at me. "My uncle had lupus, Clara. If you're having a flare-up you need rest. When were you diagnosed?"

"Over a year ago."

"Ah. Not that long then." She said it like that explained everything. "It's hard to accept."

"I've accepted it," I balked.

"Have you? Because some days, you need to rest. And some days you can't be a hundred percent. Even the healthiest people need days off and to monitor—"

"My stress levels. I know. But I also need to get this bakery off the ground."

Paloma hummed. "How long have you and Dom been dating again?"

"I ..." Calculating our fake backstory felt like a lot of work right now. "For a while."

"Right." She said it like she didn't believe me at all. "So, if you guys want people to believe whatever the hell you got going on, you might want to get that story straight."

I sat up and met her gaze and determined something. I needed a friend and Paloma was one of my very closest ones here. "Fine. You know what? Today isn't my day, and I need a shoulder to lean on now. So, you're getting burdened with all my problems."

With that, I blurted out the whole story to her. I swear her smile grew bigger and bigger as I told her every detail.

"God, I think he's really falling in love with you," she said as I finished telling her he put pictures up of me.

"He's not. He barely agreed to meet me at the floral shop tomorrow. But I don't know why I'm on his wall. Maybe he's having guests over?"

She just shook her head and all her dark hair swung back and forth to emphasize her point. "You'll see. Just you wait."

***

Unloading on Paloma gave me a little more optimism. I had a pep in my step and thought I could manage all this still. I went to bed easily and woke up ready for anything.

Dominic was meeting me at the floral shop that morning and, later, he was brainstorming with all of us at the end of the workday. Maybe it was Rita's idea since she'd sent the brainstorming invite, but the idea still made me smile. He was asking for help, taking into consideration that another person's opinion might be helpful. That, alone, should have made for a great start to the day.

Except that good days have a tendency to morph very quickly into no good, very bad days. When I had to wait a whole hour at the floral boutique for him, my hope for the day disintegrated. My blood pressure increased, my calm disappeared, and my fury took a front seat, ready to drive me off the overwhelmed cliff.

I knew he kept staff waiting. I'd seen how he'd acted in meetings too. He'd literally gotten up in the middle of them and mumbled, "We have to reschedule." His disregard for people was infuriating.

And I knew we weren't a couple. I knew he'd slept with me for fun and that was it. It didn't mean I deserved any special treatment but I did deserve the respect of a trusted colleague. Or even an employee. And he hadn't even texted me. Or called. For a whole hour.

I'd worked so hard on this and to be left waiting in the middle of a garden center was quite frankly embarrassing.

"I know you said that Mr. Hardy would be here, but maybe he got held up in another meeting? I have other clients to take care of, but I'm happy to help when you're ready. Feel free to look around."

Me: Are you coming?

Dominic: I won't be. Use discretion and get what you need. I'll let the staff know it should go under my tab.

No apology. No explanation. Just commands. I'd show him discretion all right. I bought what I wanted. And then some. And then some more.

When I got back to my bakery, I was so mad I didn't consider looking at my phone when I answered.

"Clara Milton, are you ignoring your mother?"

I winced immediately, stumbling over my steps as I went to the back kitchen to grab my bag and laptop. "Hi, Mother."

"Don't 'Hi, Mother' me. You haven't called me in weeks, and I know you've spoken to Anastasia, so you could have at least given me the courtesy of a phone call considering you've been all over the news lately."

"Right," I whispered. I didn't have time for this, didn't need it right now. I felt my heart beating faster and faster. "It's a fling with Dominic. New. I'm not sure where it's going to go and—"

"It'd better not be just a fling. Honestly, if that's the case, I really should come and make sure you move this relationship in the right direction." Her voice sounded so beautiful, so nice. I used to believe it as a child. "It's a great opportunity, Clara."

I winced. There it was. My mother's true lifetime goal, to make sure she and her daughters married into wealth and prestige. "I don't plan to marry anyone, Mom. I'm focused on my bakery. It's coming along nicely. And this has been good for me."

"Oh, please." She sighed. "Don't tell me you think this is helping you with your fake disease."

I gnashed my teeth together. "I've been diagnosed, the bloodwork—"

"My God, don't start. And don't tell Dominic about it or anyone. No one wants to be around someone who's complaining all the time about something so ridiculous."

I took a deep breath. "I'm not complaining. I'm in LA to get healthy and actually do something on my own." For some reason, I had to make her understand, maybe because no one was understanding me today.

"Doing it on your own for what?" she asked in that tone I knew meant she was disgusted. "If that's what you're telling him, fine, but—"

"I'm not telling Dominic anything. I just really want to see where this bakery will go here."

"Your sister would never pursue such foolishness when there's a wonderful opportunity for a man right in front of her. Although, I will say those Hardy brothers are unforgiving. I wouldn't be surprised if he's playing you. It's best for you to come home so I can match you up with someone of financial stability or I'll just come to meet with Dom—"

"I don't want you here."

There was silence on the other line. I could practically hear her turning into that monster I was still so scared of. "Oh, really? What is it that you want then, Clara?" Her voice was almost a hiss as she asked.

Freedom. Success. Independence. Health and happiness. I should have said all those things.

I said nothing.

"You'll regret my not coming there to help with this situation. And with your ridiculous bakery. You've never been able to design a single thing let alone a whole place. I'm warning you of that. I really hope I won't have to say I told you so but—"

Maybe I'd taken enough from Dominic that day or I'd been too tired or I was just fed up but I did something I never normally would.

I hung up on my mother, and I didn't feel bad about it one bit.

Then I checked my email, and my blood pressure skyrocketed even more.

From: Rita O'Hara <Rita.Ohara@heatresorts.com>

To: Clara Milton <Clara.Milton@heatresorts.com>

Shipping a new set of dishes for the bakery will incur an exorbitant rush fee and just won't go with the aesthetic. Have you discussed this with Dominic in detail? I suggest that we stick with the dishes already in place. Please confirm you will approve this with Mrs. Johnson by EOD.

Thank you,

Rita O'Hara

Tired didn't begin to describe how I felt going back and forth with her at this point. And maybe I made the wrong choice, but I thought about my mother's words, how she believed my taste wasn't great. I looked around my bakery, and I sort of panicked.

What if it didn't work out? What if I needed more help than I thought? Valentino had given me his number for that specific reason. I dialed it and he answered quicker than I expected. I explained that I was having issues with decor and that I needed him to assist me in dealing with Rita.

He chuckled. "Just let everyone know I'm assisting you, Clara. It will work perfectly."

The man even took his time crafting an email to send her way. I was quite pleased with him taking the reins and handling it.

An hour later, he showed up with a smile on his face and large flower planters being carted in. "Are those for the bakery?"

I couldn't help but smile. Valentino had picked out beautiful, colorful peonies for the entryway and the white stone matched the lobby enough that I didn't think Dominic would balk.

And yet it only took a couple of hours for me to receive a text from Dominic.

Dominic: Why is Valentino claiming to be your assistant?

Me: I apologize. I'll definitely get you up to speed, but he just started.

Dominic: Just started what?

Me: Assisting me with designing the bakery.

Dominic: Rita's a fucking designer, Clara. So am I.

Me: Right, but he knows what I like and does well with Rita.

Dominic: Oh really?

Me: Honestly, he just brought flowers to the bakery, Dominic. They're beautiful.

I didn't hear back. So I started baking while Valentino asked me questions about what dessert I was working on. I was five minutes into stirring the cupcake batter when I turned to see Dominic stalking toward the bakery.

The man didn't look happy at all.

CHAPTER 28: DOMINIC

So, she'd been serious. I really hadn't believed her. What did she need him for?

Didn't she know *I* was the damn designer? I was an architectural engineer. I'd studied at Cornell and had been awarded more than one Pritzker Prize.

I didn't even consider texting back once she said he'd brought her flowers. Instead, I shoved away from my desk and stood. "Let's reschedule this meeting."

No one in the room waited for an excuse or reason because they knew I wouldn't give one. "Of course," Rita chirped, standing with me. "Please, everyone, stay while Mr. Hardy attends to this urgent matter, and I'll work with you all on setting a new date."

I was out of the room before anyone could even say goodbye. I'd never have told them what this urgent matter was. Admitting that my fiery redheaded fake girlfriend, located at the opposite side of the resort, was causing my heart to palpitate wasn't something I was going to do.

I smelled the scent of her and the bakery before I even got there. Sweet, vanilla, sugar and spice. Immediately, my mouth watered, my cock twitched, and my heart lurched in a way it shouldn't. Then I saw her right as I turned the corner. Outside the shop, positioning pink and purple peonies in huge flower pots.

"Clara."

She pivoted around, still bent over the peonies. Her deep-red hair was loose and flowing today, and she hadn't straightened the waves out of it. It fell over her shoulders and landed on her full breasts. That was a perfect indicator that she wasn't wearing anything professional. The sundress dipped low enough that I could barely look at anything else, and even still, her smile looked innocent along with the sparkle in her eyes.

"Peonies, Dominic. Aren't they beautiful? Valentino said he knew exactly the thing that would work here. And he found them so fast. I think the white planters are a nice touch, and they smell so good, don't they?" She clapped her hands together and then looked lovingly down at flowers another man had given her.

The sentence didn't even feel right in my head. Then, Valentino walked up behind her and draped his arm around her shoulders. Instantly, my hands fisted. Even if the man was just acting as a friend, the interaction was overstepping. I hadn't approved him assisting anyone with designing one thing.

Still, Valentino stood tall in a collared white shirt, his maroon pants that hit just above the ankles showcasing that he spent too much time getting ready for this meeting and not enough time in his own damn restaurant. "Mr. Hardy! So good to see you. I hope you don't mind. Clara wanted to brighten the atmosphere and the scent of florals always does that for me. A small but genius trick in designing, no? Rita approved."

Of course she had. He'd probably been fucking her when he asked about it. What did I think of the flowers? They were going in the trash as soon as I could convince Clara of it. "Valentino, we don't want flowers in this walkway as it obstructs the clean view from one end of the resort to the other where there are floor-to-ceiling windows overlooking the ocean."

Valentino immediately looked confused as he glanced back and forth before he snapped his fingers. "We will move them into the bakery."

"The bakery?" I questioned and folded my arms over my chest. "Clara's bakery will be busy. And we're strategically placing as much seating as possible. If anything, we'll hang the flowers from the ceiling so as not to take up space as I believe Clara was already working on."

"Ah, but there's no way to keep flowers alive up there." He tipped Clara's chin up to look at him and it took everything I had not to grab his hand and break every one of his fingers. "These flowerpots are perfect for you, Clara. Let's keep them for now, huh?"

Clara's frown was an indication that she didn't know which way to go or what to do.

"This is your change, Clara?" I asked, waiting for her to stand up here, knowing it wasn't the right move for her or her bakery.

She took a step back like she finally wanted out of this situation. Good, she understood another man helping her in front of me was a bad idea.

"Maybe we should wait on the flowers," she said softly, frowning at Valentino. "Sorry."

"No. You're not sorry. Valentino, we're never sorry about protecting what we've built," I corrected her. "Now, Clara and I have something private we need to discuss. We'll be back soon."

"Great. I'll be here." He looked a little confused, but I didn't wait to explain.

I pulled her through the lobby and down a hall to the elevators. When I saw Paloma waving to us from afar, I stabbed the elevator button and swiped my fob before she could get any closer. I wasn't sharing an elevator with anyone else.

The doors closed, and I turned my gaze on her. "That imbecile has no taste."

"You know that's not true, Dominic."

"Why is he really here?" She sighed and didn't meet my eyes. Fine. My hand immediately went to her neck so I could bring her gaze up to mine as my thumb tipped her chin. "I want your eyes locked on mine when you try to lie this time, little fighter. Make sure you understand what the consequences of lying to your boyfriend will be before you answer."

She bit her lip and then worked it in her mouth. Rock hard was the permanent state of my cock around her but watching that motion had me throbbing, wanting her mouth around me. "I'm sick of your assistant, so I got one too."

"Really?" I lifted a brow.

"Really."

"Liar," I whispered, and then I kissed her hard, rough, and with teeth. I kissed her how I'd wanted to the last few nights I'd been avoiding her. "You lie to me, and I'm going to kiss the lies from your mouth, Clara."

"Is that the only reason you're kissing me?" She frowned and touched her lips.

I took her hand from them so I could taste her again, softer this time, slower, so I could relearn how she tasted. "That and I missed this mouth too much not to kiss it. You taste as sweet as your cupcakes, cupcake."

"I've been literally living with you for—"

"You've been avoiding."

"You've been doing that also," she pointed out, and I couldn't deny it.

When the elevator doors opened, we were greeted by a

curved desk that would seat an administrative manager. The lobby was just a waiting area with luxurious leather seating and tables set up. I pulled Clara past it all as she asked, "Is this more office space?"

"Essentially yes. When we have shareholder meetings or meetings with managers, we'll probably meet here most of the time in the future. The welcome to you all on the beach and in the lobby was purely that, a welcome."

"It was fun." She glanced around as we continued walking. "This is not fun."

"Jesus, woman. Do you enjoy sharing your opinion of my resort?"

She scoffed. "You share your opinion of my bakery. And honestly, you know I never used to share it. You should be happy I do with you."

"Mind sharing why you really wanted Valentino here today?" I wanted the truth. Clara hid what she thought people didn't want to hear. I might have been fake dating her, but I still wanted the real, raw version of her, the one no one else got.

"Maybe we should go back to avoiding each other." She worried her hands in front of me, and I caught one in mine, imploring her to stop. "You stress me out when you pry, Dominic."

"I pry because you don't offer information willingly when you should."

"As opposed to you offering your every thought even if it's negative to everyone around you?"

"I don't offer *every thought*, Clara," I ground out. I kept a lot to myself, probably too much.

She stopped in the hallway, staring at me for a minute before she said, "Give me one example."

"Well, my brothers and sisters think we're actually an item and—"

"You don't tell your brothers and sisters everything like they think you do, do you?"

"I'm the eldest. I'll always have secrets."

Her emerald eyes narrowed. "Can I have one of your secrets?"

"If I can have one of yours," I said softly, leaning against the wall of the hallway, hoping she'd give in.

She sighed and combed her small fingers through her hair before she admitted, "You didn't meet me for our meeting and then my mother called to tell me my bakery was a frivolous decision and that I never really had any design taste. With both of you doing what you did, I started to believe it."

Fuck. I'd forgotten our meeting only because I'd gotten an urgent call. I knew I owed her the explanation, but it hurt to rehash the story. "My turn for a secret?"

She shrugged, her big eyes glassy with unshed emotions welling up. I sighed. "Natya and I did most everything together years ago. I trusted her. Too much. She was partying a lot, coming to work hungover, not doing her job. I'd left my team in her hands for a week while I worked on another build and she'd assigned extra work to a former employee of mine, Susie. She'd been on my team for years, knew the job well and probably had Natya feeling threatened."

"And?" Clara asked softly.

"Susie was supposed to look over blueprints, not go to a site when I was out of town one week, but Natya hadn't paid attention to my notes. She'd been out late the night before and insisted Susie just go to the site." I cleared my throat and combed a hand through my hair, hating to relive the story. "I should have made it more clear. Anyway, Susie tripped and fell on a loose stair, breaking her hip and arm. She pretty much had to learn to walk again. Today, she fell again and her family called."

"Oh, Dominic." There wasn't disgust in her face like there should have been. I'd dropped the ball on my job and wouldn't forgive myself for it. Yet, there was only sympathy in her eyes. "Is she okay?"

I waved off her concern. "Fine. She's better than fine. She runs half marathons still at sixty. They just wanted me to know because I have her on my insurance. I pay those bills and always will. When I heard, I had to stop over there and make sure she was fine."

"You were taking care of someone?" She chewed her lip and then whispered out, "I'm sorry all that happened to you."

"I'm sorry I didn't explain it better in a text but I don't really intend to explain shit to anyone except you."

She chuckled and slumped against the opposite hallway wall. "I wish you would, Dominic. It'd make things a lot easier. I probably would have dealt with my mother better too had I known you weren't just ditching me."

"I'm sure you dealt with that woman the way she deserved."

She groaned. "I hung up on her after she told me she wants me home and dating someone of"—she waved at me—"social and financial wealth if not you. And I'm sure if she does that, I'll be bored, again."

"Again?"

"Most dates I go on, she plans. Minus Noah. And all of the guys are—" Her lips thinned, as if saying her next words would pain her.

"Go on, little fighter."

"Terrible. Most of them have a passion for how they make their money but they always look at me with pure apathy. Probably a lot like ..." She tilted her head and looked at me. "Well, probably like you have in the past."

Her assessment caused a bark of a laugh to jump out of me. "Like me, cupcake? Do you think I look at you with apathy? Or like I want to fuck you against that wall?"

"Dominic," she whispered out. "Okay, well now it's different. And honestly, your mouth is filthy, which is not a good thing considering in a few minutes we have a meeting with colleagues."

"What if your boss wants to be a few minutes late to the meeting?"

"My boss should only care about his resort reopening and I should only care about my bakery. Not screwing around. We need to get our minds out of the gutter."

Was she trying to convince me or herself? "My mind went down the drain the moment your bakery became a part of this resort, and I knew I'd have to see you every day. Let alone date you every day."

"Fake date," she corrected and smiled. "For the good of your sterile resort. Remember?"

I fucking hated that word. Yet, gone was the frown on her face as she smiled so wide, and I thought that I didn't hate it at all. "Clara, stop playing with me. Your fake boyfriend doesn't like shots at his ego right before a meeting where I'm about to ask my employees what's wrong with the resort."

She glanced around with her wide eyes as I hovered over her. "So it's really for that? You want feedback? Because I have it."

"Do you?" I growled, not really giving a shit at this point.

I'd stepped close and could smell some sweet dessert in her hair, something fruity in her lip gloss. All I wanted now was to taste her again. "Tell me then."

Her eyes lit up as she gripped my shirt and pulled me close. "You could add tiny accents of color through the resort. Like all the rooms would have just a hint of blue here and there or gold or whatever color dependent on the floor they were on. Or you could name the sections of the resort and color them that way? Maybe the frames? Or the pictures. Just a tiny hint of something." Then, instead of indulging in making out with me in that hallway, she shot off the wall and bounced with the same excitement she had when she baked.

"You want me to change everything in a few weeks' time?"

"Don't make it sound impossible." She scoffed. "You built this from the ground up, right?"

Getting a compliment from her about this place shot through me like a damn hit of the most addictive drug. "Are you saying you're impressed?"

"And definitely don't make me stroke your ego, Dominic. You get that from everyone." Didn't she know I only wanted it from the people who wouldn't give it to me?

Her. She was the only fucking person.

"Think about it. Different parts are different colors. Like the whole rainbow, Dominic. You wanted balance, right? White and black. But also, the rainbow signifies inclusion and hope and what would ultimately represent peace." She wasn't letting this go.

And my ridiculous ass was listening to her as I turned to open my office door.

She bounced by me and turned her body so she could keep her connection with me as she walked into my office. "The waterpark area could have hints of blue, the dining could have hints of pink and red." I lifted a brow. "Okay, I'm biased to pink and red, but honestly, there wouldn't be that many changes."

"Why would I do that?" I asked her, already contemplating the idea. It was something different. Something that could work well and be achieved if we moved fast. I was under the gun, and I hated that it felt like the thing that was missing in the resort.

"Because it's exactly what the resort needs!" She swung her arms around my office and then hopped up to sit her nice ass on the desk. "Do I look good on this white desk, Dominic?" Her smile was sly as her eyes dipped down to stare at the bulge in my trousers.

"You look good anywhere, Clara."

Maybe she was surprised that I'd answered positively without hesitation, because her mouth opened and shut before she whispered "Thank you" like no man had ever fed her a compliment. I needed to do it more, a lot more. "But think about how I would look on this desk if it were full of color. No one would see me. I wouldn't stand out, right?"

My little fighter didn't really realize, I think, that I was already obsessed with her and her excitement, how her skin turned pink when she started talking a mile a minute, how her eyes twinkled, how she fiddled with her dress like she was right now when she was waiting for affirmation from me. I walked toward her slowly, grabbed her legs and dragged my hands up them roughly, raising the skirt of her dress to find lace underneath. "Clara Milton, don't you know you could be in the middle of a crowd at a concert on the other side of the country, and I'd still find you, baby, because you always stand out."

I kissed her then. Hard. Rough. Much more raw and violent than I had in the elevator. This time, I wanted her to understand that I wasn't at all joking. My body gravitated toward her, was magnetized by her, and would always search for her, find her, and try to consume her. I picked her up and carried her over to my office door where I slammed it shut and pushed her back against it.

I looked at her with anything but apathy while I rubbed my cock over her entrance, and her hands gripped my shirt, shoving me back for a second. "You're distracting me, but I won't be deterred, Dominic Hardy. This is a good idea."

"Good enough idea that you shared it with your other designer?" I asked her before I lowered my head and kissed my way to the edge of her dress. I pushed the fabric to the side so I could graze my teeth over her nipple.

She gasped and her hands flew into my hair as she arched toward me. Then, she yanked my hair so she could bring me up to her face where she could take her turn devouring my lips, her hips wiggling fast over my cock. "He's just Valentino, Dominic."

"No. He's just the guy you wanted to date not too long ago."

She didn't deny it. "He's also a guy that wants what's best for the resort." Then she sucked on my bottom lip, nipped it, and dragged her teeth across it. The pain shot through me as pleasure, right down to my cock that twitched against her pussy.

"Careful, cupcake. You bite me, and I'm going to bite back."

Breathing faster, her hands were at my belt buckle. "Do it then."

She never ever backed down from a challenge with me. Others, she'd let them walk all over her, but I swear she wanted to test her limits with me, like I was the one she trusted, like I was getting a special treatment and my cock rejoiced in it. I sucked on her neck and then her tits as her delicate fingers wrapped around my length, stroking up and down, up and down. “God, I want this,” she murmured as her thumb rolled over my tip, spreading my pre-cum around.

Just then, my phone rang, and Clara’s phone beeped.

We both glanced at the time. “Shit. The meeting’s in ten minutes.” She shoved me back and I let her do so as I picked up my phone.

“Sir, we’re calling to verify that you made a purchase for $216,700.64 today at Divine Floral Arrangements. And $286,801.10 online at La Cornue. If you cannot confirm it or it is fraudulent, we can cancel the transactions.”

“For $216K and $286K?” I said the numbers slowly as I dragged my eyes over to hers. They were wide, vivid green, and had a hint of a spark. A fight in them. “No, it’s not fraud. That’s just my future wife throwing a tantrum. Go ahead and run the bills through,” I grumbled and clicked off the phone.

Fuck me, was she trying to drive me to the edge? I knew something was wrong with me because even as my heart beat faster in fury, I allowed for it. I was even smiling about it, enjoying that she had the balls to do it.

I should have been thinking she wasn’t equipped to run a bakery or have any responsibility within my business whatsoever, and yet I was on the verge of letting her keep the credit card if she wanted it.

I slid my phone back into my trousers and took two steps toward her. She took two steps back. “Clara.”

“Yes?” I heard how that rasp in her voice trembled and, fuck, I wasn’t prepared to deal with reprimanding her as her boss either because my cock instantly reacted.

“Please tell me there’s an error on my credit card with the florist and La Cornue.”

“Oh, I’m not sure, Dom,” she hummed.

"Don't call me that."

"Everyone calls you that or Mr. Hardy."

"You're not everyone. You're my future wife, remember? You're the girl who gets to spend over a half a mil on fucking flowers. So, use the name you always do when you're talking to your future husband, or I'll punish you for that too." My voice was low, vicious, and held a warning.

"No need to punish me when I'm just doing what you told me to do. The florists were very helpful in going over what they believed to be the best showcase of luxury to be hanging from the ceiling. I explained how I originally wanted pink-and-white blown glass twisting out from the corners of the bakery, too, giving a light, decadent Parisian feel. And they actually had a contact for that along with a contact for a La Cornue range."

"So, is over a half a mil for the flowers, kitchen appliances, or blown glass? What are they? Encrusted in gold?"

"Well, actually, I know how much you hate color, so most of it is silver and diamonds within the lace that will be woven through the real flowers once a week for the first year along with my pink blown glass, of course. The bakery will smell delightful and also sparkle from above. As for the appliances, a La Cornue oven is a piece of art."

"Are you out of your fucking mind?"

"You don't like the idea?" She feigned shock. "I'm sorry, Dominic. I was just trying to make sure we showcased the elegance of the hotel, married our tastes, and, well, you weren't there so ..."

"That's what this is about? That I didn't show up to help? I just said before I had that urgent matter—"

"Okay, in my defense, you didn't text me that when I was there. You just said to handle it." She shot back. "And, sorry, but that's rude to not give me a reason while I'm waiting, okay?"

"So what you're saying is because someone was rude to you, you're not competent enough to know how to pick out some—"

"Of course I'm competent enough, you asshole." There she was. I knew it was coming. Her claws came out fast and without hesitation, just the way I liked her to approach me. "I just don't like to wait a whole fucking hour with no explanation. I'm literally there twirling my thumbs apologizing for you. Like I'm some afterthought and like my bakery doesn't matter. It might not matter to you or most people here or to my mother or—"

"I'm not your fucking mother or anyone else, Clara. I've spent more time on your bakery than any other space in this resort. You know that?" I bellowed. "And I listen to your ideas more than I would anyone else's. I respect the hell out of your opinion. That should go without saying."

She gasped at my confession and then chewed her bottom lip like she didn't know what to say. "Do you mean that?"

"Of course I mean it." I threw my hands up and paced away from her before I paced back. "We have a meeting in two minutes, otherwise I'd fuck some sense into you, honestly. After it though, I expect your ass back in my office so I can teach you a lesson about spending outrageous amounts of money."

She smiled. "You know, Dominic? I'd probably rather not. We got done what we needed to accomplish for the day. I might need a nap after spending all that money."

I clenched my teeth to keep from laughing at her as she started to walk by me. Instead, I smacked her ass hard and then grabbed it to stop her so I could lean in and whisper, "If you don't come to my office after this meeting, I will punish you, Clara."

She rolled her eyes. "You wouldn't know how."

"That so? How about stalling your side of the resort opening so I can fuck you into oblivion during the time you have off?"

She gasped. I knew our marketing team had been doing social media pushes, that there were viral posts and people excited to see her pink bakery. It was a genius marketing ploy, I had to admit, but I'd only admit it to myself. "You wouldn't."

There. She finally sounded scared.

"Be here when the meeting's over. We'll take into account your frivolous behavior then."

CHAPTER 29: CLARA

Having Dominic Hardy warn me of my punishment after a meeting meant that literally anything in that meeting wasn't going to hold my attention.

I tried. I really did.

He was talking about what I'd mentioned to him, changing the colors of different parts of the resort. Everyone was scribbling notes, and I was doodling swirls on a notepad because I couldn't concentrate on a word anyone was saying.

I'd totally reacted wrong to not getting a text from him earlier that day, especially after he shared with me why. It made sense, too. He was a perfectionist in everything he did and didn't trust anyone else to do it because he'd been burned. I saw how he protected those he cared about and was realizing when he failed to do that, he held himself more accountable than anyone else would.

And now I wondered, had I pushed him too far with spending his money? I told the florist we would most likely be changing a few things but now I couldn't stop the adrenaline, the fear, and the excitement of what he would do to me after this.

"Well, that's a lot of changes in the last two weeks, right?" Rita's voice sounded high-pitched and a bit stressed, actually. Dominic's changes would have everyone working hard, but the buzz in the room seemed to point to them all agreeing with it.

"If there're no questions, I've got a little pick-me-up for you all. Dominic catered in lunch with dessert."

The announcement was followed by wait staff dressed in white and black, like always, walking in with silver trays of food. The small lunch sandwiches had flaky crescent buns and an herbed spread over either egg and ham or a vegetarian option.

My eyes locked on that food, heat rising to my cheeks. Paloma glanced over at me while most people dug in and mumbled a thank you to Dominic. No one questioned where the food had come from, but I knew right away it was a small restaurant down the street. She must have sensed my irritation because she grabbed my hand before she chewed her cheek and then mouthed a sorry before she took a tepid bite.

Could I be completely and utterly disrespectful and refuse to eat this? He'd catered in food and then after we ate that, little brownies from a bakery down the street were brought in.

Brownies I could have made. It would have been a perfect opportunity to show Valentino and the other restaurant owners that my desserts had the potential to be an option on their menus.

Instead, he'd asked an outside restaurant he didn't even care about. I lived with the man. Was about to screw him in a hallway. Normally, I would have been excited to try anything that smelled this good, but I really just wanted to shove his face in it.

When I glanced at him, he was looking at his stupid phone, taking a bite of the brownie I should have had the opportunity to make.

I heaved a sigh and stared back down at the food. The scent of it danced in the air, and I could appreciate the caramel and chocolate smell. I took my first bite and had to practically hold back a moan. My phone vibrated on the table, and I snatched it up.

Dominic: Licking your lips like that in my meeting is going to get you in trouble, little fighter.

I narrowed my eyes. Didn't he know how mad I was right now? Even if I was enjoying this dessert.

Me: Why? I'm not hurting anyone.

Dominic: No but having three men on my team watch you eat is going to get them hurt by proxy. So, knock it off.

Me: You ordered the food, not me. If I had, I know where I would have ordered it from.

Dominic: You're mad I didn't order from you?

Instead of answering, I took a big bite and made sure to lick my fingers clean after, moaning for extra effect. Valentino next to me shifted in his seat and then leaned over to whisper that the food was really good, wasn't it?

I hadn't actually believed that anyone was watching but I laughed and nodded uncomfortably before setting my brownie down immediately. I really was only trying to grate on Dominic's nerves.

Dominic: See? That moaning should only be for me. Forget my office. Just stay here once the meeting is over.

Me: Not a good idea. I'm not sure I can handle being alone in a room with you when you've so rudely ordered another person's food. I might demand you get on your knees and apologize.

It was only supposed to be a joke. I saw the way his jaw flexed, how the muscles in his neck tightened before his phone clattered down onto the conference table. "Meeting's over. I have an urgent matter that needs to be attended to."

The only person that stopped to question him was Rita. "Dom, I actually have some sketches we should glance over quickly."

Her eyes were on me, though, waiting for me to move out of the room. I didn't want the attention, nor did I want people catching on to the fact that Dominic and I had once or twice had relations in the resort. I stood, but Dominic grabbed my wrist and glared at Rita. "Not right now. Send it to my email."

"Well, then, Clara, let's go." The woman was bold even as she saw his hand on me.

"No, you." He looked at me with fire in his eyes. "You sit down. You're staying here in this conference room with me. Rita, you're dismissed."

I knew she left the room because I heard the door slam much harder than necessary. "Could you be any more blatant by demanding I'm to stay here?"

"If you want me to. I can make sure to leave the windows

transparent when I get on my knees in front of you. I won't be gentle when I apologize though. Expect that the lace is going to be ripped off of you."

"Don't be ridiculous, Dominic," I said, but my voice was breathy, and I knew I was blushing as my eyes flicked over to the windows overlooking the hallway. Our colleagues were still out there, talking and mingling.

"You worried they'll see how I can make you come, baby?"

My body reacted to his words, even if I knew it was wrong. We were in the workplace, in broad daylight, with literal eyes on us. He pressed a button that dimmed the windows a little, but I still saw their faces, still saw their bodies.

"Sit down on the table and spread your legs, Clara," he commanded.

"Honestly, my text was a joke." It wasn't. I licked my lips, and he took the back of his pen to drag it down my arm where even that touch caused goose bumps to rise on my skin.

"You don't joke about your food, love. I was trying to give you time off, not hurt you." He brushed the back of his large knuckles across my cheek.

"My feelings aren't hurt," I whispered, but they were. I needed recognition in this industry, to feel a part of the team. "I want to prove myself, and I missed the opportunity."

"To whom?"

"The team. The chefs. They think I'm where I am because of my stepdad and you."

"So, someone gave you a chance? People either make the best of opportunities or squander them, and you've been proving yourself since the day you got here."

I wasn't taking his logical train of thought right now. "Well, whatever. Like I said, the text was a joke."

"Your text was bait, and I'm taking it." He grabbed my hips and hoisted me onto the conference table.

My eyes widened and my head snapped to where everyone outside was talking. I heard someone laughing, and it felt like Valentino's eyes were on me.

"Everyone is still outside. They can see—"

"You can see them, cupcake. They can't see you ... unless you want them to." He questioned as my breath hitched where his hand dipped into the lace. He hummed. "Ah, I see. My girl likes to give a show then. Like a little bit of risk, Clara?"

I shook my head fast no, but I knew my body gave a different answer. I'd never been into exhibitionism, but with Dominic it felt forbidden and dangerous. It felt like I could have him spiral out of control much like I was. I wanted it but knew we couldn't do it.

Before I answered him, he leaned in and whispered, "I'm not giving them a line of sight to the pussy that's mine today, baby. Today, I'm selfish." His hands massaged my thighs so close to my sex under my dress, strong and rough like he knew exactly what I wanted.

When he ripped the lace from my pussy, I gasped. Valentino's face frowned at the door. He and Rita were still out there, discussing something. I bit my lip, knowing I had to be quieter.

"Don't bother wearing these to work anymore. It's not necessary when I'm going to ruin them. Now, how would you like your apology?"

"H-how?" My mind scattered in all different directions, my body on such high alert that his question caught me off guard.

I was losing the battle of resisting him when he was this close, his smell all around me, the length of him now pressing against my pussy as he stepped between my legs to murmur, "Want me to fuck the anger out of you or get on my knees to show you how much I like your food better? I'll do either."

"This ... I don't think this is helping further the resort plan, Dominic. We shouldn't be doing this here." My heart galloped at too fast of a speed. Dominic Hardy should have been the man I was staying away from. Yet, he pushed me to see my full potential, aggravated the confidence out of me, and made me express every emotion. No man fought for success as hard as him, no one commanded a room like him, no one earned respect like him, and no one touched me like him.

His sharp and intense stare felt dangerous and hot on my skin. "Are you sure? I seem to recall that you went to Valentino for advice about your bakery today instead of me. Maybe I need to establish that I know what's best for you and your bakery, not some random dumbass."

"He's not random. You chose him and his brand from millions."

"And I'm also inclined to choose to fire him if he comes near my girl again."

"Don't be ridiculous." I shoved him angrily and then tried to wiggle backward on the conference table away from him, but his hands clamped down on my thighs and yanked me back so I was directly up against his hard length. "So one guy is helping me out while you have countless women happily helping you, including Rita. Maybe you and her can—"

His hand tightened. "You think my cock gets rock solid like this for anyone else, little fighter?" he grumbled, completely serious. "You're driving me crazy spending my money, changing up my resort plans, walking around in these dresses that dance and sway with bright-ass colors that don't belong anywhere in my damn presence."

"You like the colors. It's why you're implementing my idea," I shot back as his head dropped down to suck on my neck.

"I hate them, but I like you." He thrust his cock against my clit, and I breathed out his name, not able to control myself even as both Rita and Valentino looked at the door this time. Dominic didn't stop. He actually chuckled as he felt my body tense, and then he bit and kissed on my neck.

I whisper-yelled at him, "Don't leave marks, Dominic. I don't have a sweater to cover them up."

The voice that left his body was deep and gravelly, almost near a growl full of frustration. "You didn't answer my question before, little fighter. Am I fucking you or tasting you?"

Feeling the indent of his trousers had me wanting his cock sliding into me more than anything, but I still hesitated even as my hips moved up and down against him as his tongue and mouth expertly moved over my sensitive skin. "I think I deserve both," I blurted out, my mouth obviously having no shame as I watched two of our colleagues frowning with disapproval at the door. Immediately, I followed up with, "Sorry. No. We shouldn't—"

I didn't finish the sentence. His hand sliced up my skirt to feel my pussy, soaking wet.

I fell back on my hands to watch Dominic Hardy become the man everyone knew him to be.

Determined.

Effective.

Brilliant.

And a master at everything he put his mind to. That included him getting on his knees before me and lifting my skirt. He dragged one finger up my thigh as he set about ravaging my pussy. He took his time. "Legs wider, baby. I always want full access to what's mine."

"Not yours really." But I totally spread them anyway.

He rubbed his hand back and forth across his jaw. "Might be fake dating, baby, but this pussy is mine for real."

With that, he didn't hesitate in descending on me again like the ruthless man he was. He devoured me, unrelenting as he rolled my clit between his fingers and thrust his tongue deep inside me. He didn't want to take his time here. He wanted to establish that he could unravel me within seconds. His eyes were determined as he held my gaze, one hand gripping my hip so hard I knew there would be bruises later. My fingers dug into his hair, wanting it just as badly before I went over the edge.

My breath came faster and faster. And I know Valentino and Rita couldn't see me, I knew they had no idea of my position, but there was no way my breathing was quiet enough. How her jaw dropped and then snapped up before she licked her lips and straightened her jacket before she walked off in a huff was a clear indicator they knew exactly what we were doing. I couldn't be bothered by the fact that Valentino stayed just a second longer, his jaw tensing. All I could do was try my best not to scream.

Right before I did, though, Dominic's hand was on my throat, squeezing it so tight I couldn't make a sound. I orgasmed over his tongue silently and then he let go as he came up to kiss my mouth, my sex and his saliva mingled together with mine. The taste was all-consuming, like we'd mixed all our emotions up with our desires and our frustrations and somehow found a raw pleasure in them.

He went to my ear and said, "No one gets to hear the sound of you coming on my mouth but me, little fighter. Not unless we agree otherwise."

My eyes flicked to where Valentino had been standing, but he was gone now. I guess they could wonder, but no one could confirm for sure now whether I'd been letting our boss eat me out in the conference room.

"Jesus, Dominic, we can't do that here ever again." I shook my head as my mind started to clear, but he had the audacity to press his thumb into my swollen clit.

"That so?"

I whimpered, locking eyes with his hungry green ones. "Dominic, enough. Your apology was more than acceptable. And I couldn't come again if I tried—"

"You're not trying. I am. And I don't try. I just do. Now, lie back, baby. Let your boss give you another one. This time, scream as loud as you want."

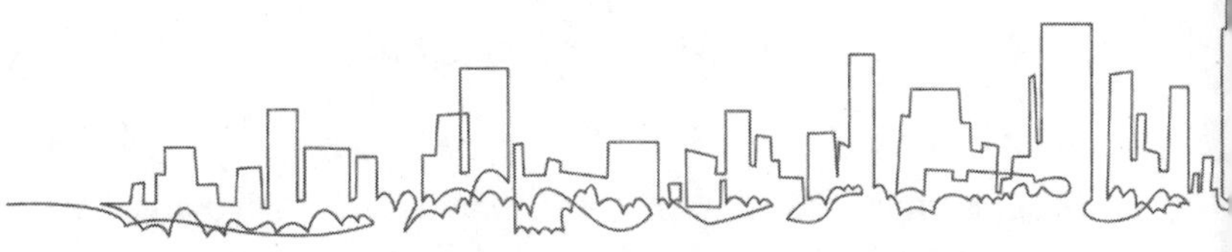

CHAPTER 30: DOMINIC

She screamed my name over and over before whimpering that she didn't care where we were at this point, she just wanted me to fuck her.

I almost did.

I was that close.

Yet, I'd wanted her all night and that meant we had to go the fuck home.

Plus, I'd seen the way Valentino had looked at her in that meeting, how he'd waited to hear her outside the fucking doors. Knowing she'd hired him to help her had me seeing red all over again.

And she'd also spent over half a million of my money. Not that it was worth shit to me. But the point was I could deliver her punishment better at home. She needed to understand that this was a real relationship, and I was really never going to let her walk all over me.

Fuck. That was a lie.

I would in fact let her do whatever the hell she wanted. Still, reddening her ass was going to give me a sick amount of pleasure.

The ride home was quiet. I don't know if she was thinking about me eating her out in the resort, like we both knew I shouldn't have, or if she was thinking about what would happen when we got home.

As we walked through the entrance, she took her shoes off

quietly, and her cats weaved their way through our legs before disappearing back into my study. She hadn't turned around to face me yet, and I was surprised that she actually started to walk to her room without so much as a good night.

Did she think we were done? "Clara, you realize we still need to discuss your purchases and your hiring of an assistant today?"

"I ..." She narrowed her eyes, and the angry fire behind her concern and embarrassment of the night ignited. "We already discussed that."

I shook my head slowly. "No. Go ahead and change, but be back out here in a minute to finish the discussion." I waved her forward and saw her jaw set before she spun on a heel and stomped to her room. The door slammed not a second later, and then she was gone for a good while.

She took her time, made me wait. More than twenty minutes.

And then she met me in the kitchen with a languid walk of hers wearing a sleep shirt that was deep red. She was basically waving that color in front of a bull. She wanted a fight, and I was about to give her one.

"You're twenty minutes late," I pointed out, trying to hold onto my anger. Most people didn't make me wait.

She shrugged. "If we're discussing our meeting this afternoon, then tit for tat."

I hummed. "Does that mean you're going to pay me back the half a mil you spent today?"

"It's for the good of your resort." She lifted her chin like she would never say she was wrong. I enjoyed that about her, how she didn't cower from me like most would.

"What about for the good of your bakery? You think your

bakery deserves it over Valentino's restaurant."

She didn't answer immediately. Instead, she folded her elegant little fingers together and clenched them tight enough that I figured she was imagining strangling me. Maybe she'd even try it by the time this conversation was over.

"My bakery is close to the lobby. It needs to make a statement. Plus, my desserts are near perfection, which means the interior of my bakery should be also."

"Confident tonight, huh?" I sat down and waved her forward. "Bake the best for me then."

"I ..." Her mouth snapped shut. "You know what? Fine."

She didn't even hesitate. She pulled ingredients from the cupboards, turned on the convection oven, and was mixing a batter within minutes. I watched her in awe and silence. I loved that here I got to see her without makeup, without the mask of the pushover she pretended to be for everyone. Here she was a masterpiece no one could replicate.

She could have fed me shit that night and I would have enjoyed every single bite of it because she baked with love and the tension in the air filled those cupcakes.

They'd taste like sex to me, I knew it. Mouthwatering, decadent sex. They'd be just as divine as she was.

When she set the timer and slid them in the oven, she finally locked eyes with me. "You know, if we're going to fight about this floral arrangement, you should know that you can just change it to fit what's best for you."

I hummed. I didn't want her to back down. I didn't want to see the fire in her eyes dim at all. I wanted to push her to make her see her full potential. She deserved everything she wanted as long as she was proud enough to stand up for it. "Remember that bridge I built? You know they didn't agree to it at first?"

"Okay." She dragged out the word.

"I might be your boss, but you're the artist. The customer doesn't tell an artist what they want. Nor does a boss. You're the artist. You're the expert."

She pursed her lips and my eyes dipped to them. Something charged both of us in that kitchen right then. Her pushing back, fighting me on my ideas of what was right versus wrong. "So, you're saying the flowers were my choice?" She scoffed. "You're obviously angry about it and honestly, I don't agree. What about when there's so many requests for something new that you have to bend to the will of who you're selling to?"

I tsked. "Still your choice when you bend or if you don't. Either way, we own our choices, and our art. We make the decisions. Not them. Don't be a pushover when it comes to your art. Own it."

She shook her head at me. "And what? Just own that you'll like it when it's installed?"

"Yes."

"Even if I own that the floral arrangement is perfect for my bakery, it seems someone"—she pointed to me—"is going to be mad." As she said it, her gaze trailed up and down my body as I got up to walk toward her. Before I did, I took off my suit jacket and unbuttoned the top of my white shirt before I rolled up my sleeves.

We let silence fill the air before I walked over to her, caged her into the island countertop and said, "You realize that a customer or a boss will always listen to you when you're confident that you're right, Clara? That they'll actually reward you for steering them in the right direction?"

We were so close to one another now that she only had to whisper out, "You can't possibly think what you're saying is true.

Haven't you heard the phrase 'the customer is always right?'"

"Of course, little fighter. It's for those who aren't willing to work to prove their idea was perfect. Want to test my theory?"

"I want to prove it wrong, if that's what you're asking." Her breath trembled as she exhaled, looking up at me with eyes that were confused but also knowing.

She knew I was going to punish her or fuck her. She probably wasn't sure which. I wasn't either. But I wanted to see which way the night would go. I deserved that with her after the day we'd had.

"Good. I've missed my fake girlfriend while she took her time coming to talk with me about her frivolous tantrum today. And she's wearing a sleep shirt that makes me want to feel what's under it. Care to be my client?"

My little fighter didn't fight at all. Our bodies were pulled to each other now, no use resisting it. I wanted to fuck her, and I knew she'd let me. Still, she shrugged like she wasn't that interested and turned to the beeping oven. She'd only made a few cupcakes, and the convection oven cooked them quickly.

She pulled them out and set them in the freezer, then she grabbed the whipped cream and the poppy petals she'd made earlier from the fridge. After a few minutes, she pulled them out and I let her delicately assemble her presentation.

"You be the client first." She handed me the cupcake. "I've updated the recipe. Tell me if they aren't worthy."

We stared at each other as I took one bite, and it was like my body surged to life tasting it. My dick hardened, my blood rushed, my taste buds practically sang her praises. She knew she had me. "They'll fit the bakery," I confirmed.

"And?" She pushed me to continue.

"And they taste as good as your pussy." I let the compliment fly. "Happy?"

She smirked and blushed at the same time. "I'll take that from you."

"Now, my turn."

She rolled her eyes like she wasn't at all interested, but that was fine. I was going to make her beg anyway. She wanted to try to prove that the customer was always right. That wasn't the case here.

I lifted her onto the island counter and then I glided my hand over her body, up to her neck, to push her back down onto the counter slowly. She went willingly and let me lift her sleep shirt inch by inch. Immediately, I realized she'd left her underwear off and I brushed my hand over her sex. "Look how you listen when I tell you something while I'm playing with your pussy. I should do that more often, it seems. Maybe you won't fight me as much."

"Please be quiet," she ground out, but her hips rocked back and forth over my fingers, her arousal coating me. "Just— I want you, Dominic."

I knew she did. She'd begged me at the office, and her pussy didn't forget that so easily. My dick didn't either, but even still, I took my time as I kissed her smooth stomach, then her ribs, then I focused my efforts on her nipples, biting them just the way she liked.

Her hands were in my hair as she tried to hurry me along, but I was taking my time here. I was proving a point. Maybe to her and maybe to myself. My cock strained against my trousers, but I didn't undo the belt. I let her pussy soak my fingers instead.

"Dominic, I'm not kidding. Please, I want you."

"Exactly what do you want now?"

"I want you to fuck me." She said it fast, but I shook my

head slow.

"Wrong. You see, I'm the artist and the expert here, baby." I knelt down in front of her. "You want to feel what you do to me first, and then you want me to eat that pretty pussy. That's what you want. And I'm going to show you. Spread your legs."

She didn't hesitate, and I realized my house had been imperfect before. Her on my island is what the house needed. She was the missing piece. I had her spread out on my granite counter, every goddamn topping of food I could want scattered around her, and I was going to use it to my advantage.

I took the whipped cream and spread it onto her pussy. She gasped at the sensation, cool sugar coating my favorite fucking dessert. Clara's pussy was going to taste good tonight. I took a petal from one of the cupcakes and dragged it over her stomach before I licked my way down to it and let it melt in my mouth. When I moaned over her skin, she trembled.

Then, I took my time sucking the whip cream from her clit, savoring the flavor of how she wanted me with the sweetness of the dessert.

"Sweetest dessert I'll ever have, Clara. I don't want to eat anything of yours but this pussy."

I tasted her long after I'd licked her clean. I felt her body clench as she moaned and screamed my name more than once. And even when she thought we were done, when her body tried to relax, I took more from her. "Not done, baby. Far from done. Ride my face, pretty girl." She whimpered she didn't know if she could anymore. I smacked the side of her ass. "Oh, you're going to. Right here, right now." I pulled her closer to the edge of the counter. "Ride it hard and rough just how *you* want."

I winked at her, and her eyes narrowed, but her jaw set as she lowered her pussy onto my mouth. I yanked her even closer as I sucked that clit hard. I was telling her just what she wanted and, God, her body agreed with me.

The next orgasm had her convulsing around me, her back arching as she begged over and over for something she didn't even know she wanted. When she tried to pull me off, I smacked the side of her ass again. "Have I not taught you? I know what you want better than you know yourself."

By that point, though, I was drawn to the reddening of her side. I flipped her over and murmured, "How many times should I redden this ass to prove a point and make you see, baby?"

She wiggled against the cool countertop, but she didn't move. If anything, her ass arched out further. "Make me see what?"

"Make you see that you're an artist." I smacked her once and she gasped. "That you need to own what you do." I smacked that cheek again. "That I believe in it. And that spending any of my money for your vision is not only condoned but necessary. Want to know why?"

She whimpered, "Why?" as I smoothed my hand over her.

"Because you're mine, and I only claim perfection. Beautiful imperfect perfection."

I let my hand drift between her thighs and found her arousal dripping down the sides of both of them. "God damn you're wet, baby. You like when your boss punishes you, don't you?"

Without a second thought, she breathed out yes over and over.

My finger slid into her without much resistance at all. "Look how you take me. Your pussy loves it. You think it would redden if I smacked it, too, baby? Pink to red, just like your bakery?"

I'd never see it the same now. Not as I delivered two small slaps to her sex and watched it darken as it glistened with her slickness.

She was crying, begging, moaning for me to fuck her. Instead, I thrust another finger in her and commanded, "Come, pretty girl. Show me you liked your punishment." She screamed my name and my cock strained against my trousers. "Fuck, cupcake. You scream for your fake boyfriend like you want him to be real. Such a damn good girl."

I started to kneel before her to taste her again, but the vibration on the counter had her tensing before she reached over and tipped the phone to see before she said softly, "Your ex is calling."

No one was ruining this moment. "Ignore it."

She shook her head and hopped off the counter so she could pull her sleep shirt back down and take a deep breath, like she was trying to center herself after her orgasm. Then she turned around and hopped back on it so she could look me in the eyes probably to study how I reacted, "No. You said you always ignore her. Answer her instead."

And then Clara did what I wasn't expecting. She pressed the green button and answered the call herself. "Hello?"

My eyes widened as she chewed her lip.

"Yes, he's in his study. Can I ask why you're calling?"

More silence.

"I'm aware of who you are. Are you aware of who I am?" She asked it nicely enough and there wasn't fear there. Natya wanted fear and I was proud Clara wouldn't give it to her.

"Right. Well, now you know it's serious and the reason you don't get a hold of him is because he's quite busy."

She tipped her head and listened, but her hand went to undo my trousers and then grabbed my cock. She rubbed it up and down. Up and down. And when I shook my head at her, trying to explain this wasn't the time, she murmured, "An artist knows. I'm just owning it."

Then she turned the phone back to her. "He's here. You can definitely talk to him about coming to the reopening."

As she handed the phone over, I growled at her, narrowing my eyes. "You want to play?"

"Maybe. I want to fight."

CHAPTER 31: CLARA

No one owned me but that man in that kitchen at that moment. I was his and his alone. This wasn't fake. This was real. And my heart was ready to fight anyone for it. I wanted him to see that.

I lifted my legs, moved to the middle of the island counter, and spun around to lay on my back. Then I hung my head from the side of the island.

"Clara," he said cautiously even though his eyes looked hungry as they took me in, lying there upside down on that counter. He was supposed to be listening to his ex on the phone, not whispering to me, "What are you doing?"

"What I'm sure my boyfriend is going to enjoy." I reached my hand out to pull his cock near my mouth and murmured up at him. "You trust the artist, Dominic?"

He growled and breathed out hard before his hands were pulling at my shirt as he held the phone between his shoulder and his ear. He whispered back, "The question is, do you trust me?"

I bit my lip and stared at his thick length that I held in my hand, so massive I knew I'd choke on it if I didn't relax, if he didn't slide into my mouth and throat at just the right angle as he worked my body.

"Baby, you have to say you trust me."

I took two breaths before I nodded and then I pulled him forward. I heard Natya muttering something on the phone. I knew she was there. I knew deep down maybe she always would be there, a barrier between us, but I wanted to have him now, even while she tried to get him back. I wanted to be the first woman on his mind now because I knew I wouldn't be first in the future.

He groaned and then swore over and over. The phone clattered to the counter as his hands gripped my breasts hard. Natya's voice was near my ear. "Are you listening, Dom? You know you won't last with her. I need you back."

His cock slid further into my throat and one of his hands slid down my stomach to pinch my clit, to pull it, to work in rhythm with how he fucked my mouth. Deeper and deeper he went to the back of my throat, slow at first, and then faster, more erratic.

"I'm going to make you taste every part of me, baby. No one is ever going to fuck your pretty mouth the way I do. You understand?"

I hummed in approval.

"That's right, cupcake. Take it all. Take every fucking drop of me." I swirled my tongue over the head of him, tasted the salty cum that built up right before he thrust hard, so hard my eyes watered as he came down my throat. I came with him as he pinched a nipple and thrust one large finger in me, curling it fast with his release.

One of us should have been hanging up on Natya or worrying about the fact that we'd both come over the phone for his ex to hear. Yet, neither of us seemed to care as he pulled away from me but reappeared almost immediately to wipe a warm damp towel over my sex. Then, he asked, "Need anything before bed?"

I bit my lip and started to sit up from the counter as I glanced around. "Have another cupcake before we go to sleep?"

"Don't want one." He shook his head and I frowned.

"Are you kidding me? You loved these the first time you tried them, and you just said they would do in the bakery."

Dominic glanced at a jar over in the corner of the kitchen and had the audacity to walk over to it, open the lid, and pop a chocolate *I had not made* into his mouth.

Motherfucker. My jaw actually dropped before I stomped over to snatch the jar and grab a chocolate for myself. "What's so good about these? You told me you don't like chocolate."

"No. I said I don't like to indulge in it. There's a difference."

I popped one in my mouth and chewed it. Then I turned to spit it out into the sink. "These are terrible."

"Pretty much abominable," he confirmed.

"Why would you eat these over everything I've offered you?"

"I'm already addicted to your pussy, baby. It's the best dessert you offer. I don't need to be addicted to anything else."

I rolled my eyes. He chuckled and scooped me up like a baby. "Come on, little fighter. You're sleeping in my bed."

I shook my head, laughing at how ridiculous he was, but my gaze landed on the wall of pictures he'd put up just a few days ago and I blurted out, "Why are those pictures there? Are you having guests over because if so—"

"I just wanted pictures up of people I care about."

I think I lost my heart there. Lost it all to him. "But I'm up there."

"Yes. Well, I think I might care about you most."

Nothing should have been intimate with my fake boyfriend. We should have gone to our own separate beds and forgotten about the sex we'd had that day. But his words and his actions imprinted themselves on my heart. Those pictures on his wall were in color.

Bold.

Beautiful.

Devastating color.

He would have told me just weeks ago a picture of color on his walls would have marred his whole home. Now, they hung there like a statement piece. My heart was fueled by it, consumed by it, and probably hypnotized by it.

From that point forth, he'd become my real boyfriend. I couldn't help it. I made him breakfast, hung out with him through the day, laid in his study while he worked in the evening. We laughed. We discussed the resort. We made changes together. It felt real. It felt good. It felt like a space I wanted to be in for the rest of my life. There and in his bed. It's where I slept every night until the reopening of the resort.

CHAPTER 32: CLARA

Just a week until the opening, I got the call that the flowers were being installed in the ceiling of the bakery along with the Sugar and Spice Bakery sign.

Standing there and seeing it happen was supposed to be a happy moment. I stood on my own and watched them work since Dominic had a meeting and Paloma was at her store.

Without anyone by my side, I took it in. The sunlight on the bright-white curves of the lettering popped against the black backdrop. They'd woven small red, orange, and pink poppies through the last couple of letters, accenting it perfectly.

As more and more flowers threaded with lace were carted in and a crew stood on ladders to position everything correctly, I tried to hold back the stinging behind my eyes, especially when it was all done and one man came up to me to say he thought it turned out beautifully.

I offered all the workers poppy cupcakes, and they gushed over the unique recipe.

Something about watching the final touches happening to the thing I'd worked so hard to accomplish had tears streaming down my face. Both happy and sad ones. The happiness of completing it warred with the sadness that this part of the journey was over, that the climb to the top had ended. I didn't want it to end even though I knew it was just beginning. Each first step was a final one and with its finality came a sadness I hadn't expected.

By the time I walked into my bakery and took in the floral smell mixed with the spices I'd added to a few drink concoctions this morning, I'd cried more than I wanted to admit. I took a couple pictures and sent them to Evie, who'd been begging to see, and then I posted a snapshot of the ceiling to social media.

I sighed as I turned to the wall I still had to tackle. If I finished this, I could rest for the day, or maybe two days, before the reopening. I pulled at my neck and winced as some of the pain traveled through my body.

I'd already bought a white paint can and cracked it open. I took my time lining the blue tape the best I could and even watched an online video on how to keep it nice and straight with a paint brush. I was halfway through and feeling quite proud of myself when Dominic walked in.

"Clara Milton," he sighed as I turned to him, coughing just a little. His gaze narrowed on me. "You told me you were hiring someone to do this."

"I can do it myself," I retorted and turned back to the paint.

"Really?" He walked up and pulled back some of the blue tape. That's when I saw the white was now bleeding onto the pinks. "You didn't line the walls correctly and it's still a skill that—"

"I'll do it again." I stood up and shooed him away as I winced.

"Clara," His voice was low. "You need to quit working and go home. The bakery looks stunning, and we can finish the rest tomorrow."

"Stunning?" That's all I heard.

He tsked. "I won't say it again."

"Why are you here then if not to keep complimenting it? Don't you have work to do before we open?"

He nodded. "I came by to give you this." He pulled a small red box from his trouser pocket and shook it in front of me as I wide-eyed it. Then he grabbed my wrist and set it in my dirty paint-speckled hand.

"What's this?" I whispered.

"A gift."

"For what?"

"For perfecting Sugar and Spice. It's everything you wanted to accomplish and more."

His compliments never came willingly and were so far and few between that this one meant the world. I also knew he meant it—that he truly was as happy as I was with it.

I think for someone to truly appreciate the highs in their life, they have to experience the lows. I'd graduated from culinary school without my mother in attendance. I'd had birthdays with no cakes, no mentions of it, and no apologies for forgetting.

My mother and sister didn't call to get an update on the opening of my bakery. Instead, it was to ask about Dominic.

In comparison to those lows, the high with Dominic and his gift was remarkable.

Tears streamed down my face as I opened the box and saw a gold cupcake hanging from a chain.

"Dominic," I whispered. Smiling through the tears, I said, "Please put it on me."

He turned me around and undid the chain to lay it over my collarbone where his hands brushed softly against my neck. I held my hair up and he latched the clasp before murmuring into my ear, "Cherry on top because your lips taste like them. And if you don't let me taste them now, I'll be pissy the whole rest of the day and not let you fiddle with this stupid wall."

I jumped up and kissed him hard, squeezing him tight and breathing in the scent that now felt like home. He might have been my fake boyfriend but he was everything I'd ever wanted, what I never knew I needed.

When I pulled away, Paloma was in the doorway with puffy eyes that looked like she'd been crying. "Paloma, what's wrong?"

"Just a bad review in an article about the name of my store. It doesn't matter." She waved it off now and her brows slammed down before she breathed out my name in concern. "Clara, do you have a death wish?"

"What?" I tilted my head confused.

She rushed in and rounded the counter to turn on my back kitchen fan before she closed the paint can and then turned a furious glare on me. "You have lupus. Do you understand? Painting with no ventilation is—"

"What?" Dominic's question sliced through the air cutting off Paloma halfway into her rant.

I winced and Paloma's mouth snapped shut. When I turned to look at Dominic, in his face, I saw a flurry of emotions. Disbelief, then anger, then sadness, then something that looked a lot like fear.

He said the question again, softer this time but no less lethal. "What did you just say, Paloma?"

She shook her head fast when she realized what she'd done. "Sorry but you need to wear a mask. Or hire someone! Breathing that paint is bad for anyone and lupus doesn't have one-size-fits-all triggers." She started to backtrack out of the bakery and hurried to say, "Talk to you later. Your bakery with the flowers and the sign looks beautiful. Love you, bye."

Willing myself to start this conversation was like gearing

up to face one of my bullies head on. Hiding my condition, which was probably what I should have admitted I was doing, was easier than sharing it, than recognizing it, than accepting it. I'd avoided the sign from my body when I hurt, I told myself I was fine over and over, and I talked myself into believing no one needed to know.

"So, it's not a big deal but—"

"Are you fucking kidding me?" He bellowed. "Don't start the conversation with bullshit, Clara Milton."

"I'm not. This is something I've been dealing with and it's not really something my boss needs to be burdened with." I looked away, unable to meet his gaze with me obviously attempting to remind him of the barriers between us.

He wasn't having any of it.

"Your boss?" he repeated in a whisper. Then he barked out a laugh before rubbing his jaw. "You sleep in my fucking bed. We live together. Call me just your boss again, cupcake, and I'll bend you over this breakfast bar to remind you who I really am. Go ahead, see how it works out for you."

I sighed and folded my hands together, trying not to get emotional. "Fine. I just didn't think—"

"I don't even want to know what you thought, Clara. You have a goddamn disease, one that's hurting you every single day, and you didn't tell me?" His tone was full of pain, not anger.

I met his gaze finally and saw how every muscle on him was coiled with some sort of grave emotion along with his anger. The room practically shook in fear of his wrath, and I felt his fury deep in my bones as I tried to diffuse the situation. "It's really actually not that big of a deal. My doctor back home—"

"You're painting without a mask—with that fucking cough—knowing you have lupus?" He seethed. His eyes grew wider as he glanced around. "Do you have any of your ventilation fans ever going?"

"Okay, Dominic, you need to calm down. Like I said, my doctors back home—"

"Back home?" he cut me off. "Does that mean you haven't seen one here?"

"Well, okay." I waved off that question. "We've been pretty busy."

He paced up to me and snatched my hand into his. "We're going to the doctor right now."

"Erm, no thank you," I replied and turned to go back to painting, then stomped my foot when he yanked me back around. "Are you kidding me right now?"

"Do I look like I'm kidding?"

"We're days away from Sugar and Spice opening and—"

"We could be minutes away from it, and I wouldn't care. I wouldn't give a flying fuck."

"Okay, so you're mad." I tried a different angle. "But if we finish painting—"

"You're not finishing shit today, Clara," he corrected.

"Dominic, this means a lot ... to all of us."

He sighed and pinched the bridge of his nose. "It means nothing to me without you healthy. We'll hire someone."

"I can't hire someone! I don't have the—" I wasn't about to admit I was actually painting because I couldn't afford painters at this point.

"Don't have what?" he pointedly asked, enunciating each word, and his jaw ticked up and down as if he was egging me on to finish the sentence.

"Well, you know since you already so rudely dug into my finances that we all don't have grotesque amounts of—"

"Didn't I tell you once if you think you need something that you should own it and buy it under my damn tab?"

"Okay, but that was in the heat of a moment." I blushed at remembering how he ate me out on his island countertop just a few nights ago.

"But I meant it for every moment." He frowned at me like I should know better. "You're done for the day, cupcake."

"No. But I—"

"Actually, you're done for the whole fucking week." His voice ricocheted off the walls of the bakery, loud and powerful. "Until the opening. If you want to, you can stand in the lobby, but you're going to rest and get that cough checked out."

"It's not even a real cough!" I tried to reason with him, but he was storming out of the lobby and dragging me with him, and I was actually really pretty tired, so I didn't fight him too much.

When he got me into the SUV, he turned on me again, his eyes that piercing green, like he was going to search my soul for answers. "How long have you had this?"

"Dominic, it's not really your concern, and I have it—"

"How long?" he asked, punching a fist into his thigh.

"I was diagnosed on the same day as the will hearing."

He winced like I'd hit him with a ton of bricks. "And you didn't tell me?" The lines on his face deepened as he frowned at me and pulled at the collar of his shirt before he unbuttoned the top of it. "I would have—"

"You would have what, Dominic? We hated each other then."

"Still, I was hard on you and—"

"You're hard on everyone because you know it produces the best results. A diamond without pressure is just a rock, and you made my damn bakery a diamond with me."

He shook his head like he was tormented by something, and instead of him consoling me about having lupus, I grabbed his hand and pried open his fist. "What's really wrong?"

Suddenly, that pain he hid so well was back in his eyes. "Nothing, Clara."

"You're a terrible liar, too, Dominic." I patted his thigh. "Let's talk over a cupcake when we get home."

And maybe that night my disease was what we needed. It cracked his fortress enough for him to be vulnerable. First, he made me shower. When I said no, he pulled me in there with him and took it upon himself to wash every part of me. He tsked at some of the rashes he saw on my arms that had popped up today. "They're minor," I told him, and he just shook his head as he toweled me off before he bundled me in a massive robe and told me I needed to see a doctor very soon. Then he carried me to his bed where he laid me out on top of him and started the story of him and Natya.

How he loved her. How he thought she was everything. How he believed they had it all, but then the story curdled into the lies she told, how he couldn't be enough for her, how he tried to protect her from the fame she kept seeking, how she tried to yank him into it, and ultimately, how she lied about being pregnant to keep him around.

He'd failed her though, he told me. He hadn't been able to save her from her own ego. And now he wasn't even doing a good job of being a good fake boyfriend and saving me from working too hard with my disease. I started to see how Dominic Hardy took every burden from everyone he cared about and made them his own. If he didn't fix their problems, he felt unworthy.

He was a good man, a man I shouldn't want but did.

***

The next morning, he said he'd send a driver to pick me up late in the afternoon but that I would only be able to walk around the resort, not work.

He told me to book a doctor's appointment.

I ignored that but appreciated the extra time to get ready for work. Under the stress of the reopening, I could feel my body needing more time for everything. Even so, I took my meds and did my best to make it to work.

When I got there, Dominic was in my bakery, hands covered in pink and red and white. The ombré had been accented further, and the corner lines were immaculate. "What's this?" I whispered.

He stood and hesitated. "We needed more pink and some red, right? Bold and beautiful like you." He shrugged and then turned me toward the door. "It's drying. No breathing the paint. Go console your friend and tell her to check the papers today about her store."

I checked the headlines myself on the way and found most news articles raving positively about the sentiment behind Paloma's name. When I showed her in her store, she started crying and I cried with her. "You realize he didn't do this for me, right? He did it for you."

I shook my head. "No way."

"Yes way. You balance him and he loves it."

I shook my head at her and at my heart that was galloping away with her words. "It doesn't matter though. Your store and you deserve this."

Paloma nodded and looked around. "You know all the reds and greens he helped me pick out? He walked in here the other day and said they'd match your hair and eyes. That's not coincidental, Clara. You're on his mind all the time."

I told her there wasn't any way he wanted that. I told myself the same thing all the way home because I felt myself starting to hope for it, to want it more than I had ever wanted a relationship before.

And wanting what I couldn't have was dangerous.

That night, I asked him about Paloma, accusing him of stuffing the headlines for the good of her store because I couldn't get it off my mind. "You did that for her. Why?"

He took off his eyeglasses, sitting at his desk and shrugged. "She's your friend, right?"

"Of course."

"It made her happy?"

"Of course."

"And you too?"

"Yes, but—"

"Then why does it matter why I did it? Just be happy." He went back to working, but I wasn't done.

"Because you don't do that." I tried to reason with myself. This wasn't the man I knew when I'd first met him. "You were ruthless when I met you. You made us all feel inadequate."

"And now? Now, we're ready for the world. And you're all a part of my world, right?"

"So what? Now, Paloma's close to you?"

"She sits by me every morning." He replied matter-of-factly.

"You barely talk to her!"

"So?"

"Is this how you've been? Quietly fixing everybody's problems behind closed doors and then acting like a freaking jerk to our faces? Is this the oldest sibling in you?"

"My siblings know I don't do anything they don't deserve."

I narrowed my eyes. "You think your siblings deserve the world though!"

His smile sliced across his face like he was happy I was starting to finally understand him.

I truly think I was.

CHAPTER 33: DOMINIC

My little fighter had been battling a silent war the whole time I'd known her without ever giving me a heads-up.

She was strong. So strong that I was sure she'd be able to move a mountain if I goaded her into it. And it was brilliantly beautiful to see even if it was infuriating.

She'd kept the biggest secret of all so that I wouldn't treat her differently not knowing that I treated her differently already.

Didn't she get that? She was living in my house. I literally was eating sweets to try to curb my addiction to her and her treats.

Me: Did you know Clara has lupus?

Declan: Evie may have mentioned it once or twice.

Me: I'm going to fucking kill you.

Izzy: Cade said if you need help with that, he knows a guy.

Me: That's not even funny, Izzy.

Declan: Well, it kinda is. It's also funny that you didn't know your own girlfriend had lupus.

Dex: That's because, like I said, pretty sure it's his fake girlfriend.

Dimitri: If she's fake, I think they've made it pretty believable thus far.

Izzy: I read enough magazines and hacked enough data to know it's fake, you guys. Dom's just trying to be the big brother.

Delilah: Except he's screwing it all up.

Me: So, you were all talking about this shit before I texted?

Izzy: Of course. Half of us are home with kids and bored.

Dex: I'm just trying to make sure my casino deal doesn't get fucked in the next couple weeks. So keep it together.

Me: You're all assholes, you know that?

Delilah: In our defense, you lied first.

Declan: Not that it was even a good lie.

Declan: Let us know if Clara needs us

to come to town to get her away from you. Pretty sure you've probably stressed her out enough.

Dex: If she fake dumps you, can I fake date her next?

Me: You think that's funny? What if I said I was going to date Keelani?

Dex: Why would I care? I told you at the club, I'm into someone else.

Me: Good. Because that casino company wants singers in some of their casinos. She'd be a great fit.

Dex: You better fucking not, Dom.

I knew my brother wasn't going to fix his own love life, so I'd have to do it myself soon enough. Keelani and he were meant to be.

We all knew it.

Plus, his ass was goading me so I was going to push back.

Now we all were angry. This was why no one started the day off talking to their five younger siblings. I just knew they were setting the stage for a shit day after that. Case in point: when I got to the lobby of my resort, a large shipment was being hauled in.

"We didn't order this," I told the delivery man who frowned down at his tablet.

"It is addressed to Sugar and Spice Bakery." He squinted

and then shrugged. "A Clara Milton."

I knew damn well who it was addressed to. "No one but me is authorized to have deliveries here." I cracked my neck before I continued, trying to dissipate the anger flowing through me as I stared at the bubbled wrapped figure behind him. "That will have to be returned."

"Fuck me," the guy grumbled as he clicked his tablet off and turned to his friend. "We need a signature for this, or can we just leave it?"

Just what type of delivery service had Clara even hired? "You can't just leave crap on my property."

"The address says here, man. We got other shipments. This one is already a pain in my ass."

I'm sure it was. I knew that Clara had ordered more colorful blown-glass figures to be placed throughout the bakery, but this was too much.

Of course she was hustling down the walkway on her way back from visiting with Paloma right then to sign and then actually *hug* the delivery drivers.

"Why the hell are you hugging them?" I grumbled.

"Because it was probably hard to carry and not break." She glanced over at them, and they nodded with large smiles on their faces.

"Get the fuck out of here," I told both of them.

"Oh, wait." She waved her hands wildly. "Can you please help us hang them? We need them up today."

And that's how the rest of my day got taken up by her bakery. Hanging blown glass from the corners of her painted wall under floral arrangements that cost me half a million dollars.

The only saving grace to my being there was every time she

tried to stand up and lift something or start to work, I pointed at her. "Get up and I'm breaking your blown glass. Sit your ass there and rest."

Of course she didn't see that as helping. She fought me about it the whole time, going on and on about how I was too overprotective for no reason.

She knew the goddamn reason.

Now that I knew her diagnosis, her smaller symptoms were more noticeable. She took time getting up and down every day, she moved consciously after cooking a while to stretch her joints. And she avoided certain foods. Granted, she didn't have a doctor and had stressed herself out for months working tirelessly on this bakery, but I couldn't fault her for that.

I was more than attuned to her late nights to the fridge now, and every time I followed her out there, she sighed and told me to go back to bed. Finally, yesterday she admitted that sometimes pain was worse at night so she got up to get water or move around to keep her mind off it.

I'd also caught her trying to cover up a rash on her face the other morning with concealer and had to snatch the makeup from her hands. She'd looked tired, broken, frustrated, and vulnerable as she curled in on herself, bowing her head to try to hide the redness of her cheeks. I lifted her chin and tsked before telling her to wait. I'd bought specific creams now and she didn't fight me much when I rubbed them over her butterfly rash.

If she wouldn't take care of herself, I would. I'd scheduled her acupuncture and massaged her back before bed. Then I fucked her slow or fast dependent on how she wanted it.

Most nights, we wanted it fast and hard, like we were trying to get as much of each other as we could.

Then I held her close. Every single night.

I shouldn't have. No sleeping together had been my rule and the original plan. Also, no kissing women and staying the night had been my rule too.

Yet, there were no rules with Clara. She wasn't really my fake girlfriend anymore. She was just mine.

Most people knew that. I'd made it quite clear by being in her bakery every day but that day specifically, Valentino seemed to want to test the waters. He stopped by to "lend a hand" and flirt with her. He complimented her necklace, how the bakery looked, gave updates on assistance emails with Rita, like the guy was actually helping her. He was a damn chef on the top floor of this resort, not her personal helper.

And yet even with my frustration throughout the day, as the work day came to an end, she turned to me with a tired smile on her face. "Let's go home."

She said it like that place was ours. I was pissed that I loved hearing the words that way, that I loved seeing her smile, that I loved how she threaded her fingers through mine in the car and whispered, "Thank you for believing me when I told you I had lupus. Thank you for still being the you who's a complete jerk about your resort but also being the you who cares."

How could I tell her I wasn't me anymore? That we weren't us? We were something more.

I worried about her day in and day out, wanted to spend every second with her. Hell, I researched lupus more than I'd researched angles of a new project that I needed to start working on. And through all that, she still managed to push the limits of my temper and keep me on my toes most days.

We'd finally settled in my study, where we spent most evenings, when I grabbed my phone to take a call. "Clara!"

I bellowed loudly and threw my phone down instead of answering. "What in the hell is that?"

"We've been in here for like twenty minutes, Dominic. You're just noticing?" She actually sat there with a pout on her face like she had a right to be irritated.

"Did you rearrange my books?" I shot up from my chair and threw down my eyeglasses before pacing over to the wall-to-wall shelves. I'd had classics printed in black leather binding, their white pages facing out to match the room, literally spent hundreds of thousands to make it all work together and the middle row was a fucking rainbow of colors.

"No. You said I could make myself at home, and I was at a garage sale the other day and this woman was selling a whole collection of romance novels. They're all color coordinated, and I thought it was literally perfect for making me feel at home here."

"You knew damn well it would make me furious. Where are my books that belong there?"

"The books you don't read?" She curled her lip.

"You have no idea if I read them or not."

"Name one on that shelf."

"Clara, I swear to God—"

"Fine." She cut me off and stomped one red-colored sock. The fact she even wore bright red on her feet around the house almost had me smiling. Fuck, I was getting soft. "I'll put them all back up on your stupid shelf," she pouted. "Just know though that all the ones I have up there now, I've read more than once. They're amazing, and they deserve a spot."

Such passion about a book or two for the content rather than the aesthetic. "What's the book you're reading now about?"

I held out a hand, but she stepped back fast and held it to

her chest. "None of your business."

"You're blushing, cupcake."

"I am not." She spun and went to sit back on the couch. "Go back to your work."

Instead, I walked over, tipped her book up so I could read the title and then started typing it into my phone.

"Wh-what are you doing?" she stuttered out.

"Downloading the book to my Kindle."

"What for?!" She jumped up and tried to snatch it away, but I held it out of reach.

"I want you looking at me like that soon. Means I've got to read what's in that book."

She groaned and plopped down onto the couch. "Whatever, Dominic. It will be good research for whoever you decide to bother with your time after the reopening."

"Is that so?" I chuckled to avoid thinking seriously about her leaving. Didn't she understand she'd changed everything in my life? That I wouldn't be able to go back to what I was before her? She'd waltzed in quietly, hoping not to be a disruption, but she'd been a beautiful tornado of change.

She was with me most of the day, challenging me, questioning me, conversing with me in a way I never knew I wanted. When life was comfortable, pushing into the unknown was difficult, especially when the unknown had hurt before. I hadn't wanted a relationship before her, would have sworn my life was fine without it. Now, my heart beat much too fast thinking of her leaving.

"Remember, Clara. I don't date," I said it to remind myself too.

She sighed. "Right. Me neither. No dating and no marriage. That's why these books are nice. I get to have the romance for a bit."

"I ..." I snapped my mouth shut. For some reason, her not wanting to date me didn't sit well with me. I waited for her to elaborate, but she didn't. "You're reading romance?" Didn't I romance her enough?

"Yes." She shrugged. "Anyway, they also can teach you a thing or two about how to satisfy your partner for once."

Teach me? My head snapped up from my desk, and I caught her smirking. "Hm, very funny. If you need a reminder of how I satisfy the fuck out of you, keep it up."

"You're a very accommodating fake boyfriend." She laughed, trying to keep the conversation light but her bringing up the fake part of it was a sour reminder for me.

"With the Pacific reopening, we'll be dealing with a lot of publicity."

She stared at me. "Safe to assume Natya will be there?"

"Along with my family, potentially yours if you invite them, and most noteworthy reporters."

"If you're concerned I won't be ready—"

"I'm not ..." How did I say I didn't want her to be ready? That I didn't even fucking want to go? That was the point of our whole charade but it didn't feel like the point at all anymore. "You don't have to deal with this publicity if you don't want to."

"Why would I not want to?" She frowned at me. "I'm upholding my end of the bargain, Dominic. It won't be that hard. I'll open the bakery, get ready, and be on your arm. No problem."

I took my eyeglasses off and rubbed at my face. "Right. No fucking problem," I grumbled. I should have pushed her more to see everything that could go wrong but I was focused on something else. "Why don't you want to be married? And why don't you really date anyone, Clara?"

"Probably the same reason you don't."

"Natya broke my trust. You know that. Did someone break yours?"

She chuckled but the sound was sad. "Maybe my family did. I never really tried hard to date because my mother wanted it so badly for me that I think I avoided it. Why would I want to fall in love the way she did just so that someone can ruin my heart the way hers was?"

"Fair." I hummed. It made sense. Still, I said, "What if they won't ruin your heart though?"

"Would you take a chance on someone else after Natya? She hurt you, right? So, tell me. Is it worth it?"

Yes. In my heart, looking at her, the answer was a loud, resounding yes. And that scared me. "No. Natya ruined me."

"And the idea of ruin has ruined me too."

CHAPTER 34: CLARA

Ruin was coming.

Life wasn't this good. It couldn't be.

And the reopening was that very day. We'd planned our schedule, laid out how we'd be there very early in the morning because guests would be arriving. I'd baked the night before, had extra staff to help me, and couldn't help but be excited.

Dominic brushed a hand over my cheek outside of Sugar and Spice Bakery and murmured, "Own it, Clara. She's a stunning representation of you, and it will be a hit."

I nodded once and then again to try to reassure myself. When I squinted at my bakery through the glass, though, I saw a glint of something that wasn't there the night before.

I rushed to swipe my fob and push open the door.

Inside, on every table and lining the walkway up to the register, were gold roses and gold petals. "What is this?" I whispered.

"A little extra." He shrugged, his hands in his pockets. And I just spun around in silence until he said softly, "Do you like it?"

His question was hesitant, like suddenly he cared what someone else thought of his addition to the design. Gone was his confidence, and in its place was vulnerability I never expected from him. "If I said I didn't?"

"I'd expect that. But it'd hurt about as badly as you calling my resort a sterile hospital." He chuckled but his gaze didn't meet my eyes.

"You're not kidding, are you?" I squinted at him trying to figure it out.

"For some reason, I'm not. I care about your opinion much more than others."

"Because it's an honest one?"

"Because it's yours," he corrected.

I took a breath and glanced around again, trying not to give in to the tears that were forming in my eyes. "No one's ever helped me accomplish exactly what I wanted in the way I never knew I needed. It's beautiful, Dominic Hardy."

He stared at me, didn't take his eyes off me as he said, "Yeah, it really is."

It felt like he was saying it to me, and my heart beat faster as my face heated because of it.

I shook my head at him and my perfect red curls that I'd spent extra time on today waved back and forth too. "You shouldn't be here making me feel better about my bakery. You have a million things to do. Aren't you nervous?"

"For what?" He smirked. "I'm the artist. I tell them what they want, right?" He kissed me then and when he pulled away, murmured, "Remember, own it. I'll see you at nine, cupcake. Don't be late."

With that, he was gone. He backed away down the lobby, in that three-piece suit looking like perfection under the massive chandelier that now had hints of silver and gold in it. Every fiber of my being still felt him there with me, in the roses, in the paint, in the blown glass he'd hung, in everything. Dominic had helped me achieve my dream, and I think I loved him for it.

Loved him. Not liked. Loved.

I stared out at that lobby, trying to catch the sparkle

of the chandelier even though the sun wasn't in the sky yet. Dominic hadn't changed much with the lobby because it was his statement to the guests. Clean, luxury, elegance. The new gold accents just enhanced the sparkle of the chandelier. It drew everyone's attention, much like Dominic intended for it to.

I took a few deep breaths and got to work. When it was time for me to open the doors, I let the crowd outside in the lobby be an indicator that I'd be a success, and then I tried not to cry for the next nine hours of pure chaos.

People ordered everything on the menu and then moaned and whispered sweet nothings to my cupcakes the way I'd always dreamed they would. Declan waltzed in with Evie and their baby, and the tears flowed freely. She'd brought flowers to match the place and cried happy tears as she shooed away her husband so we could have a moment together.

We only had a minute in the back while staff took orders, but she hugged me tight and told me she was proud of me, that I'd bled color all through the resort just like it needed. Dominic's resort had splashes of color everywhere now, it was true. Just enough that people understood the concept and completely embraced it.

He'd overworked himself—and all of us—to make perfection and I had to try not to cry thinking about it. "He did really great work."

"Oh no. Don't cry, or I'll cry again," Evie warned.

"I know." I took a deep breath. "It's been a lot, but it's all been worth it."

"You did it."

I owned it. "Yeah, I really did."

She squeezed me again and then whispered, "Now get through tonight and don't either of you let each other go. Fake dating or not, he's yours."

She backed away before I could correct her, before I could ask how she knew. I'm guessing the Hardy family had figured it out, but I was too tired to inquire. The night had to be the beginning of the end for Dominic and me, and it seemed Evie and probably the rest of his family knew it.

When the last customer filed in and grabbed a coffee to go, I let out a sigh and pulled at the cupcake necklace Dominic had given me. Cleaning up with the staff didn't take much time at all, and as I waved goodbye to them, I saw Valentino hurry over just as I was about to exit the resort.

"Clara." He pulled me in for a hug. "I don't have much time, but I wanted to see you and your bakery on the first day." He stepped back and looked me up and down. "Gorgeous. Sugar and Spice Bakery was a hit, no?"

I smiled softly. "It seems that way."

"You'll come to my restaurant soon and have me cook for you then?"

"Oh." I tilted my head, not sure what he was asking. "I'll see if Dominic would like to come."

Why I felt the need to invite him along was silly. Yet, my feelings for Valentino had never grown past simple admiration for his attributes as a chef.

"Yes. Or not." He shrugged and winked at me. "You decide, huh? Also, I got you a little something to compliment that necklace."

He held out a box that housed another necklace, this one longer and with one small diamond. It was nice but generic and also felt a bit slimy after he knew Dominic had bought me one.

"Thanks. But I can't accept this." I eyed the necklace cautiously. "It's—"

"Oh, of course you can." He pulled me in for another hug and told me he would see me at the beach tonight, leaving me there with another necklace, confused. When I turned to leave though, I saw Mrs. Johnson was standing in the lobby smiling at me with Mother and Anastasia alongside her.

Mrs. Johnson patted her gray hair as she stared past me before she walked up in low heel pumps to give me a hug. Then, she handed me an envelope. "Your mother and sister found out I was making a trip here to give you an update on Carl's will. Of course, I said they could come to congratulate you on the bakery with me. You invited them to the reopening right?"

When I didn't answer at first, she pulled away to search my eyes. Then, she whispered, "Oh, darling. No need to explain if you didn't. Do me a favor and don't open that envelope in front of them, okay?"

Maybe I'd been caught up in my bakery, maybe I'd been caught up in Dominic, maybe I'd been caught up in my fake life, but I'd stopped thinking about them.

Maybe.

Or I'd blocked them out, knowing now that my physical health relied heavily on my mental health.

"Anyway"—she patted my cheek as she stepped back to take in the bakery again—"you did it. Carl and I knew you could. Anastasia and Melinda, isn't her bakery beautiful?"

"Sure." They came forward and my mother's eyes along with Anastasia's were glued to the envelope as she asked, "Should we catch up at your house?"

"I have to get ready for the party tonight at the resort," I said softly.

"Then, we should come to that right?" Her tone was expectant.

I should have said no but saying that to a mother felt wrong. "Sure. It's here tonight. Your names will be on the list."

A smile snaked across her face as dread snaked through my bones, fast and ready to prove that all my luck had run out. I felt it like a viper, slithering through me, ready to strike.

CHAPTER 35: CLARA

Dominic: I'm on my way back home.

Me: What for? Don't come back for me. I can just have Callihan drop me off.

Dominic: My future wife needs to be on my arm when I walk into the biggest party of my life, Clara.

Me: Probably not how you should refer to me since we're going to have to break up in a month or two.

Dominic: No one needs to know that.

Me: Right. Natya is sure to attend?

The thought of her in the resort he'd worked so hard to build when all she wanted to do was tear it down or be by his side made my stomach churn enough that I rubbed a hand over it.

Dominic: Don't worry about her. The public really seems to like us,

cupcake. Maybe I should keep you for a few months longer.

I was sitting in Dominic's study, petting Sugar and Spice when I should have been prepping for the night. I told myself everything would be fine even though I didn't feel it after inviting my mother and sister. The tabloids had been nice already. To them, Dominic and I were meant to be. A match made in heaven. Dominic was calmer, smoother, and more accommodating in interviews about his plans for the HEAT empire. Not only was this resort going to be a success but partnerships after it too.

Me: As if it's only your choice.

Dominic: So, I need to persuade you?

Me: Let's focus on what you think the press is going to ask us.

Dominic: They'll ask if you're my future wife.

Me: Don't you have to worry about how people are receiving the aesthetic or something?

Dominic: Nope. My work here is done. We make a show and then leave. Design, invest, manage, and then watch it all work seamlessly for HEAT.

Me: Carl would be proud.

Dominic: Proud that I'm thinking of a way to get us out of this resort gala so I can have you to myself?

My thighs instantly clenched, and I knew I had to stop texting him if I was going to be ready in time. Thankfully, my hair naturally held a decent curl, and so I kept it dry as I popped in and out of the shower, and then stared at my gala dress. The last time I'd worn it, she'd been there, seen us, and had tried to make me feel small.

I took a deep breath and pulled the dress on, letting the heavy fabric glide over me as I stared at myself in the mirror. My cheeks were flushed in a healthy way. No flare-up now, my body felt tired but strong, and still my heart raced.

Tonight was going to be a war. I knew it.

I jumped at hearing Dominic's throat clearing in the doorway of the bathroom.

"What are you doing here?"

"If I didn't come, Evie and half my family were going to. Something about girls getting ready together, and then Izzy was with her, mumbling that family was family and if I wasn't going to pick up my future wife—"

"Izzy's saying that now?" I squeaked. Although Izzy was Dominic's sister, she felt like an Armanelli to me—dangerous and beautiful all at the same time. She'd married Cade Armanelli, a man that was so volatile people didn't even glance in his direction. He could end a life with the touch of a button and supposedly had once or twice. The Armanelli name was one people spoke of with respect, but also fear. "She's here?"

"Along with Cade and my other sister, Lilah. And her husband Dante."

"Dante Armanelli?" I breathed out. "Just how many of them are showing up?"

"I think Rome and his wife are in Italy, so they won't be there. But Bastian will be." He shrugged and I tried not to gasp at the name. Sebastian Armanelli was the leader of the mob, and I knew my stepfather had done business with them, but not like this.

"Are you ... close with them?" How did you ask a man if he knew that his brothers-in-law were killers?

"Close enough." He chuckled as he leaned against the doorframe of the bathroom. "You scared, little fighter?"

I scoffed and turned back to the mirror where I tried to steady my hand to paint on some lip stain.

Dominic came to stand behind me, his hands sliding up my dress and murmured, "This is my territory, cupcake. You know I'll protect you right?"

I stopped what I was doing to stare in his eyes. "Do I need protection?" I whispered.

He hummed like he wanted to goad me. I knew he did because his length hardened against my back. It was foreplay for us. "Maybe." He gazed at me, his eyes seeming to pry into my soul. "But not from them."

Did he know that I needed protection from losing my heart to him instead?

I looked down and grabbed my lash kit. "I'm just going to finish my makeup, then we can go. My mother and sister are here. I invited them to the beach."

He tsked. "Still being nice to people you shouldn't be."

"They're family, Dominic. Plus, I really didn't know what

else to say. They were here with Mrs. Johnson and asked to come. Maybe they're genuine in wanting to come support me."

He nodded once and then twice before he kissed my forehead and murmured, "I like you better when you're fighting for what you believe in instead of lying through your teeth, Clara. I also like you with freckles rather than makeup, but you're still stunning." He stepped to the side and smacked my ass hard before grabbing it and pulling me close. "Especially in this dress."

"I appreciate you getting it for me." I held my hands out wide because I was holding a tiny lash and the glue. "I still have to get ready though."

"Fine, but hurry." He rearranged his trousers, and I took a second to look at his suit. All-black jacket, vest, and collared shirt. He appeared sleek and refined but so big, and his eyes blazed so green and penetrating that I doubt anyone would be able to look away from him tonight.

"I like your gold accents." I pointed to his pocket square and then caught a glimpse of his cuff links. "They suit you."

He hummed but straightened the cuffs of his shirt. "Clara, I don't want you sweet, okay? I want to hurry to this event, show everyone my girlfriend, get questions out of the way, and then bring her home so she can ride my cock mean and hard into oblivion."

"Jesus," I whispered, trying my best now not to get wet from his words.

He murmured, "You opened your bakery, baby. And I want to celebrate with you. Not a bunch of people I don't give a shit about."

"Your family is here—"

"Sure, but they'll be around next week waiting to celebrate

with us then. Want to go to a resort with me next week?"

"Wh-what?"

"I'm going to check out a resort up in Big Bear. You'll come. We'll celebrate there, okay?" I was so thrown off by his request that I didn't really answer. "But the longer you take, the longer till we're back home in this bed."

My fake boyfriend wasn't acting fake at all and I needed him to. I didn't trust that he'd love me enough to stay, or that I was good enough to keep him around. My mother and sister had instilled that in me.

I was just getting my footing here and had to protect my heart, especially considering this was only supposed to be fake.

I should have told him there was no point to us sleeping together anymore, that we should actually be sleeping apart more now since we'd have to go back to getting used to that. I should have told him that grabbing my ass while we weren't in public was unnecessary too. I tried to remind us both the best I could, "I'll be ready to be your fake girlfriend in five."

His jaw ticked. "Well, then. In five minutes, cameras start rolling, huh?"

It wasn't a question. It was an omen.

***

The Pacific Coast Resort Gala was like nothing I'd seen before, and I'd been to a few. My stepfather had hosted some, and we'd been invited to others. This one was bigger. We made it just in time to sit front row for more than one performance by some of the biggest singers in the industry.

Beautiful people, beautiful lights, out-of-this-world performances, and then we were directed to the black-and-white carpet—no red because I knew Dominic had made sure of it. He held my hand the whole time, and we smiled for cameras and pulled one another close while his hands drifted where they wanted and my body reacted how it always did.

They asked if I was truly his future wife, and he didn't bat an eye as he said, "Of course." Without even a smile on his face, Dominic was still a man of few words, but now, the world swooned over every single one of them.

We filtered into the blocked-off beach area where bouncers in suits let us through but checked most everyone else to confirm they could be at the event. We were greeted with ice sculptures, white and black tables, and tented off areas that still allowed for the beautiful backdrop of the ocean horizon. With the resort jutting out over the ocean and rising up into the sky, it was hard to know which way to even look. Beauty was all around us.

I was introduced to the Armanellis again and then the Stonewood brothers. Each family owned more than half the country, it felt like. With them partnering in the HEAT empire, I knew the Hardys were at their status level. As all the men talked in front of me, I saw why. Their confidence, their appearance, the way they held attention was like a gravitational pull that couldn't be ignored.

"I'd complain that my husband abandoned me, but he did say he got me the best seats for the performances tonight and he'd helped make those performances happen. So now I don't really give a shit what he does." Victory Stonewood was striking in her high heels, light blue dress that fluffed at the waist, and long blonde hair. Her friend and sister-in-law, Aubrey Stonewood, stood next to her, smiling softly, in a demure black gown. She didn't say much of anything to anyone, but Victory talked enough for them both.

Evie pulled me to her side and whispered, "Victory supposedly let Izzy paint all of Jett Stonewood's computer monitors on a floor of his building when she was mad at Jett and Cade while working under them."

I snorted. "Really?"

"Yes." Izzy appeared behind both of us, and I jumped before turning to see her smiling big in a skintight black dress that matched her black heels. The dress was short enough that most men were glancing at her toned thighs even as Cade came to stand right behind her. "I did paint them because he was a total dick."

He wrapped his arm around her and set his chin on her head while glancing at Evie and me. The man was drop-dead gorgeous in a dangerous tattooed sort of way. "She's right. So, I'm not arguing with her about it. How long are you two gracing this party with your company?"

"Oh, I'll be here all night. I want to make sure my bakery is on everyone's radar."

He narrowed his eyes at me, and I felt like my insides were being pried apart. Cade didn't seem to know social boundaries at all. He didn't look away, didn't comment, didn't even look apologetic as he stared. "You know that fake dating Dominic is helpful, but your bakery would have been on everyone's radar anyway. You're talented with your marketing and how you pushed it. And so far, the reviews are not at all negative. The resort is going to prosper."

"Um ..." I almost melted into a puddle at his words, but I didn't have time to dwell on them as my mother and Anastasia approached.

They congratulated me, gave me a hug, and my mother whispered that she wanted to have lunch the next day. All smiles and no frowns or sneering.

Sometimes, I just wanted to believe. I didn't want to give into my gut feeling. I wanted to suppress it and hope. The abused get great at that—focusing on the good rather than the bad.

I let Dominic steal me away to my seat as the MC announced that there would be speeches before dinner. We sat at linen tables set up under a tent. The Hardy brothers stole the show, each of them giving a speech thanking my stepfather, Declan thanking his wife, and Dominic taking a bit more time to thank each one of us. He smiled at me, and the few approved cameramen took pictures over and over as he said, "Clara's been a bit of the yin to my yang. The black to my white, if you will."

Everyone laughed at that, but my heart beat a mile a minute. This wasn't planned. He wasn't supposed to talk about me, yet he thanked me specifically, as if my input truly meant something to him. When his gaze cut to the ocean halfway through, I turned and saw her.

Natya Fitch.

"The white and black, curves and straight lines are the balance in my resort. The spectrum of color represents inclusivity and I wouldn't have come to the realization that this specific Hardy resort needed that without Clara. I wouldn't have come to the realization that it needed anything, just like I thought my life didn't need anything either. She changed that by consistently challenging me, provoking me, and persuading me to take the risk. I'm indebted to her for that, but I get to spend the rest of my life paying her back for it. So, to her and to the rest of the team, we've done it. It's been an honor to work with you all." With that, he handed the microphone to what appeared to be another shareholder and made his way back to our table.

I didn't say anything as he sat down next to me. How could I when he'd directed that whole speech at her? Was he putting on a show just for her to believe? If so, that somehow hurt my heart most even knowing that's what I'd signed up for.

Somewhere along the way, I'd started to believe something different, and now I wasn't sure if he'd meant any of it. Could it have all been fake?

The question swirled in my mind over and over, turning into a tornado rather than dying out as just a breeze of a thought. I didn't know if any of it was true or if he'd been flaunting a love he didn't have for me in order to push hers further away. When I glanced at Dex, his eyes were ping-ponging between us. "Just so we're clear, the casinos have agreed to the deal in Vegas. The lawyers are drawing it up as we speak. Their team just walked out."

"I saw them leaving as I was giving my speech," Dominic said without much emotion. Which was fine since I was feeling all of it for both of us. Playing pretend was something I'd loathed until I'd loved it, and now I was back to loathing feeling a damn thing when I wasn't sure if he felt for me the way I did for him.

Instead, I focused on the plate of food in front of me as a soft, sultry voice started from the stage.

"What the fuck?" I heard Dex mutter. Then louder, "What the actual fuck?" His eyes were filled with fury as he slammed a hand down on the table and glared at his brothers.

Each of them shook their head until Dex's eyes skirted from Dimitri to Dominic, who pointed back to Dimitri. "It was mostly his idea," Dominic said.

Dimitri's smile grew. "She's a good singer, bro, and she needed a few gigs. Pretty sure your casino is going to hire her too."

"Are you fucking kidding me?" Dex stood abruptly. "You know I hate her."

But he turned to look at Keelani, his muscles tense, as she stared right back at him. Her voice held edge as she hit a high note, never breaking eye contact. So much emotion was in the song and as she sang, half the audience whispered about her range.

When her song finished, Dex stormed up to the stage as she mumbled she'd be back after a break. He waved her over and she rolled her eyes before sauntering to the edge of the stage where he grabbed her hips and plucked her right off it.

Dimitri chuckled. "He's going to cave one of these days."

Dominic cracked his neck and shook his head. "We're probably playing with fire, Dimitri."

"Am I?" His brother glanced at me and then to the back of the tent where I knew Natya had been. "Or are you?"

With that, Dimitri got up to leave, and Dominic cleared his throat. "Want to dance, cupcake?"

I took a few breaths, reminding myself that I was here to make an impression. This was the solidifying of our relationship before we separated. The world would know Dominic and I were together, and the resort's reputation wouldn't suffer, even if suddenly I didn't want to pretend anymore.

I didn't know what I was pretending. Whether I was his girlfriend or whether I enjoyed pretending to be his girlfriend when really my heart was crumbling as I considered the fallout.

I put on the face everyone wanted to see, reminded myself that I'd painted on cat eyes with a little extra concealer, curled my hair again and pinned it up so that only a few soft tendrils fell over my shoulders. I looked the part tonight. I had to act it too. I ran my hand over the necklace that was pure elegance and no cupcakes. Today had been about my bakery, but tonight I'd thrown on Valentino's just so I could complete the look and then I slipped on the dress Dominic and I had picked out together.

Tonight was about the resort.

I knew the reopening of the resort would be talked about in every magazine, on every news station, and the approved press on the beach were snapping pictures through the night. When Dominic pulled me to the dance floor, the flashing continued. His fingers skirted up my neck before he murmured against my lips, "Did you like my speech?"

"It was a good one for show." My stomach dipped and twisted as his hands dug into my hips.

"What if it wasn't for show, little fighter. What if now this is just for me?"

I frowned at him, not understanding. I'd seen how he looked at his ex, how he'd smiled at them all, and then came back with less emotion in his eyes, like he was tired.

His hand dragged across the necklace that wasn't his. It was simple and elegant and had no personal touch. Perfect for the night. "Why not the cupcake I gave you?"

"I figured this was better for tonight. Tonight's not about my bakery."

He hummed and then he flipped it over. The pendant was not something I had really even looked at, but then he whispered out, "Congrats from Valentino?"

"Huh?" I glanced down but couldn't see it. Its length was much too short, but I felt how his grip tightened on the chain around my neck, saw the fire in his eyes as I glanced up at him.

"A gift from him?" We were still moving together across

the dance floor, but the stare between us was so charged, I didn't know if anyone else was still on the dance floor, in the room, in the whole resort.

All I saw was him. Dominic Hardy, larger than life, so overpowering that I'd forgotten about anything else. I'd lost my concern for lupus, ignored my mother and sister, snuffed out my worry of offending him or anyone else with my opinions, and began to implement what I wanted everywhere. He'd given me the confidence, the fight, the drive to own it.

I stepped with him across that dance floor, meeting his moves match for match, sway for sway, twist and turn for twist and turn. "It's just a necklace, Dominic."

"Do you think I want to see another man's jewelry on you? And soon do you think it will be just a coffee? Just a date? Just a fling?"

I narrowed my eyes as we stopped, his hand low on my back like he was about to dip me. "Are you jealous when you know this is about to end? When you goaded me into doing this for that very reason?"

He didn't answer me, just bent his knee and dropped me faster than most lead dancers would. I gasped at the feeling of my body falling along with my heart, with all the butterflies, with all the feelings I had for him flying around. No part of me was safe from him anymore, either, because when he yanked me up, his mouth took what he knew was his.

That kiss was searing, possessive, and territorial, and I clung to the lapels of his suit jacket, trying not to be conquered by the man who had knocked down every barrier I'd built. I melted into him without putting up a fight for my heart. It was his already. I wasn't his little fighter anymore. I was willing instead. "I'll always be jealous of another man's jewelry on my neck. It's mine, Clara. We haven't broken up yet."

"Dominic—"

"If it's not gone by the time we're home tonight, I'm ripping it off you, cupcake. And I'll deliver it back to him myself."

The music ended with his words, but we stayed in the middle of the dance floor, staring at one another for far too long. His statement felt like it held weight, like we should talk through it, like maybe we were going to figure it all out, but then the press walked up.

Not just one of them ... all of them.

"Natya just gave us the exclusive."

"You took on building this resort after you lost her."

"You wanted a baby, right, and couldn't have one together?"

"Was that why you put your heart and soul into creating this masterpiece?"

The press wasn't supposed to be this aggressive as they stuck a mic in his face while Natya stood behind them smiling. She crossed her arms and flicked her gaze at me before lifting a brow while the vultures continued.

"Would you consider IVF with your soul mate? Adopting?"

"Natya said a baby with you is all she wants."

They were just words. Words supposedly couldn't break you. Sticks and stones, right? Yet, words ate at your heart, they bled-out your soul, sliced at your mentality if you let them. Words.

I think they broke what was left of Dominic and me right there in the cool breeze of that summer night. When he didn't answer, when his stare turned violent and vicious, the paparazzi knew they'd overstepped. They backed away fast, but Natya didn't.

She walked right up to him and whispered for only us both

to hear, "I can make it seem like we had a miscarriage too. Just because it isn't true doesn't mean they won't believe it."

Her eyes were wild and full of vengeance and jealousy. She wanted him, and she wanted to prove she could get him by any means necessary. "You loved me, don't you remember? I ruined you, sure, but I put you back together. Remember that. And then, just because you found out I told you a little lie, you were more than happy to abandon me. I didn't deserve it. Not when we had everything together. We can try to work this out, or I can tell them just that."

"Natya—" Dominic warned.

"No. Don't *Natya* me. You haven't answered my calls, Dom. I don't deserve that. I loved you. And I'll tell them that over and over again."

"We'll talk later. Just handle the press." Dominic's jaw ticked. "You know how to do it right, Natya."

She smiled at him, her hand drifting over his chest before she said, "See? We work as a team. Even if you had to have a little fun with her. And I'm sorry about faking the pregnancy, okay? But don't make me fake a miscarriage with the press now." She eyed me warily. "Answer my call later, Dominic, or the press will change its tune."

It didn't matter that she promised to help, Dimitri was already escorting paparazzi off the premises. People were already leaving the party.

The night air had shifted. And something in Dominic's eyes had shifted too. "Let's walk down the beach. Let the staff take care of the rest of the party."

My feet were frozen there as I stared at him. "I think I should go home, Dominic. Actually, I should stay here and then ..." I could afford an apartment now. I could afford the penthouse for months if I wanted. "Mrs. Johnson delivered an envelope with updates from the will. I'm ... I'll start looking for an apartment."

He whipped around to glare at me. "You think it's going to be that easy?"

Leaving him would be the hardest thing I ever had to do. I felt it in every part of me, the physical ache beginning. "No. I think it's rather difficult, Dominic. I honestly think it will make me physically ill."

His eyes flared with concern before he swept me up to go down to the ocean with me, away from the lights, away from the resort. He walked with me in his arms for minutes upon minutes.

My fake boyfriend held onto me as if I was real on that beach, and the feelings I had for him felt almost too real to bear.

CHAPTER 36: CLARA

"It was the last lie she told me that did us in." He confessed as we watched the water wash up to shore. "I'd almost been ruined by her blaming Susie's injury on me publicly but I didn't care. That was my fault anyway."

I stayed silent, not sure what to say.

"That baby though? The way I thought I was having a mini me. Do you know I bought the crib, the blankets, the little pacifiers? I researched what she should be eating, drinking—everything. I even got the car seat set up." His voice cracked with pain. "Natya said she was only eight weeks along, but I didn't care. I wanted that kid. I wanted that life. I wanted her."

The tide was high, and the waves crashed close to our feet. In and out, cold water and cool air, over and over again as the city around us went to sleep.

"She lied about all of it." I said it as a statement because she'd admitted it in front of me. Her words had been vicious, yet he hadn't so much as flinched, like he was used to her in the way that I was probably used to my family's twisted emotional abuse. He even told her to handle it, like he still trusted her to do so. I asked him, "Do you think she'll actually tell the press what we want?"

"Yes, because she'll save her reputation. She's not stupid. She knows how far to push me."

I didn't know if there was respect in his words. "She knows all your buttons, it seems."

"My weaknesses too." He dragged a finger up my arm, and I shuddered. I hated that I didn't pull away, not even when we were talking about her. "I wanted the perfect life with her. We'd mapped it out. I thought she wanted that too. Now, maybe she does."

Could I be jealous of the idea of another woman? What he thought she was? Because I felt like disappearing into the sand as he said those words, burying myself under there so I didn't have to hear how his heart broke for her.

I didn't know what to say other than, "I'm sorry she hurt you." I took a breath and held his hand in the silence, breathed in and out while the water rushed up and then back.

His silence was heavy with something, and I hated to think it was regret. He'd pushed her away this time with me, but maybe he really loved her. "She still wants you, Dominic. Maybe you could call her and work through it."

I think a person must really love another when they're willing to sacrifice their happiness for that person's. They relinquish their heart, break it up into pieces, offer what they can to make the other person's heart whole.

He didn't say one way or the other if he wanted to make it work. He stared out at the lights flickering off near the resort. "I don't think I can love a woman like I loved the idea of her," His gaze turned to me, and I saw the desolate emptiness, the sorrow, and the pain. "I don't want to love someone like I did her ... not ever again. I risked my career, hurt people, hurt her, and lost the idea of something I wanted more than life itself."

The words sliced through my heart and soul. The breath I took in was shaky as my eyes filled with tears I knew I couldn't shed in front of him. He turned back to the water like he couldn't bear to see me cry over him, but when I tried to pull my hand away, he held it. He didn't let me stand up but instead pulled my body close to his. We sat with that heavy silence weighing us down for too long that night.

I knew Dominic had embraced the darkness as he gazed out at the ocean. His soul had waded out to sea and left the flickering light of the city behind. He didn't want the light or the path back to salvation. He wanted to drown in his pain. I tried to understand it, but I'd left the darkness behind, and couldn't drown in it with him if I wanted to survive.

I wouldn't.

Sure, you could die of a disease, but I think people could also die from heartbreak.

Love and heartbreak. Those were two emotions you couldn't hide. I felt them both at that moment. "I can't stay with you like this, Dominic." I forced myself to say those words.

"Like what?" His eyes suddenly sliced over to me.

"I don't want to be a second thought or the girl who took only a piece of you. Not when I deserve all of you. And I know this is all for show—"

"What I feel for you isn't all for show," he ground out, but his confession was full of anger.

"Do you want to feel that way?"

"Hell no," he bellowed and that was enough for me.

"Exactly," I said, and I felt the stinging in my eyes that I didn't want. "I've always been a second thought or around when someone doesn't want me to be. But I won't be anymore. Not here. I'm not willing to be the person you wished you didn't like, Dominic. I want someone to enjoy liking me. Love liking me. Or love loving me. And just me. Not the idea of what we could be if you mold me into what you want."

He frowned. "Clara..."

"No. Let me just say this. I'll never be the person who'll live up to the idea of what you thought you could have. I'm *me*. That's what you get. And, honestly, I've built this palace that I'm finally alive in, Dominic. I was so proud of myself today in that bakery, and I loved it, loved me for doing it. I want someone to just love me too. I can't sit by you, worried I'm not enough or worried you're holding back because of an idea you wanted in your head. I want to just be enough for someone. I deserve to be."

He nodded solemnly. "If I hurt you or you hurt me, Clara..." He sighed. "No one enjoys feeling like someone could rip apart your damn life at any second. It's happened once before and—"

"And it won't happen with me again," I summarized for him, cutting him off so I didn't have to hear the rest of what he said. I didn't want to. "You'll drain my happiness, Dominic. I can't play second fiddle to all this nor can I live up to it. I won't." My voice shook as I said the words. Standing up for myself after so many years of standing idly by was terrifying but liberating too. I'd learned that with him, fell in love with it because of him, knew I needed it in order to be happy now.

Never again would I tie myself to the weight of someone else and let them drag me down. I'd tied myself to too many anchors, had gone down with the ship too often, hadn't been willing to throw myself onto a life raft to find an island on my own.

I stood from the sand and brushed myself off. When he tried to stand, I held his shoulder. "Don't. Let me go."

I felt his whole body tensing against it. "You can walk away so easily from me?" he whispered, and his words were tortured.

I stared down at him, and before I knew what I was doing, I raised my skirt and lifted one foot to swing over onto the other side of him. I stood over him, looking down at the man I loved as he looked up at me.

"Do you know I love you, Dominic Hardy?" I said softly into the wind, but he caught the words.

"Clara—"

"No. Don't say anything." I shook my head and then slowly lowered myself so I could straddle him. "I love you so much that I'm not walking away easily. I'm leaving my heart here in the sand with you, don't you see? I'm going to walk away and let it wash into the ocean where it can drown with you and your fear and your sorrow."

He hummed that hum I loved so much, and when I felt the tears streaming down my cheeks, I didn't stop them. I pulled him close instead by the collar of his shirt and kissed the mouth I knew I wanted but wouldn't be able to have after this night.

His big, rough hands skirted up my dress, desperate as they gripped at my thighs. When he found nothing underneath, he didn't laugh this time or call me a good girl. He shook his head and swore. "I've become obsessed with how you listen to me, cupcake. Obsessed with how you don't. Obsessed with how you feel, how you sound, how you smell. Obsessed with you."

"But you hate that you're obsessing over me." I summarized. Our relationship wasn't a good thing to him.

He didn't answer the question. "I don't want to lose you. I'll fucking hate it."

Yet, he didn't say he'd try to keep me either. Didn't say he wasn't going to let me go. I didn't know why either, maybe it's what he thought I wanted. Maybe we were both doing what we thought the other needed in that moment.

Love. It makes you do what you hate.

I cried in his arms as I scooted back to unbutton his

trousers. I pulled his thick length from them and pumped my hand over him once, watching his eyes darken in the night. If I didn't own him anywhere else, I owned him here under the moonlight with the sea breeze blowing between us.

I leaned closer even as his hand brushed over my sex, rubbing back and forth to work me up to spiraling down into oblivion. "I don't know if I'll ever get over losing you," I admitted.

"You won't, little fighter. We're not made to be apart." He ground out and then he lifted my hips and jerked them forward onto his cock. "Feel that? It's me with you."

I nodded as I cried and rode him. My sex ached for him, my body curled around him, and my soul felt whole there in the sand with him. Then, I shook my head no, not able to believe it, not wanting to believe it and then crumble when it wasn't true. "Do you actually believe that, Dominic?"

I rocked back and forth on him faster now, gripping his shoulders tight, the sounds of our bodies colliding growing stronger and stronger. His eyes looked wild, his muscles tensing as my pussy squeezed against his cock and even though my orgasm hit, the sound of his whisper hit harder. "I want to believe it, cupcake. I really want to believe."

One last thrust, so hard, I felt him hit every sensitive spot within me, before I cried out his name.

He let out a string of swears as he bowed his head, and his forehead touched mine as he kept murmuring that he wanted to believe.

I nodded with one last tear streaming down my face and said, "That's not good enough."

CHAPTER 37: DOMINIC

She was right. It wasn't good enough. She deserved everything.

I couldn't believe we belonged together when she deserved a man who could give her everything, who could give her less baggage than I could.

Yet, damn, I wanted to believe.

Still, when Clara tried to get off my lap, I gripped her hips. "Give me one more minute of you, cupcake. Please."

I knew I was broken, knew this might end, and knew I wouldn't survive it if it did. So, I begged for more of her, and she sighed into my arms, wrapped hers around my neck and snuggled in.

She gave. I took. She shined light on my darkness and I swallowed it up.

I laid back with her there on that beach for longer than I should have, listening to those waves, wondering how to make this right. How to survive without her, because I was too scared to admit I was vulnerable again. More vulnerable than I'd been before.

Nothing mattered anymore but her. Not the hotel. Not my career. Nothing was more important than giving her everything.

And maybe that's when it clicked for me. I'd never be good enough but no man would ever try the way I would for her. I wasn't letting her go.

I didn't just want to believe that. I knew it.

When her breathing slowed and I saw her eyes were closed, peaceful and calm without tears in them now, I didn't even contemplate getting her a hotel to stay in. We were going to our home where she belonged.

With me.

I righted our clothing and carried her to the car where Callihan stood stoic and quiet as he opened the door for me to fold us into.

He was older and didn't say much but when he got into the car he murmured, "She gave me a cupcake the other day and I decided she's the only girl of yours I'll drive now."

I chuckled and stared down at her. She trusted me to take care of her after being this fatigued and I hoped she'd trust me with even more very soon. I pulled her closer to my chest and smoothed away her hair. "She's the only girl I'll allow you to drive now."

"So, she really your future wife?"

"If she'll have me. And even if she won't, I'm going to try forever to change her mind."

Once, I was seated in the car, she didn't hear me whisper against her hair that I loved her, that I hated loving her the way I did, and that I wouldn't let her go.

When I laid her down in her own bed that night, I stood at her doorway for far too long. It was fucking ironic that I'd avoided sleeping with her, and now all I wanted to do was lay behind her and pull her as close to me as possible.

We both needed space, because I knew that all the things Clara had said to me were right. She deserved to have a man without a past that would dim her light. She deserved the whole world of color, and I needed to find a way to avoid infusing my darkness into it.

I'd been a perfectionist for so long that I wanted to give her that too. The need to do so rattled through my bones. I knew she was mine and I was hers. I just had to pave the way accordingly. My heart beat for and belonged to her, even if it was barely beating from how cold it'd gotten over the years. Natya may have frozen it, but Clara thawed it out, had brought it back to life.

I backed out of the room on a new mission. I called my brother-in-law and Izzy. I told him I wanted everything pulled on Natya. I told them I was done fucking around.

"Finally. Do I get to leak it to the press tomorrow?" Izzy squealed into the phone.

"Hold it."

"But she's fucked us over enough," Izzy whined. "And I can see right here she's laundering money."

Her husband interjected. "If he needs to show mercy, let him. It's not our problem. We're going to bed, Dom." He clicked off the phone before I could say anything else.

It was the only arsenal I needed, one I hadn't used before because getting my hands dirty hadn't been worth it.

Clara, though. I'd go to hell and back for her. She was worth it.

I called Natya, and she purred into the phone, "Well, you got the resort, Dom, and got to fool around. You happy? Because I know you used her to push the narrative in the press for your reopening. It's obvious," she hissed.

I sat down in my study and poured myself a finger of whiskey, knowing I'd need it for the last conversation I'd ever have with my ex. I was ready to dig myself out of this hole of darkness so I could find the light with Clara.

"Of course I used her. She was a perfect girlfriend for the

press. Wouldn't you say so?"

"She did the job, but she's not going to stick around when she figures that out."

"She agreed to it, Natya. Agreed to move in with me too. She agreed to everything."

Natya scoffed. "Did she think you'd fall for her? You can't love her like you loved me, Dom. What we have is—"

"Nothing." I cut her off. "I told you I'd never love like that again. And I don't, nor would I ever want to. With you, I enjoyed it and pursued it. With her, I hate it and have tried to avoid it."

"Why?" she whispered, almost like she was scared to hear it.

"Because I know the love I feel for her won't simply hurt me like yours did. It will destroy me. And even still, it's the only love I want for the rest of my life."

I waited a beat to hear if Natya would respond, if she would finally realize now was the time to apologize and try to let me go. All I heard was silence though.

"People thought I was joking when I said she was my future wife. Natya, I'm not. You so much as look at my future wife wrong after this, I'm coming for you. I will tear apart your career, go to the feds about your laundering, and hang you out to dry for the lying piece of shit that you are. You get me?"

"Dom, I would never—"

"We have evidence of everything you've done, Natya. Don't fuck with her or me. Ever. Again."

I hung up.

There was nothing left to say to the woman. I didn't care about her enough to listen to anything else she wanted to tell me.

I had to plan how I was going to make Clara my wife, and

that meant I was going to have to grovel and make her believe she was it for me. I started with emails first and stayed up late into the night before I gave her the space she requested and went to my own bed.

But when I woke in the morning, Clara was gone.

CHAPTER 38: CLARA

"Of course I used her. She was a perfect girlfriend for the press. Wouldn't you say so?"

And he'd actually waited for her response.

More silence.

"She agreed to it, Natya. Agreed to move in with me too. She agreed to everything."

He still had such emotion, such anger, such a feeling toward her that it hurt to listen anymore.

"Nothing. I told you I'd never love like that again."

I backed away. The reinforcement of his statement, the doubling down of his emotions, the fact that he contacted her in the middle of the night. This all left no room for me.

I packed quietly, sent emails off quickly, and texted Evie early that next morning for Dex's number.

She called immediately. "What's wrong?"

"I just need a place to stay. I can't be here with Dominic after what happened with Natya last night."

She waited in silence, but I wasn't giving any more right now. "Well, we have an apartment building in LA that Declan and I are staying at. Come here. I'll make sure the doorman lets you up."

"No. I need to find my own apartment and ..." I took a deep breath. I hated telling someone no, but this was survival. Survival didn't have formalities or expectations attached to it.

"I get it. I'll get you a furnished place. The doorman will

have your apartment number when you get here. You realize, though, you own shares now, Clara. You get that right? All this is yours too," Evie explained to me.

I hadn't even looked over the paperwork Mrs. Johnson delivered well enough to understand. And the thought made me almost feel as if I couldn't breathe. There were too many things changing, too many pieces of my life I still had to fit together, too much pain I had to comprehend to figure out my finances now. I cleared my throat. "I ... Right."

"We'll figure it all out. Go to the apartment. Rest. Call me after, okay? Do you need—"

"I'm fine. I just need time alone and some sleep. I can't think when I'm near him and—" I tried not to cry, tried to hold together my soul that was breaking.

"Oh, Clara. It'll all be okay."

I assured her it would. I tried to feel it too. But when I got to the apartment, it felt so empty even with its beautiful high ceilings, wall-to-wall windows overlooking the city, and the custom leather furnishings.

I didn't want muted tones with cleanliness everywhere. I wanted my furballs running around while my rainbow accents clashed with Dominic's black and white.

When a soul shatters from hitting the ground after falling in love, I don't know if there's a remedy other than surrounding yourself with the people you love. And family is supposed to be that. Familial bonds are comfortable, ingrained from childhood, and what we strive for in adulthood. It's why when my sister texted to meet me for breakfast, I thought it would be fine. I thought inviting her to my apartment would maybe bridge a gap if I told her I'd broken up with Dominic.

When I laid in my bed to wait for her, his text came

through.

Dominic: Where the hell are you?

Me: I got an apartment. I'll be back to pick up all my other things soon and the kittens.

Dominic: You're not picking up anything.

Dominic: Especially not the cats.

Me: You know Sugar and Spice are mine, Dominic.

Dominic: Those cats are ours. And you're mine. Get your ass back here now.

Me: Dominic, we discussed this.

Dominic: No. You discussed it. I barely even fucking processed it.

Me: This is best for both of us.

Dominic: Speak for yourself. I'm left with a rainbow garden and bookshelf that's not in the right order.

Instead of crying, I was growling in anger now.

Me: I didn't leave your place a mess, Dominic. And you know it. Plus, I said I'm coming to get my things soon. If there's something you need me to take care of, I will.

Dominic: You're not taking a damn thing out of this house, Clara. Get back here so we can figure out everything. The media outlets are taken care of now. We just need to take care of us.

Me: No thank you. I'm tired, Dominic. And I've got to get all this moved. For me, it takes a lot of effort.

I was only affording him that honesty because he understood it and had been compassionate about it in the past. He'd let me feel comfortable sharing the aches and the pains before, and now, with the stress of knowing I wouldn't have him in the near future, I felt my body bending to the will of my condition.

My phone rang immediately. When I answered, he didn't even let me say hello. "Are you okay?"

"Fine," I said softly, but my voice cracked. "I just need space."

"That's the one thing I won't give you, Clara. I'm coming over. Text me your address."

"No. It's the one thing you have to give me."

"For how long?"

"I don't know." I took a shaky breath. "Maybe an hour or

maybe forever. We'll see how strong I am."

"You're my little fighter. The question is are you fighting for us or against us?"

"You can't honestly think we'd win this fight, Dominic. You haven't gotten over her."

"Her?" he growled. "It's not about her."

I murmured that I had to go and hung up on him.

I laid down to try to take a nap, to just forget all that was happening.

Time passed but my eyes never drifted shut. Sleeping without him near was much too hard already.

When the knock at the door sounded, I welcomed the distraction and went to open the door for Anastasia ... and my mother. She sneered at me, "So he left you?"

"I'm leaving him," I started, but I was looking at my sister, trying my best not to let the unshed tears roll down my cheeks. "You said it was just you coming."

"So? Mom wanted to come too." She shrugged and walked in, waving my mother in after her and leaving the door wide open like they had servants to take care of it. "Is he putting you up in this apartment to be gracious?" I wouldn't tell them that I owned it now. The sliver of hope I'd had at finding resolution with them was gone. "I really thought you might be of some use to us, Clara. I honestly did, but you're fucking useless." My mother shook her head in disgust.

"What?" I murmured.

"Oh, don't look like you're going to cry. It's obvious we want our HEAT membership back, and we were hoping you could get to Evie's ridiculous status with Dominic maybe. Evie married Declan, and now she gets to act like she's above us. If you married Dom ... Well, that's not happening, is it? You've ruined that too."

"I ... I guess so." I shook my head, mad for even subjecting myself to them again, for falling for their act at the reopening.

"And what's with this rash?" She poked a finger into my red cheek and then pushed it hard. "Go cover it up. No wonder he's leaving you. If you're not going to take care of yourself—"

"That's what I'm trying to do!" I screeched and both of their eyes widened. "Why do you think I moved away from you? You're triggering—"

She smacked me clean across the face with a lot more power than I imagined she had at this point in her life. When she wound back up to do it again her hand was yanked from behind.

Evie had my mother's hand behind her back and her chest on the ground in one fluid move. I knew Evie practiced self-defense and could restrain most if need be. My mother was no match for her even though she tried. "I'm not letting you up, Mrs. Milton. Dominic, call security." My stepsister's knee pushed into my mother's back as she squirmed further.

"I'll press charges if you don't let me up. I'm having a conversation with my daughter."

"No. You *hit* your daughter, Melinda. And it's illegal, even if she allowed you to do it," Evie said, her eyes searching mine with sadness and then turning on Anastasia with malice. "What sort of sister are you?"

"Excuse me?" Anastasia scoffed. "I wasn't doing anything—"

"*Exactly.* You just stood there. You're her older sister. You're supposed to protect her—"

"Evie, it's fine." I shut my eyes for a second and then opened them to catch Anastasia's gaze. "Actually, it's not. Why did you bring her here?"

"Well, I ..." She looked shocked that I wouldn't let it go. "It's not a big deal, Clara. You know how Mom is."

"Yes, she's like *this* with me. Not you. And you brought her here knowing that she'd be angry."

"You're useless," my mother screeched. "Of course I'm mad. I have a daughter that can't do anything right. She's lost us the HEAT empire. She's useless. Useless. Useless."

"Mrs. Milton." Dominic's voice cut through the room and ended my mother's whining. His eyes were on me, vivid green and full of so many emotions I couldn't pin one of them down. Then, he walked right over to me and kneeled so he could lower his face into her view since Evie wasn't letting her get up. "Do you know your daughter left me and practically stalked her this morning to figure out where she was? That I showed up to be here for her? That I'll always be here even if she doesn't want me to?"

My mother tried to say something.

He cut her off. "Do you know she'll be able to ask me for the rest of her life to jump, and I'll ask how high? She could ask me to give someone a membership to HEAT although it's an unbiased lottery and I'll put the names through expedited just for her. Better yet, you know that your daughter already has that luxury, and do you know why?

My mother stopped squirming. "What?" Her big eyes widened as she glanced at me. "How?"

"Clara, would you like to tell your mother, or should I?"

I chewed my lip before shrugging and owning it. "I am officially a major shareholder."

The paperwork I got still hadn't completely sunk in from Mrs. Johnson.

"And that's because she was able to design and run a world-renowned bakery within the resort. She's not useless. She's fucking *priceless.* And as a major shareholder, she also owns most of this apartment complex that you're in. You're on her fucking property."

The security guards came to the door.

My mother whispered out, "That can't be right. I mean, Clara, you know I didn't mean what I said."

"Mrs. Milton and Anastasia, I'm going to say this one time, and I want you to listen very carefully before you're thrown out of our building. My future wife may allow you to treat her badly but let me be crystal fucking clear: *I* won't ever allow it again."

"But you're broken up—" Anastasia started.

"Doesn't mean I'm not going to marry her, Anastasia. I am going to. And I'm going to spend the rest of my life protecting her from feeling the pain you delivered today. Do you understand?"

Neither of them answered because they probably were so embarrassed for being called out on their actions, they thought they could be silent in hopes it would disappear.

"I said, Do. You. Understand?" Dominic repeated pointedly this time. They muttered yes and Dominic turned to me. "Cupcake, would you like your security to escort this woman and her daughter off the premises?"

"Clara, be reasonable—" my mother whimpered.

Evie scoffed and I shook my head. Reasonable was finally seeing the truth and acting on it. "Yes. I'd like them escorted off the property and a record filed on their behavior."

When they were waved toward the door, they went willingly and Evie followed. "I'm leaving you two to discuss this 'future wife' thing. And Clara"—she pulled me close and hugged me—"Sorry, I told Dom where you were when he called but I love you. Remember, I love you."

When I tried to say thank you, she held up her hand. "There's no thank yous in families." And then she was gone too.

In their place was silence, heavy with questions and pain and echoes of what had just happened in that room. I tried to fill it with lies. "It doesn't happen often that she—"

"You're a shit liar, Clara. I've told you that time and time again."

I took a breath and then one tear rolled over my reddened cheek. "Right."

He was there within a second to pull me close. To let me break down and expel whatever pain I had. It was the pain of losing a mother and a sister, the idea of them that I thought I could create. "I guess you know what it means to love the idea of something," I murmured.

He nodded over my head and smoothed my hair. He then whispered, "But sometimes the real thing becomes better than the idea ever was."

I thought of Evie and me, of how she'd been my estranged stepsister for so long but still stepped into the line of fire for me in a way my sister never had. Sometimes choosing a family instead of keeping the one you were given was the right choice.

Yet, I didn't know if he was talking about Evie and me. He might have been talking about me and him, but how could he when he wasn't sure we were even made to be together? He wanted to *believe* it. That was all he'd said that night on the beach.

And then, his phone call with Natya solidified it. My heart lurched thinking about it. "I don't want to talk about ideas today, Dominic. I just need space and time to think."

I couldn't.

"I'm staying over today." He didn't wait for me to invite him. "And we're lying in bed for most of it. You need rest. Were you packing all night?"

"No ... Well, maybe." I sighed. "You used to never want to stay in your bed with a woman, Dominic."

"Yeah, and now it's only my bed if you're in it." He pulled at his neck and looked toward the ceiling. "Please, Clara. I don't beg, but I will for you. Let me sleep here, and then I'll leave you alone all week if you want. You have my word. One week for you to think."

I chewed at my cheek and then rubbed away the tears but winced at the rash forming there.

"Fuck, baby. Let me take care of you. Just for today."

"I don't want to talk about us at all." It was too much right now.

"Fine. If you agree that you're going to go to a doctor about that rash."

I nodded because it was all too much. I was so tired. Too tired to fight him on sleeping arrangements. I was too tired to fight against what my heart wanted when it was latched to him anyway. I fell back into my bed, "Stay on your side, Dominic Hardy."

He got into the bed and even though I was on the edge of my side, he grabbed me and yanked me over to his so he could spoon me. "Only if you're on my side with me."

***

I slept like a baby, and the next morning, he'd made me breakfast with paprika in my eggs and a note on the counter.

Breakfast for my cupcake.

Don't say I left before the sun came up unless you also

admit that you were going to kick me out anyway.

One week, cupcake. That's it.

Trying to cover the rash on my cheeks and the joint pain through the workweek would probably have been impossible, so I didn't really bother. Although I went to work as much as possible, my staff was there to pick up the slack when needed, which was most of the day considering how busy opening week was.

Every day, I settled more and more into my routine. Every day, my flare-up symptoms subsided a bit. I knew lupus showcased itself differently and that I wouldn't always be able to control my flare-ups. That sometimes they would appear even during the most relaxing day. Yet, I found contentment in controlling the parts of my life I could, that I'd been strong enough to do that. I could and had created a healthier life here without my mother and sister.

Even if I knew my ultimate heartbreak was near. Dominic wouldn't always be around. He'd have other projects, more responsibilities outside of this resort. I would be able to prosper here without him because I loved baking for people who appreciated the hint of spices I added into their specialty drinks and their chocolates. I enjoyed the children coming in from the waterpark begging for poppy cupcakes. And my heart melted when an older couple who bought the cupcakes for each other and told me they danced in the California poppies one night fifty years ago.

Good food created memories and reminded people of the

ones they'd had in the past. I knew that. Yet, the memories of Dominic were all around me and I was still trying to forget.

So, on Friday, when Valentino came in to pout about how I'd not come to his restaurant yet, I told him I'd make my way there that night after I closed because I wanted to show him I was proud of all of us.

I wasn't really thinking about how it would look. I didn't think he would, as the head chef, sit down and dine with me.

I wasn't thinking until I saw my ultimate heartbreak, green eyes blazing with fury, in the doorway of the restaurant.

CHAPTER 39: DOMINIC

One week.

I thought I could last a week. And at one point, she texted me that she was coming to get the cats, but I told her no. I got my whole damn week.

So, that solidified that I needed to hold out.

But I'd seen that woman endure an abusive mother and sister, a move, and many flare-ups caused by the stress she'd been under. I'd watched from afar as she powered through a crazy opening week with the bakery and somehow managed to push through the pain I knew she was feeling.

If I didn't walk by her bakery to catch a glimpse of her stretching and flexing her hands every now and then, I watched the security cameras.

I wasn't above it.

I called my sisters and brothers to handle Anastasia and Mrs. Milton because I knew they still owned some family shares of our spas, and I wanted them out on their asses in the meantime. I also made sure that our PR team handled releasing any sort of media about Clara.

The resort didn't matter anymore.

"What do you mean the casino deal isn't a go?" I growled into the phone when Dex called me.

"I don't want Keelani anywhere near it. So, if you guys brought her in for a gig there, I'm pulling out."

"You're pulling out of a multibillion-dollar deal because

you're mad Keelani broke your heart when you were a fucking teenager? Man the hell up, Dex. She's been a family friend for years."

"Fuck you. You just told me to handle the press with Clara and that you didn't care if the casino deal fell through either."

"Clara is different. They can have the whole resort for all I care when it comes to her. I'm going to fucking marry her."

"So now your precious baby doesn't matter?" He sounded like he was in disbelief. Then he sighed.

"What about your precious casino deal?"

Dex's security and tech industry was unmatched. It was why he'd been given the casino deal in the first place. With that partnership, we'd have his HEAT security systems in place at all the casinos in the country.

"I don't want Keelani fucking near it—"

"Sign that deal, Dex." My hand all but crushed the phone as he said it. Had he been in front of me, I would have punched him. "And quit being a baby. She got over you. You need to get over her."

"How do you know she's over me?" Now he sounded devastated.

"Jesus Christ. I'm not telling you her business—"

"Is she in Vegas now?" he demanded. When I didn't answer fast enough, he growled, "I'll check the cameras myself," and hung up.

My brother had lost his mind to the girl he loved. I couldn't blame him. I was losing mine too to Clara. I texted the family that Natya was backing off, but we needed to push out statements about the resort and that no media outlet was allowed to talk about Clara. I wanted everyone to make sure their PR teams knew that.

She didn't need the stress. I wouldn't allow for it.

Then I saw her with Valentino.

In his restaurant.

I'd just waved a red flag for my brother about the girl he loved, and now I was seeing the same thing with the one I loved.

She was smiling. She seemed happy. I should have been the one making her smile.

I glanced at my watch. It was Friday. That was a full workweek. Still counted as lasting a week in my book. My future wife was sitting with another man in his restaurant, though, and that man was going to pay a hefty price, no matter that he smiled at me as I approached them.

"Dom, I didn't know you were still here tonight—"

"I'm where my future wife is, Valentino." I cut him off as I stood at their table. I knew my anger was palpable, knew the stare that most shrank away from was drilling into Valentino.

He chuckled nervously and motioned for a server to bring a chair. "Please join us."

"Do you think I need to be invited to a dinner within my own resort?" I asked him softly and then I tsked. "Get out of my chair."

His eyes widened along with Clara's but here was the lesson they needed to learn. When they'd met me, I'd been an asshole about the design of my resort. I was ruthless when it came to that. It benefited them all wildly. Now, they needed to learn I was also an asshole when it came to what was mine—and anything involving Clara was exactly that.

Even so, Valentino learned fast. He stood from the chair and offered me the seat. "I didn't mean any— Why is everyone leaving?" His voice was high.

"Your restaurant is closing for the night. It may be

closing for the future too," I pointedly said. "Don't ever give my girlfriend a gift again, Valentino. And if you invite her to a meal without me, know that I'll ruin you. You may feed all these people, and you may be a world-renowned chef, but I feed you. Have you heard the saying? Don't bite the hand that feeds you. "

"Yes ... I—"

"There are millions of good chefs in the world, do you know that? Millions who could take your place. But there's only one of her. You understand?" I lifted a brow, and the man nodded, his own brow sweating now. "Leave."

He didn't even say goodbye, just rushed out.

"You've got to be kidding me, Dominic," I heard from across the table as I waved over the last waiter still there and told him to get me two fingers of whiskey. "That was the most ridiculous territorial display of—"

"Why are you still fucking wearing that necklace?" I cut her off. My eyes were on it. I couldn't look away from it, couldn't unsee her with another man she'd viewed as a potential beau when I knew all I wanted was for her to be with me.

Her small fingers floated over it. "I honestly forgot with everything going on and haven't thought about changing it—"

My hand snapped out to twist the gold chain around my fingers. Then, I yanked it fast. The motion was swift enough that the necklace gave way and broke so I could fist it. She gasped and grabbed at her neck, but it was too late. I dropped it into the champagne Valentino had been drinking. And when the waiter stopped by, I waved at the glass. "Pour it down the drain where it belongs." I held her eyes as the waiter scurried away with the jewelry in the glass. "It should only ever be my necklace or fingers touching your neck. Nothing else."

I saw how her breath hitched, how her pale skin blushed,

and how her nipples hardened under that thin dress fabric. “Dominic, you know you haven’t given me a week—”

“A work week,” I corrected her.

She rolled her eyes. “That’s not a whole week.”

“Semantics.” I glanced down at the food.

“So, I get my kittens back today?”

I didn’t answer that. “How’s your flare-up doing? It’s gone down a bit.”

I studied the emotions flying over her face, how she touched her cheeks that I knew she covered up because of the rash but I also saw that it had faded. “You noticed?”

“I notice everything about you,” I told her and meant it. Every moment I caught with her was beautiful and I didn’t want to miss a single one. Clara Milton was stunning in her strength to overcome every obstacle that had been thrown her way.

“I’m not used to people noticing, I guess.” She picked at a linen napkin on the table before she cleared her throat. “Anyway, I’m okay. I’ll meet with doctors next week.”

“Good. I’ll come if you’ll let me.” My jaw ticked. I couldn’t command her here like I could within the resort and with her bakery. Her life was hers, but I wanted her to trust me enough to allow it.

Her eyes sliced to me then, studying me. “Since I’ve been here working with you, you’ve told me to own it, Dominic. So, I’m going to. I heard your conversation with Natya the night I left.” Her voice was shaky.

“Okay?” I dragged out the word, not sure why it mattered.

“You said you used me,” she whispered. “On the phone with her, you said I was the perfect girlfriend to her.”

“What?” I frowned. “What are you talking about?”

“I keep wondering if you just nurtured and pretended to

like me so I would do all this perfectly?"

"You didn't hear the whole conversation then, Clara." She couldn't have or she wouldn't have looked so broken. "Of course I would have done anything for this resort, but we agreed to all this together, and then—"

I saw how her mind was racing as she frowned though. "You taught me how to hold myself confidently, to relax into your touch, to be the idea of what you thought was the perfect girlfriend. But I'm not *just* an idea, Dominic. I just got away from my mother and sister treating me just how they wanted."

Her and this thing about ideas, I was starting to get it though. Clara had been a tool for her family for too long and she was feeling the same with me. "If I was only molding you into the perfect fake girlfriend or real one for that matter, Clara, I wouldn't have had you change all the colors in my resort and put a bakery in the center of it that everyone is obsessed with. We agreed to start out like that, okay?" Didn't she see that?

"No. That's not fucking okay." She blurted out and then looked shocked that she had. "I fell in love with you, Dominic. I fucking loved you."

"You do love me. Don't do that." Her use of the past tense had my jaw tightening, my throat burning.

"How could I love a man who was using and molding me into some idea as I fell for him?" She replied and then she leaned back in the chair to look me over. "You know that Valentino asked me tonight what I saw in you? I saw the artist, the man that wouldn't stop even when everyone told him something wouldn't work. Having a resort taller than the tallest, one that jutted out into the ocean, or a completely transparent bridge. You proved everyone wrong, and I looked up to that, respected it. You know why? Because you defied logic, and you owned it.

You told me to own it too. Over and over again."

I didn't say a word. Her lip trembled, and I knew there was more coming.

"I've felt undeserving my whole life. Not good enough. Too big, too small, hair too red, too many freckles, too much or little of something. And I wanted to defy that logic too. I started to believe I could with you. You're a master at it, defying logic, constructing something beautiful from something not. But now, I think... I know, I don't want to be anything but myself. And now I'm not sure if everything you want me for who I am or who you want me to be. Was all this a lie?"

"They weren't lies, Clara." My teeth clenched together. "We're not a lie. Take it back."

"I won't," she whispered. "Because I don't know. You said you *wanted* to believe we were meant to be together on the beach that night. You didn't say you *did* believe it, that you would *fight* for it, that you would fight for me."

She tried to stand up in her anger, but I caught her wrist before she did, and she sat back down to listen to me. "You think I haven't been falling too? Of course, everything was real, even when I didn't want it to be. You're the damn light in my world that I didn't want. *You.* Nothing else. I told you that. I knew I was going to be that black hole that snuffed out your light, babe. I didn't expect you to instead explode within me and fight off all the darkness."

I closed my eyes for a second, trying to wrap my mind around how I felt for her and explain it. I heard her sigh and start, "Dominic, maybe we—"

I cut her off. "I said I *wanted* to believe we were meant to be that night only because I don't believe *anyone* is good enough for you, Clara. But I'm going to try every day to be good enough. Don't you see? Every idea I thought I wanted out of my life was obliterated when you stepped into it. You changed the trajectory of everything, and I fought to keep my sanity, to not fall victim to what I had before because loving you is much more fatal than loving anybody else. Any idea or person. If you leave, I'll lose the life you gave me back."

She stared at me for moments. Maybe minutes. Her mouth opened then closed. Then she asked softly, "You want me to apologize for being lovable?"

"Yes," I bellowed. "I want you to apologize for making this resort something I don't even give a damn about. The papers could write that the resort was my baby for days and I wouldn't give a shit now. They could rip me and the resort apart and if they left you out of it, I'd be happy. I'm obsessed with only your well-being. With being with you. And you've done that. You can apologize for being irresistible. Being you. Being everything I wanted but don't deserve."

"You don't deserve me if you were trying so hard not to fall for me," she whispered, and that shit broke my heart because she was right. I couldn't even correct her.

"No one deserves you. But I tried not to fall for you, Clara, because of the fear I feel now at losing you." I told her and then looked at the table between us, at the restaurant another man had invited her to. "But I'll be damned if anyone tries to have you over me. I'm yours and you're mine."

"You don't get to make that decision alone, Dominic."

"I know, but I'm going to show you that over time." There was a brilliance to Clara Milton, and I was sure no one could compete with it. They'd have been stupid to try. But I could show her that.

Words never showed anyone anything. I knew that. I

built structures that inspired the masses because they wouldn't believe it if I just drew it on paper.

They needed to see it. To witness it.

So did she.

I wouldn't say more. Not now.

Not yet.

I cracked my neck before I looked down at the food. "Was your meal good?"

"Before I was so rudely interrupted?" Her foot under the table nudged my leg in irritation but it also seemed to be a sort of truce. We'd discussed enough tonight. Plus, any touch from her was wanted, and I smiled at it.

"If my girlfriend goes on a date with someone else, I'm going to interrupt."

"Fake girlfriend. And now ex."

"You really think you're breaking up with me?" Fuck, it hurt even when it shouldn't have. This had been the plan before. We'd break up and Valentino would swoop in. I'd predicted and pushed for it at one time.

Now, I'd die before I let that shit happen.

She didn't answer as she glanced around. "Was there a reason the restaurant closed?" She lifted a brow.

"Other than because you were sitting here with a man who's trying to fuck you? No. I own the restaurant. And I'll close it any time another man glances in your direction the wrong way."

"Possessive with all your exes?" I saw the sparkle back in her eyes.

"Just one ex ... because she's not going to be an ex for long."

"What's she going to be?" Her voice came out a breathy whisper.

"My fucking wife," I growled, no hesitation at all. I wasn't letting her go, and I knew I was gaining ground because her breath caught at my words.

"Don't be ridiculous." She finally said softly.

I let it go for now. "Plus, I figure I'm saving them from a fight, cupcake. Protecting the public, actually."

She smirked and then glanced around. "The restaurant is beautiful."

"Have you seen the chef's kitchen?"

She shook her head and I stood, holding a hand out. I needed her to take it, to accept who I was here as much as who I'd be in the future. This was the first gesture of many I would make, but I was establishing a boundary too. She needed to know she was mine or that she was at least learning to be mine.

When she set her soft hand in my palm, my whole body relaxed. I pulled her close and walked her back through the steel doors. With only a few of the staff left, I commanded that everyone leave, and the kitchen emptied quickly.

Clara's eyes twinkled as she took in the stainless steel, bright lights, big stoves, and the large metal island top in the middle. She let go of me to drag her hand across it. "The setup is perfect. He's got everything he needs in here." She turned her eyes on me. "He's an amazing chef, Dominic. I really do like his food."

"So, are you saying I shouldn't fire him?"

"You're not going to fire him," she said as I placed two hands on the table behind her so that I'd caged her in.

"Is that so?"

"Yes, because it's his restaurant and if you do, I'm going to be furious."

"Hm. You know I love when you fight me, cupcake. Go

ahead, be furious," I murmured as my lips touched the soft skin of her neck and she shuddered. Then, my hand went to the back of her neck, and I grabbed a fistful of her hair, pulling it to expose the column of her neck to me.

I sucked the skin there as soon as she did and then bit hard. I wanted it to be painful, to show her the pain she'd inflicted on me over the past week, to show her this skin was mine, even if she kept it from me.

Her hands were on my shirt as I did, and she moaned into the fabric, "Dominic, this isn't us giving each other space or working out the problem."

"I never wanted fucking space. I thought that was clear when I texted you and then came to stay with you that day. I'll give you it but I don't want it," I ground out, my hands at her hips as I lifted her onto the table, "Instead, I want you every single day, and I'll want you every day for the rest of your life."

She stared at me like she was trying to believe it, like she was working through if she could. "Are you sure you won't just want the idea you created?"

Clara had been used her whole life and molded into what she didn't want from her family. I vowed right then to break her of the concept.

"Don't you see the idea I created would have never been you, love? It would have been easier, it would have been smoother, it wouldn't have been me worrying about you and craving you and missing you every day. It would have been a woman never fighting me, but you do at every turn." She whimpered when my hand went up her skirt; I felt nothing there, as always. "Damn, it would have been you wearing underwear when you're at dinner with another fucking man, Clara. Did you go without them for him or me this time, little fighter?"

Her eyes narrowed. "I didn't even know I was going to dinner with him tonight but if you think this was for him"—she spread her legs wide so I could feel how wet she was and then a sly smile crossed her face—"then it definitely was."

Fuck.

She rolled her pussy into my hand and yanked me close to her mouth. "I'm still mad and I'm still not sure about us. So, make me forget, Dominic. If only for a second."

"You won't ever forget anything between us." The words came out rough as I pinched her clit and she gasped. I kissed her then, devoured her lips. Our tongues warred against one another, our hands rough, our movements fierce as we sought out pleasure from the other body.

"I'm going to fuck you on this table, little fighter, so every time you step into Valentino's restaurant you know who owns you. Who's never been your fake boyfriend but only the real one. Who actually owns this pussy of yours. You won't forget that."

I think we'd both been lost without one another over the week, both wanted the fight, wanted to feel one another, even if it was painful. "Or maybe Valentino will own it," she countered.

I lost it then, growling as I stepped back to turn her to face the table and bend her over it. Then, I grunted in her ear, "I'm going to fuck you rough for that, cupcake."

She put her hands on the table and looked over her shoulder with fire in her eyes to goad me, "Do it."

I smoothed my hand over her ass before I lifted her skirt and took in her perfect ass, such smooth round globes. Then, I dragged a finger over her sex. "Look at you. So wet that you're dripping down your thighs, Clara. You think Valentino could own you like this?"

She just shook her head.

Good.

At least she knew. “This pussy is practically weeping for me to give you exactly what you need.” I undid my pants to pull out my length. “You know what that is, baby?”

I pinched her clit when she didn’t answer. “You. I need you, Dominic.”

“Yeah, me. Only me. No one else.” I let her feel the tip of me at her entrance, sliding my cock in her slickness. “I’m going to fuck you so rough. This pussy will be feeling me for days after. It’ll be sore, baby, but wet too. Want to know why? Because I belong here.”

I thrust into her swiftly, all the way in. I buried my cock as far as it would go because I wanted her to feel me everywhere in her. In her pussy but also her mind and her heart. “You’re mine. Only mine. Do you understand?”

She shook her head. “It was fake and it’s over.”

Fake. I hated that word.

I fucked her harder, smacking her ass and gripping her hips before I pulled completely out and dragged my cock between the cheeks of her backside. She shuddered at the new sensation. “You want it, Clara?”

She whispered yes but I wanted more from her.

I smacked one ass cheek again hard enough that I felt the reverberation on the other and on my length.

“Louder. Say you understand this was never fake. Say it, Clara.”

I felt her arching for my cock, but she wouldn’t say it. She wouldn’t admit what we were. And, fuck, she was stronger than me because I growled and slid inside her again without hearing her say the words. Her pussy clenched around me, and I heard her moan my name, but it wasn't enough.

"Don't you understand that only my cock belongs inside you, baby?" She didn't respond. "That you fit around me perfectly?"

"Please just make me forget," she said instead.

Her begging for that just made me fuck her more desperately.

And she cried out, "Harder, Dominic. Harder."

I was gripping her hips so tightly, I knew there would be bruises but she met each thrust of mine with her body, like she couldn't get enough. "You feel that? Your pussy feels who owns it for real, little fighter. You can't fight this. Tell me you understand."

Again, she didn't respond.

"So, I guess you're going to make me prove I own it."

She nodded right as her sex clamped down on me like a vice.

I thrust in twice more as I ground out, "That's it, Clara. Take my dick, baby. Just how you like it. Just how it's meant for you. You do it so well."

I emptied all of me into her.

It's the only place I would do it from this point forward anyway.

And I was going to prove it.

CHAPTER 40: CLARA

He said he had something to show me after we'd made a complete mess of ourselves in Valentino's restaurant, that we deserved a weekend away to figure everything out.

I wasn't so sure. Could you figure out love and heartbreak at the same time?

I was only sure that suddenly I was strong enough to endure them both. I'd confronted him. I'd lost myself to him again. And I'd picked myself back up.

That week, I'd also stood up to my family, opened my bakery, taken what I wanted finally, and managed to get through it. I wasn't just surviving, I was thriving here, and I wanted to thrive with or without him.

I owed that to myself. Everyone did. Our hearts and souls deserve for us to be our number one advocate. If you don't fight for yourself, who will?

I agreed to go with him under one condition. "You bring Sugar and Spice over after if we don't work all this out, no fight."

"Clara," he warned, but I was ready.

"They're mine, and they need their mother."

"When do I get to see them if you're not happy after this weekend?" He looked so desperate in his pursuit of me suddenly and my heart yearned to just give in, but I had to be sure.

"Well, I can bring them to the bakery, I guess." I tried not to laugh because I knew he would totally disagree with cats in his resort.

His jaw ticked, once, twice, three times before he ground out, “Fine. At least two days a week.”

I think my eyes bugged completely out of their sockets, but I tried to hide it by blinking over and over again at the tears that were filling my eyes. “Fine. I’ll go with you this weekend.”

“There was unexpected weather there so I’d like to see it now if possible. Two days. Make sure your staff can manage without you this weekend.”

I had to clarify. “I’m not staying with you.”

He narrowed his eyes. “We’ll see.”

That’s how I ended up in the SUV with Callihan driving us up the side of a mountain that weekend. When I got in, I started, “It’s probably best to clear the air.”

He just shook his head, laptop already open as he typed away. “Wait until we get to the resort I want to show you. I’m working on something.”

“Working?” I questioned and he just nodded. “Didn’t you invite me so we could talk?”

“No. I invited you to show you something at the resort.”

I huffed but figured I would just ignore him until then. So, we didn’t talk for the two hours it took to weave out of the city and up through forests and mountain terrain. Until I was so awestruck, I couldn’t contain it anymore. “Dominic, there’s snow.” I squealed.

He looked at me confused. “I said there was snow.”

“You said ‘unexpected weather.’”

He shrugged. “Well, right. We’re going to see if we can get the HEAT brand established somewhere in Big Bear. I’m thinking a boutique ski resort. There are three mountains, apparently, so we need to assess which area would be best.”

“It’s so pretty.” I was literally bouncing in my seat.

He closed his laptop and took off his eyeglasses. I still hated those things because every time he wore them, I wanted to literally climb on his lap and ask him to study me instead of his computer. That's not where my focus should have been at all. "California has very diverse terrain. I've got to finish this email, so anything else?"

"I'm so excited! My mother hates snow. We never learned to ski or snowboard. I've never even been sledding. Did you sled as a kid?"

He pointedly looked at his laptop and then nodded. "Sure. I also got buried by my brothers and sisters in an igloo once. They did it on purpose, claimed I was being an annoying big brother. When I held my breath under there for about thirty seconds, they'd all dug me up, and my sisters were crying."

"That's sort of mean and terrifying."

"Well, they learned that day to not only own their actions but the consequences of them too."

"Are you always trying to teach everyone to own it?" I asked.

"Maybe." He thought about it. "I think I tried to teach lessons until I had to learn them myself."

We let the silence linger a little, and he grabbed his glasses and reopened the laptop but I was now considering the attire I'd brought. "How cold do you think it's going to be over the weekend?"

He groaned and snapped the laptop shut again. "I'm not going to get done what I'm working on, am I?"

"Probably not." I shrugged. He'd invited me. "Do I need to get a winter jacket?"

"You didn't bring a jacket?"

"No. I just thought it would be like LA."

He lowered the partition and told Callihan we needed to stop at a store.

I wrinkled my nose. "Is it going to be expensive?"

"I swear to all that's fucking holy, Clara, it doesn't matter. Do you know how much money you have now? How much money I have? I have one more email to write and then—"

"For someone who invited me along, you're really not making this at all enjoyable." I crossed my arms. Then I unbuckled my seat belt to move over one seat, distancing myself.

Two minutes later, he snapped his laptop shut again, and unbuckled my seat belt—even when I batted at his hand and said, "What are you doing?"

"Moving you back where you're supposed to be, little fighter."

"Where's that?" I said, but it came out breathy in a way it probably shouldn't have. We hadn't discussed where this was going, but somehow, it felt like we were back to dating and back to me being concerned about what he needed in life.

"Right next to me, baby. Always." He reached across me to grab my hip closest to the window and pulled me toward him.

Right then, though, we passed another patch of soft snow that sparkled across a sloping hill. "Can we stop?" I whispered.

He stared at me for a second and then nodded before he told the driver to stop. I jumped out of the car. There's something about seeing a landscape painted all white, the sun shining brightly on it. I felt the breeze on my skin, the cool air filling my lungs, and took in how quiet it all was.

"That white I love sometimes can blanket things beautifully, right?" Dominic said, his voice close.

When I turned back to look at him, he was smirking at me with a twinkle in his eye.

"And sometimes, there needs to be a little something to mess up all the perfection right?" Before he could answer, I ran fast into the snow and moved through it, spinning around and around. I dropped to scoop up a pile of it and threw it over my head giggling at how cold and light it was.

Dominic shook his head the whole time at me, but I just yelled at him, "Come run with me, fake boyfriend."

He rolled his eyes and chuckled as he walked out into the field, his black suit a stark opposite of how I must have looked in my maxi dress blowing in the wind. "I'm not your fake boyfriend anymore, Clara."

"Right. What are you then?"

"The real one."

I looked down at my hands as my vision blurred, and it seemed like they were turning gray. I flexed my fingers, but color only came back to two of them. Everything turned gray and faded away. "I don't feel right, Dominic," I murmured, and then I passed out.

CHAPTER 41: DOMINIC

She took one breath. It was a gasp, full of fear, full of surprise, and then her hand reached out before her body collapsed right as my heart about stopped beating.

I already knew that Clara wasn't just an annoying piece of my puzzle that wouldn't fit into my life, but this confirmed it. She wasn't just a piece.

She was the whole puzzle.

My whole life.

I hadn't been ignoring her in the SUV to work, I'd been planning how I was going to grovel and make her mine for good up in the mountains. I might have hated the way she infused her color into the black-and-white of my life and hotel, but I loved hating it.

Proving that to her didn't matter in those moments though.

When the person who lights up your world has their life dance with death in front of you, the reaction is catastrophic. I crumpled with her into the snow as I caught her before she hit the ground. It was only seconds that her eyes fluttered closed, only seconds of loss, but they were the most important seconds of my life, the ones that imprinted on me forever, tattooed the feelings on my heart, and solidified that I'd never let her go.

She tried to brush it off as she came to and said she was going to the doctor this coming week, but I'd already called 911. I sat in the ambulance, helpless, as they checked her vitals, as they went over her prognosis saying something about Raynaud's syndrome on top of lupus. I squeezed her hand the whole time.

Now, sitting in that hospital room, I wondered if she knew the risks she'd taken, if she was aware how fragile a life could be. Maybe I hadn't been aware either until that very moment.

"Your person to contact in case of emergency, Ms. Milton is—"

"Me," I cut off the nurse.

She glanced tepidly at me and then Clara. "And is he your—"

"Future husband," I finished before Clara could clarify.

Her eyes narrowed like she wanted to fight me, but she didn't when I waved to the nurse to get the paperwork. She was in a hospital bed and not supposed to be dealing with any of these things right now. "Some of her paperwork is in the system, but we'll need an updated medical history as it looks like you're from Florida?"

"I am," Clara confirmed, but when the nurse left the room, she crossed her arms. "Stop telling people that!"

"Why?"

"Because we weren't even together and we broke up."

"Hm ... I don't recall being broken up when I fucked you on Valentino's table."

Her eyes flicked to the door of her room. "Dominic, now's not the time for your mouth and—"

"I was there when you fell and fainted, okay?" I closed my eyes tight for a second, reliving how it felt like she could slip through my fingers now, how I had to make sure she didn't. "I'm here now. I need you to let me handle this, because I know maybe your family didn't in the past, maybe you've felt like an afterthought or undeserving or like an idea, Clara. But to me, you're not. You're my *only* thought. Does that make sense? Let me have you for real now, okay?"

Her mouth opened once, then she snapped it shut. Another nurse came in during the silence and so it went. She smiled at the doctors giving her updates, nodded at the nurses, and even let them talk over her a few times when they asked about her symptoms.

I tried to let her handle it for the most part. A whole day of them doing it, and then they said she needed to stay overnight as they ran tests.

When she slept, I fielded updates from the doctor. "With her kidney damage, we most likely will be diagnosing her with lupus nephritis."

"Which is?"

The doctor sighed. "A kidney disease that can potentially lead to kidney failure, dialysis or a transplant could be—"

Were they aware of the amount of stress these visits could induce? "How can you check if I'm capable of being her donor?"

"The risks are quite high." He frowned at me.

"I'm aware. The risks are quite high of losing her, and without her, I lose myself. Schedule the tests for me."

When she woke, I was shown again how Clara was stronger than most gave her credit for. And she navigated most situations with more grace than I ever could. She balanced me with it, made me see the world had more to give if I allowed for it. Yet, sometimes, I balanced her too.

The doctor was there again, asking about the loss of blood in her fingers.

"I've had numbness in my fingers before, probably on and off with the rashes for three or four years but I wasn't diagnosed then and I just didn't—"

"You just didn't what?" The doctor's tone was

condescending, out of place, and definitely out of line.

I cleared my throat and glanced over my glasses as I closed my laptop slowly. My voice came out low. "Watch the way you speak to my future wife, doc."

"Excuse me?" he stuttered out.

"She may be sweet, but I'm not. I have no problem putting you in your place."

"You do realize I'm the head doctor in this—"

"I don't care at all who you are. Don't make me report the way you talk to patients."

That shut the fucker up. He apologized and explained that if her symptoms were showing years ago, her kidney function had probably also been declining then. When he left, Clara chided me, "Dominic, he's probably tired. It's petty to say you'd write in a complaint. What if he lost his job for that?"

"He just might. I do my job well, and I expect others to do theirs well too." She sighed. And later that night when her mother and sister requested a visit, I finally stood up. "Absolutely not."

She glanced at me like she was considering it, and then I saw the little fighter in her come out. "What he said." There she was, brilliant and beautiful. "I don't want to see them. I'm not sure how they even found out."

"Right." I considered if the press had found out something. "And we're done here, actually. I want private nursing set up at home. And that's it. A doctor's visit once a week," I commanded.

The nurse explained, "Oh, you can't just request—"

"This is a Hardy hospital, correct?" I was willing to throw my name around now.

"Um, yes." She shrugged like the name didn't matter.

It did.

"I'm Dominic Hardy. So, tell your management what I requested and get it done. Or the management of your management, aka *me* will start having people fired." Her mouth hung open for a minute too long, so I commanded, "Now!" before she left the room.

"Jesus, Dominic. I can't live with you," she whispered, and when I turned to her, I took in her beautiful red strands of hair and her freckled face where the makeup had been worn away.

"Why the hell not? You already were."

"Right, but I'm—" She waved at herself. "I'm a freaking burden now."

"A burden?" I shook my head at her. "Clara, I'm taking you home. You tell me who you think the burden is then."

She wrung her hands most of the time and stayed quiet.

Before we got out of the SUV though, I grabbed her hand. "If there's something you don't like, tell me, okay?"

She squinted at me. "Okay?"

I didn't elaborate.

She'd understand soon enough.

CHAPTER 42: CLARA

I thought Dominic was talking about how he'd set up the house for me being sick, which didn't make much sense. I was still who I was, just a bit sicker.

They were changing the meds, we were going to regulate better, things would progress the way they were supposed to. Or so I hoped.

I'd driven forward the last few months on hope, and I was going to keep going on it. Sometimes hope shows in the day with the sunrise or the sunset, sometimes it shows in the tasks you complete or the ones that are left, sometimes it shows when you push yourself hard enough and you see still that you have the strength to keep going. And sometimes it shows in others.

In him. Dominic Hardy.

He opened the door for me, and there were no lights on, but candles with gold petals on the ground—so many I couldn't even see the white flooring. "Dominic?" I didn't walk forward.

"It's one of the only colors I enjoyed before you. Follow them, huh?"

I followed them forward into the living room to see the wall he'd had a few pictures hung on was now filled with them. Tons and tons of snapshots. Framed photographs of us in the bakery, of us in the club, of us everywhere. "Why?"

"Why not? They're for the girl who puts up pictures of everyone but herself. I figured she needed a wall with her in them."

"Where did you get all these?"

"Mostly the press. They can capture us in the best lighting, but when I offered them six figures for the photos along with a lawsuit in exchange for printing them, they agreed pretty easily." He scooped up Spice when she meowed by his leg and petted her as I squinted at the wall connected to the study.

"You painted?"

It was a soft peach pattern, not black or white at all, and it appeared familiar like a spotted sweeping mountain that sort of reminded me of the California horizon. He hummed. "It's not done but I'm considering keeping it just like that."

"What is it?"

"Your freckles babe. Just your freckles. One of my favorite parts of you."

"But why?" It was all I could ask. "When?"

"We worked on it all week since you've been gone. If I couldn't have you, I wanted the idea of you."

I shook my head because tears burned at the back of my eyes now, and my heart beat faster, and my mind was going a mile a minute. "Dominic, this is—"

"This is our home, and I wanted you to feel that when you're here healing."

"You don't have to take care of me, you know that? I can take care of myself."

"Right, but if I don't take care of you, who's going to take care of the shell of a man I become, Clara? Who's going to take care of me being a complete asshole all the time? I need you as much as you need me." He pointed to his study. "Don't forget to look at the study."

I chewed my cheek. "Why did you do all this?"

I knew before he answered that this was how Dominic

proved he loved me. He showed people through action, not words.

"I wanted it this way. And I want my girlfriend back. Is that a good enough reason?"

All I could do was nod because I already saw color so vibrant and brilliant in that study that I hurried to push the double doors open and stare at it. Floor-to-ceiling, wall-to-wall books, all colors of the rainbow, sorted beautifully to match one another row by row by row.

"What did you do?"

"Made my study your study, I guess."

"Oh my God."

"Do you like it?" he asked, and I genuinely think he needed to know, as he stood there with his brow actually sweating.

"If I said I didn't?" I turned to him finally as I pried my eyes from the bookshelf.

"I'd stay up all night changing it like you did for me."

"Right. You hated that I'd changed it."

He hummed.

"You hated me and a lot of the things I did when I first moved here," I reminded him but a smile was forming on my face that I couldn't hide because a feeling was growing in me that I couldn't hide either: trust and comfort along with my love. I realized Dominic created perfection for me, did all this for me. And he did it for me despite the hell I gave him.

"Hated you?" he asked, taking a step toward me.

"Well, yeah. I don't know." I shrugged.

"Don't know?" He smiled as he rocked back on his heels and stuck his hands in his trouser pockets before he said quietly, "You know, when I heard the will being read, I hated that I couldn't get rid of your bakery the second it was put in my resort. I hated that you tried to infect the rest of my resort with your flair. I hated how I agreed. I hate that now whenever I walk in that place, I smell your signature cupcakes and your damn coffee that I literally crave. I hated that I went to bed wondering where you were, I hated that I woke up searching for your body next to mine, I hated you. I hate that I hurt you, I hate that I can't take it back, that I can't let you go, that I'm not even considering it at this point. I hate that you deserve someone better than me."

I tried to stop him there with tears streaming down my face at his words.

He held up a hand. "But you're not going to get it, Clara, because I'll kill another man. Do you get that? I'm no better than the men I've judged who lost their tempers in jealousy. And I'm not joking with you about it."

"Dom—" I started.

He paced back and forth now. "I mean it. You think Valentino will survive without his precious restaurant up there? You go on another date with him, I'll close it down. I'll destroy him in any way I know how." I tsked to chastise him but he wasn't listening. He was still pacing. But then he stopped to glare right into my eyes. "You've brought out my emotions, good and bad. I'm not proud of it, but I've owned it. I loathe you, little fighter, and that's how I know I love you."

"You hate that you love me?" I whispered.

"Absolutely. I loathe how much I love you, Clara. I hate color, and yet I'm obsessed with everything you wear. I don't like to eat sugar, but I'll devour anything you put on a plate in front of me. I'm exhausted, but I'll stay awake thinking about you just to catch one more thought of you running through my mind. What is that? Love? Because I loathe it. Loathe that I know I can't live without it, that I want it for the rest of my life with every fiber of my being."

"Well, I loathe that I love you too." I said it softly, feeling everything that he was. He was as scared to lose himself to this feeling of love we were both feeling. I pushed him away because I didn't want to find out later he loved me for something I really wasn't or couldn't be. Really, though, I was just scared to love him without that love back.

Love is a risk. We might hate taking the risk but we won't feel the love unless we do.

"So, when I get down on one knee, will you loathe saying yes?"

I bit my lip and then smiled as I said, "I will. But at least I'm owning it."

EPILOGUE: CLARA

With every happy ending, there's a new beginning, and with every up there's a down, a yin to the yang, an opposite to attract.

Dominic and I went through the ups to our downs. It was only three months later, I found out that he'd signed on to be my kidney donor. And that I needed his kidney. Lupus affected us daily, sometimes in a tiny way and sometimes in a big way. That day, it'd been a big down. Catastrophically big.

We'd fought about him giving me an organ for days but, in the end, he wouldn't lose that fight. Within a week's time, his whole family was there acting like I was a part of the family too. His parents hovered around, his brothers and sisters made themselves at home, and no one listened to him at all when he yelled that he wanted them all to go home. They stayed and were there for us through the surgery. It was a testament to the highs coming with the lows. I had a new family that would always be there for me.

And kissing him before surgery, crying in his arms, that might have been a down. But seeing him wheeled into my hospital room after the surgery, that was a ginormous up. Especially when that gorgeous man smiled at me, laced his fingers through mine and said, "Well, I owed you my life, and now I got to give you back yours. Guess I'm a part of you now, huh, little fighter?"

We were back in our home healing, but after five weeks, I'd felt ready to get back to work. After three more, the bakery was back to normal. And we both were living a healthy life.

Although Dominic didn't seem to understand that I was able to do anything with that life even on the days he was supposed to be flying around the world while I handled our wedding preparations.

"What are you doing?" I heard his voice at the front of Sugar and Spice Bakery.

"Why are you here?" I questioned as I set the finishing touch on the cupcakes I was making.

"No. That's not the question. Why the fuck are you here?" he growled as he walked in and then around the counter to the kitchen door to shove it open angrily.

"Don't be a grouch, Dom," I mumbled but didn't look up because I was concentrating on frosting the last cupcake.

"It's midnight." I'm sure his jaw was ticking.

"I'm aware that it's late. Your flight was supposed to be coming in tomorrow." I took a step back and stared at the art. I'd started taking event orders for the resort and this order was for a six-year-old girl having an unicorn party. The mother didn't seem to care if the unicorns were done to perfection on top of the cupcakes, but I did. And it'd been an extremely busy day, so the only time to get this order done for her daughter's birthday at the resort tomorrow was now.

"The bakery opens up at six." Was his shoe tapping, too, like he was waiting impatiently for a response?

"Can you come here and tell me if the eyelashes look like the unicorn is smiling?" I ignored his statement because I needed help. I hadn't done cupcakes like this in a while.

When I finally glanced up to take him in, I almost gasped at the way his hair looked like he'd combed his hands through it numerous times, the way his muscles bunched in frustration, and how his eyes drilled into my soul.

For a second, his brow furrowed, and he opened his mouth like he was going to say more before he snapped it shut and rounded the counter to come to the back of the bakery.

I attempted to step to the side, but his hand shot out and gripped the stainless steel prep table blocking my way. His body shoved up against mine, and his other hand went to the metal too, caging me in. Dominic surrounded me, looking over my shoulder at the cupcakes, and there was no controlling how my breathing picked up the pace. "You stayed here to make cupcakes until midnight while I worried about you across the damn country? Do you answer your phone ever?"

"I put my phone and watch away today. They were bothering me."

"How am I supposed to check on you then, cupcake?" His hand wrapped around me, and he nestled into my neck.

I sighed but couldn't hide the tremble in my breath. I dragged a finger across the cool steel edge of the table, trying to focus on that rather than the equally hard man up against me. My thighs quaked from how close he was, how I felt his cock right up against my back. I let my hand drop off the table just as it was about to touch his though. I couldn't feel his skin against mine right now, knew if I did, I would indulge in what I shouldn't. "I'm an adult."

"And you're my fiancée. I need to make sure you're okay 24-7, because knowing you, you'll be out planting flowers without sunscreen or painting walls without a mask or, in this case, staying up way too late working."

I scoffed. "We actually do need to plant flowers tomorrow outside, and I needed to get this order done so that it can be off my mind over the weekend."

"No. We're not going out in the sun with—"

I rolled my eyes. "Don't start, Dominic. Being outside is good for you. The sun provides us with vitamin D, too, which—"

He turned me to face him and placed his hands on either side of my face, his thumbs rubbing back and forth on my cheeks that I knew were reddened by the sun just today. "You love the sun, and yet you're practically allergic to it. It's life's biggest joke. Just like it's life's biggest joke that I'm so in love with you that I can't say no to you even though it's what should be done."

"So, does that mean you're going to say yes to a lattice above our wedding walkway?"

He groaned immediately. "Why are we discussing a wedding that I told you I wanted to plan after our lives have settled down?"

"Because it takes a long time to plan."

"How long?" He frowned.

"I don't know. Probably a year. We have to send out invites and—"

"I'm not waiting a whole year to marry you, cupcake," he growled. "We don't need a big wedding, and you have a whole resort and all the staff to plan it for you. Marry me this summer."

"Dominic, what if your family can't make it?" I said it with a smile though because I didn't want to wait to marry him either.

"I can barely get my family to leave me alone, Clara. They'll make it. We're getting married in three months."

"What if I want a certain band. They book out," I pointed out, just to irritate him now.

He shook his head and stepped close, grabbing my ass, and yanking me against him. "I'll get whatever band or singer you want. Just let someone else plan the thing. Actually, I'll take care of it. I don't want you stressed."

I felt his length growing against my stomach. "Or you want me focused on other things." I pushed away from him and turned to pick up the last tray of cupcakes to put away. "You also are going to agree to the opening of four more Sugar and Spices, right? And we're pushing the poppy cupcakes to be sold at bakeries around the country, correct?"

He eyed the open refrigerator and pointed. "Give me a poppy cupcake, and I'll think about it." He said it like he truly had a say. Dominic had watched me grow in the past few months fast, in a viral way almost. He'd told me every time I got nervous, "Own it, Clara. They see your worth. It's time for you to see it too."

And I'd started to. I'd just started negotiating with large brands, pushing my product into the right hands, and wasn't hesitating to tell anyone no if I felt uncomfortable. I'd done it all on my own, and Dominic had stood by to watch, smiling the whole damn time.

I played with his cupcake necklace on my neck as I acted like I was thinking about it. "I don't know if you deserve a cupcake. You didn't give me my present yet."

"Present?" he questioned.

"You got my necklace there?" I murmured and glanced at his hands.

Confused, he flicked his gaze over my neck and then saw where I was staring. Immediately, he smirked as he flexed his hands before he slid one up my neck. "I thought I'd wait to get you home but forget it. My wife in her bakery taking the cock that's hers is all I really want. I'll say yes to everything else for you just to get what I want now."

I hummed, "Good, the flower walkway in our wedding is going to cost you millions," I told him as I lifted my skirt, holding his gaze over my shoulder as I bent and arched my back a little.

"Don't give a fuck, cupcake. You can have anything you want as long as you take this cock."

I laughed. "At least you're owning it, future husband. At least you're owning it."

-THE END-

Want to see who Dominic brings to the wedding? Keep reading for the bonus scene!

BONUS SCENE: CLARA

"Sugar. Spice, come on. You'll get a treat." He kneeled down in front of me, full three-piece suit and all, and rubbed his fingers together. Wearing tiny boxes on their collars, both of my furry gray cats trotted up the red-petaled aisle within one of the grandest resorts in the country to my almost-husband. When he scooped them up and pulled our wedding rings from the boxes, my tears started.

I don't know how Dominic managed to have our kittens here in Vegas for our wedding, but he'd done it. Every single human and animal I cared about was present. He'd made that happen. I wasn't sure what the officiant was saying, but I mouthed, "I love you."

He smirked as he turned to hand the cats to his brother, Dex, who I'm pretty sure scowled at him and grumbled, "I hate you."

Izzy started laughing behind me with Evie and Lilah. I turned to scold them but chuckled too. Through tears and laughter was exactly how I wanted my wedding ring to be slid on my finger by the man I loved.

Our wedding was small with only about fifty people, but we had the grand room, the perfect arrangements, and the best people for me there.

Finally, the officiant announced. "I now pronounce you man and wife. You may kiss your—"

Dominic Hardy didn't wait for the end of the sentence. Under my flower archway in the ginormous ballroom of Black Diamond Resort and Casino, my lawfully wedded husband yanked me against him and dipped me before he kissed me in front of everyone.

Devoured me. Consumed me.

I kissed him back with the same fervor and then cheered with our family and friends. Dominic scooped me up and announced that drinks and cocktail hour with photos would be on the top floor. "We'll be back in twenty minutes." His brothers and sisters groaned, and I wiggled in his arms. He didn't care. He beelined out of our own wedding. "Stop fighting me, little fighter."

"We can't leave our own party. Where are you taking me?"

"To our suite," he said in a matter-of-fact tone as he carried me into the elevator and swiped his key fob.

I stared at the elevator light as it turned green, then we were shooting up to one of the top floors. "Dominic Hardy, we're not leaving all our guests during our wedding to ..."

"To what, cupcake?" He smirked down at me, and his green eyes sparkled with mischief.

"You know what!" I smacked his shoulder. "We're supposed to sleep together after the wedding."

"Yeah. I just married you. I said 'I do.' You're now my wife. And now, I'm going to fuck you like you're my wife. Want to know why?"

"Why?" I asked because, who was I kidding? I wanted him just as badly as he wanted me.

"Because you're fucking mine, little fighter."

The elevator door opened to a lavish penthouse suite with mostly black silk and velvet furniture. It was a sexy, decadent vibe that matched the casino and resort throughout. When Dominic set me on the black counter and stepped back to take me in, I bit my lip as my eyes roved over him too. His suit was all black today—black tie, black shirt, black suit jacket and pants. I'd worn all white with red lipstick and ruby red earrings. His complete opposite. The yin to his yang.

I leaned back on my hands and said, "Well, husband, are you going to retrieve your garter now or later tonight?"

"Now," he growled. "No one gets to see me lifting that skirt." He said as he unbuttoned his suit jacket, discarded it, and then one by one, rolled up his sleeves slowly. My pussy clenched, watching his forearms flex.

When he stalked up to me, I whispered out, "It's your favorite color."

"That right?" He tipped my chin up and rubbed a thumb across my bottom lip. "Then it must be as red as these lips, or as green as your eyes, or as pink as the blush on your cheeks."

“Not black?” I pouted.

He kneeled before me. “Should we find out how much your husband likes any color wrapped around that thigh of yours?” His hands were skilled enough that they skirted under the many layers of my wedding dress toward my pussy.

And his smile was devious before he disappeared under it all.

***

We were absent for much more than twenty minutes.

Still, neither of us apologized when we made it back to our own reception. A seventy-foot chandelier of millions of crystals and black diamonds sparkled above us with the seven-piece band playing music. We’d made sure it was just instrumentals because we wanted their lead vocalist for later that night.

When we walked in, the cheering from the small crowd of fifty felt like a million, loud and brilliant, because I knew every single person in that room wanted us happy in a way a family should.

My mother and Anastasia weren’t present, nor were they invited. The love from Evie and my sisters-in-law was more than I’d ever wanted anyway. They’d more than accepted me in as a part of the family, they’d embraced me. For the good ... and the bad.

Izzy, Lilah, and Evie rushed up to me as soon as I was free from Dominic. Lilah said, “So, Dex is going to be pissed. Izzy you take the fall.”

“Me? No. I’m not dealing with him.”

“All because she’s singing?” I squeaked. “You’re kidding, right? It’s a wedding, and she’s a family friend.”

“Right.” Izzy nodded, a small smile playing on her lips. “It’s your wedding. He won’t be mad at you. You tell him.”

Before I could refuse, Lilah smacked Izzy in the arm. “No way. It’s her freaking wedding. Let’s just blame the person he can’t get mad at.”

“Um ... Dex gets pissed at everyone.” Izzy looked at her like she was an idiot. “He didn’t talk to us for like a month after I fiddled with one of his security systems. Remember?”

“Right.” Lilah paused and when she smiled, I was reminded

of how lucky Hardys were in the gene pool. "He can't be mad at Keelani though."

Evie had been quiet next to me, but she pointed at both of them then. "That's evil and brilliant. We're doing that."

"Doing what?" Dominic asked as he and Dex walked back up. Dominic's arm slid around me, and I leaned into him.

"Lilah has something to tell you," Evie blurted out and wide-eyed her.

"Oh great. Make me do it." She sighed but then turned puppy eyes on Dex. "Keelani wanted just one chance to sing here. We know you said no, but—"

"Lilah"—his whole face, all smiles a second ago, turned stormy—"you didn't."

"Not me specifically. But Dominic needed a band," she spit out fast.

"I needed a band?" Dominic repeated. So, Lilah was throwing big brother under the bus. Great idea.

"Right. We needed a band," I chimed in. "Dominic said she's so close to the family, and he loves her voice."

"You love her voice, asshole?" Dex glared at him, and his hands clenched immediately into fists.

"I'm fucking married, Dex. Get a grip. She's singing our first dance song." His eyes narrowed. "Then, she's singing at this casino. Then"—he glanced at all of us women and smiled—"I put her in the same apartment building as you for the next six months. You know how Keelani is. She gets a bit crazy when she's somewhere new. So, keep an eye on her. Mom and Dad love her, and you don't want her parents thinking we didn't take care for her while she was working in our—"

"I don't need anyone to take care of me," I heard from behind me. Keelani's voice was distinct, low and raspy in a sultry sort of way. When I turned to see her standing there in a deep-purple dress, I knew Dex was going to have a hard time.

She was stunning with dark-brown hair, tan skin, and eyes that were so dark you couldn't tell the color.

"You don't need to be in Vegas trying to take care of yourself," Dex said to her through clenched teeth.

"Dex, honey, what could you possibly be worried about?" She smirked at him and then gave Dominic a hug before she pulled me in for one. She whispered to me, "Sorry I couldn't make the wedding and if I'm a little off-key tonight, I swear I'll make it up to you. The Hardy brothers always put me on edge."

She didn't elaborate, but I knew she meant one Hardy brother in particular. "You'll do great."

She backed away quickly after that, but I saw how Dex's eyes darkened as he stormed after her when she hooked an arm in Dimitri's not much later.

"They're all screwed." Dominic shook his head after Dex and Keelani.

"Are we good enough matchmakers to throw them together like that?"

"Nope," Izzy answered as Cade walked up to her and pulled her close.

"Izzy's terrible at everything except being my wife and causing chaos in the world. So, expect this casino to implode with Dex not on his game because his heartbreak is here."

"It better not," Dominic grumbled. "It's my wedding day. You all need to keep this shit together."

Cade laughed. "You fuckers merged with Black Diamond Casino, brother. There's no way you're keeping this all together."

"Fuck off," Dominic said and steered me away from them to go sit at the head table.

On the way, I asked, "Should I be concerned?"

"No. My brothers and I will handle all that. You worry about the bakeries, cupcake."

"We're married. It's never going to be just yours to handle or just mine to handle again. We're in it together," I told him as I threaded my fingers through his.

He stared at me for a second and then pulled me close to kiss my temple. "You know I can't stand you pushing back sometimes when I'm only trying to keep you from worrying."

"Well, I can't stand you babying me. So, we're even, dear husband of mine."

"We're even," he murmured and then ran a finger over my cupcake necklace. "And that's why I love you, beautiful wife."

ALSO BY SHAIN ROSE

Hardy Billionaires

Between Commitment and Betrayal

Between Love and Loathing

Between Never and Forever - coming March 2024

* * *

Stonewood Billionaire Brothers

INEVITABLE

REVERIE

THRIVE

* * *

New Reign Mafia

Heart of a Monster

Love of a Queen

* * *

Tarnished Empire

Shattered Vows

Fractured Freedom

Corrupted Chaos

ABOUT SHAIN ROSE

Shain Rose writes romance with an edge. Her books are filled with angst, steam, and emotional rollercoasters that lead to happily ever afters.

She lives where the weather is always changing with a family that she hopes will never change. When she isn't writing, she's reading and loving life.

Sign up for her newsletter:shainrose.com/newsletter